SOCIAL SECURITY

SOCIAL SECURITY

IMMACULATE DECEPTION - A NATIONAL DISGRACE

ROBERT JAMES KARPIE

Outskirts Press, Inc.
Denver, Colorado

This is a work of fiction. The events and characters described herein are imaginary and are not intended to refer to specific places or living persons. The opinions expressed in this manuscript are solely the opinions of the author and do not represent the opinions or thoughts of the publisher. The author has represented and warranted full ownership and/or legal right to publish all the materials in this book.

Social Security
Immaculate Deception - A National Disgrace
All Rights Reserved.
Copyright © 2009 Robert James Karpie
v5.0

Cover Image © 2009 Robert James Karpie / B4HEART Publishing
All Rights Reserved. Used With Permission.
Cover Image Designed by Robert James Karpie & Christopher O'Neill.
All Rights Reserved. Used With Permission.
Cover Image Painted by Christopher O'Neill.
Author Photo © 2007 Bob Mussell
All Rights Reserved. Used With Permission.

This book may not be reproduced, transmitted, or stored in whole or in part by any means, including graphic, electronic, or mechanical without the express written consent of the publisher except in the case of brief quotations embodied in critical articles and reviews.

Outskirts Press, Inc.
http://www.outskirtspress.com

ISBN: 978-1-4327-4339-0
ISBN: 978-1-4327-4826-5

Library of Congress Control Number: 2009931809

Outskirts Press and the "OP" logo are trademarks belonging to Outskirts Press, Inc.

PRINTED IN THE UNITED STATES OF AMERICA

"Before a problem achieves recognition as such, it has to go through three stages: In the first one it is laughed at. During the second it will be fought against; until in the third, it is accepted as being-self-evident." --- Schopenhauer

Contents

Synopsis		ix
About the Author		xiii
Preface		xv
Acknowledgement		xix
Dedication		xxi
Chapter 1	Hell	1
Chapter 2	Genesis	15
Chapter 3	Intrusion	33
Chapter 4	Uncertainty	59
Chapter 5	Acceptance	83
Chapter 6	Fate	97
Chapter 7	Confrontations	113
Chapter 8	Peace and Closure in Paradise	143
Chapter 9	Compassion, Mercy and the Confession – Plus	161
Chapter 10	Thee Awakenings	203
The New Mission via B4HEART — A Spiritual Revolution		247

Synopsis

Synopsis
Four old codgers are sick and tired of the abuse and neglect which occurs daily in their old-folks-home. Max has a broken leg for getting involved as he tried to help his buddy Thomas with his bed pan. Unfortunately, Thomas is now in the intensive care unit at the county hospital. He's in a coma. Another resident, Marge Taylor; has been repeatedly beaten and raped and hasn't spoken a word since her tragic ordeal started. She was too afraid to report her cruel and inhumane treatment.

Loss of morale dictates as anxiety and pessimism have set in to say the least; thanks to the agony and shame that has been inflicted upon them by the so called system. Eventually, the shit hits the fan in protest and arrest. The press is having a field day, the old folks are demonstrating and the *Four Amigo;* Clarence, Max, Sarge and Henry are playing cards, conspiring to overthrow the system and make change by taking matters into their own hands as they vow to conquer *Hell --- Prudent-Paradise*.

They actually hire a lawyer, Chi, Clarence's grandson who sues the state as well as the owners of *Hell*. The residents go wild with the idea and unite as they pool their resources and purchase *Prudent Paradise* in the *Name of Love*. They change its name to *Social Security* and become one big family; with a bar, pool, hot tubs, pets, the *O-zone*, and a *Laugh Room*. They learn to live and enjoy life again as sex is on their minds.

Clarence and his *Amigos* have their hands full. Sometimes he wonders if they bit off more than they can chew. He falls in *Love* which seems to be contagious. Unfortunately, life is dangerous. Together, they continue to address uncertainty as they confront destiny; in spite of its ups and downs. Their goal is to make change; before it's too late and out of control. Thus, they devise a plan to challenge the troubles that are plaguing America today; which most citizens choose chose to ignore as the *'Elite Powers That Be'*; herds us like cattle into organized chaos.

This *Novel* is a little obscene, dramatic, provocative, and educational through a historical review, including several unnerving *National Disgraces* which have infected the world; but were covered up in the *Name of National Security*. On a lighter note, it is also funny as well as bitter-sweet and a bit violent but then again, that's *Life*. For as *Mark Twain* proclaimed:

"Man is the only animal that blushes, the only one that needs to."

Hence, you will laugh and you will cry, but my aim is to STIMULATE your brain, connect the dots; so to speak and make you think. This is but a *Wake-up Call*. Frankly, the system itself is consuming the consumers. We are becoming slaves economically as our Individual Rights & Freedoms are cannibalized from within by own government; an unforgiving act of Immaculate Deception.

Unfortunately, Americans have lost their faith in our government as well as our system of justice and the rule of law? Wake up my fellow Americans; it is time to support and defend the U.S. Constitution! United, it is time we implement the system of *'Checks and Balances'*; which were designed by our founding fathers as they established a *'Separation of Powers'*, on purpose.

Ultimately, the *'Power'*, was designed to be shared between our three branches of government and each branch has the right and the duty to challenge the actions of the others; a safe guard to prevent excessive power grabs by either the judicial, legislative or executive branch of our government. Ironically, our forefather's greatest fears are coming true? Why? Because --- 'We the People'; have fallen asleep. We have forgotten about the 'Power of the People'; our Duty to Question Authority and Demand Answers. We should not fear our government; they should fear us, We the People!

    Alas, God help us if we laugh now and cry later. Especially since Life is a matter of Good verses evil. Ironically, Truth is akin to Cool, as both are Repulsive to the Un. It's Time To Open Your Eyes & WAKE-UP!

About the Author

About the Author
Robert James Karpie is a student of the human condition, wielding the written craft to enrapture the mind much like an artist wields a brush. The pages are a blank canvas on which to draw from a talent heralded by many and matched only by an imagination that rises to the task. *Social Security* is a gut-wrenching drama with epic proportions; that is sure to bring tears to yours eyes as well as joy to your heart.

   Bob is a former U. S. Marine and has been married to his lovely wife Susan for over thirty-five years. They have two daughters and seven grand-children! Bob was born and raised in Buffalo, New York. He worked for the Buffalo Board of Education for twenty-three years as a computer operator at city hall.

   At present, he owns B4HEART Publishing / www.B4HEART publishing.com. He is also the creator of www.B4HEART.com as well as www.A-National-Disgrace.com, www.Truth-About-Alcohol-Fuel.info and www.YourWorkFromHomeSolutionCenter.com

   Mr. Karpie is a preferred author on www.writing.com/authors/b4heart. This is his second book; his first novel. His first book is entitled Surprise and can be found at the following --- Outskirts Press, Amazon or Barnes & Nobel. The web addresses are below: http://www.outskirtspress.com/webpage.php?isbn=1598009427
      http://www.amazon.com/Surprise-Robert-James-Karpie/

dp/1598009427/ref=sr_11_1?ie=UTF8&qid=1234892884&sr=11-1

http://search.barnesandnoble.com/booksearch/isbninquiry.asp?r=1&ISBN=1598009427

You can watch a video trailer of *Surprise* on *YouTube* at the following addresses:

http://www.B4HEART.com

http://www.youtube.com/watch?v=McorPEGfrHc

Bob also has another short story for children ready to be published entitled: *Mayan's Paradise*.

E-mail bob at bob@b4heart.com

Preface

Preface
Evolution

Life is a *Divine Privilege*. It is but a gift from God as every moment is precious in its own rite. Man is but a work in progress just as government, which is a by-product of man and both must either evolve or self-destruct. Historically, government has a tendency of holding mankind back as a whole through politics, religion, and science as lobbyist's corrupt morals. To add insult to injury, it's outrageous when much of our so called free press - mainstream media - steers, persuades, preaches, promotes and instills governmental policies via fear tactics, ridicule, disinformation, conjecture, propaganda, and censorship by ownership as *"knowledge is power"*.

Unfortunately, "power corrupts" and, *"absolute power, corrupts absolutely"*--- in the name of greed, the ultimate evil as they protect their sacred cash cows, hidden history, dishonest agenda, and government secrets. Systematically, the masses are controlled through outright blatant lies, rhetoric, institutions, manipulation, fear and intimidation as we bestow our trust in a system which is plagued by temptation and choose to ignore, forgive or forget about resulting transgressions, foolishly. Ironically, we as a society have progressed to organized corruption, better known as corporations; which play god on impulse. God help us.

Frankly, in the beginning, there was --- *The Word*. However, throughout the annals of time, man underestimated the power of the *Magnificent Word of God*. Spontaneously, curiosity wondered, ventured and experimented on and on and as a result, eventually, man was defined as --- "Homo Sapien, Man the Thinker".

Consciously as well as subconsciously, we perceive to reason and learn. Cognition instills knowledge. But consciousness is more that mere observation as rationality and understanding are the driving forces behind possibilities. Consciousness is *Divine Energy*. Perhaps Harold Sherman defined it best in his book *'You Live After Death'*:

'...consciousness is intelligence in action and all consciousness has feeling'.

Essentially, we are blessed with potential --- *Reason and Free Will* as *Imagination Creates Inquiry*. And so, the search began as philosophy was born in search of Truth / Wisdom. Thus, the Classical Greeks proclaimed philosophy as --- "Love of Wisdom".

But, *William James* professed that philosophy was:

"...an *unusually stubborn attempt to think clearly.*"

Consequently, philosophy is in fact an enigma, but so are politics, science and religion, not to mention man, government or its institutions. After all, there is surely a gap between policy and practice, between sin and crime, between morals and morale as ethics are suspect in the name of economics. Especially, since man has a hard time practicing what he preaches.

How many mean what they say and say what they mean? How long are we supposed to put up with this *Maleficent Bull-shit*? Ideologically, when the *Rule of Law* can be manipulated to benefit the *Powers That Be* - especially at the expense of the masses (We, the People), or interferes with *Humanity* or denies *Necessity* - it's time for a change.

Thus, man is at a crossroad: obedience or moral choice? Pathologically, we hurry and worry about our own individual rights and neglect our personal responsibilities to each other. Incomprehensibly, far too many also deny or ignore both the responsibilities and the liabilities of government as civil liberties' / rights become extinct or obsolete. Perhaps *Horace Walpole* summed it up best with his testament when he realized that: *"Life is a comedy for those who think... and a tragedy for those who feel."*

Ironically, destiny waits patiently as change is constant and social identity evolves; as *Love* is *Absolute*. Inevitably, the establishment's man-made-laws are subject to, technicalities and double standards. But, *"love worketh no ill to his neighbor; therefore love is the fulfilling of the law," (Romans 13:10)*.

Ultimately, man is obliged to *Love*. Honesty, good-intentions and an open-mind will not suffice. Man must open his *Heart*. *Love* cannot be tailored, it fits all, but one must choose to sport it via *Humanity*. Phenomenally, man is blessed with the *Power to Love,* and therefore he can govern himself. There is no substitute for *Love!*

Robert James Karpie

Acknowledgment

Acknowledgement

From birth throughout history, even still, man is his own mystery, a rare breed which is filled with wonderment as it longs for *Information*. Thus, in the field of life, there are two pertinent factors which are more important than reading. The first is writing, but most imperative, is the prevailing destiny of the *Naked Truth*. Ironically, while some search for the *Spirit of Truth*, others seek and strive for success. But, how does one measure and define success? Especially since man is not born to impress, emulate or antagonize anybody, not even --- *Him-self*.

Over the years, scientists have discovered that there is a direct link between nutritional health and viral mutation. Naturally, a malnourished body provides an accommodating breeding ground for intruding mutant viruses as undernourished bodies are rendered helpless and thereby susceptible to infection. But what about an undernourished mind and soul; are they not more susceptible to ignorance and evil and therefore unintentionally responsible for self-destructing impulses as diseases or *Dis-Ease* per malingering existence?

Haphazardly, both ignorance and evil are also mutants as they vary and change in degree naturally. Dynamically, man is a predefined biological mechanism which unlike any modern computer - is a divine complex interacting system of not only hardware and software; but also --- *Latent-Eternal-Ware*. Thus, a coexisting affiliation of body, mind and soul, which unlike any computer; is responsible for its actions.

Systematically; like all computers --- *"garbage in, garbage out"*. Therefore, we receive, compile and transmit accordingly; as parity is pertinent to harmony. Ergo, as a matter of peace and tranquility; we must balance all of our emotions and never under-estimate the under-current of our powerful minds as we have a choice.

Unfortunately, physical illness as well as ignorance and evil result from psychic disturbances, which are a manifestation of a *Spiritual Imbalance* of body, mind and soul. Ignorantly, mankind is so negligent and thereby --- *delusional-ally arrested*. Hence, *Plato* proclaimed: *"if you want to heal the body, you must first heal the mind."*

Ultimately, *"from the clash of differing opinions comes the spark of truth!"* Life is indeed a transition as we humans endeavor to survive. Afraid of being lonely, we long to be loved as we compete for place, acceptance and recognition. Conversely, man fashions to be understood as we seek answers, proof, reassurance and confirmation.

Ironically, judgment is only a matter of opinion, as reasons are many and forgiveness --- a measure of maturity as jealousy is ignorance. History speaks for itself. But in the name of convenient rational, far too many history books are full of crap. One must learn to read between the lies. All must deal --- face to face with self. *All must do his part in the Name of Humanity. Thou Shalt Not Lie to Thyself by Denying Truth!*

Hence, *Thoreau* --- the Philosopher, surmised: *"if a man does not keep pace with his companions, perhaps he hears a different drummer....' Thus, to each his own Tempo.' ... let him step to the music which he hears, however measured or far away."*

Dedication

Dedication

I dedicate this book to mankind in the Name of Humanity. I don't claim to be any kind of prophet or saint. Some may even think that I am crazy, but to each his own. No two perspectives are exactly the same. I just tells it like I sees it and it's awfully Fucked Up. It is time for a change. For at the rate that we are going; God help us.

I don't consider myself to be a democrat or a republican. I am but an Earthling. I do believe in God, but I also believe that God is Love. And, I believe that each and every one of us is here on Earth for a reason.

We are here to learn to Love. Ironically, all are blessed as Divine Courtesy Calls; however, few listen and even fewer - Answer. Intuitionally, we must answer the 'Call'. My mission, my calling is B4HEART.

B4HEART --- Humanity Envisioned And Realized Together!

"Whether small or great, and no matter what the stage or grade of life, the Call rings up the curtain, always on a mystery of

transfiguration ---- a rite, or moment, of spiritual passage, which, when complete, amounts to a dying and a birth. The familiar life horizon has been outgrown; the old concepts, ideals, and emotional patterns no longer fit; the time for passing of a threshold is at hand. "
Joseph Campbell,
'The Hero With a Thousand Faces' --- 1949

CHAPTER **One**

Hell

Chapter 1   Hell

"We have rights!" "We have rights!" "We have rights!"

"No more abuse!" "No more abuse!"

"Close that darn window, I can't concentrate on the cards." Henry sighed as a nurse granted his prerogative.

"Damn it guys, I worked all my life, over fifty-some years; half a century, and for what? I certainly did not intend to be a victim of society; a by-product of neglect and broken promises. We're fucken inmates. We're prisoners of the system." Clarence complained lividly.

"What goes on in this community is beyond belief. Every time you turn around, it's sign here; sign there, rules, rules, and more rules. Keep your mouth shut and do as you are told. Obey all the rules like good boys and girls or else. It's a fucking outrage, a travesty."

"I signed all of my money over to my kids, house and all." declared Max.

"Yeah, so did I," Henry interjected. "Sometimes I think that they can't wait to collect my life insurance."

"I haven't any family." Sarge confessed. "I chose to live here, but I must admit; I had more freedom in the *'Crotch'*."

"And what thanks do we get?" Clarence asked sarcastically. "Welcome to *Hell*."

Ironically, they all started to laugh as *Hell* was the nickname of their retirement home --- *Prudent-Paradise*. Unfortunately, there wasn't anything prudent about it and the only pleasure was the thought of the alternative as the truth would set them free --- destination death.

"I want my money back!" Max shouted.

"I want a shot and beer!" Sarge reminisced.

"I want out of here!" Henry admitted.

"Let's do it," exclaimed Clarence.

"Do what?" echoed the other three.

"Go for the gusto, the whole enchilada." Clarence replied.

"Normally, I tend to mind my own business. Trouble is easy enough to find, but when trouble invades you, enters our mutual home; it's time to do something. Enough is enough. Only a fool negotiates with his integrity as he sacrifices his dignity. Tomorrow morning, I'm going to renege with a change of heart and try and get my money back. I intend to enjoy my twilight years."

"Then what are you going to do?" Henry asked reluctantly. "Are you going to get drunk, buy some *Viagra*, hire a hooker and rent a hotel?"

"You'd be better off hiring two hookers!" Max advised. "You haven't lived until you had a *Menage a trois*. In fact, I got a hankering for one myself; since it's been a while. What you say *Nursey-Poo*; why don't you go and find Sexy Sarah and meet me in my room, say in about half an hour?"

They all laughed together; everybody but the nurse that tried to pretend that she was minding her own business and Clarence, who was as serious as a heart-attack.

"Ha-ha-ha," Clarence mumbled. "Don't be so damn insolent or skeptical. I'm serious. I have a need; we all have needs and desires, and I'm going to fulfill them. Who will support us if we don't support ourselves? There is strength in numbers. We must take matters into our own hands and create our own safety, ensure our own destiny."

"United we stand!" yelled Sarge. "But, what the heck are you talking about?"

"Our very own private, retirement / nursing, *Commune!*" Clarence shouted.

The nurse started laughing ignorantly as Clarence continued. "Including bar, in-ground pools, hot tubs, coed-rooms and whatever we decide on. After all, we are adults. Why should we forfeit our rights, our hard earned money as we suffer in disgrace and misery while our colleagues are beat, raped and neglected at random on any given chance; behind closed doors?"

"It's so hush, hush as image is lucrative and silence ensures secrecy. I don't know about you guys, but I'm fed up with living in this tragic nightmare. God helps those that help themselves. We're not invalids."

"Amen!" Max shared his sentiments. "I need some *Lovin*, every now and again --- *ASAP.*"

"God bless the 60's!" Henry declared. *"Free- Love, Peace and Rock-n-Roll.* Those were the days my *Amigos.* Those *Hippie-chicks* would go all night and day. They always put out. It was pure heaven as they worshiped cool, older, mature and distinguished men. In fact, I married one."

"Cool?" Sarge asked dumbfounded and somewhat appalled with askance eyes.

"Yeah Man," Henry professed proudly. "I had a ponytail, stash and pierced ear. Back then, I was *'With It'*, so to speak --- *Hip.* I wooed the chicks with shyness; it was my style. My wife was twelve years younger than me. God bless her soul. As a matter of fact, I've been called *Sensitive.*"

"Sensitive? Shit, your not one of those damn bleeding-hearts? Don't tell me that you were protesting while I was fighting the VC's in Viet Nam." Sergeant Satire fumed aghast; pounding his fist on the table, feeling somewhat insulted again, for risking his life in the name of U.S. policy.

"You're damn right!" Henry snapped back in rapid fire. "I was against that outrageous farce from day one. The defense contractors made billions upon billions of dollars; war profiteering at the expense of young and old innocent lives on both sides. President Johnson prolonged the war as he never intended to win."

"When it comes to war," Henry continued, "I'm skeptical indeed. Especially since there is a very fine line between *National Security and Corporate Security*; the bottom line is the almighty dollar. Man is such a greedy animal that is obsessed with money, power and the control of others."

"Relax!" Max interjected. "You're absolutely right; however let's deal with Clarence's ideal for now. I'm fed up with deprivation, uncertainty and peril. I thought that I put up with enough shit in my life; being married and divorced three times but this is hideous and out of control."

"I got tired of taking crap from my wives and I don't intend to take anymore from anybody. Frankly, I just don't like being told what to do and what not to do. You can't negotiate with a system that is out of control. It must be straightened out or else."

"Let's pool our money." Clarence interrupted. "Let's form a non-profit organization, doctors, nurses, staff, and the whole works; an elite - *Social-Security*, run by a board of directors."

"You can be our spoke person." Sarge laughed skeptically. "All you have to do is speak slow and softly and carry a big bottle of Jack."

"Let him continue." Henry demanded. "It sounds interesting. *Hell* is so dysfunctional."

"I bet that there are some philanthropists out there whom would help us." Clarence argued his case convincingly. "After all, it is a humane issue. Treat us, we the elderly, with dignity and respect; not as inmates. Prohibition is dead. We have rights. No is our option, our choice."

"Do you think that this state investigation will shut *Hell* down?" asked Henry.

"No way," replied Max; "payola, payola, payola. They'll do *Jack-shit*."

"They'll make some changes --- new staff and lookout for us for awhile until the media and the people forget about it, and forget about us." Clarence answered. "But what does anybody really expect wholeheartedly when the help is entrusted with our safety for meager wages. They can probably make more money walking dogs. Poor Marge hasn't spoken a word since she was beaten and raped and Thomas is still in intensive care because he shit his bed. Max, you're lucky that you only broke your leg."

"I know! I know already!" Max vented. "But back in the day, I would have kicked his ass. He'd be lucky if he landed in the hospital; instead of the morgue."

"Such is life, as it sucks being old." he continued. "I'm sick and tired of being a victim; violated and presented with danger, with indecency. We literally live in fear but, why? Maybe it's time we do stand up for ourselves."

"'One for all and all for one'," Henry shouted as the nurse shook her head in disbelief. "We must vow to stick together --- dependability. Your idea sounds promising." he continued. "We have to stop these creeps from doing creepy-things."

"It's ridiculous." Sarge grunted apprehensively with an intense look on his face. "It's preposterous. Your families will surely commit you guys to a mental hospital. Didn't you see *One Flew Over the Cuckoo's Nest*? Nobody is going to give me shock therapy. It's sad enough that they try to medicate us. I'll roll with the punches. Thank you, but no, no, no thanks!"

"I thought you had balls, Sarge." Max queried wryly. "What'd you do; lose them in *Nam*? Where is your courage, your sense of pride? It's imperative that we take a stand. I'm with Clarence!"

"Me too!" exclaimed Henry. "The kids can fend for themselves. It's a matter of principle; justice for the geriatrics. My heart bleeds for this cause for concern for we the forgotten has-beens. There should be no shame in growing old, but living like this is surely a damn shame."

"Don't get me wrong, I don't want to be young again, but I want to be free to fuck-off if I wish. Go to bed when I want, eat when I want. Drink in moderation or get drunk if I chose to. Hell, I want some young nurse with big tits to give me a sponge-bath. Not some fat old slob, young punk or perverted fag. I'm going to get my money back too!"

"We can pull it off Sarge!" Clarence emphasized with excitement. "Don't jump to any conclusions. *Cuckoo's Nest*, dealt with a bunch of nuts. Why we aren't even senile yet. Besides, who is going to commit you? We can hire a mouth-piece to deal with our families and all the legal work. Chi will surely help us."

"Shit, we'll even go public if we have to. After all, people love causes. Many will be begging to enlist and jump on the band-wagon. Just listen to the uproar out there, ruckus galore; rapid fire echoing through the crowd, demanding reform. It reminds me of the 60's --- TV cameras, protesters demonstrating with signs. It's riot-like; half of them will invest with and or support us. And I'll even surf the net at the library for more support."

"OK, OK, I'm in!" Sarge reconsidered. "But I'm in charge of the bar."

"So be it!" They all agreed as Max took out a flask of Jack Daniel's and the *Four Amigos* toasted their spiked-lemon-aid to *Social Security*; the opportunity to decide for themselves.

Suddenly, Max started laughing.

"What's so funny?" Henry asked.

"You should have saved that old ponytail!" Max teased with a shit-eating grin. "You could have had it made into a rug and pasted it on your bald head."

"Ha-ha-ha, very funny," Henry whimpered; agape while blushing as the other three *Amigos* roared.

Needless to say, they all woke up early the next morning. In fact, none of them actually slept as each was too excited and all refused to take any type of sleeping aid. After breakfast, the four conspiring reformers piled into Clarence's Buick and drove off to see Chi, Clarence's grandson who was a civil-rights lawyer.

Clarence was God in Chi's eyes. Shit, he wanted Clarence to live with him but Clarence didn't want to impose or be a burden. Perhaps deep down, Clarence knew that he had to fulfill his destiny; it was his duty to make --- *Change*.

"What's up *Amigos*?" Chi asked as the four frustrated radical rebels marched into his office unannounced; determined with fire in their eyes. It was no surprise that Chi didn't care about the interruption. He was always warm and receptive to their concerns. Time with his family and friends were more precious than money to him.

Ironically, he didn't charge half his clients, and yet his practice was booming, lawsuits galore; as everybody was being sued. Nobody messed with Chi Kharisma. The *Four Amigos* had come to the right place for resolution and they knew it. They meant business and they wanted their dignity back.

"Sarge wants to be in charge of the bar!" Clarence said nonchalantly.

"And we want our money back!" Max added.

"And we all want out of that *Hell-hole!*" shouted Henry. "Inaction sucks."

"We have rights!" Sarge interrupted." It's time to act --- now; immediately!"

"Wow, slow down men, you'll get your blood pressures sky-high." Chi warned. "What's this all about? What bar? What money? What hell-hole? And, what rights?"

Chi just couldn't help but sense how frantic and desperate his *Amigos* were.

"We want to love life again, live life and have fun before we die. But we got troubles." Clarence clarified. "We're sick and tired of being sick and tired. We want to take charge of our destiny, invest in our safety, our future. We long for peace and comfort but unfortunately, we live in fear, antitrust and disgust. The living conditions are intolerable."

"It's insulting." Sarge's tongue was sparking from his mouth. "You ain't heard nothing yet. Our fate is in the hands of unconscionable bastards. *Gandhi* said *'you should judge a civilization by the way they treat their animals'*."

"How would he classify our society for the way it treats its senior citizens? Ironically," he continued, "*Truth* is, but akin to *Cool*, as both are *Repulsive* to the *Un*."

"Some of us," Henry interjected, "are even praying --- *Hail Mary full of grace, get me out of this crazy place, controversy.*"

Chi just laughed. But the *Amigos* were serious, as they were hot under the collar and had their sights on the *Truth* or else coup d'état. Loss of moral, anxiety and pessimism have corroded *Prudent-Paradise*; thanks to acts of ill-wills. It was in fact, a time for a change and they needed Chi to answer to their prayers. It wouldn't take much more to convince him, but they continued by stating their case with a great argument, concerns and facts.

"We've seen the light so to speak," Max added, "a reality check. We are trapped in an absurd predicament. We are neglected, over medicated, physically violated, mentally anguished and some are sexually abused. It's a fucken nightmare."

"We actually fear for our lives." he continued convincingly. "It's time to fight back, hold them responsible for their actions. We intend to file a class action lawsuit on behalf of all the residents of *Prudent-Paradise*."

"I just flew in from DC an hour ago," replied Chi. "We were there for two weeks, the whole family. But I did hear something on the radio in the car on the way here from the airport; something about protesters demonstrating."

"I had no idea it was of this magnitude. I was going to stop over this afternoon to investigate. Why didn't you guys consult with me sooner? Never be afraid to call me. What happened to your leg Max?"

"He got Involved!" Henry shouted. "Now we all want to get involved. We had it. 'Oldage', according to Cicero: *'is the crown of life, our play's last act'* and we plan on going out --- kicking and a swinging if necessary, but hopefully --- partying."

"We intend to control our own destiny, make a difference between peace and misery. For you can't negotiate with evil; it thrives on negotiation. Will you please help us set the record straight as ominous expectations are terrifying?" Clarence was adamant.

"I'm in your corner!" Chi assured. "Now what's this about rape and physical abuse? *Prudent-Paradise* has the best reputation on the east coast. It's state of the art, paramount to being a class-act."

"It's a fucken prison with hush, hush bull-shit. Talk is cheap; rhetoric and broken promises are more like it." Sarge fumed again with his sharp tongue.

"Some of the residents are so doped up that they don't even get out of bed. Those of us that do mingle, mind our own business. Especially in the last six months, since the staff cuts and changes. I don't know where they hired the new help from. They are so impatient, so cruel and lack experience."

Chi shook his head in total disgust and astonishment. He felt their frustration as Sarge continued.

"Shit, I don't think that half of them can read let alone give needles without missing the vein a few times or take blood pressure accurately. They spend most of their time bitching and complaining about the job and how they deserve a raise. They laugh if we complain about or question their abilities."

"They relish in bad-attitudes." Max agreed. "They're selfish, inconsiderate, rude and nasty-mean; void of values, without soul. I don't know whether the state or feds cut back on funding or what, but something is wrong. Malfunctions? We are in deep shit literally as our lives are in the hands of a bunch of mishaps."

"Three days ago," Henry added: "Thomas O'leary got beaten to a pulp because he shit his bed. He's in a coma now, in the intensive care unit at the county hospital. Two days before that, the same demented bastard that beat Thomas, pushed Max over a bunch of tables for helping Thomas with his bed pan. He declared that Max fell on his own because he was goofing around."

"It was his word against mine. That's when I broke my leg." Max cried. "That crazy lunatic is in jail now and we found out just the other day, that he had been beating and raping Marge Taylor for three or four months."

"She is so scared," Clarence informed, "that it's no wonder she hasn't spoken a word since it all started. The fucken prick was caught raping her right after he beat Thomas. Rumor has it that he was on some shit called --- crack."

"The shit is hitting the fan. Everybody is anticipating more scandal. We are suspicious and skeptical of the whole staff. Paranoia is prevalent. Chaos is pending. And we want out."

"Rest assured, your wish is my command." Chi promised as he sympathized with their plight. He sensed the ominous feeling of discontent in his *Grand-fathers* voice.

"Lawsuits, new staff, state and fed investigations, etc. etc. Now let's go have a talk with the administration and put the fear of God into them and guarantee your safety."

The *Four Amigos* felt relieved. They were all glad that they told it like it is, got it off their chest. They summed it all up --- page, chapter and verse; as they were all gung-ho. They may be old, but they were ready, willing and able to make a difference as their hearts were in the right place. They were up for the challenge.

They wanted to clean house, disinfect the germs, and abolish *Hell*. It wasn't a pleasant picture or a hopeful future. Compromise and attitude adjustments were out of the question, not options; as they weren't the answers to their problem. They had a *Grand Plan!*

"Not so fast," Clarence insisted, "that's not the answer. There is more, much more to deal with."

"OK, something about money and a bar?" Chi didn't forget. "However, I haven't a clue what you guys are referring to," he continued. "But I do sense the anxiousness; the extreme urgency in the matter. Enlighten me."

"Well," Clarence replied, "we were all naïve and too hasty in our original decision. We want all of the money we signed over to our families back. We don't care about tax laws, inheritance penalties, medical costs, etc. etc."

"Ironically, we tried to pull a fast one and save some money for our families by beating the system. But unfortunately, the system is beating and abusing us literally. It's our money, we earned it and we deserve to spend it by choice ---- freely. We need it and we need it now! What ever amount we can get back, will help."

"Actually," Henry elaborated, "we wish to invest it."

"We want to incorporate our own safety!" Sarge exclaimed. "In foreign countries, the old are held in high esteem, worshipped for their wisdom with honor and respect. Unfortunately, here in the US, we are treated like burdens --- senile old fools. A fart gets more respect."

"We are determined to exercise our duty and help each other." Max vowed. "It's time for a change. The *'System;'* sucks. Together, we shall establish our own privately owned retirement / nursing *Commune;* with doctors and nurses on staff, along with a bar, hot-tubs, pool, coed rooms and whatever we agree upon."

"We are willing to go public, but we prefer to be a nonprofit organization." Clarence insisted. "We'll solicit philanthropists, barter, beg, borrow, steal or do whatever we have to do to succeed."

Chi scratched his head and then, he started to laugh again. He laughed so hard that it was contagious as everybody joined in. The commotion was so loud that it caught his secretary's curiosity as she came a sniffing and a snooping into the room.

"Hold all of my calls Suezy." Chi commanded. "I'm in the fight of my life. These guys are on a mission. *'May the Force be with us?'* "

"Amen!" yelled Henry.

"This calls for a toast." Sarge suggested.

"But of course," Chi agreed as he pulled out a bottle of *Jack*.

Suezy got six shot glasses and they all toasted to their emancipation; a dedication in the name of *Social Security, a Little Peace on Earth --- a Last Hurrah*.

After the short celebration, Chi followed his four *Amigos* back to *Hell* and literally put the fear of God into the administration; which guaranteed their safety. He promised to talk to all of their families regarding their prior money; since he handled all the legal matters in the first place. He didn't anticipate any problems in getting most of the money back as he knew all parties involved.

He assured them that he'd use his reputation to put the screws to any resister --- if necessary. It was a moral issue which involved principles, a matter of life and death, peace and happiness. Chi vowed to represent all that needed his help in any way to get this project realized. After all, he loved his *Pa-Pa* as well as the other *Amigos*.

SOCIAL SECURITY

It was pandemonium at suppertime in the mess hall when the word got out --- an elated uproar. The excitement was cause for disorder. The seniors acted like a pack of teens.

"No more victims of circumstances!" someone yelled.

"Victory shall be ours!" added another.

It could have gotten chaotic if Clarence didn't calm them down. Finally an *aura of peace* prevailed. Every coherent resident wanted in. United they all vowed to stand. They even agreed to take care of the incoherent.

The following morning, the *Four Amigos* paid a visit to the *County Hospital* where Thomas was still in the intensive care unit. Miraculously, he came out of his coma during the night. Clarence got a call just before breakfast from Chi, who was already on the job.

When they got to Thomas' room; he still looked a terrible mess, all bruised up, black and blue, IV bags, etc. But needless to say; he was glad to be back. He was elated with the *Amigos*' brainchild --- *Social Security* and he also had some good news.

"The doctors said that I should be out of here in a few weeks." he whispered in a frail voice to his buddies. "According to them, I should be able to walk out on my own two feet. Look!" he laughed as he wiggled his toes.

The *Amigos* were grateful with Thomas' recovery as was the entire *Commune*; when they heard the prognosis. They had a welcome home party for him when he got out of the hospital. Unfortunately, he returned to the *Commune* in a wheelchair. He got all of his feeling back, but he had trouble with his balance when he tried to walk. The doctors said that there was a fifty / fifty chance that he would fully recover back to normal; considering his age.

Regardless, Thomas was content and hopeful. He was pleased to be home. He had a new outlook on life. When you face death, life has new meaning. When you are bed-ridden, you have plenty of time to think.

You pray for a *Second Chance* and promise not to *Fuck It Up*. He realized that he got his *Second Chance* and vowed to never complain again. He pledged that he would live each day as if it were his last and enjoy it for what it was. He looked forward to *Social Security,* a fresh start for the *Commune*. And he prayed that the rest of the residents; would *Realize How Precious Life Truly Is*.

Unfortunately as might be expected, there was a variety of egos that lived at the *Commune*. Some were bright and cheerful old souls while others were sad and miserable; living in the past. They were mad at the world and life itself.

But, who was to blame; God? Chi had his work cut out for him. But in the name of *Love and Justice*, failure wasn't an option.

CHAPTER **TWO**

Genesis

Chapter 2   Genesis

They say that patience is a virtue but the natives were restless as anticipation lingered. They had something to live for again, however time has a way of making some people impatient. Fortunately, hope kept their dream alive and faith in God, self, Chi and each other made it a reality as optimism set the tone.

It was Sarge who came up with their motto. Being a former *Marine*, a retired lifer, it was only natural to adopt *Semper Fi*, (*Always Faithful*) for *Social Security* --- their new *Retirement-Commune / Nursing Home*. Active participation was paramount and pets were welcomed. A garden was mandatory; especially since homegrown veggies are the healthiest.

"All for one and one for all," Clarence yelled as he christened the newly renovated building, which was sold to its former inmates.

"Amen!" Echoed the crowd as they all rejoiced in the big parking lot at *Social Security*.

"It's ours, it's ours!" somebody hollered.

"Congratulations Pa." Chi praised as he shook Clarence's hand. "Good Luck."

"Thanks," Clarence replied. "We're going to need it."

Cameras were all over the place, everywhere; media galore as the elders had had enough and took matters --- destiny into their own hands. Creativity was their savior as they bonded in togetherness.

"Speech, speech," the crowd chanted; as Clarence neared the podium with Chi and the *Mayor* of the city.

"Congratulations fellow citizens for your efforts and your achievement. On behalf of all of the residents here in the city of Buffalo, New York; we are proud of each and every one of you inspired reformers for your courage. We wish you the very best of luck and I am privileged to present your *Commune* with these two hand-carved, golden engraved plaques to hang; one over your door and the other over your fireplace."

"The first plaque is adopted from *Peace Pilgrim*; as her philosophy is the *Sacred Way of Peace*:

*'Overcome evil with Good,
Falsehood with Truth,
And hatred, with Love'*."

The crowd went berserk. "Peace! Peace! Peace at last!" they all chanted until the *Chief Magistrate* continued. "The second plaque simply reads:

*Social Security
Our
Home Sweet Home!* "

"May *God Bless* and protect each and every one of you."

Again, the crowd went crazy. "Peace! Peace! Peace at last." they shouted.

Clarence stepped up to the podium, waved his hands to get their attention, but they only got louder.

"My dear, dear friends," he interrupted, "I understand that we are about to receive a couple monetary gifts. Actually," he specified, "two generous donations. May I introduce Eon Adams from *IARP*, and Quincy Johnson, from *Humane International*? Let's give them a warm and hardy welcome."

The crowd cheered as the two men came up to the podium. Mr.

Adams spoke first. His presentation was short and sweet.

"It is an honor to be here. On behalf of the *International Association of Retired People*, I am pleased to award your *Commune* with this million-dollar check."

"Thank you!" "Thank you!" "Thank you!" the crowd cheered.

Next, Mr. Johnson gave an identical speech and on behalf of *Humane International*, presented Clarence with another million-dollar check. This time though, Clarence gave the: "Thank You."

"United we stand." Clarence shouted.

"United we stand," the crowd roared back.

"Blessed is he," Clarence continued, "who is dedicated to our *Legacy of Love; a willing effort and a will to share.*" Clarence knew how to work the crowd, but he had no intentions of exploiting his captive audience. His motives were purely spiritual --- in the Name of Humanity.

"Dedication, dedication, dedication," the crowd promised.

"As you all know, we wouldn't be here today, if it weren't for my grandson Malachite Kharisma; better known as Chi."

"Chi, Chi, Chi!" the crowd chanted as Chi approached the microphone and addressed his clients.

"I am proud to represent *Social-Security*. Your *Constitution of Love* is simple and as sacred as any constitution anywhere. It puts all the others to shame. Courtesy, commitment and communication are edifying."

"Your pledge to honor, serve and protect each other is precious. Betrayal is evil. Evil is ugly. Live up to your promise to stand up to evil. You have a right to bare arms. You have a right to own pets as well as a bar, sunken-hot-tubs, coed-rooms and --- no curfew."

"Freedom, freedom, freedom," the crowd cheered!

"*Hell* is history!" Chi continued. "But its evil was no mystery. For as Mark Twain warned: '*Loyalty to petrified opinion never broke a chain or freed a human soul.*'"

"Your silence only fanned the flames of its dirty secrets. Your silence became consent. And don't you ever forget it. For evil must be confronted --- always. We must demand accountability,

accountability, accountability; in spite of plausible deniability and pretentious intentions."

"When *shit happens;* you must deal with it. When *Grace Happen;* you best enjoy it. Savor your *Blessings.* Beware of the power of suggestion. Consent is precious. Don't get conned. Choice is yours --- 'To do or, not to do?' It's your responsibility. And remember that the secular powers that be --- fear the power of a crowd; the power of the people as well as the power of conscientious objection."

"United, you succeeded. You took charge of your destiny as you invested in your future; your safety. You realized that co-dependency is sacred and dependability is divine as care, concern and compassion ensure relationships."

"Never underestimate the *Power of Love.* Embrace each other --- Always. Love is the *Divine Word of God.* Love heightens awareness and enhances the quality of interactions. Chivalry is a code of courage, a charismatic vow --- to defend the weak and challenge the strong. Charisma is a *Gift of Grace;* influence. It must be utilized wisely."

"In closing, I leave you with a thought to ponder: --- Does respect have to be earned? Or is respect a mutual given until --- it is forfeited? *Thank You* and *God Bless Your Peaceful Co-Existence."*

The crowd cheered and applauded until Clarence stepped up to the mike and yelled. "Who's hungry? Dinner is being served as you listen. I spied the Mayor sneaking over there. Look, there he is stuffing his face. Go and get your share, but save some for the press and me."

The first day was hectic to say the least. It started out in chaos as family members were bringing *pets* for their *Loved-Ones.* Sarge slipped in a puddle of piss. The noise was unbelievable, fighting was inevitable; amongst the creatures and the *Commune* was divided in bickering concerns as war broke out.

Clarence had to call a special meeting to address the issues, certain particulars. Compromise was necessary. It wasn't easy but rules were agreed upon and established. Responsibility was mandated as boundaries were set. The pet problem was dealt with swiftly and satisfactory; proper edicts.

Unfortunately, that was just the beginning as Max put on a CD of --- 'Lets Get Drunk and Screw' (by Jimmy Buffett) and four men and three women got drunken shit-faced. Three of them puked all over the place. Two of the women got in a catfight over one of the guys. Sarge pulled what little hair he had had left out of his head. He barred all seven of them.

Needless to say, too many of them prayed to the porcelain gods. Bar rules had to be established. No more free booze; deterrents were necessary. No more alcohol allowed in the sunken bar at the pool. Somebody got tipsy and fell into the water. The lifeguard saved her.

Sex was going on in half of the rooms. Two of the condom dispensers jammed, but at least they were practicing safe sex. One resident gave *Viagra* to anybody and everybody who wanted it. One of the male residents got so excited that he literally had a heart attack. Thank God, he didn't die.

Eventually, sex had to be subjected to protocol; as precautions were necessary. The majority had spoken as you needed a special ID pass and permission from your doctor to participate in the O-Zone; a 1960's type of *Free-Love-room* --- including incense, candles, hanging-beads, strobe-lights, VCRs, couches, vibrating chairs, heart-shaped-Jacuzzis', etc.

Unfortunately, you can't please all the people all the time as freedom entails responsibility. But at least most of the *Commune*, felt alive again. And all savored the atmosphere of safety, comfort and love --- *Quality Time Together*.

All in all, believe it or not; other than a few plugged toilets and an asthma attack, no other major incidents occurred that first week. Perhaps the excitement wore off or perhaps they could behave like adults after all. But, maybe one party a week was all that they could handle. Time would tell; as the staff didn't know what to expect next.

At times, they got a good laugh but other times, they were startled as the elders exploited curiosity and went with the flow. Their adopted thesis was choice of desire --- *'when in Rome, do as the Romans do.'* It was a menagerie of *'Monkey see, Monkey do.'* How long would it last - *Peer-Pressure?*

Clarence was having a bad day. In fact, it was a rough week. He thought to himself; *what did I get myself into? I haven't had time to take a decent shit on the throne.*
Suddenly, he was struck by an idea!
"That's it," he mumbled, "it's time to slow down;" as he pondered Oliver Wendell Holmes:
'What lies behind us and what lies before us are tiny matters compared to what lies within us.'
Things will work out in due time; he assured himself. All I need is a little fortitude; the strength to persist, the courage to endure. Faith is the Key. Bold Belief. Fear and doubt are Divine No-No's. And then, he remembered and prayed the 'Serenity Prayer':
'God grant me the serenity to accept the things I cannot change; the courage to change the things I can and the wisdom to know the difference.'
He was sincere as he vowed to himself --- I'll do my best, but I'm letting go and letting God. The ball is in His hands now. So be it.
Nonchalantly, Clarence spotted the *Baby Grand Piano*, just sitting there in the huge living room. It was anonymously donated six weeks ago. It's been collecting dust, fifteen feet from the stone fireplace, unnoticed, untouched; pure neglect.
Shame on us, he surmised; but to his surprise, it was in perfect tune. After all, he should know since he pounded the ivory before he could talk. Without hesitation, he played the first solo that he learned, *Chop-Sticks*.
He got so involved that it was if he were back in time, practicing it over and over and over again and again until he realized he had had a huge audience. He stopped and they applauded as fate interjected.
"Please continue. Do you know anything else," said a strange voice? Clarence was dumbstruck as he was bitten by the *Luv-Bug*.

"It, it, it's been a long time." he stuttered.

"Mind if I join you?" she asked seductively.

"No, no, not at all," Clarence admitted shyly as he moved over. She slid next to him and they played *Double Chop-Sticks*; as her smell of perfume drove him wild.

"What's your name?" Clarence asked curiously.

"Peggy Austin," she replied.

"Oh yeah," he remembered as he stood up politely for a brief moment to shake her hand and she obliged.

"I'm Clarence Kharisma and I sort of help get things organized around here at *Social Security*. I am pleased to meet you."

"Likewise," she responded.

"You're here for the position of *Director of Nursing Staff*," he continued as he sat back down next to her.

"Your resume is quite impressive, your credentials --- outstanding. The board approved and we did an extensive background check. And you already seem to fit in here. Just look at them smiling faces."

"You're hired, if you wish Ms. Austin. Your hours should be a steady routine so it shouldn't interfere with your social or married life."

"It's a pleasure to meet you too," she replied. "I've seen your picture in the paper several times and I think I'm going to like it here. Yes, I wish but, please call me Peg."

"Your wish is my command Peg," Clarence granted.

"Thank you," Peg responded. "By the way, I am a widow and I don't mind any extra hours; if I can help out in any way. I encourage and endorse what you are trying to do here."

"Your presence is most welcomed." he assured while he pounded out more *Chop-Sticks*; one final time as Peg rejoined him again.

"Lucy, my secretary will show you to your office. Shall we go find her?"

"Why certainly," Peg agreed as the duet rose together and got a standing-ovation from their audience.

"Encore! Encore!" they shouted.

"Later," Clarence promised. "We all have some work to do. Now

SOCIAL SECURITY

go tend to your duties."

"Slave driver, slave driver," yelled Chi who caught their performance; unbeknownst to them.

"Pa-Pa, Pa-Pa," little Jim-Jim, the apple of Chi and Clarence's eye came running and jumped into Clarence's arms.

"Can I do dat?" he pointed excitedly.

"No, not now Jimmy," shouted his mother ---- Brandie; Chi's wife.

"Leave him alone," ordered Clarence. "Of course you can play with the piano."

"Come here Jim-Jim," yelled Lucy. "You can teach me how to tickle the *Ivory*."

"Oh no Lucy," Clarence verbally chastised her gently. "You have to get Peg situated --- show her the ropes. Jimmy can learn Pa-Pa."

"Slave driver, slave driver," Lucy verified.

"Sorry *Tyrant*," Chi interjected. "But we --- you and I have business to attend to. They made an offer but I think we can get more. Besides, Jimmy and Brandie are going to the zoo."

"So are you and I." Clarence insisted. "We can talk there with the animals as our witnesses. I might need some extra special advice, some divine inspiration as we frolic freely."

Everybody just laughed as they went about their business.

In the SUV, on the ride to the zoo; Clarence was at peace. *What a difference a couple of hours can make*, he thought. *At 9 AM, I was overwhelmed; I felt so burned-out. But now --- 11 AM*, as he glanced at the clock on the vehicle's radio; *I feel so wonderful. Thank you Jesus!*

Jim-Jim broke the silence of the quiet travel.

"Can I tell Pa-Pa da secret?"

"What secret," asked Clarence curiously?

"Go right ahead Jimmy!" Brandie insisted.

"Mommy gonna have a baby!"

"Oh my, my, congratulations to --- each and every one of you," Pa exclaimed with joy! "When is the *Blessed Event*?"

"There is plenty of time." Chi assured. "But there is another surprise. Enlighten him Bran."

"Well, I've been soliciting donations for the *Commune* for the last six months, without any luck until today. Nelson Brinkworth from Jersey, the rich and famous philanthropists, just wrote a check for $10 million!"

Astonished in disbelief, Clarence was flabbergasted with elation over the generosity.

"Oh my, my," he shouted! "Thank you Brandie! Thank you Nelson! Thank you Jesus!"

"Amen!" Chi interrupted. "God works in mysterious ways; patience is a virtue, persistence divine. The insurance offer is tempting Pa, but I think that we should refuse it; as patience, in spite of its rather exceptional generosity."

"You have the final say. However, this $10 million donation will more than cover all the upgrades as well as the new equipment. *Social Security* is solvent. Besides, the state suit is still pending. We can afford to wait. It would be stupid to jump on the first proposal and stupidity is an unforgivable sin."

"You're the expert," Clarence replied. "Our welfare is in your hands. We trust your proficient judgment, second to none."

"Thanks Pa," Chi answered modestly yet proud that the *Commune* cherished his evaluations. "I shall decline the offer and see them in court if need be. The jury will act as our power of persuasion. They'll surely re-negotiate, as they can't afford negative publicity; since they still own another dozen facilities."

"I'll drag this through the media upon media, multi-media-galore; until they beg --- settle, settle, please. They can't deny the facts, the ugly truth. They are liable. *Hell* was evil as its wrap-sheet / record, speaks for itself."

"How are Marge and Thomas doing?" asked Brandie sympathetically.

"Marge sulks in silence. She still hasn't spoken a single word and Thomas gets out and about in his wheelchair. Unfortunately, his legs are still shaky; his balance is unstable?" Clarence cried. "The doctors don't know if he'll ever be able to walk again."

"That bastard should be castrated." Chi declared with a voice of anger. "He hasn't any conscience in any size, shape or form. His willful disregard for others is diabolically evil. What he did is unforgivable. Justice is not compensation and compensation is not closure, but it's a start."

"Marge's, Thomas' and Max's lawsuits are all separate issues. Each of them will go in front of a jury. Negligence, neglect and rape as well as mental and physical abuse are serious charges."

"Ggarrffs, ggarrffs, giraffes, giraffes," Jimmy pointed as he tripped on his tongue!

"That's right Jim-Jim." verified Pa-Pa. "Do you want to feed them?"

"Can I? Can I?" he cried.

"But of course," Pa assured him with delight.

While Jimmy was feeding the giraffes, Clarence smiled to himself. The apple-of-his-eye had a twinkle in his eye. He recognized that look, that innocence --- *Blissful Ignorance*. After all, he raised his family and he was there as Chi grew up. It was as if he were going back in time --- memories and sweet memories.

Clarence shared his wisdom with Chi and Brandie as he explained that: "When you look into the eyes of a child, you see pure-passion; a lust for life, hope, trust and curiosity. A child," he continued, "is the essence of beauty, an entrusted miracle; longing for *Love*."

"Inadvertently, they know that they must adapt and grow up, but they also learn that death is ordained. Sometimes they learn it the hard way as death can be so sneaky. We can try and dry their tears and comfort their sorrows. But unfortunately, we can't do their crying for them; no matter how bad they hurt. And believe me; it is hard when you lose a parent at a young age. Even the loss of a pet can be somewhat devastating for a while. Ironically, death has a funny way of giving you a new-out-look on life. "

"Enjoy him," he advised, "because he'll grow up fast. And watch over him as there is plenty of evil in this world that is watching and waiting; anticipating if and when to lure upon, abuse, corrupt and / or manipulate him. There is nothing worst than burying your child.

I shed my share of tears over the years and each has its own story; some happy, some sad but regardless, life goes on."

"So, encourage his dreams and learn from his innocence. Set an example and teach him the value of *Love by Giving him Love*. Never give up on him. If he gives up on him-self; give him a swift kick in the ass and then hug and kiss him. There is no substitute for *Love*. Unfortunately, we can't make choices for our children. They must make their own mistakes. Experience is the best teacher. Everybody gets knocked on his ass; every now and then."

Brandie had tears in her eyes as she listened to Pa's concerning discourse and patted her pregnant stomach. She knew that Clarence lost a teen-aged son; William. Chi put his arm around his emotional wife as Pa helped Jim feed the giraffes and continued with his rational.

"Ironically," he exclaimed, "society also infringes upon their innocence as well as their dreams; just as it does to its seniors. Is it not a vicious circle? Oddly enough, so many old revert back to being a child as subconsciously, we all long for the safety and comfort of *Mother's womb*. As a matter of fact, some even curl-up into the fetal position --- longing for *Love*. May God bless them all, both the *young* as well as the *old?*"

Suddenly, Clarence picked Jim-Jim up and cradling him in his arms, he added: "We are all *Mysterious Miracles of God*. Someday, mankind will learn the difference between *Curiosity* and *Compassion*."

Chi and Brandie are touched by Pa's sincerity. They hug and kiss each other and then; Chi jokes: "Brandie sleeps in a curled-up-fetal-position."

"Ha, ha, ha," she mumbles as they all laugh and then; she smacked him on his chest.

Speaking of miracles, Jim-Jim got the biggest kick out of the two baby giraffes, as he was tickled-pink.

"Can I ride them Pa- Pa? Can I, can I, Please?"

"Sorry," Brandie spoils his plan. "You can't ride giraffes. They're not like horses."

SOCIAL SECURITY

"Yes you can!" insisted little Jimmy.

"Can not."

"Can too! I rode one on the Merry-go-round."

Brandie, Chi and Clarence just busted out laughing again.

"From the mouths of *Babes*," Pa warned. "Beware as *Innocence can be Embarrassing*. The *Truth* will set you --- fleeing in a Hurry."

"We already experienced a few episodes --- when we wanted to crawl under a rock and hide." Chi admitted.

"Like *Father*, like *Son*," Brandie teased.

"Like *Grandfather*, like *Grandson*, like *Great-Grandson*." Chi shifted the blame.

"It's hereditary, DNA doesn't lie; it's in the genes." Pa confessed officially.

"I'm hungry." Jimmy growled.

"Me too," Pa agreed.

"What do you guys want to eat?" asked Brandie.

"Cotton-candy and a snow-cone," Jim-Jim demanded!

"How about we get some hot-dogs and French-fries first?" Dad suggested. "Then you can have anything your little heart desires."

"Really," he asked?

"Really," Dad promised!

"OK but I, I want a hambrgg with mustrdd with my Fench frays and a milk-shakkk!" Jimmy replied as all responded in another elated uproar.

After they finished lunch, Jimmy decided that he wanted a huge stuffed-animal --- *Gorgeous Gorilla*. Pa granted his wish and Jim-Jim wanted to go home and play with it.

"So much for the Zoo," Mom said without any doubt.

"We can come back --- Tomorrow!" replied the *Apple-of-Their-Eye*.

"I guess determination and initiative run in the family too." Pa surmised. "Sometimes parents have to respect the wishes of their children."

"Ironically," he warned, "The *Bible* commands: *'to Honor your Mother and Father.'* But, did they honestly earn your respect? Are they truly worthy of your honor? How about your pity?"

"Shouldn't we honor our children? Will we earn their respect? Or, will they pity us? Isn't every child a precious interactive part of the *Circle-of-Life* as we *En-Trust* them with *Our Future*? Unfortunately, pay-back can be *hell*. So behold as an *Understanding Heart* is a *Cause for Concern*."

Both Chi and Brandie nodded as if to heed Clarence's advice as he continued. "Beware of the terrible-twos' and threes' as they require *Love and Patience*. And, beware of the terrible-teens' as they require more *Love and Patience*. Love is the *Stellar Force of Nature*. Love should be held in the highest reverence; awe, affection and veneration as *Love Ensures the Beauty of Life*."

"Never," he continued, "never break a young and innocent spirit with conformity as his passion shall become --- dull routine. But encourage that same young and innocent spirit with *Love and Understanding* and his passion will exceed --- our *Wildest Dreams*."

Brandie and Chi both promised to do their best as Pa let them in on his little secret. "I believe in reincarnation and I also believe that we all choose our own *Parents*; before birth as part of a *Spiritual Goal*."

While Pa-Pa was giving his little sermon, Jim-Jim fell fast asleep in his mother's arms, cuddling his *Gorgeous Gorilla*. Clarence was extremely proud as a peacock; of his pro-creations. He closed his eyes too and contemplated on his experiences here on *Mama Earth*; a little soul-searching.

He had witnessed his share of life and death; the joy and the pain of daily existence; grief, sorrow and acceptance, as well as struggle, rejection and deprivation. It was still hard to comprehend, perhaps even harder to swallow. The good times are great, but they seem to fly by too fast. He came to realize that *life is a matter of Truth or Consequences; 'To do' or 'not to do', per reason, free will and conscientious objection.*

He valued his *Intuition*. He recognized the significance, the importance of getting involved. Each and everybody have a duty to

SOCIAL SECURITY

make a difference, to risk his life if necessary in the name of truth, justice and the humane-way.

Why is man so mystique, so obscure? He asked himself. *Peculiarly, man is the mystery himself. We make life so complicated. Why?*

'The Fall' was no accidental coincidence --- waiting to happen. It was inevitable. For when curiosity and greed unite, it is like water and oil; which don't mix. It is a sure recipe for disaster. God help us, please. Where are we headed? He wondered?

Intuitively, Clarence perceived that 'Freedom isn't Free', and 'Need knows No-Season'. Ironically, sometimes life can be so ugly; even unbearable. But it's an awful crying shame when humans make it uglier. It's just plain evil when they don't get involved or just sit back, laugh and do nothing about it; poverty, need, greed, corruption, neglect and abuse of power. Ironically, life is a living hell thanks to both the sins of commission as well as the sins of omission.

Suddenly, Clarence awoke from his meditative state and shared his revelations with Chi since Brandie was also asleep. Chi was impressed with Pa's wisdom and shared his convictions exactly. But they had other issues to address; they didn't have time to save the world. Not now, perhaps later; perhaps when *Social Security* was smooth, without doubts or confusion.

"What do you think about Peg?" Chi changed the subject.

Clarence beamed with embarrassment. He felt uneasy, somewhat self-conscious and yet anxious, but downplayed his excitement as he literally forgot about her.

"Ah, she's OK." he mumbled as anticipation set in and his mind wondered again --- *Maybe, just maybe* he hoped. *But shit, was she too young;* he pondered with doubt?

Would she reject me? She must be in her mid fifties? Damn it, I can't ask her, her age. That's a No-No.

Chi just laughed in silence as disappointment appeared on Clarence's face. It was obvious that he was frustrated until Brinkworth's $10 million donation danced in his head. He couldn't wait to tell the others.

Why, he thought to himself; *why didn't I let go sooner and let God --- Always?*

Peg greeted Clarence when he got dropped off; back home at *Social Security*. His heart pounded like crazy and then skipped a beat or two. He felt stupid. He was clumsy, weak in the knees as he almost awkwardly tripped over his own two feet. "Calm down," he told himself as he headed for a *Jack*.

"Sound the *Cause for Celebration!*" he commanded with excitement as Sarge tolled the bell and asked:

"What happened to the slave driver?"

"There is a time to work and a time for play." Clarence replied. "But this isn't either. It's a time to celebrate," he shouted as the bar got filled with curiosity.

"We got a donation and I mean a donation, $10 million, tax free; complements of Mr. Nelson Brinkworth. It's a wonderful day."

"Thank you Jesus," somebody yelled, as everybody was so excited!

"Drinks are on the house!" announced Sarge as Peg strolled over and congratulated Clarence. He thanked her and everybody toasted cheers to *Social Security*; in the name of Mr. Brinkworth. And then, someone put a CD in of Louis Armstrong's famous solo, *What a Wonderful World*.

It was unbelievable as everybody sang; everybody except Marge and some incoherent patients on the second floor.

*** *What a Wonderful World*
*** **'What a Wonderful World'**, is a song by Bob Thiele (using the pseudonym George Douglas) and George David Weiss. It was first recorded by Louis Armstrong

I see trees of green, red roses too
I see them bloom for me and you
And I think to myself, what a wonderful world.

SOCIAL SECURITY

*I see skies of blue and clouds of white
The bright blessed day, the dark sacred night
And I think to myself, what a wonderful world.*

*The colours of the rainbow, so pretty in the sky
Are also on the faces of people going by
I see friends shakin hands, sayin' "How do you do"
They're really saying "I Love You"*

*I hear babies cryin', I watch them grow
They'll learn much more than I'll ever know
And I think to myself, what a wonderful world
Yes, I think to myself, what a wonderful world*

Oh Yeah.

When the song ended, Peg had tears in her eyes. The participation was so electrifying, poetry in motion. Clarence looked at her and she jumped in his arms and gave him a big hug-n-kiss.

"I'm sorry." she apologized as she shocked the living shit out of him. "I, I, I just couldn't help myself. I'm just so happy for all of you. You have something very extra special here. I'm proud to be aboard. It's *Divine!*"

Clarence was in *Puppy-Love-shock*. He was utterly speechless but decided to play a hunch; as he trusted his gut instinct --- *Intuition*, which never failed him.

"I need a confidant," he confided. "Somebody I can trust with extra special activities. Loyalty is pertinent, even critical for the *Commune*. Are you interested?"

She closed her eyes, took a deep breath and said. "I am but let me sleep on it first."

"OK!" Clarence agreed. "We'll talk tomorrow. Now then, do you want to dance?"

"I do!" She giggled like a teen with butterflies in her stomach, as Clarence was quite the charmer.

They were both goo-goo-eyed; as they danced in delight until well past midnight. In fact, nobody left early as they all deserved it --- *Good Time Rock n Roll*, liquid spirits, pizza, wings, subs and *Friendship*.

Clarence insisted on Peg getting a ride home from the night staff driver. He told her to leave her car here and that the day driver would pick her up at 8:30 AM sharp. Then he kissed her on her forehead and said "good-nite," as she went gaga into a daze.

She felt a bit tipsy and left with the driver as Clarence requested. She never drank *Jack* before. Asti was her usual preference of choice. Ironically, the bar emptied instantly as if everyone would turn into pumpkins at any minute; everybody except the *Four Amigos*.

"Hey Romeo," Sarge yelled over to Clarence who was gloating in delight. "Was that private property or what?"

"I think he's in *Love*." Henry interpreted. "Did you see them dancing and gawking at each other all night as if they had nothing better to do?"

"Bedroom-eyes but no balls," Max made it unanimous. "Why don't you ask her if she wants to play strip-poker with us?"

"She's special." Clarence retaliated. "She makes me feel young again. You guys are just jealous with envy. She's a fox. Her class shines brightly. But regardless, we need her here; it's destiny. I like her a lot and I'm going to target her heart --- one day at a time."

"You going to roll with the punches," Sarge joked as Clarence walked over to the piano?

"I think he wants to roll her in the sack and jump her bones." Max assumed.

"Ah, leave him alone." Henry sympathizes with jealously. "It looks like they got something pretty special."

"Why thank you for noticing Henry." Clarence replied. "Its magical, I'm on Cloud 9, my destination is --- *Love*."

Clarence began to pound the ivory and sing as his buddies all laughed. But he had the last laugh by the time the night was through. Without effort, straight from his heart, he composed a love song for Peg and it was a beauty.

CHAPTER **Three**

Intrusion

Chapter 3   Intrusion

Needless to say, word spread fast about the *Commune*'s $10 million windfall. It made the front page of the local newspaper as well as TV and radio stations. The media was fascinated with their new liberal lifestyles.

Clarence didn't like the publicity. He was glad that he and his *Amigos* were qualifying tomorrow on the range for their pistol permits. Soon, they would be *Comrades-in-Arms* and he could relax a bit.

Shit by all rights, he thought to himself, *there wasn't any cash here. Nothing to worry about, but then one never knows; what warped or immature minds might think. Besides, the book-making operation was almost ready to go --- full force and that's strictly cash.*

The four comrades were drinking coffee in the sunroom when Peg drove up in the corporate-car. Max whistled at her as she walked up the drive. She blushed beat-red.

"Do you know much about flowers?" Clarence asked her stupidly.

"Good-Morning to you too," she snapped.

"I'm sorry." Clarence apologized. "It's good to see you."

She smiled and greeted the other three *Amigos* who echoed likewise.

"I need a head gardener." Clarence cried.

SOCIAL SECURITY

"I'll take care of it." Peg assured. "Is there any coffee left?" she asked.

"It's on the table next to the grill." Henry enlightens.

"Will you have time to find a *Gardner*?" Max asked kindly.

"I'll manage." she responded confidently.

Ironically, nobody mentioned last night. Clarence was too shy. Sarge, Henry and Max --- minded their own business and Peg was all business-like.

Was she a little hung-over or is she playing hard to get? Clarence wondered. *Women can be so mysterious.*

"I see *Social Security* made the headlines," Peg commented softly.

"We don't need that kind of exposure." Clarence insisted sincerely.

"Clarence," Lucy's voice called out on the intercom system.

"Already," Clarence mumbles as he picked up the phone on the table? "Yeah, yeah, Ok, yeah, I'll be here." he barked.

"Who was it," Sarge asked?

"It was the phone company." he replied. "They want to hook up the lines; upstairs in the *Laugh-Room*, and in the offices on the third floor."

"I can't wait!" Henry laughs. "Hey baby," he continued as he disguises his voice, "do you want to hear how I masturbate?"

"I most certainly do not; you, you repulsive perverted-pig." Peg hollered as she stormed out of the room.

"Wait, wait, hold on, and please give me a chance to explain." Henry pleads as he is lividly embarrassed into blushing shame, literally. The other *Amigos* laugh and laugh and laugh until finally; Henry joins in.

"Don't worry about it." Max harasses him sarcastically. "I'm sure that she will avoid you like the *Black Plaque*. But we know that you're not a sexual predator."

"You do have some splaining to do; right quick." Sarge warned trying to ease the worry on Henry's face. "Perhaps you should pick her a bunch of flowers."

INTRUSION

"I'll explain!" Clarence interrupted jealously. He didn't want anybody infringing upon or giving any presents to Peg but him as he had the *HOTS* for her. He didn't need any competition.

Suddenly, there was a big commotion in the garden; too many chiefs and not enough Indians. Everybody was excited about planting the veggies. Everyone was a self-proclaimed expert.

Pushing and shoving would of ended in actual fighting if it wasn't for Peg, who insisted that each have their own specific task and personal little gardens for whoever wanted one. She sure knew how to delegate. The situation was under control by the time the *Four Amigos* arrived and they respected her for that.

"Wow." Sarge whispered. "She put each and every one of them in their proper place --- peacefully. We could have used her in *Nam*. There is nothing worst then dissension; it can be disastrous. Leadership is critical. She is a natural. She's special indeed. Her diplomatic resolution is precious."

"Ironically," he cautioned, "humans can be as delicate as flowers. Sometimes you have to tip-toe through their egos which are so fragile. They like to be pacified. But, sometimes you must crush an ego or two or they will spread like a poisonous wild fire."

The other three agreed with his sediments, but Clarence was on *Cloud 9* and Henry wished that he was invisible; as he was still sincerely embarrassed, agonizing in shame and self inflicted humiliation.

Nonchalantly, Max warned Clarence, "You best make your move before I play upon her sympathy for my poor old broken leg. Maybe she'll push me around in a wheel chair?" he joked.

"Ha, ha," Clarence laughed. "But you better watch it *Old Buddy*; can the *sympathy strategy* or else you WILL end up in a wheel chair."

They all laughed together as Peg asked: "What's so funny? Is the pervert sharing his dirty gross and offensive secrets?"

Henry just wanted to die again; he was a nervous wreck and felt as if he should crawl under a rock. "It's all a big misunderstanding." Clarence tried to assure her. "Please, please let's all go inside and we will translate the whole thing to you."

She hesitated but followed them into the bar. Suddenly, Sarge announced, "The bar is now officially open. Come sit, wet your whistles. What are your pleasures?"

Peg gave him the evil eye. "A bit early to drink; don't you think?" she replied as she stopped to stand her ground with her hands on her curved hips, looking straight into Henry's eyes.

"I, I think I need a *Jack*." Henry stutters.

"This better be good." Peg reminds them.

Sarge set up five rock-glasses but Peg declines as he only pours four bourbons. Henry downs his like an ordinary shot and says "I'm going to have one more and then I think I'll go and hide in my room."

"Ha-ha-ha," Peg laughs as Sarge sets him up again. Peg sits on a bar-stool while Clarence tries to rectify the situation.

"Believe you-me, it's not what you think. Do you remember when I told you that I could use a confidant?"

"Yeah but," she replied as she planted her arms crossed --- together firmly beneath her well rounded breasts.

"Well," Clarence continued, "that's part of it."

"Well then," she insisted, "I want no part of it!"

Suddenly, she gets up off the bar-stool abruptly and started to walk away again.

"Wait, Wait, Please," Henry shouted!

"I, I, I'm sorry; honest!"

"Give him a chance to explain." Sarge pleaded.

"OK. OK," she responded. "But I warn you."

"Soon you'll be laughing with us." Max budded in.

"Perhaps we should all go and sit at the table." Clarence points.

"Well, spit it out." Peg demands. "Make my day; I could use a good one."

"The *Commune* voted," Clarence tried to clarify and defuse the issue; "and we all decided to go into business. Actually two businesses and one of them, is sort of kinky."

Peg was curious, yet confused.

"You're not pimps. Are you?" she cried.

"Hell no," Clarence assured her! "The first business is going to be run in an office on the third floor. But we didn't get the computers hooked up yet. Besides, we still have research to do. We need a website and a supplier as we plan on selling lingerie and sex-toys."

Ironically, it was Peg's turn to blush with crimson embarrassment as Max interrupted. "We're going to call it *Erotic Delights*."

"That's funny?" Peg asked sadly.

"No, but the other business is." Henry interjected radiantly. "It's something, which the whole *Commune* is looking forward to in anticipation."

"You caught Henry practicing." Sarge joked.

Peg was more confused than ever? "Wha-wha,what," she mumbled out loud?

"We are only going to operate it on Friday and Saturday nights," Henry continued, "in a huge room on the second floor. We named it the *Laugh-Room*."

"It's for shits and giggles," Max grinned. "Everybody wants to participate in *1-900-sex-chat*."

Peg burst out loud; she almost busted a gut. "I guess *Bingo* is obsolete." she surmised. "It, it is brilliant. What a form of entertainment."

"Profitable too," Henry beamed with relief!

"Marvelous, may I participate?" she begged.

"Absolutely, by all means," Sarge assured! "But you better not talk dirty in front of Clarence; he might explode."

Clarence was in shock. He felt like a shrinking violet. He bit his lip with perplexity as he held his tongue. He just wanted to vanish; become invisible or at least change the subject. But, he was speechless.

Peg couldn't believe her ears as the other three were rolling on the floor --- trying to catch their breath.

"What am I going to do with you guy's," she asked? "Maybe I should wear earplugs?"

"You'll get used to us," Max insisted. "We shall surely grow on you."

"That's what I'm afraid of," she responded sarcastically. "Count me in -- *El Confidante.*"

"Alrighty then," Sarge yells! "Can I pour you a Jack?"

"No, no, no *Jack* for me, thank you." Peg refuses.

"Party-Pooper," Henry teases.

"I'll have an Asti, please."

"That's my girl." Clarence says spontaneously without thinking as pure emotions escaped him from his heart again. Peg looks at him with open-mouth observation; as the other three *Amigos* don't dare say a word. Suddenly, she gives Clarence a big kiss and says:

"*I Love Wild-flowers.*"

"It figures." Clarence remarks smartly as he puts his arm around her, looks into her eyes and says, there is more."

"What do you mean --- more?" Peg asked.

"Well, first thing first," Clarence clarified. "With all of those beautiful flowers in the garden; where the hell am I supposed to get wild flowers from, around here?"

"Grow some, Mr. Smart-ass," she replied. "Surprise me. I'm worth it."

They all laughed as Clarence elaborated that there was a third business, which was illegal. Peg was somewhat disappointed, yet concerned. She was irritated but intrigued.

"Detail, details," she demanded. "Spit it out."

"It's my idea." Sarge confessed. "I've been involved in book making, off and on --- my entire life."

"Book-making, of all the nerve; why didn't you say so in the first-place." she responded! "My Granddaddy was one of the biggest bookies in Cleveland --- fifty years ago."

Wow, what a relief. Clarence thought. *Should I ask her to dinner?*

"Are you going to play your new song for Peg; the one that you wrote for her?" The other three *Amigos* echoed in conspiracy, simultaneously.

"What song?" Peg asked anxiously.
"He practiced all last night, after the party." Henry tattled.
"Well," Peg demanded with sparkles in her eyes. "I'm waiting."
"Thanks a lot guys," Clarence mumbles as he drags his heavy legs over to the *Baby Grand* and, without hesitation --- belts out *Destination Love;* flawlessly.

DESTINATION LOVE

I'm on a mission
An old tradition
My destination is your love
I got my eyes on you
I got my mind on you
My target is your heart
I'm gonna wine you and dine you
Treat you oh so right
Each day and every night
Cause I'm on a mission
An old tradition
Destination --- Love

I'm gonna whisper sweet nothings
And think of the some things
That'll sweep you off your feet
You'll get lots of hugs and kisses
And I'll even do the dishes
If that's what it takes
To generate --- a spark
And penetrate --- your heart
Cause I'm on a mission
An old tradition
Destination --- Love

SOCIAL SECURITY

I got my eyes on you
I got my mind on you
My target is your heart
I'm gonna wine you and dine you
Treat you oh so right
Each day and every night
Cause I'm on a mission
An old tradition
Destination --- Love

So fall with me
And we'll be
Destination --- Love
It's just a mission
But what a mission
Destination --- Love

Clarence was quite the crooner as his serenade was fascinating, a welcomed surprise which summoned curiosity. When he finished wooing Peg; the other three *Amigos* were proud as they envied their pal. Needless to say, the crowd cheered and applauded; including four men from the phone company, who were eyeballing the bar.

Peg was awe-struck by *Cupid* as Mr. Kharisma literally swept her off her feet and enraptured her heart.

"Oh," she screamed as she ran over and jumped into his arms conceding --- *"It's Beautiful, Simply Beautiful!"*

They made such a cute couple. Their *Love* for each other was quite obvious as they locked lips and gazed into each other's eyes --- intoxicated.

"Drinks are on the house," yelled Sarge. "It's party time ---- again, a habitual event. Name your poison."

Even the telephone crew joined in --- gladly. Somebody put a CD in and soon, the dance-floor was packed; including the two *Lovebirds* as well as Henry and Lucy.

Ironically, it was Lucy who dragged Henry out to cut a rug as Max and Sarge egged him on. Peg pointed to the pair as she and Clarence swayed with the music. He laughed, until she whispered into his ear:

"Incidentally, I can hook you up with both a web-site-designer and a wholesale lingerie supplier who also deals in joy-toys and dirty-movies."

"Ooh," Clarence fantasizes, "connections and a bit naughty. I think I like that. Any more secrets you want to confess?"

"I'll take the fifth." she pleaded.

"I suppose you're computer savvy too." he joked.

"But of course I am," she replied.

He kissed her and tells her that she is a God-send. Then he asked. "Are you?"

"Am I what," she giggled?

"My Girl!"

"I hope so; if you insist?" she consents. "We both have the same destination --- LOVE. And besides, I don't dance with just anybody."

"You don't make exceptions?"

"Only with your permission," she assured.

"Will you marry me?" he asked sincerely from his heart.

"You drive a hard bargain," she hesitated. "Let me sleep on it."

"Take your time *Baby*," he backed off. "I got a few good years left."

They both laughed until Clarence is rudely interrupted as he is called upon to instruct the phone men. He kisses Peg on her forehead and says,

"'See ya later kid.'"

"I'll be waiting *Pops*," she affirms as she is in *7th Heaven;* wedding-bells dancing in her head.

Clarence does an about-face to go tend his business, but suddenly he yells back to her --- "Dinner tonight! I'll pick you up 8 PM, sharp."

"Aye, Aye Sir," she shouts back as she goes off making her rounds.

The residents accept and respect Peg with open-arms as both she and Clarence are the new talk of the *Commune*. They sense her sincerity, her compassion as well as their *Love* for one another. But a few are jealous that she is Clarence's girl. Peg has to earn Eva, Edna and Betty's confidence; their friendship. Until then, her relationship with them is unremarkable as time runs its course.

The staff was somewhat skeptical of their new boss at first. But they were impressed with the way she charmed Clarence and was impartial amongst the other *Amigos*. They realized that she would run a tight ship as they already seen her put two doctors in their place.

Peg didn't believe in bullshit. She was high-spirited, had clout; influence and they knew it. She was proactive and proved to be productive.

Clarence was late for lunch as he was held-up; learning the different communication systems. *I'm too old for all this complicated technology;* he thought. *But ah, cheer up Pops; you got a date tonight with Peg.*

Suddenly, reality set in. *What am I going to wear? Where should I take her? Wild-flowers? It's been such a long time since I had a real concern.*

God, has it been ten years since my wife died? Time sure flies as life goes on and on and on regardless of the loss of a Loved-one. You learn to accept it, but you never get over it.

"Well, well, well, look whose here; the smooth charmer himself." exclaimed Henry as Clarence joined his pals in the mess hall.

"We thought you were pumping iron or having your back shaved or something relating to your date tonight." Sarge teased.

"Don't forget your Viagra." Max warned. "Are you going to take Peg to the *O-Zone?*"

"Non-Sense, absolutely not, don't be so crude," Clarence snapped. "She's not like Sexy-Sarah. Romance is a different ball game, its major-league stuff. I'm playing for keeps."

"Does she know about the *O-Zone?*" Henry asked with worry on his face.

"No, I don't think so." Max cried. "We forgot to tell her."

"Not to worry," Sarge assured. "It's just a little consenting, adult --- fun and games. She will understand."

Max and Henry agreed with hesitation. But Clarence was nervous. Especially after witnessing how furious she was when she thought that Henry was a pervert.

"I'm glad you need an ID card to enter." he confessed. "I couldn't imagine her walking in there by accident. She'd probably flip out and quit. I better warn her tonight."

Coincidently, Peg was just a few tables away; helping some resident with a walker. She caught the last part of their conversation. On her way out of the mess hall, she smiled at Clarence and said.

"Lucy informed me all about your *O-Zone* and rest assured; I shall stay clear --- *Away*."

Clarence was relieved, he felt as if some burden was lifted; as if he confessed some dirty little secret. But why; he never even participated in the *O-Zone?* Honesty was his only policy. You could ask Sexy-Sarah, who propositioned him more than once and he turned her down each and every time.

Clarence was old fashion and never tried to pretend to be something he wasn't. To him, phoniness was taboo. To each his own, but don't push your luck. He hated bull-shit, lies and people who made broken promises on purpose.

He minded his own business and despised classical fools --- hypocrites as well as those who think that their shit; don't stink. He firmly believed that hypocrisy was the root to evil as controversy was the spice of life until; the *Truth Sets Man Free*.

Unfortunately, he learned from experience that sometimes the *Truth* hurts. Sometimes you deserve it as stupidity is your own fault. Many times you don't, but you should never lie to or try to fool yourself.

He was grateful for his *Amigos*. True relationships are sacred. Thus, he smiled as he knew that *he was right where he was supposed to be in life*. The other *Three Amigos* just laughed as they realized that Clarence was delivered from stress.

"So," Henry asked, "where are you taking Peg on your really special happening tonight?"

"I haven't any idea," he confessed. "I haven't been on a real date since my wife. God I need help; an agenda. I feel somewhat insecure. But, I shall prove adept at exceeding by my *Will to Love!*"

"Just relax," Max suggested. "Let *Nature* take its course. You got to pace yourself. If I didn't have this bum-leg; I'd go in your place."

"Like hell you will," Clarence responded with jealousy. "Don't be so absurd. I'm going to marry that woman."

"Marriage," Sarge asked? "Why you two don't know anything about each other; there's no intimacy yet? You must be getting soft in your head and I don't mean your little-guy."

"I've been married three times," Max warned. "Don't fall in love without thinking. We all have weak moments, but you better be careful before you jump in. I hope Peg doesn't go into *Bridezilla* Mode. I've been there too and the wedding cost me a fortune. But, divorce is worst. It is war and war is hell."

"My first wife was running around on me as I was working two jobs. I was a good husband, loyal and sober, until one Christmas Eve; I found a present under the tree. I opened it up and surprise --- I found divorce papers and our bank-book with a zero balance. She ran off with a guy twice her age --- to Las Vegas. Thus, I became a male slut because of the cold-hearted bitch."

"It was a good thing that we didn't have any kids. I hooked up with her best friend shortly after she fled. She was my main-squeeze until she too left for Vegas. Apparently, my ex's boyfriend dumped her, but she was making a lot of money hooking. And my main-squeeze went to join her. So when it comes to *Love* and marriage; I speak from experience."

"*Love* speaks for itself!" Clarence clarified as he interrupted with excitement. "I already proposed and she is going to sleep on it!"

"Wow, the M – *Word* again! God, this is serious," Henry surmised.

"Shall we head for the bar and celebrate?"

"We can't," Clarence reminded them. "We have phone-calls to make and I have to educate you guys about the new technology. Peg is going to take care of *Erotic Delights*. We're almost ready for business."

"Entrepreneurs," Henry shouted. "Who would have ever figured; especially since I've been retired for over twelve years?"

"Vice Moguls, sounds more like it." Max joked.

They all laughed as they headed upstairs to attend to last minute details. By suppertime, all systems were --- Go; for both the *Bookmaking Operation* and the *Laugh Room*. Commercials for *1-900-SEX-CHAT* would start airing tonight --- for Friday and Saturday nights.

Rumor already spread throughout the *Commune*. Everywhere you looked, you'd see groups of elders, laughing, joking and practicing on each other. The anticipation was anxious; everybody was excited as they couldn't wait to get involved.

The *Four Amigos* couldn't believe their eyes or ears as they encountered a bunch of old pretending perverts; on their way to check out Sarge's phone lines. Sarge was extremely pleased with the new system behind the bar. It was state of the art and its automatic, up to the minute point-spread-system would save him a lot of time. They were connected with the big boys.

He assured the guys that they'd get plenty of action; starting tomorrow as word was already out on the streets. He had contacts and connections to cover any unbalanced bets. They couldn't lose; as the 5% vig, was a sure thing --- cash money in the bank.

"Cash makes me nervous." Henry admitted. "It sends mixed signals, temptation; it's an invitation to danger."

"Relax!" Sarge tried to reassure. "Tomorrow we'll be armed and dangerous."

They all laughed as all four entrepreneurs were glad that they would be getting their pistols. But they weren't so happy with their new cell-phones. Perhaps they were old-fashioned. Perhaps they didn't want to be bothered. Regardless, they all agreed that both the

SOCIAL SECURITY

guns and the phones were necessary evils -- vital to *Social Security*.

"It's almost 6 PM *Romeo*," Henry warned. "You better shit, shower and shave; or else."

"Damn, already," Clarence mumbled. "Where the hell am I going to find wild-flowers in two hours?"

"Good Luck." Sarge interjected.

"Thanks," Clarence replied. "I need a miracle to pull this off."

"Do you want me to call Peg and tell her that you are sick with cold feet?" Max harassed.

"Ha, ha, ha," Clarence responded.

Suddenly, Lucy enters the bar with a beautiful bunch of *Wild-Flowers*, a bottle of Asti and a poetic card. Clarence's face lit up and glowed with delight.

"Thanks Lucy! I owe you --- *Big Time*. Where the heck did you find them?"

"At the lake, *Passion Point*; they thrive there. Peg would love it; you might even get lucky." she replied with a wink and a nod.

"OK, Ok," Clarence blushed. "But how did you know about my predicament?"

"You can thank your *Amigos*." Lucy confessed. "Henry gave me the scoop --- after Peg flew out of here. It was their idea to rescue you. Besides, we all like Peg. We decided to surprise you; help you make it a memorable night."

"'One for all and all for one'," Henry exclaimed.

"Share and share alike," Max joked.

"When you're in Love," Sarge added; "you don't think before you act. So we did the thinking for your hot date. We encouraged Peg to leave early so that she could get ready. She refused at first, but we all insisted."

"We chipped in and bought you a new suit, shirt, under-ware, socks and tie." Max informed.

"I took your favorite old blue suit with me for an example." Lucy admitted with pride. "The tailor assured me that it would be a perfect fit. It'll be delivered here before 7:15 PM."

"And," Henry announced; "you have dinner reservations for two at the *Lobster's Claw* for 9 PM. The night driver is going to chauffeur you *Lovebirds*."

Clarence was emotionally misty-eyed. He was speechless. Sarge pulled out a fresh bottle of *Jack* and Lucy and the Guys toasted --- "Good-Luck," to Clarence; whom literally cried.

He was grateful but mere words couldn't explain or express his gratitude. They all understood as he smiled, wiped his face with his sleeve and walked upstairs to get ready. As he left, Lucy yelled:

"Don't worry, that *Jack* will put lead in your old pencil."

The suit came on time as promised. Henry got the honors to take it to *Romeo*. When Clarence came down at 7:30, the living room was crowded with curiosity as everybody was waiting to greet him. Even Marge and Thomas; whom sat in his wheel chair, were there.

Clarence looked stunning, dashing and debonair. He got plenty of whistles and cheers as he waved and exited with the night-driver; for his date with destiny, the *Moment of Truth*.

They arrived at Peg's home right on time. Both Clarence and the driver were impressed with both the luxurious house and the neighborhood. *God, Clarence thought; she must be worth mega-bucks? She couldn't possibly afford this place on her salary.*

"Maybe she is a high-class hooker by night?" The driver joked.

Clarence was simply appalled, really pissed at Gino. He was chewing nails and spitting screws. "Watch your mouth son, or I'll shove my fist down your throat. That is no way to talk about a lady. Just stick to your driving and forget the lip."

"Sorry Sir. But, I was only kidding." replied the so-called chauffeur.

"Forget about it." Clarence calmed down. "But remember," he continued. "It's nice to be nice."

Clarence didn't like Gino's cocky-attitude from the start. There was something about him; a chip on his shoulder, disrespectful. *Forget about him,* he thought to himself. *Enjoy your date!*

Mr. Kharisma was quite a gentleman. He rang Peg's bell with the wild-flowers hid behind his back. Both were awed when she opened her door. Peg was absolutely gorgeous; all dolled-up, and was pleased at how handsome Clarence was; all clean-shaved and slicked-up. He looked so suave but he felt vulnerable as he was tongue-tied by her elegant beauty.

He handed her the flowers in silence. She giggly-screamed like an adolescent --- "Oh, they're so beautiful," and thanked him with a great big kiss.

Finally, after gaining his composure, Clarence cleared his throat and declared that they had "Dinner reservations at 9 PM."

"I hope you like lobster-tails?" he asked.

"Adore them." she admitted.

"Alrighty then, cause we're headed to the *Lobster's Claw*."

"Oh my," she replied. "That's my favorite restaurant."

"Great," he was relieved.

Peg put the wild-flowers in a vase of water, grabbed her purse, a light sweater and activated the security alarm as they headed to the caddy. Once inside the vehicle, Peg commented on its license plates.

"What does the *B4HEART*- acronym stand for?" she asked.

"I had them made up." Clarence admitted articulately. "They're special plates. They have special meaning to me. It's my philosophy, my ideology, and my dream. Everybody should --- Be for *Humanity Envisioned And Realized Together!*"

"Wow!" Peg responded, "That's so profound."

"Thanks." Clarence replied. "But *Life* itself is so *Profound*."

"It sure is," she agreed.

"Nice neighborhood," Clarence remarked as they drove off. He was dying to know.

"I've been here for twenty years." she replied. "My late husband was a State Supreme Court Judge. He died two and a half years ago. It was a heart-attack. I guess he couldn't handle the heat in the bedroom."

Clarence was stunned and it showed. He felt awkward as he thought. *God, is she kinky? Can I handle her? Shit, maybe she'd kill me in bed too?*

"I'm only kidding," she laughed. "But he did die of a heart-attack. And besides, I owed you that for this morning and for not warning me about the O-Zone."

They both laughed as the driver drove in complete silence. They exchanged bits and pieces of their lives as each achieved respect for the others sentimental attachments. After all, memories are precious. Before they knew it, they were at the prestigious restaurant.

Dinner turned out to be quality time. After a short while together, they were lost in conversation as they indulged deeper into past histories. Both time and the butterflies flew away as both Peg and Clarence felt calm and completely relaxed. It was as if they had known each other forever.

Peg confessed that *she liked to sleep naked and take bubble baths with candle light and a bottle of Asti*. Clarence just laughed and listened attentively, but in actually, he was a little bit embarrassed. He didn't share any of his secrets.

The ambience was exquisite, lavishly elegant and refined. Their lobster-tails were incredibly delicious, but neither of them had any room for any dessert. They didn't stay for dancing. They didn't want to tie up the driver. Besides, it was a beautiful night and they agreed to hang out in the *Garden* for a while at *Social Security*.

After all, it had a surround sound system and Clarence had another bottle of Asti just waiting to be indulged. They could dance there under the stars. It sounded *Romantic as Love was in the Air*, but Clarence was sorry that he didn't bring his own car.

When they got back to the *Commune*; Clarence made it clear to the driver that he himself would personally take Peg home in his car.

"Yes Sir." Gino replied sarcastically. Actually, he was somewhat relieved since his idle mind did some ominous thinking while they were enjoying their dinner date. The more he thought about it, the more he realized that Clarence assaulted his sensitive pride.

In fact, unbeknownst to Clarence or Peg, he planned on quitting the next day. Perhaps he put his foot in his mouth once too often ---- OOPS. Perhaps, he was just jealous or full of animosity? Or perhaps, he was some sick, sinister bastard with a hostile plan?

The couple walked out back to the *Garden*. Clarence was so

proud of his girl. Peg couldn't believe how affectionate he actually was. She never met anybody so sincere and full of compassion for others. He was so unique, so smooth and amiable; well rounded. He was an original, a keeper. She wondered if *he would make a move and proposition her.*

Perhaps I am a bit naughty, she laughed as she wondered *how big his pedigree was*. She wanted to check out his package. She was willing but she figured that he was too shy --- yet.

Suddenly, a shooting star fell across the sky. It was a sight for bedroom-eyes. A divine sign, which set the mood as they embraced passionately; until they realized that they had company. Marge just smiled from across the *Garden* as she politely left so that they would be alone.

"Poor woman," Clarence cried, "she is mortified in a melt-down-mode. I feel so bad for her. This *Garden* seems to be the only thing that comforts her."

"Lucy told me all about her nightmare." Peg informed. "It is so sad. She seems so lonely, so withdrawn?"

"Unfortunately," Clarence interrupted, "she alienated herself in guilt and shame; a shadow of frustration. She blames herself for being sexuality molested."

"Sometimes," Peg surmised, "life can be so unfair."

"Perhaps," Clarence replied, "but *'what goes around; comes around'*. So I wasn't surprised when I learned that the sinister bastard-lowlife that terrorized her; got his last week. Three skinheads raped and beat him to death in prison on some work-detail."

"*Karmic Justice*," Peg surmised.

"Amen!" Clarence agreed, "*Poetic Justice.*"

"Got any music Maestro?" Peg asked as she looked up at all the stars twinkling brightly in the sky.

"But of course," Clarence assured. "We best not waste this precious moonlight."

He left briefly to turn on the surround-sound and returned with two glasses and a chilled bottle of Asti. They toasted to the *Full*

Moon in the night horizon and then, they danced and danced from one end of the *Garden* to the other --- to the beat of their hearts. It was a *Cosmic Chemistry*. Ironically though, Clarence forgot to turn on the music.

Suddenly, he starts to laugh as he realizes that he was absent-minded. Peg just smiles and says "Yes I will!"

Clarence is confused. "I forgot the music."

"It doesn't matter." she insisted. "Didn't you hear what I just said?"

"Wha,wha what?"

"Yes," she replied, "I'll marry you!"

Needless to say, that led to another passionate embrace; which was all it took for Clarence to invite Peg to spend the night in his room. She accepted and they consummated their *Love*.

It was a perfect night, quite memorable and so rejuvenating; thanks to a little help from their *Amigos* and --- *Mother Nature*. In the morning, when she awoke, Peg felt awkward; perplexed in an embarrassing dilemma. She wasn't accustomed to being mischievously permissive. Neither was Clarence. But they were in *Love*. They trusted their hearts and each other.

Peg broke the silence as she told Clarence that "She was confused when she heard him mention the *Laugh Room*. I couldn't figure out what a Laugh Room was?"

They both laughed as they cuddled and found comfort in setting a wedding-date. They were grateful spirits, glad that they found each other. They made passionate *Love* again before they got dressed.

At breakfast, in the mess hall; the guys wanted to know all about his date and especially the intimate details. "How sweet was that?" Max asked as Clarence gave him the *Evil-eye*.

But Clarence wasn't one to *kiss-n-tell*. He was direct and to the point. He thanked them for their thoughtfulness, which led to a wonderful date. Then he announced: "We're getting married! She said yes!"

They all congratulated him as he gave them the date and word spread fast; throughout the *Commune*. Ironically, rumor hadn't even spread --- yet, that Peg spent the night. She had another uniform and her work shoes, in her assigned locker; so nobody suspected the contrary.

Clarence promised to drive her home when she finished her shift of duty, and that is how the cat got out of the bag. Prior to that, only a few knew, but they were content with minding their own business; as they kept silent. Sometimes silence is golden.

However, neither Clarence nor Peg gave a damn. After all, she was sassy and he was bold. They didn't care what others thought; as it was their business, their lives. Together, they made a perfect couple, *Soul Mates*; willing to take on the world if necessary.

After the *Amigos* finished their morning meal; they piled into Clarence's Buick. They were nervous yet anxious about qualifying for their pistol permits. Everybody except Sarge; he was an expert with firearms.

"Thank God for friends," Clarence remarked in regards to a new county requirement. With some help from Chi and a quick call from Peg to an influential judge, an acquaintance; they had permission to be eligible for a carrying license --- personal protection which was hard to get. Being old and entrepreneurs; were power for their cause.

They got their application reviewed and processed as well as background checks in about six weeks instead of the usual six to eight months. But the judge insisted that they take and pass a safety course. They all agreed and assured him that they had clean criminal records.

Everything went according to plan, but unfortunately; not all of the guys qualified. Sarge put the instructor to shame. Clarence and Max were both quite impressive. But the course proved depressing for Henry. He couldn't hit the broad side of a barn.

"*Maggie's Drawers*," Sarge joked every time he missed the target.

Henry got frustrated. It was so annoying. However, as it turned out; his eyes were the culprits. Old glasses or cataracts were the suspects as the instructor gave him an old fashion eye-test.

INTRUSION

Henry felt better when the instructor assured him that he could come right back and qualify again as soon as he got his eyes corrected. He was pleased that he wouldn't have to wait to fill out another application. His character references, fingerprints, passport photos and the various background checks were good for at least ninety days.

"Maybe I'll take you as a pinochle partner again." Max joked. "I owe your brain an apology. Your eyes weren't cooperating Quincy."

"Ha-ha," Henry laughed in comic relief. "Who the hell is Quincy?"

"Mr. Magoo, the famous nearsighted cartoon character who was as blind as a bat!" he answered as everybody roared in reminiscing laughter.

With permits, licenses and registration in hand; three quarters of the *Amigos* purchased their pistols right then and there on the second floor at the shooting range. Even Henry picked his out in anticipation of future results. Actually, they all bought forty-fives, with a magazine which held seven rounds each.

But Max had to be different as he insisted on having a special quick-release-spring-fed-holster. "*El'Caramba,*" he shouted as he named his piece, his new *sidekick*!

The *Comrades in Arms* felt powerful on the ride back to the *Commune*. They respected their persuaders; their new items. Even Henry felt safer. But little did they know what a blessing in disguise; they would turn out to be. For at that moment, malignant forces were in cahoots; plotting in conspiracy to rob *Social Security*.

The night driver was so coy, cold and calloused. He called Lucy and told her that: "he had to quit." He said that: "his father was dying --- *out on the west coast and to tell Clarence that he was sorry about last night.*"

But in actuality, he was infuriated and jealous about Clarence. He wanted payback; revenge if not compensation for his macho remarks against his wounded ego which felt insulted. Gino feared Clarence. He was a scared coward, with a vendetta.

Unfortunately, he needed the audacity to recruit others to do the dirty deed. He masterminded in premeditation and engineered the whole scheme. The article in the front page of the local newspaper about *Social Security's $10,000,000.00 donation* was convincing temptation.

It was all the inspiration and motivation that they needed to get involved. How malicious could they be? Brutal potential, probable cause; destine to be?

Ironically, idle minds can be dangerous, more dangerous than just one and very dangerous when they have empty pockets between them as the devil dances in their heads; *Subtle Insistence.*

"Easy marks," he assured his younger brother Lou and his two low-life crack-head friends; Derek and Dennis.

"Pushovers, a quick fix; I'll get you in and out as I lay it all out for you guys. Just tell the guard at the gate that you are here to surprise your Uncle Clarence Kharisma. I'll drive the get away-car." he exclaimed with a save-his-own-ass; play it safe precaution.

"All you gotta do; is follow my instructions. Trust me, Gino will never stir you wrong." he assured them. "When you get in there; you must grab the *Amigos,* see --- remember these faces, tattoo them in you brain."

He made them memorize their picture, which was in the paper.

"The *Four Amigos* are always in the bar playing cards at the time that we plan on striking; routine recreation. Put a gun to Clarence's head; he is the leader. Him," he pointed! "It'll be an unexpected surprise."

"Then take them upstairs on the third floor and pistol-whip them until they open the office and get the money out of the safe. They're all loaded," he continued. "You should see Clarence's girlfriend's customized house. It has the best of everything. And the restaurant that I took them to last night was high-class, *Big-time.*"

The would-be thieves were getting excited as their adrenaline was a flowing. Gino was pumping them up, motivating their confidence into false courage. He was an ignorant, corrupt and demoralizing lost soul.

"Kill Clarence if you gotta make an example. Then they'll know that you mean business. It's easy money. Take the whole shebang."

"Yep," Lou put his two cents in, "I hear that old people don't trust banks because they can't forget about the *Great Depression.*"

"Oh yeah?"

"Fucken-aye!"

"Cool man, sounds good."

"Hell yeah; awesome."

"OK then!" They nodded obediently as all agreed and then; they decided to pull it off tonight as Gino opened up a small duffel-bag and handed them each a loaded *Li'l Buddy*. In theory, it was a dramatic plot but time would tell; destiny?

The *Amigos* arrived back home just in time for Clarence to drive Peg home. They were all famished yet surprised when they realized that Peg spent the night. They were cool about it as *Bold* and *Sassy* left together.

On the way to Peg's, they stopped for pizza and exchanged details about their separate day. Peg felt sorry for Henry, but she was glad that the guys were armed. She even confessed that she too was packing.

When they pulled up to her driveway, she got a sudden-urge and invited Clarence in --- for a quickie. He accepted; they did the wild thing and then, he left. They were both exhausted since they were up half the night.

On the way back to *Social Security*, Clarence got his second wind from his ego, which felt great.

Three times in twenty-four hours, he bragged to himself! *Maybe Jack does put lead in your pencil? Fuck that Viagra shit. Maybe I'll take it in ten years or so.*

He smiled proudly to himself as he pulled up to the security gate and waved to the guard who let him in. It was a quiet night and he looked forward to some relaxation. When he entered the complex, Henry introduced him to Phil; the new driver whom Peg hired. He was pre-approved and had impeccable references. Nobody suspected anything about Gino, who quit.

Clarence was harassed and pressed for details again, relating

SOCIAL SECURITY

to him and Peg. But he was a gentleman again, always discreet. He was the center of conversation; as gossip and whispers prospered until destiny struck.

The guard at the gate phoned the new driver; instructing him to: "open the door for three unexpected visitors from out of town; who were there to surprise their Uncle Clarence."

He was told to: "let them in quietly so that he didn't spoil their unexpected awe."

The *Amigos* were getting ready to play cards. Sarge was behind the bar getting a new deck. The others were already seated at their favorite table, when the three low lives recognized their prey by the etchings, embedded in their brains.

Gino's foot soldiers rushed into the bar, armed with their marching orders, trembling with their guns drawn. They rudely interrupted the *Amigos* routine with a disturbing blood-bath. Unfortunately, the perpetrators had a rendezvous with death.

Well, at least two of them did as the robbery was a possibility, but not probable. Their plan proved implausible as it was stymied. For the *Amigos* proved to be a force to be reckoned with; thanks to their elements of surprises.

It was an explosive situation as *El'Caramba* and the *Comrades-in-Arms* responded without any doubt. They were a team, a deadly combination that hit their marks. Unfortunately, the wanna-be-thieves made the biggest mistake of their young lives when Lou grabbed Clarence's neck by his shirt-collar with one hand and put a gun to the back of his head with the other as he stood behind him and told him to: "Stand up."

Without hesitation, instinctively as he stood up; Clarence gave him a cocoa-butt with the back of his head --- breaking his nose immediately. He continued his reaction with an elbow-blow to Lou's mid-section; then he bent down low and grabbed him and flipped him eight feet over his shoulder.

The other two panicked as both the card table and all of the JD's spilled all over as Max fell to the floor, cast exposed. They didn't pay any attention to him as he pulled out *El'Caramba* and shot one of the crack-head's right in the heart while Sarge put a bullet in the middle of the other crack-head's eyes. Both collapsed dead --- instantly on the spot.

Clarence finished his reaction as he dropped to his knees and shot Lou in the stomach as he jumped up to his feet in utter shock; nose dripping blood. Clarence stood up slowly. He was sweating profusely, contrary to the bone-chilling ordeal.

Sarge walked over to him and felt his pulse. "He is alive but it's critical. Gut-shot wounds are very dangerous. It's touch and go." Then he checked to see if Lou had any other weapons on his possession.

He also checked the other two bleeding bodies; to make sure that they were dead. He then picked up all three guns that were flung across the floor during the fiery massacre. Sarge was afraid that Lou might try to crawl to get one of them and get revenge or end his own misery.

Someone called 911 for an ambulance. Somebody else called the police directly; who arrived quickly as they were patrolling the area. The guard and Phil felt like fools as it took three old men to foil the planned plot in motion.

"Maybe," Sarge exclaimed, "Dr. Martin Luther King Jr. was right. Maybe someday *'Unarmed Truth'* and *'Unconditional Love'* will *prevail?* But until then, I'll keep *El'Carambas'* cousin."

"I need a shot of Jack Daniels." Henry confessed. "I think I pissed my pants."

"Me too," Max admitted as he puked his guts out.

"Poor bastards," Clarence added as he shook his head, "misguided victims of ignorance. "Misspent youth; what a waste? Set up a round, Sarge."

Sarge obliged and the *Four Amigos* tried to regain their composure.

"Fucken *Bone-Heads*," Max cried. "Because of their brazen stupidity, they wasted four perfect glasses of bourbon, Alcohol abuse, and now they're *Dead-Heads;* literally. I hope the other bastard makes it."

SOCIAL SECURITY

"If you do," Henry cried out to Lou as he walked around him, stopping for a brief second or two to look him straight in his crying eyes: "Maybe next time you will think twice before you try to pull off such a malicious act. Essentially, you had to learn the hard-way; that crime doesn't pay."

Needless to say, it was ugly chaos; a variety of disorders, reeking havoc. People fainted, some cried, others were in literal shock or disbelief. Blood was all over the place. It was a living nightmare, a gruesome sight; two dead bodies and one clinging to life in pure pain, wailing like a baby.

Eventually, Lou was rushed off to the hospital in an ambulance. One of the night-staffed nurses did what she could to stop the bleeding and make him more comfortable until the medics got there. Soon thereafter, about a dozen crime-scene investigators littered the *Commune*.

They taped off the death display, took pictures and drew chalk marks. Then they took statements for hours; right, wrong and indifferent as perspective varies. The coroner from the county medical examiners office bagged and hauled the bodies away after he got the OK from proper authority. Clarence was told to:

"Hold off on the clean up and to keep the door locked per the pending inquest." They didn't want anybody to enter the bar area but, "Not to worry; as it was only police procedure."

CHAPTER **Four**

Uncertainty

Chapter 4   Uncertainty

Nobody slept that night as reporters from television stations and newspapers swarmed outside, like bees. Both Peg and Lucy heard about the tragic ordeal on TV and came back to help out as quickly as they could. The guard and the police suspected a forth suspect, an accomplice; a get-away driver. They'd seen a car peal off and flee the scene without its lights on.

Clarence became suspicious when he learned Lou's last name --- DeAngelo. The detectives eventually apprehended Gino and brought him to the station for questioning. He took the fifth, hoping that they all died; so that they couldn't finger him. He also declined a lawyer; bragging that: "I'll be released in forty-eight hours or less --- by law."

Peg couldn't believe that for the second time in three days; the *Commune* and the *Amigos* made the front page of the local newspaper. Ironically, it was the first article; that instigated this outrageous incident. *Social Security* was targeted because of it.

Chi stopped in while Peg was having coffee and reading the culprit's latest piece. He despised all the press and news crews; hanging outside. "No Comment." he echoed several times before he entered.

Except for the day staff, everybody else was upstairs --- trying to get some sleep. Even Lucy was up there; she was exhausted from

SOCIAL SECURITY

trying to calm everybody down. It was one hell of a night.

Chi assured Peg that the deaths were justifiable homicide, self-defense amid a felony in progress; armed-robbery. "The *Amigos* are Heroes in the *Eyes of the Law.*" he said. "*Common Sense* dictates that they were victims, so called easy prey; exposed to evildoers."

Peg felt relieved. She thanked him and he told her that he'd be back later to talk with the *Amigos*. He also promised to: "Put some pressure on the press to --- *Back-Off.*" Then he left.

At 9 AM, the new gardener reported for duty. Peg had another old acquaintance run a personal as well as a criminal background check on him. He was cleared as a stand-up guy; responsible.

Max and Henry left the grounds at 10 AM with the day driver. Max was getting his cast off and Henry needed his eyes checked. As it turned out; he only needed new glasses.

Several detectives came back at about 11 AM with some lab equipment. "Just routine," one assured Lucy. Then he gave her *the OK to have the area cleaned*. She called a professional cleaning company.

By suppertime, Max had his cast off, Henry was *Hawk-Eye* and the bar was spic and span. At dinner, Sarge informed the Guys that in spite of the horrific night, the book-making operation was a success. They *took in $8500.00 in action. $425.00 was their profit*.

"Not bad for our first day of business!" he commented. Then he estimated the weekly profits to be roughly $4,000.00, explaining; "*double action on the weekend.*"

The *Amigos* were pleased, but they were still in shock; as his prediction didn't even excite any of them. But, Sarge was just doing his duty, keeping them informed and trying to cheer them up. Actually, he also felt depressed as well as sickened by the whole incident.

Chi stopped back at 7 PM. He was pleasantly pleased when he heard that Clarence and Peg were getting married. One of the residents spilled the beans.

He congratulated his *Grand-Father* who asked him to be his best man. He accepted with honor and gave Clarence his *Blessings*.

UNCERTAINTY

Then he assured the *Amigos* that neither they nor the *Commune* had anything to worry about.

He told them that the police already closed the case. "Lou made it through surgery. He is going to be all right. He went into shock when he was shot and was unaware of anything that was going on around him. But, when he awoke from his surgical operation, he went hysterical as soon as he found out that Derek and Dennis were dead."

"'That Fucken Gino!' he screamed from the top of his lungs. 'It's all Gino's fault, it was his idea; he was our getaway driver.'"

"I knew it!" Clarence's mouth dropped.

"Relax Pa," Chi interjected, "he's a coward. He cried when the police arrested him for conspiracy, armed-robbery, and attempted murder. He denies everything and he is mad at his brother for ratting him out. He threatened to get even with him for furnishing incriminating evidence by lying."

"Although," Chi continued ---"he is in jail now, but he'll probably make bail. However, the good news is that the two deaths are officially ruled as justifiable homicide; self-defense."

The *Amigos* were relieved, but Clarence was concerned about the bail issue. He didn't trust Gino; who was a smart-ass from day one. He knew that he didn't have any previous record but now, he believed him to be a walking-time-bomb. Unfortunately, nobody expected his homicidal tendencies.

Clarence was sorry that he didn't trust his intuition as he felt guilty. He wondered out loud, *"Did Gino infiltrate Social Security --- just to case it out?"*

Chi and the others became suspicious too; as they also wondered with his rational and vowed to be alert. Chi assured them that: "He would warn them if and when he made the bail." Then, he left.

The following morning, Henry went back to qualify for his forty-five. His buddies cheered him on as he became an elite member of the *Comrades in Arms*. He didn't get into *Maggie's Drawers*.

But technically, he was still a virgin. He didn't have any notches

SOCIAL SECURITY

on his belt. Regardless, he felt the power and the prestige of his *Enforcer*.

'Make my day', he thought to himself, referring to Gino. Henry was oh so ready to --- *Rumble. Let him just try something. Anything; I'll be waiting.* Ironically, at that moment, Clarence got a call from Chi --- "Gino just made bail."

When they got back to *Social Security*, they went to the bar and toasted to Henry --- *'all for one and one for all'*. They seemed to put the bloody incident to rest as they soaked in the sauce. Ironically, the *Jack, El'Caramba* and his three cousins calmed their nerves, but Gino was on each and every one of their minds.

They decided to have security cameras and motion detectors installed throughout the outside perimeter and in the hallways and main lobbies. They needed a – *Round-the-Clock-Surveillance;* just in case somebody jumped over the fences or gates. They all agreed that just the sight of them would be deterrents; which would make Gino think twice and ease their fear-factor.

Suddenly, the phone behind the bar rang. Sarge answered and took some bets for that night. When he hung up, he said; "Incidentally, we made $488.00 last night."

"Easy money," Max replied.

"We'll make a grand tonight." Sarge assured. "Payday always makes people itchy. Money burns holes in their pockets. TGIF, its party time --- sex, drinking and gambling; all weekend long, vices galore, poisonous passions."

"Shit," yelled Clarence. "It's Friday? We have to get ready for tonight's action in the *Laugh Room.*"

"Oh God," Henry responded, "with all of the commotion around here the last two days; I forgot all about it."

"So did I," echoed Sarge as Max nodded.

"I better remind Peg." Clarence thought out loud.

"I'll remind Lucy." Henry vowed. "She said that she wouldn't miss the debut for anything."

"I'll give her some JD," Clarence interjected sarcastically, "oil for her pencil sharpener."

UNCERTAINTY

They all stated to laugh. All but Henry, who seemed offended and yet; was too meek or shy to say anything about it?

"I heard that, Lucy and Peg were working with all the residents; regarding the perverted performances," Max exclaimed. "And that they all agreed that --- *if somebody should get a good caller, they'd put it on the speakerphone so that everybody could hear and get a good laugh as the others busy out.*"

"How many calls do you guy's think we'll get?" Sarge asked curiously as everybody was clueless. "How long will the conversations last? And, what should we say?"

"I don't know." Henry admitted with ignorance. "But the longer we keep them on the line, the more we make. How many perverts are there in the world?"

"They are just lonely people." Peg interrupted as she handed Clarence some papers and a bunch of lingerie-catalogs to perusal. "Some will be longing to get-off. It's the same as *Erotic Delight's* joy-toys, and your *O-Zone*. It's only adult fun and games. But, a lot of the calls will be lonely people just looking for someone to talk to."

"It would be cheaper for them to see a shrink." Max surmised as Clarence looked through the catalogs. "$4.95 a minute adds up quite fast. Don't you think?"

"It's convenient and private and besides, it's their money." Lucy interjected. "However, if and when some lonely soul calls; we can get their phone number and call them back to talk for free."

"Sounds like a plan," Clarence acknowledged. "We'll just play it by ear --- so to speak. We have plenty of ready, willing and able participants --- just raring to go. We have eight lines; six set up for male callers and two for females."

"And," he continued, "I heard that some are willing to disguise their voices and pretend to be the opposite sex. It should be interesting if not amusing. *'May the force be with us'*; again. If somebody needs a little help getting-off, then so be it."

"But," Clarence warned as he amplified his point across. "We better make sure that all residents realize that this is strictly fun and games. I don't want anybody falling for some *Sick-O*; going out with him or her and getting hurt or perhaps even killed. We don't need the money that bad. And if and when we decide to call back some old lonely soul and they become friends; I want them checked out --- first."

Everybody agreed with Clarence's concerns. They all vowed to keep an eye on all the other residents and decided that it would be a good safety measure to make it mandatory to work in pairs. There would be a meeting tonight at 7:30; to inform all the others and to address any other questions or suggestions.

"What do you think about the catalogs and the web-site proposal?" Peg asked Clarence as he passed them around to the others.

"The catalogs and the price-lists are great." Clarence replied. "And this web-site layout is quite impressive. Go with it unless anybody has any objections or suggestions."

Nobody opposed or disapproved but Max suggested that: "Peg should model some of the lingerie for the *Amigos*." Everybody laughed except Clarence whom was pissed until he changed the subject.

"Ladies," he warned. "We have a serious situation. Gino is out on bail."

The women were up-set to say the least. "Oh my," they echoed in disbelief.

"We decided to get motion detectors and video cameras installed throughout the *Commune*." Henry tried to reassure them and ease their tension.

"I'll make some calls and have somebody out here first thing in the morning to install them." Lucy promised.

"Good." Peg sighed with relief. "But," she continued, "I don't think he has the guts to come around here. He's a chicken; purely yellow. He'll probably flee the country."

"Thus, I don't plan on losing any sleep over him. I have two calls to make," she tried to change the subject, *"Erotic Delights* shall be up and running in about a week or so."

"We mustn't take Gino lightly." Clarence warned. "Consider him

UNCERTAINTY

armed and deadly dangerous. He got the shit beat out of him in the holding-center. They almost raped him. The guards saved his ass."

"He's extremely bitter and scared as he has two black-eyes and a semi-dislocated shoulder. There is no telling what on *God's Earth* --- he plans on doing next. He's a wounded savage with a wounded ego. There is legitimate cause for worry."

"Worry shall get us no where, no how." Lucy advised. "We mustn't belly-ache over Gino. We must focus, be alert and prepare. Yesterday is gone; tomorrow will come soon --- regardless. But in the meantime Clarence, don't you fret about my old pencil sharpener. It doesn't need any oiling from *Jack*. However, perhaps Henry could pacify her?"

"Wow, that sounds like a proposition if I ever heard one!" Sarge exclaimed with excitement as Henry was floored by shocking embarrassment --- again. "Why don't you two hook-up in the O-Zone. She's drooling over your sexy physique."

"Ha, ha," Henry snaps back while Clarence was snickering. "But my room will suffice. What do you say Lucy; you want to get lucky and stain my sheets? Are you in the mood --- for a little hanky-panky?"

"Wait! Wait!" Max interrupts. "We can have a three-some."

"Not in this life time!" Lucy shrieks as she sneers at Max. "Not in your wildest dream would I even allow you to bite me ---- Never." she laughed. "Not even if my life depended upon it."

"Relax girl. I'm only fooling. I'm practicing for tonight's entertainment." Max backed off.

Everybody started to laugh and then, Lucy grabbed Henry by the arm, winked at him and said: "Let's go get naked;" as she led him off for some afternoon-delight.

"You go Girl!" Peg hollered as they exited the room with big smiles on both of their faces.

When they were out of sight, Peg informed the rest of the *Amigos* that: "Lucy was crazy about Henry from day one. She thought that *he had a great set of buns*. She tried her damnedest to get his undivided attention, but according to her, he was so bashful, shy and timid."

The three *Amigos* started to laugh as they recollected Henry's style. Peg elaborated as she explained; "She confided in me yesterday, that she was going to make a drastic move --- soon. But, I never imagined that she'd be so blunt."

"What the hell," Max interrupted, "she made her move and now she is making Henry's day. God Bless her. After all, none of us is getting any younger. We best enjoy and make the best use of what time we have left."

"I'll drink to that." Sarge yelled as he went to fetch another round.

"Me too!" echoed Max and Clarence.

"Don't forget about me," Peg reminded, "Asti please."

"But of course," Sarge replied as he granted their prerogatives and the four of them toasted to Henry and Lucy as well as *Happiness*.

7:30 PM rolled around fast. All were excited about show-time. Everybody except Henry and Lucy as Lucy never went home. She didn't even call for the surveillance cameras.

She and Henry had to be woken up. They knocked each other out and fell fast asleep in each others arms. But when they awoke, they were energized, completely rejuvenated; as they both felt simply --- *Great*. It was an erotic encounter, vibrant, and healthy.

Tardy, the new item joined the rest of the *Commune*. The meeting was almost over, but they got a standing-ovation. Max wanted to know if Lucy was free tomorrow afternoon. Henry made it perfectly clear that she was now officially off-limits as a romance was in bloom.

Sexy Sarah acknowledged that she was free and they, Max and her; made a date for the O-Zone. Another couple offered to join them and they accepted. Ironically, Sarah warned that she had only one rule when it came to sex.

"What is it?" Max asked curiously.

"The 24 / 7 Rule," she replied! "I'm *Ready, Willing and Available* 24 hours a day, 7 days a week. I'm a gluten for porn; *Punish me Baby, Consent* is my middle name."

UNCERTAINTY

"But," she continued, "I want it on record that I never had any STD's. However, I must confess --- I did have crabs --- once. It was way back at *Woodstock*. I got them from some musician's mustache. The band use to sing a song entitled *Crabs In My Mustache*, and dedicated it to me."

Everybody laughed. Even --- Marge as Sarah was a true slut, an authentic nymphomaniac and proud of it. Nonchalantly, Sarge yelled, "Drinks are on the house! Does the *Sexaholic* want a double?"

"Are you trying to get me drunk and take advantage of my innocence?" she joked in preparation for the performance.

Peg suggested that "Sarah be in charge of the *Laugh-Room*." she proclaimed her as the *"Resident Sex-Expert."*

Everyone agreed since there wasn't anything that she didn't know about sex. Besides, she was dressed for the part as usual --- red-wig, false eye-lashes, make-up galore, cheap perfume and a skimpy negligee. She was every bit a woman, pleasantly plump, a round-rump and voluptuous huge-knockers.

Suddenly, Peg remembered why Sexy Sarah looked so darn familiar. She was a blast from her past. She couldn't place her at first. After all, she did put on a few pounds. Quite a few to be exact, but now it was perfectly clear. Ironically, they partied together with the same band at *Woodstock*.

Peg started to sweat profusely as she became quite uncomfortable and a bit nervous. She felt as if she were sitting on pins and needles. What will Clarence think; *Sexy Sarah and Piggy Peg?*

Woodstock was her wilder days. That's when she got knocked-up with her illegitimate-daughter; Helen. It was her secret. Not many knew but she was dying to tell Clarence --- before the wedding.

Shit, she thought to herself. *Should I come clean now and reminisce with Sarah? Or should I confess in private? Perhaps I better sleep on it, and decided; guilt or shame.*

Consequently, her decision wasn't that easy as Helen was on her mind. *She is so beautiful and Harley has been a good father and great provider as his generosity is outrageously beyond any expectation.* He showered them both with gifts and luxury trips over

SOCIAL SECURITY

the years. Actually, it was just a drop in the bucket as he could afford it.

"You can't spoil a child." He always insisted as he welcomed his *Little Princess* with open arms when he found out --- three years after the fact.

Unfortunately, he was overseas touring with his band when Peg got married to save-face; protecting her reputation. She married an older gentleman, a wonderful husband and understanding father. Peg had to make a choice; *save face as an abortion was never an option.*

"What are STD's?" whispered Betty as Eva and Edna giggled in confusion.

"Sexually transmitted diseases," Peg explained; as they all blushed in silence.

"Oh my, I forgot to ...." Lucy shouted as she realized that she was derelict of her duty.

"Not to worry," Peg assured her that it was alright since she took care of it.

"A crew from *Security Plus* would be here at 8 AM tomorrow morning." she elaborated. "They are familiar with *Social Security's* plight via the newspaper."

Lucy was relieved but apologized for her negligence, her dereliction of duty. Everybody forgave her as it was an understanding *Commune*. After all, helping, caring, and sharing, forgiveness, trust and respect, were all woven in their hearts. Besides, she had a good excuse, *The Call of the Wild*.

Every seat in the house was packed as disappointment never arrived. The phones rang and rang as liberating laughter bounced back and forth --- off the walls. Sexy Sarah proved to be an instant star, a seductive success with her clients whom vowed to call her back, again and again as she knew how to *Talk-Dirty*.

She got more people off then all the other residents combined. She was a Pro; "Hey there big boy, what can I do for you dear? I am Sooo HORNEY; ya gotta help me right away!"

"I'm coming, I'm coming," echoed off her speaker-phone as she ended each call.

UNCERTAINTY

The entire *Commune* was having the time of their lives as customers shared their secret fantasies. It was a sight to be heard. Humans can be such perverted creatures, so bizarre. We are, but strange animals with selective memories. Disgusting seems to be popular to pleasure.

"How big are your tits?"
"Are you a bad girl?"
"Will you masturbate for me?"
"Can I knock at your back-door?"
"You wanna drain my vain?"
"Are you a bad boy?"
"Can I check out your package?"
"Will you be my dirty little secret?"
"Can I ---?" "Can ---?"

On and on it went as they took turns pacifying obscene urges. Some residents were naturals, others were pathetically sad. Most callers were literally satisfied, pleasantly pleased. Some were disappointed, but whose fault was it if they couldn't get it up or get off?

"'You can satisfy some of the people all the time,'" said Sexy Sarah as she paraphrased ol Abe. "'But you can't satisfy all the people all the time.'"

"However, I'm always able, willing and ready to go for the Gold; the *Happy Ending!* Ironically, I've gone to bed --- broke, tired and hungry, but only a fool falls asleep --- *Horny*. You got to keep in touch with yourself. All it takes is a little effort and allot of practice. I abused myself last night, but I knew that I needed it!"

Everybody roared spontaneously as Sarah could get raunchy, but she was honest. She was a sex machine. Lucy got the best call of the night which turned out to be the last. It was a hilariously gross finale.

Some gay-guy called and she pretended to be another guy. The caller wanted her to toss his salad? He insisted that Lucy describe how wonderful he smelled and tasted. It was all on the speakerphone.

Lucy was utterly confused until Sexy Sarah explained that "He desired her to lick and suck his ass-hole/scrotum area until he came." She got lividly offended.

"Go get a bottle of Jack Daniel's and down it till you toss your cookies!" she shouted. "Then stick the entire bottle up your naked-brown-eye, without *Vaseline*."

He thanked her as he screamed --- "God, I'm cumming, I'm cumming!"

The entire *Commune* was dying in delight as tears as well as bodies were rolling on the floor. Henry laughed so hard that his false teeth fell out.

Max warned him to: "Be careful tonight."

"Why?" he asked.

"Lucy might stick that bottle up your ass if you piss her off or don't satisfy her. Ouch!" he chuckled as he cringed at the thought which reminded him of his last colonoscopy.

If *'laughter is the best medicine'*; then the *Commune* was medicated for the rest of their lives. They were on such a high; they couldn't shake the rush as nobody was tired. Suddenly Sarah yells out loud --- "Why does a dog lick his balls?"

"I do not know." Betty answered so concerned.

Nobody knew the answer.

"Because he can!" she enlightened as everybody laughed again and Betty blushed beat red.

It was 2:30 AM when they decided to dispatch the night driver. Clarence instructed him to: "Fetch the bus and bring it out front; destination --- *Mr. Denny's*."

Interestingly enough, it was a sight to be seen as sixty-three hungry entrepreneurs marched into the restaurant; including three in wheel chairs and two with walkers. Marge led the way as she wheeled Thomas through the door. He warned the manager that his: "Establishment was being invaded by a bunch of old perverts;" as they filled most of the tables.

Both the patrons as well as the night staff got an experience of a life time; an unwanted education. Boring was out of the question

UNCERTAINTY

as conversations were out of control. The residents were fired up beyond any drunken talk that the servers normally have to put up with in course of a weekend night.

Besides being propositioned and over-hearing perverted topics about earlier events that evening; people were quite shocked by their behavior. Sexy Sara flashed her tits at one of the cute young waiters before she re-buttoned up her house coat and then; asked one of the waitresses: "If she knew how to - *Toss The Salad*?"

"But of course." she replied innocently as all of the residents roared. Peg wouldn't let her elaborate.

Eva commented nonchalantly, trying to make-out with another one of the waiters that she was proud to admit that: "I never had any STD's."

"Neither did I," echoed Betty and Edna as Clarence and his *Amigos* were ready to crawl under their table.

"Wow?" he politely responded as he declined to tell her that he thought that *it was too much information* as he passed out the menus. He scurried away as he bit his tongue, trying not to laugh in front of them. In fact, he actually sent someone else to take their order.

He waited on Clarence and his buddies instead as the three *Sex-pots* kept winking, waving and blowing kisses at him. It was getting so annoying and needless to say, Clarence was some what embarrassed as were several others. But what the heck, they were still having a little fun and games. But then again, Clarence couldn't help but wonder: *What are we creating?*

When the food came, they finally clamed down and dug in like a pack of hungry wolves. Without any doubt, they were the talk of the restaurant. When they were finished eating, Clarence paid their bill with their corporate credit card and left a big fat tip for the entire staff; for putting up with their abnormal manners as the *Tribe* exited to their bus.

It was almost 6 AM when the bus rolled back home. The cooks were pleased as coffee, tea, fruits and juices were about all that was requested. The *Laugh-Room* was the center of conversation. To most

SOCIAL SECURITY

of the *Commune*, it was a blessing, something to look forward to. It sparked a new interest as *Social Security* bonded in laughter via perversion.

By 7 AM, downstairs was a ghost town as most vanished to their rooms to catch a little shut-eye. Lucy bunked with Henry and Peg with Clarence. Max and Sarge held the fort as they volunteered to instruct the crew from *Security Plus*.

In the mean time, they restocked the bar then went over the recites for the *Bookmaking Operation* and the *1-900-Sex-Chat*. The sports betting netted just over a grand, but the action from the *Laugh Room* blew their minds. It grossed $10,500.00 in credit card transactions. After sales tax, charge fees, phone expenses and commercial advertising, they cleared $7,800.00.

Half of the *Amigos* were elated with the take. They couldn't wait to enlighten the others. They had a gold mine. They agreed that this called for a special celebration. Something exotic for the entire *Commune* as cost was not an issue. *Social Security* deserved it.

Sarge had a great idea. He had one of the most incredible experiences of his life --- Overseas in the Philippians.

"Besides the naked broads and the booze," he exclaimed, "the natural hot-springs and mud-baths were out of this world. It was right after I received a *Dear John Letter*, from my wife. I thanked God that we didn't have any children and then, I died and was in *Heaven on Earth*."

"Sounds like a plan," Max shouted with enthusiasm. "We can propose it and put it up for a vote Monday, at the *Commune's* next council meeting. But," he asked, "Aren't there any natural hot springs here in the US?"

"Why certainly," Sarge assured. "I'll find us a nice hide-away. I figure $2,000.00 a head ---round-trip for a week."

The owner of *Security Plus* arrived at 7:45 AM with an entourage of three cargo-vans and a crew of six. They scoped and surveyed the grounds with Max and Sarge. Henry and Clarence relieved them at noon as most of the residents were strolling down for lunch in their PJ's.

UNCERTAINTY

The *Four Amigos* each had a *Bloody-Mary* together as Max and Sarge updated the other two; then headed upstairs to crash. Neither Clarence nor Henry expected such results from either operation. Both were extremely pleased as they agreed with the forth-coming proposal. The *Commune* definitely deserved to be rewarded indeed.

The outside perimeter was secured with cameras and motion detectors by 6 PM. The Forman assured Clarence that they'd be back on Monday at 8 AM to finish inside and fine-tune everything. He went over the new updates to the existing system with the *Amigos* before he left.

Saturday night turned out to be an encore performance, so entertaining as well as profitable. In fact, both businesses made more money than the night before. Needless to say, everybody went straight to bed --- pronto. They were all literally exhausted and besides, they had an outing tomorrow morning.

Instead of the customary brunch of Champaign and OJ (Mimosa), Bloody Maries and buffet; Sunday's breakfast was plain and simple. The bus was on the road again by 9 AM as they were headed to the country for a picnic. It was a day of relaxation --- outdoors, reading, sunbathing, fishing and swimming. They arrived back home at 5 PM, just in time for dinner.

By noon on Monday, all systems were going as the security system was operating in full-force. Even new alarms were installed. The monthly council meeting commenced at 7 PM sharp. Since Henry was treasure, he went over all finances with the tribe except for the *Bookmaking Operation*. It was illegal and the *Amigos* didn't want anybody to get in trouble because of their viceroy.

Secretly, all *Four Amigos*, decided in private to donate all of the profits from their gambling enterprise to *St. Jude Children's Research Hospital*. It was Clarence's idea and besides, they never needed the money; like they originally thought they would. They vowed to send a cashier's check anonymously, ounce a year starting on the next anniversary of the opening of *Social Security*.

Henry elaborated on the profits from *1-900-Sex-Chat*. The

residents went wild. They couldn't believe how they could actually make so much money and have so much fun at the same time.

When Sarge made his proposal, all the residents were overwhelmed. He told them that he did some detective work and came up with options as well as prices. They voted to charter a private plane for a 7-day round trip up in the Mountains in Aspen, Colorado. It would be perfect; hot and sunny in the day for mud baths and chilly in the night air so that they could appreciate the pleasure of the natural hot springs.

The air-fare was $19,500.00 and the package price/group rate for room and three buffet meals at *Paradise Lost*, was $88,200.00. It was well below the $2,000.00 a head goal and it was voted upon unanimously. However, they decided to hold off for a year. They didn't want to jeopardize the *Laugh Room*.

Concerning the rest of the agenda; they declined both a nudist-colony trip and the forming of a bird-watching club. They agreed to have two separate trips to strip-joints; one for the guys and one for the gals. It seems that sex was a priority.

Their final issue involved forming a *Sun setting* and *Sun rising* club. It was optional as all you had to do was show up. When Henry adjourned the meeting, everybody pigged out on pizza and wings as usual.

On Tuesday afternoon, Peg assured the *Amigos* that *Erotic Delights* would be up and running Monday. She was tending to final details. She already contracted a major advertising campaign.

Clarence asked her if she: "Wanted to do dinner and a movie?" Lucy and Henry tagged along as they double-dated. Max had another date with Sexy Sarah in the O-Zone and Sarge disappeared as usual for a few hours.

By the time Wednesday rolled around, Gino had been stalking Peg for two days --- unbeknownst to her. He realized that *Social Security* was untouchable as he cased it out and witnessed all the surveillance. But he still wanted revenge --- now, ASAP as animosity ate at his heart, poisoned his brain.

"Peg would do just fine," he thought out loud to himself. "She and

Lucy are the weak links. However, Lucy doesn't have any real money."

He needed cash. He was running out of patience and frustrated. Jail scared the living shit out of him and he vowed that --- *he would never to go back.* He just *wanted to get the hell out of Dodge, leave the fucken country.*

He decided to take forceful action with ill-will. His plan was to force himself on Peg, rob and kidnap her, then flee to Mexico. He knew where she lived; what time she was supposed to work as well as the route that she took to and from the *Commune*.

But since Clarence was her man; Gino never knew for sure if or when they'd go out together or spend the night with each other? Thus, he had to play it cool, one day at a time --- watch her, lay low and creep about. His best option was to follow her until he could grab her in some secluded parking lot --- shopping or perhaps at the bank.

"*Relax,*" he told himself, "*I'll get that tight-ass bitch.*" He was an arrogant cold-hearted, self-centered, deviant with no conscious sense of guilt or shame. And, he was running out of patience, time and money.

Unfortunately, Friday turned out to be *D-Day*. Peg made a serious mistake. She didn't watch her back as she exited the bank and walked back to her car. Gino was oh so sly --- baseball-cap, dark sunglasses, just waiting for her to get in.

"Excuse me," he interrupted; "do you have the time?" he asked as he disguised his voice.

"5:37," she answered without any fear or concern.

"Wrong answer," he retorted as he put a gun in her back.

"Gino," she eked as her heart pounded a mile a minute? He pushed her to the side, opened the door and unlocked the back.

"Get in Bitch." he commanded. "It's payback time."

She got in the front and he sat in the back. She was scared to death. She feared him, especially since he seemed so desperate and out of control.

He was shaking like a leaf, gun trembling against her back. She never matched wits with a moron, but she was determined. She wasn't looking for trouble but sometimes, it sneaks up on you as shit happens.

'Tough Babe', flashed in her head. It was her old nick-name --- way back when she was a teen.

"Be strong," she told herself, "calm down! Think? Now is not the time to fight back."

"What do you want?" she asked, voice trembling with fear. "I have money! Take it!"

"Shut-up you fucken slut. Hand me your purse, start the car and go straight to your house."

She engaged the engine and proceeded as ordered.

"Please don't hurt me." she pleaded with him. "I'll do what ever you say."

"You're gonna blow me bitch." he replied repulsively.

"God, you're so pathetic, so disgusting." she charged back without thinking via angry emotion.

"Don't give me any of that God shit. You're gonna need a miracle to save your sweet ass. Why don't you look for a *Burning-Bush.*" he laughed.

"You don't believe in God?" she asked coyly.

"Hell No, I don't believe in anything that I can't see, touch, hear, taste or smell." he replied arrogantly.

"Don't you feel in your heart? What happened to your conscience; your moral principles?"

"I feel with my dick. A stiff dick hasn't any conscience."

"Don't be so gross." Peg snapped again, at him.

"Don't tell me what to do or how to feel - *Bitch.*" he warned her.

"But," she insisted, "*Love* makes the world go round."

"Love is for fools." Gino disagreed. "You have that perfect dream until you wake-up as reality sets in. Life is but a night-mare."

"Do you mind if I pray?" she asked.

"Ya ya yah, pray all you want, but do it in silence." he laughed. "In fact," he added, "put the radio on --- now."

She obliged and whispered an *'Our Father'* and a *'Hail Mary'*, to

UNCERTAINTY

herself as he ransacked her purse --- looking for cash, bankbooks, credit cards and weapons.

When she finished praying, her mind wandered as she thought of *her daughter, Helen, as well as Clarence and their wedding plans and the Commune.*

God, Please Help Me, I have so much to live for.

Suddenly, she realized that she had to make a move or else. Soon she would be home. Essentially, she devised a plan as *Desesperado* and her *Trouble Bush;* danced in her head. For she was a survivor, he was a total eclipse of a brain.

"Is this $400.00 all the cash you got?" he asked disappointedly.

"I have a few thousand dollars at home."

"That's a start; however I'll need a lot more. I plan on staying out of jail and you're gonna help me. Your platinum credit cards should do the trick, but I thought that you'd be packing heat. I guess you're too holy." he laughed again.

When Peg pulled into her long driveway, past the gate; she thanked Gino for allowing her time to pray. He grinned, eyes dazed in anticipation as he felt powerful. After all, he was in control now. Soon he'd be her master in the bedroom and she knew it.

"You think God's gonna help you?" he asked. "God is but a dog spelled backwards."

"I'm prepared for death." she replied. "Are you?"

"I'm the one who has the gun." he bragged. "But whatever happens; happens. Death can't be any worst than my life."

"I prayed for you." she lied.

"Big deal; so does my mother and grand-mother." he retaliated back verbally. "I went to catholic school for awhile, until they kicked me out, cause my father died and my mother couldn't afford the tuition. At first, Father Dominic was oh so nice, so concerned. He even made me an alter-boy."

"He said that: 'I needed a father-figure in my life' and that 'God wanted him to comfort me.' He took me to a few ball games and I thought that he was my friend. He insisted that friends should always hang out together and trust each other."

"Soon after that, he gave me wine and showed me dirty-movies. Then one night, he raped me. I was eleven years old. Where was God then when I needed him?"

Peg just shook her head in disbelief --- *Horrified*. "He raped you?" she asked pathetically.

"It was my word against his. Go figure?" he added, "Nobody believed me. The lying bastard kicked me out of the school and laughed at me."

"I don't believe in any God that took my father away. You have no idea how hard it is growing up without a father and seeing your own mother working two jobs, praying and crying all the time; feeling sorry for us, for herself. Just looking at her was enough to make me puke. I finally left home at seventeen and haven't seen her since."

"According to my brother Lou, the bitch never remarried or dated; ever again? She lives out west, somewhere with my younger brother. What she needs is a good fucking or a good beating to knock some sense into her, bring her back to reality. Shit, God knows that my father kept her in line and on her toes. He beat the shit out of all four of us, all the time."

Peg was shocked. Gino was bitter and he had a right to be since that evil parasite that hid behind the cloth; fucked-up his mind as well as his life. But, she wasn't about to let him, Gino; fuck up her life.

"I thought that you don't believe in God?"

"I don't, He's just an old habit from my younger days at catholic school."

"I'm sorry." she interrupted with concern, "Betrayed and literally priest-ridden? You poor ba"

"Don't you worry about me *Bitch*. You're the one who has troubles now."

"Ah, but I have a *Trouble Bush*!" Peg exclaimed. "I never bring my troubles into my house."

Gino scratched his head, perplexed. "A *Trouble Bush*," he asked all confused?

"But of course," she replied. "It's a family tradition. I'm the third

UNCERTAINTY

generation to practice it. It would be a mortal sin if you wouldn't let me perform my religious ritual before we entered. Besides, you might learn something. What do you have to lose?"

He looked around; the area was secluded by *Nature* --- vines, brush and trees galore.

"Nothing," he hesitated as he got courage from fingering the gun which was hidden under his jacket which he was carrying. "I am curious. But make it quick, you got a nice ass. I'm getting horny."

It's now or never, she thought to herself as they got out of the car simultaneously.

"Where is this *Trouble Bush*?" he asked sarcastically with a sinister smile on his face. "Next to your *Burning Bush*?"

"Please," she pleaded, "it's a sacred routine ritual. Can't you be serious for just a few precious minutes?"

"Ya ya yah, blab, blab, blab," he pacified her as he bit his lip.

"It is over there next to the porch." she pointed nervously.

He followed her as she proceeded toward her elaborate plan. She just hoped that *Desesperado* would come through.

When they reached the bush, she stopped and egged him on with reverse psychology.

"Now don't you dare laugh at me; as I do my family's secret sacred ceremony? It may seem stupid, but it is a simple procedure that makes me feel better. I'm at peace when I'm all finished. Observe as I cleanse my thoughts and put my troubles on hold."

Gino couldn't help himself as he started to giggle. Peg started to chant.

"*Om! Om! Om!*"

Then she looked up into the sky, sun fading-off-west. She put her arms up into the air as if she was reaching for the stars.

Gino was getting bored. "Hurry-up," he mumbled." I gotta take a piss."

Nonchalantly, Peg put her arms down to her side, looked over at Gino and smiled. Then she put them straight out over the top of her *Trouble Bush* and started shaking them over and over and over again and again in a circular motion; shouting: *"Be Gone, Be Gone, Go, Purge."*

Gino is more curious than before. He laughs and laughs as he thinks that she is crazy, but he is running out of patience.

"I'm shaking all my troubles away before I walk into my house. When I leave, I'll pick them up off the bush and take them with me. It is a mutual agreement between me and the bush."

"Enough is enough!" he shouts as he moved closer towards Peg to stop this nonsense.

Suddenly, she screams from the top of her lungs --- **"Desesperado!"**

Gino jumps a step back and she kicks him square in his balls as she continues in a planed motion - sliding down on her derriere purposely; grabbing for *Desesperado*, in her ankle-holster.

He bends over, grabbing his family-jewels with both hands --- dropping his gun, agonizing in both pain and shame.

"Stand up slowly, you degenerate bastard." she commanded. "Blow you. You probably can't even get it up, you morbid freak. You're a fucken loser, a menace to society." she shouted as she jumped back to her feet.

Gino was stunned in ballistic disbelief. He starred in a silent gaze for a brief moment with eyes that looked as if they had no soul. His jaw dropped as he was literally in shock. He underestimated her and she played him for a fool. She insulted his ignorance. He was lividly infuriated, but Peg was in charge now.

His nostrils were flaring out, vibrating constantly between breaths. She had the power, the control. Would his twisted mind submit to surrender? Was jail his only option? Or, did she light his short-fuse?

"You Bitch." he snapped as he straightened back up. "I'm not going back to that fucken jail."

"Oh well," Peg replied, "but I insist with pleasure. Death is inevitable, *Life* is optional. Today, you get to choose. Make one false move and I'll blow your ass away with my insurance policy."

"Meet *Desesperado*," she continued as she waved her *Beretta 708*; pointed at his mid section. "He takes care of my lite-work; God handles my heavy work. One wrong maneuver and we'll send you to meet your maker --- dick-less."

"You ain't got the nerve to shoot me." he retaliated.

"Don't insult my intelligence," she replied boldly. "Call my bluff if you have the balls to find out. I'll give you a free trip to oblivion. Submit or die, it's your choice."

He anticipated wrongly as he charged at her in desperation with a scared look of fear on his face --- taking three slugs to the groin; flabbergasted dead. Trouble eliminated instantly --- *Sudden Death* as one less dangerous disgrace to *Humanity*. Blood oozed out of his wounds as Peg screamed: "Oh God, what have I done?"

Several neighbors heard the shots and came out running; comforting Peg. They escorted her into her house as somebody covered Gino's lifeless body with a blanket. The police arrived shortly. Peg was on the phone with Clarence. They were familiar with Gino and his alleged involvement in the *Social Security* case; which was pending. They sent the ambulance away and called the county morgue.

Peg explained to the detectives *that Gino abducted her at the bank in the parking lot.* She said that she loosened the strap on her ankle holster from under her pant leg as she drove home while he went through her purse. "Preparation was subtle," she confessed. "*Desesperado*; was my *Element of Surprise*, my *Savior*."

The police concluded that it was self-defense by the time Clarence and his *Amigos* arrived. They took Peg back to the *Commune* to spend the night. She cried on the way there as the guys tried to console her. Clarence held her close as Sarge assured her that her nightmare was now over for good and nobody had to worry about Gino any more.

When they got home, they all headed for the bar. Even Peg drank Jack Daniels. Henry proclaimed that he was sorry that she had to experience such an ordeal. But, he admitted, "I wish I had shot that slimy creep, myself."

They all laughed and Max asked, "Do you want to talk about it?"

The whole room was filled as word spread fast and even Lucy returned for support. Peg got it off her chest as she relived the whole incident for her precious friends.

When the residents heard about the amazing *Trouble Bush*; they just had to have one. It was unanimous, but they decided to get a dozen of them as so to make sure that trouble no longer lingered over their heads. They would become their *Symbols of Peace* with themselves. Tomorrow morning, twelve *Trouble Bushes* would be planted throughout the grounds.

Peg was relieved. She was quite content, as she felt safe again. She didn't feel guilty about killing Gino, but she did feel sorry for him.

His life was a living horror. His mother carried a heavy load, an ugly burden. Blame was irrelevant but Gino lacked faith in God, himself or mankind for that matter as he avoided *Love* since he was afraid of being hurt again. Thus, his values were shallow, superficial and shameless.

How many Gino's, she wondered *are there in this world ---- because mankind as a society, corrupted them as it robbed them of their childhood as well as their dreams as they live in shadows of shame? May God have Mercy on them! May God have Mercy on us!* She prayed to herself with tears in her eyes.

Clarence sensed her emotions and suggested that she go up to his room and take a nap.

"Yeah," Sarge agreed, "then you can shit, shower and shave your pits and legs so that you're fresh and alert for tonight's action in the *Laugh Room*."

Peg giggled as she wiped the tears from her eyes and exited upstairs. On her way up, Max hollered out to her: "It would be a pleasant surprise if all the gals dressed up tonight like Sexy Sarah does!"

CHAPTER **Five**

Acceptance

Chapter 5   Acceptance

Friday night's performance in the *Laugh Room* was a splendid success in spite of the horrific ordeal. It was both profitable and quite entertaining. The residents assumed aliases last week and some callers requested them personally. Especially *Sexy Sarah* who didn't change her name.

As a matter of fact, the gay guy, called back for his *Tossed Salad* and *Bottle of Jack Daniels*. Lucy recognized his voice and promised him that *if he was a 'Good Boy', she'd buy him a gerbil for Christmas*.

"Oh Baby!" he cried as he got off --- Again.

After the last call of the evening, Thomas proclaimed: "I'm Hungry!"

And so, off to Mr. Denny's they went pronto. When the bus rolled back home about 6 AM, everybody crashed for a few hours. The *Commune* was like a ghost town, deserted with silence.

Peg woke up about 9:30 AM and left with the gardener in the pick-up truck. They returned with a variety of *Trouble Bushes*. After lunch, she got a crew of volunteers to plant them; two in front, three on each side and four in the garden. It only took about an hour and then suddenly, the ceremony began as the entire *Commune* assembled outside.

All twelve bushes were utilized. One by one they stood in line,

SOCIAL SECURITY

taking time, taking turns to rid themselves of their troubles; all but Marge. The poor woman looked frustrated as she lingered in her shadows of shame ---- watching all of the shaking and shouting.

"Be gone!"

"Off you go!"

"Go away!"

It was a personal purifying, a *Purging of Thy Soul*, a pack between *Humans* and *Nature*. It was a sight to be seen – the cleansing of one's ideology, bad thoughts and or sins.

The *Amigos* took their turn one at a time, after Peg and Lucy. They atoned in delight as did the rest of *Social Security*. It was fun to say the least. An *Aura of Peace* was in the *Air* as everyone vowed --- 'never to bring trouble inside ever again'; everybody but Marge?

Clarence watched as she fidgeted in pain. He knew that she wanted to participate, but she just wasn't ready yet.

"She needs a little time," Peg surmised as she put her arm around him. Clarence nodded and predicted:

"She'll come around. I hope. Her mind is haywire --- in some disabling fixation. She's cognizant of her surroundings, us, *Social Security*, the whole *Family*, but she's either unwilling or unable to forgive or accept and go on --- yet? All we can do is hope, wait and see."

"I'll pray for her." Peg promised.

"I'm sure that most of the *Commune* does." he replied, "Including me. But," he continued, "it's been so long. It is over a year and a half and that's a long time to suffer."

"God works in mysterious ways." Peg assured. "Adversity is but an adventure. Blessed is he whom overcomes without hate or regrets. But, how can one forgive evil? Poor Marge! I can't imagine, poor Gino, Poor Gino's *Mother* and *Brothers*?"

"I killed somebody's *Son* and a *Brother*. Would they, could they possibly forgive me?" she continued until she started to cry.

"They know what Gino was." Clarence replied as he hugged her and she melted in his arms.

"I Love you." she replied gratefully. "It's nice to have a shoulder

ACCEPTANCE

to cry on; somebody who cares."

"I Love you too." he dittoed as they headed back inside. Peg went upstairs to shower and Clarence headed to the bar to go over the books with the guys.

Clarence was shaving when Peg informed him that she needed some things from her house, including her car. He agreed to drive her, but only after she compromised her weight for some buttered stone-crabs.

They drove to the *Crabby-Shack* on the *Lake*. It was such a beautiful afternoon. After they ate, they decided to take a quick swim since they each had shorts on. But first, they locked their valuables ---- his wallet and her purse in the trunk of his car.

Once in the water, they felt free as water has a way of conforming regardless of age and *Love*, makes you feel as if nothing else matters. They swam like two little fish, stopping every now and again to kiss. In fact, they actually got hot and bothered and decided to hurry off to Peg's; where they could pacify each other in private.

The beach was too packed to chance it, but they made a promise to each other. They vowed to come back some night, under a *Full-Moon* to skinny-dip and make *Love* in the *Water*. They sealed their deal with a passionate kiss.

As they departed the water, Clarence had a hard time walking with a hard-on rubbing between his legs. Peg teased him all the way to the car. He had to walk nonchalantly slow; as if he had a stick stuck up his ass.

When they pulled up in her driveway, Peg became hysterical as she seen her *Trouble Bush*. Gino's bloody body flashed in her mind. Clarence wanted to drive off, but she insisted on going in, and quickly grabbing enough clothes and personal items for a week.

"It's going to take time." he consoled her. "It's like you stated earlier this afternoon; referring to Marge's healing as God does work in strange ways, but it is man who does the dirty deeds."

"Unfortunately," he continued. "Gino's ego possessed his soul. Ironically, life is but a war with self? Its ego verses soul as '*Inner-*

Peace is a prerequisite for World-Peace'."

"Hence, *Father Pierre Teilhard De Chardin* professed: 'we are not human beings having a spiritual experience.' 'We are spiritual beings having a human experience.'"

"It sounds as if man is his own worst enemy." Peg surmised. "*'To do or not to do'*, in route to perfection or devastation as Humans are so unpredictable. Perhaps, fact is stranger than fiction?"

"*'Thou Shalt'*; is but a *Dragon* as he drove *Nietzsche* insane." Clarence exclaimed. "Each must learn to tame his own 'Thou Shalt'."

"You can stay with us at the *Commune* for as long as you wish; move in my room with me. United, we can help each other *Hope* and *Cope*. Together we can tame *Thou Shalt*."

"Perhaps, I think I should sell this place." she concluded. "How will I ever forget, as my poor *Trouble Bush* has turned into a *Trouble Reminder*?"

"Then so be it!" Clarence agreed. "Call the realtor Monday. *Social Security* is our *Family-Home*. I *Love* it there."

"So do I," Peg admitted as Clarence escorted her inside past the bush. She packed two suit-cases; including make-up and some surprise. Clarence carried them out. Peg got in her car and he followed her back to the *Commune* in his.

When they arrived home, they informed the other *Amigos* and Lucy that Peg was moving in for good. They were all overjoyed. Suddenly, Lucy interrupted the excitement with more excitement.

"Henry asked me to marry him!" she screamed ecstatically as her face glowed in delight.

Sarge got the *Jack* and Asti.

"Why don't the four of you have a double wedding," Max joked as usual. "It'll be cheaper and you can have an orgy in the O-Zone."

"Ha, Ha!" they retaliated but then; ironically agreed with half of his idea as September 30 was fine with Lucy and Henry and Hawaii sounded fabulous.

They all toasted in honor of the new engagement and Peg's

new home as Sexy Sarah entered the bar. Sarge poured her a JD. Max couldn't take his eyes off her. She had on tight jeans and was proudly sporting a camel-toe. He asked her if she wanted to: "knock off a quickie."

"Absolutely," she replied without any doubt. However she explained; "I'll meet you in your room in about ten minutes. I have to confer in private with Peg and Lucy."

"You best be ready for action. I go crazy for a man who knows what he wants. So, you better decide whether you want to be the 'spanker'; or the 'spanked'. I'll bring the whips and chains for a little pain and a whole lot of pleasure."

"*Oh Baby!*" Max exclaimed in anticipation as the three women left the bar area. The other three *Amigos* laughed as they shook their heads in disbelief.

"You two are nuts." Henry analyzed for free.

"You better be careful as that wild sex can kill one of you." Clarence warned.

"Ah, to each, his own," Sarge mumbled as he excused himself for a personal rendezvous.

"Another hot date," Henry queried Sarge as he left in silence?

"She must be a dog." Max surmised. "He's either afraid or ashamed to bring her around."

"He's just old fashion." Clarence defended his pal. "Sex is a private matter. Mind your own damn business."

"I'm sorry." Max apologized as he exited for his beating.

"Is Lucy going to move in?" Clarence asked.

"I don't know." Henry replied. "We didn't discuss it, but let's go up and take advantage of the girls since we have the chance."

"I'll race you upstairs!" Clarence responded as they flew up to get *Lucky*.

The three women crept out of the men's rooms, as they were all fast asleep; *according to plan*. At least Sarah didn't kill Max; as she just knocked him out cold.

"Why does sex act as a sleeping pill for men?" Lucy asked as they walked down the hall towards Sexy Sarah's room; to get ready.

"God only knows." Sarah replied. "But, Max will never forget about me. He won't be sitting straight for a few days."

"You didn't whip him? Did you?" Peg asked with shocking concern.

"Hell No," she responded. "He wanted me to give him a hinny-lick, toss his salad. So I took a bite out of his ass, his right cheek to be specific. He screamed like a little sissy."

"Ouch?" Peg shrieked out with empathy as they all started to laugh until Sarah confessed.

"And then, I tossed his salad, but it wasn't a brown-eye; it was a pink-eye."

Peg continued to laugh so hard that she bent over --- holding her stomach as she literally pissed her pants. Lucy was on the floor, holding her own privates.

"What's so funny?" some doctor asked as the gals were hysterically dying in delight.

"Sexy Sarah just performed an oral-rectal-exam." Lucy exclaimed --- shutting down his curiosity as he gawked at the negligees which both Peg and Lucy had in their hands and at Sarah; who was wearing hers. He just shook his head in disbelief as he continued about, making his rounds.

Sarge got back at 8:15 PM. Just in time to wake the other three *Amigos*. After a quick shower, they met in the bar. It was 8:45, fifteen minutes before show time and not a woman in sight. Two dozen plus men marched upstairs scratching their heads. Thomas and some guy with a walker took the elevator. All the guys were confused? They began to panic. Where were the women? Were they already in the *Laugh-Room*?

"Maybe they are on strike?" Henry joked.

The door was locked. When Clarence opened it, it was dark? He turned on the light and **SURPRISE** ---

All the Women had sexy negligees and make-up on, including Marge. The guys all hooted, hollered, whistled and cheered:

"Hot, hot, hot!"

ACCEPTANCE

"Fuck the phone calls," yelled Max! "Let's all have an orgy. All the girls are hot to trot; Dynamite ---Ready to Explode."

Everybody laughed but then, suddenly the phones began ringing and ringing and ringing as it was business as usual except; Sexy Sarah brought a prop.

Throughout the night, she waved a big dildo around --- obscenely; in various gestures. Almost everybody wanted to borrow it, but she was stingy and overly protective of her joy toy. Ironically, some of the women blushed with curiosity as she compelled caller's imaginations, regarding her pacifier; by telling tall tales.

Clarence saw the look in their eyes – bulging, a sense of wonder. Eva, Edna and Betty were thirsting for knowledge as satisfaction was the motive behind curiosity. But they weren't alone as Sarah's persuader looked so inviting, so enticing yet intimidating, appealing and compelling as it invoked desire.

After all, every form has its function and it looked true to form as if ready willing and able to find a need and fulfill it. Denial would be betrayal as you live and learn. Sometimes, vulnerability is but an excuse to explore.

He laughed; as he knew that *Erotic Delights* was destined for success. He surmised that its first customers were ready, willing and able --- right here at home. Ironically, he thought to himself, *masturbation use to be a gingerly subject --- strictly taboo. But know, thanks to Sexy Sarah, it seems like the thing to do. After all, Sexy Sarah never squandered her time.*

Suddenly, Max yells, "I can't take it any longer." He grabbed Sarah by the hand and led her to his room. In fact, every body hooked up with somebody or ended up in the *O-Zone*; everybody but Marge and Sarge. Marge headed to the *Garden* and Sarge to the bar as Lucy busied-out the phone system a bit earlier than usual.

In the bedroom, Peg was nervous as she decided to spit it out. "Clarence," she exclaimed, "I have something to fess up to. Honesty is sacred. Thus, I must come clean."

Clarence was cool, calm and collective as he let Peg speak her

SOCIAL SECURITY

Peace. And then, he said: "So what! I can't wait to meet Helen." He even suggested that she'd *invite* Harley *and his band to the wedding*. She giggled as they hugged.

After they made *Love*, Clarence began to laugh. "What's so funny?" she asked.

"I can't believe that you use to hang out with *Sexy Sarah*."

Peg was embarrassed but knew that Clarence was only joking. Suddenly, she replied, "Whose idea do you think it was to ban the bra?"

"It had to be Sexy Sarah's." Clarence surmised.

"But of course," she assured. "We became *Liberated Together*."

They both had a final chuckle before they fell fast asleep. Peg awoke, up early. It was 5:40 AM and she felt great considering the noisy stormy night. Her burden was lifted as Clarence was oh so understanding.

She decided to take a walk in the *Garden* in spite of the rain; especially since the thunder and lighting subsided. After all, she loved the feel of the raindrops amidst a warm summer breeze. The *Garden* was so peaceful as she got lost in the serenity and beauty of the flowers and the falling showers, until she was disturbed by short and sudden outbursts of cries.

"Go away! Be gone! Leave me alone already!" Marge yelled in a weak frantic voice between her tears and sobs as she shook her hands over and over, again and again.

Peg was stunned as she investigated the situation. For it was an irate effort on Marge's part; very daring.

"Marge?" she screamed as the poor frail woman hurried over to another bush and encored.

"You poor *Dear*; you're soak-in-wet. You'll catch a cold."

Marge was distraught, sobbing in sorrow, agonizing in shame. Her pain was traumatic. She was exhausted and yet, seemed determined, but will power was not enough. It was preoccupied by doubt, guilt and hate. Unfortunately, it refused to surrender --- to *Peace* as *Ego* was in control --- wryly.

Peg felt sorry for her as the *Trouble Bushes*, were useless. She needed affection and support as a part of her was dead. Ironically, faith, hope and discipline died as she was sadly hysterical.

Peg tried to comfort her as they embraced. Marge shook like a leaf and cried like a baby. Peg was at a lost for words as she realized that Marge was out here for over three and a-half-hours. She led her inside and gave her a sedative. It kicked in slow but surely as Peg sat next to her bed, holding her hand while singing her favorite song --- *Moon-River*.

By the time she finished singing it for the second time; Marge was out cold. Peg felt awful. The *Trouble Bushes* put Marge through *Hell* as they endangered her health. Peg couldn't believe that that little old lady braved all the rain, thunder and lighting; that ruled the night. And yet, there was no end in sight for her misery.

She knew that she had to go face her own *Trouble Bush*, --- Alone. Or else, she'd end up in *Denial* --- lying to herself. Ironically, you can run from your *Trouble Bush*, but you can't hide from your troubles. Eventually, they shall imperil and cause havoc if not confronted.

Peg prayed all the way to her house. She asked *God for strength and hoped that she wouldn't panic.* Her heart pounded as she pulled into the driveway. But courage was with her as God answered her prayers. Without doubt or hesitation, she performed her *Family Ritual* --- perfectly.

Suddenly, she had an eerie thought. *Was death the only answer to Marge's prayers? Is death the ticket to Peace or is misery lurking --- beyond the grave horizon? Can man take his doom and gloom with him? Is Thou Shalt, invincible? Is Consciousness invincible?*

Peg scratched her head --- puzzled. *Why are life and death so complicated?* She wondered. *What is their relationship, if any; Karma?* She believed that *God Is the Source* and she hoped that He was the destination.

She stared at her *Trouble Bush*. Innocently, it remained silent as usual as if nothing special was required. She bent over and kissed it and then, miraculously, she had a reckoning, an epiphany.

She smiled as she spontaneously realized that *all people have* a few things in common; everybody is different and yet, we are all special as each of us is unique. But, **'Forgiveness' is the Gift from God that is a 'Divine Option'.** We must choose to use it. Actually, all humans must learn this little secret and forgive themselves as well as those that trespass against us. Thus, she forgave Gino and then suddenly, she felt at *Peace* with the *Universe*.

At brunch, in the mess hall, Lucy announced that she was moving in. Everybody was delighted; all but Marge and Sarge. Marge was fast asleep and Sarge was no where to be found. Peg kept silent about Marge's ordeal but planned on telling Clarence later on.

"Where's Sarge?" Henry asked.

"His bed wasn't slept in." Max informed. "I knocked three times, but there was no answer so I peeked with concern. He too, must of gotten horny --- last night."

"When are we going to meet his *Secret Lover*?" Lucy asked curiously.

"Maybe she's shy?" Peg interrupted. "Maybe we should invite her on our next outing; break the ice so to speak with --- hospitality. We should encourage Sarge to bring her around."

"You can take her next month on your trip --- to the male strip joint." Max joked. "That is if Sarge will let her go?"

Everybody laughed until Lucy spoke. "I think next Sunday's picnic is more suitable."

"That sounds like a great idea." Clarence interjected as they all agreed with him.

After brunch, Henry and Lucy went to Lucy's house to pack some cloths. Monday, it would be on the market. They decided to take advantage of the bed, but settled for the couch.

After they were alone, Peg told Clarence about Marge's ugly ordeal. He was upset with grave concern. She brought a temporary smile to his face when she revealed that she made *Peace* with herself and her *Trouble Bush* as she forgave Gino.

"Do you still want to live here?" he asked.

"Absolutely," she confirmed! "I'm calling the realtor tomorrow for both houses."

ACCEPTANCE

"Lucy's selling too?" Clarence asked.

"She said that it's too much to handle. We have the same sediments exactly." Peg assured. "Besides, we found our *Family Home*."

"Very well," Clarence exclaimed with joy! "It's settled then. Now all we have to do is support and comfort Marge with *Love*. She'll come around. She has to. For when one member of a *Family* is hurting, we all hurt."

"I Love you." Peg whispered in his ear.

"I Love you too." Clarence dittoed. "Whata you say, do you wanna go get some afternoon delight?"

"But of course," Peg replied with a smile. He took her by the hand and led her out the door.

"Where are we going?" she asked.

"Ice-cream," Clarence clarified with a twinkle in his eye. "Do you think I have sex on my mind all of the time? There are other pleasures in life."

They both laughed as they drove off --- headed for the lake.

Sarge came home at suppertime. He got the third degree from both the guys and the gals, but he was so ornery and miserable, that they let him slide off of the interrogation. He told them that he already ate and politely excused himself.

Lucy suggested to him as he was leaving the room that: "You might want to bring your girlfriend to the picnic next week." Either he didn't hear her, or he chose to ignore her; which left everybody puzzled? Nobody said a word as they continued eating.

Silence prevailed until two doctors interrupted dinner with disturbing urgency. *'Marge has pneumonia. She is on oxygen and intravenous antibiotics'.*

Peg was sick to her stomach. *If Marge dies,* she thought, *it's surely my fault.* **'Oh God Please,'** she prayed; **'Don't let Marge die. She's not ready yet. I'd never forgive myself. Please God, Please have Mercy, Spare her Life until she Heals - Spiritually.'**

Clarence sensed that Peg was upset. He held her in his arms. He

SOCIAL SECURITY

knew that she blamed herself.

"God works in strange ways." he reminded her.

"I have to be with her." Peg insisted.

Clarence walked her to Marge's room but Peg wanted to be alone with her for awhile. He understood and headed for the bar. The *Amigos* were there waiting for him. They were confused until he enlightened them about Marge's experience.

"That poor woman," Lucy uttered. "What was she thinking?"

"Misery is so disgraceful and dreadful." Sarge professed sympathetically. "It masquerades but evidently, it can't be denied. Them *Trouble Bushes,* served a purpose as Marge confronted herself in spite of the thunder storm. Now, all she has to do is forgive herself and that degenerate bastard that raped her and let it --- Go Away."

"It's easier said than done." Clarence surmised. "Her pain is so deeply ingrained. She is helpless. Hate and anger can eat away at you literally and rob you of your sanity. What can we possibly do to help her; help, herself? Ultimately, we must all answer to our-selves as forgiveness is divine. Ironically, we must live and die with self."

"Doesn't she have any family?" Henry asked sadly.

"She lost both her husband and daughter in the same year to Tuberculosis in the early fifties." Lucy informed. "She never remarried after that. As far as I know, there is no one else."

"We're her *Family!*" Max assured. "And she knows it. She trusts us, but she seems afraid to ask for help. At times, she seems cold and confused as if she is afraid to open up, express her feelings."

"She's afraid of getting hurt again and again." Clarence added. "Distance is her protection as she fights her feelings. But you can't fight *Unconditional Love.* Love is all that matters. God is Love. Love is Truth. Truth is Peace. Unfortunately Marge is afraid of Truth. She needs a lot of TLC *(tender loving care)."*

Everybody retired early that night; all but Peg. Clarence checked in on Marge before he went to bed and Peg prescribed that she was spending the night with her. Marge was half awake and smiled when Clarence kissed her on the forehead before he left. Peg

ACCEPTANCE

remained behind nursing and singing off and on throughout the night --- *Moon-River*.

Monday rolled in on schedule. Marge struggled to sit up and strained as Peg helped her force some soup down for breakfast. Peg then entrusted her to the day nursing staff; since she had to tend to *Erotic Delights*. But first, she called a friend of hers; a realtor whom agreed to represent both homes.

By lunchtime, *Erotic Delights* was up and running full force as orders came quickly. Drop-shipping was a breeze and the high-priced advertising; all over the internet, paid for itself ten-fold. Peg informed everybody that it was against the law to send dirty movies through the US mail. They opted for UPS.

Eva, Edna and Betty were naturals as their curiosity took charge. Clarence was right; all the women had a field day with catalogs. Each of them ordered several sex toys; all but Marge and Peg.

Nonchalantly, Peg reintroduced herself to Sexy Sarah. The day flew by as they reminisced about *Woodstock*. Sarah mentioned that it would be great to see Harley again after Peg spilled her secret. That convinced her to invite him to the wedding, but she didn't tell Sarah.

At supper time in the mess-hall, Lucy announced that *Erotic Delights* was a success. "Orders are coming in as we speak," she informed, "twenty-fours a day, seven days a week, via --- the information highway. The average order is $60.00. We took in $1,000.00 today. 60% is pure profit --- $600.00."

Everyone was delighted, but Peg was exhausted as she didn't get any sleep last night. Sarge called for a celebration. All accepted except Peg, whom excused herself and went to check on Marge. Then she headed to bed for the night.

The party was typical as nobody wanted to be the first to leave. Ironically though, nobody got drunken-shit-faced. It seems that experience led to tolerance or respect. Regardless, they all had a good time; all but Marge and Peg.

Day by day, several weeks came and gone as business went on lucratively in spite of the fact that Marge was bed-ridden. She was strong enough, just in time for the strip-joint outing as she made a remarkable recovery, but opted to stay home. Peg and Lucy stayed behind with her. Especially since Sarge's *Lover* declined their hospitality --- Again.

Sarah and the gals had a ball and the X-rated pictures to prove it. They went to the *French-Ballet* in Canada; where the men take it all off legally. The following week, the guys headed for Canada and Max had the pictures to prove it.

Summer was winding down fast, but the *Commune* was grateful as Marge recovered fully. There was a good hot month left; when Peg and Clarence honored their promise to each other. The skinny-dipping was quite refreshing, so romantic and tempting.

Irresistibly, they couldn't take their hands or eyes off each other. Perhaps it was the spell of the *Full-Moon*. It was so exciting, so inviting as it drew them together --- sexually engaged.

"I Love You Clarence!" she moaned as they came together.

"I Love You Too!" he replied. "You're the light of my life."

"Oh, Oh Clarence, you make me so happy." she jumped into his arms, hugging and kissing him all over his neck and face until --- Busted. They got caught by the State-Police. Obviously, an adventure of that magnitude involves risk and it proved to be embarrassing.

The troopers chuckled as they escorted the couple off the beach. They were polite enough not to write a report, let alone a ticket, but explained that it was their duty to patrol the beach at night.

"Sometimes that current picks up at night." warned one of the officers, "Especially under a *Full-Moon*."

Peg and Clarence understood as they took their lecture like adults and promised not to do it again. The other officer joked: "Teen-agers usually give us problems."

They laughed all the way home. Peg admitted that she was embarrassed about her *Point-E-Out-E's* while Clarence confessed that he too was embarrassed since he shriveled up as both of them were cold when they exited the water amidst the night breeze. They vowed to keep it their little secret.

CHAPTER **Six**

Fate

Chapter 6 Fate

It was July fourth and all were excited about the pig-roast. Sarah joked that she wanted the penis and testicles. Everybody laughed, especially the renowned French Chef, Jacques. They hired him specifically for the occasion. Peg read an article about him retiring and moving from Paris to the US. He was promoting his new cookbook and just happened to be in town for what was to be the end of his book tour.

 Peg bought his book at a local book store and had a chat with him after he signed it. He seemed shy, especially for someone being so famous. His dishes were widely known; held as highly esteemed. He told Peg that he didn't need the money, but he just loved to cook and was thinking about opening up a restaurant; here in America.

 Peg listened attentively; then told him about their up and coming event. Jacques volunteered to cook for free, but Peg insisted on paying him. They came to a mutual agreement. Thus, she hired him for the fiesta which turned out to be most enjoyable.

 No appetite was deprived --- chef d' oeuvre as he lived up to his illustrious reputation. In fact, a dozen or so residents ate so much that they accidentally took a siesta as it was a lazy, relaxing occasion. Jacques was proud and the *Commune* got their moneys' worth.

 When it got dark, they had a sing-along --- around the campfire. A few of the residents played their guitars; one had a banjo, and

SOCIAL SECURITY

two had harmonicas and Carlos had his maracas. It was actually quite impressive as talent is in the eye or ear of the beholder.

During the old fashion hoe-down, Sexy Sarah took the initiative and snuck off with Jacques. She exposed her Twins as she introduced him to the *O-Zone;* seduced him and then, took him *Around the World*. When they finished, he asked her if the *Commune* needed a *Chef de Cuisine*. The tribe put it to vote around the flickering flames and he was hired.

Suddenly he confessed with delight: "I've been around the world --- literally. But tonight, the sex was the best I ever experienced. Bar-none!"

Everybody busted out in an uproar --- again. Sarah was proud; she still had it in her as she nabbed a frisky Frenchman, a horny little-devil, twenty years her younger. For she not only knew how to talk the talk or walk the walk, she danced every dance. Bar-none!

The summer ended and fall began as the resident's bellies became spoiled when Jacques moved in. Even breakfast was gourmet / cuisine, especially Sunday Brunch. Nobody complained but Max was a bit jealous as the chef shacked-up in Sarah's room. Regardless, time flew by as Saturday September 30th, finally arrived and everybody put on a few pounds.

The brides were splendidly beautiful in their simple yet adequate gowns as the grooms looked distinguished and handsome. Clarence wore his surprise suit, which the *Amigos* bought for him as Henry sported a new suit, which was also purchased through friendship. In fact the residents chipped in and paid for everything except the honeymoons. Sarah offered her birthday suit as a wedding present and even the minister laughed.

Jim-Jim was the *Ring-Bearer* for both couples and Lucy's *Great Grand Daughters* --- Jamie and Cheyenne were the *Flower Girls*. Chi and Max were the *Best-Men* and Helen and Sarah; the *Bride's Maids*. Clarence's three *Sons* --- Robert, David and Michael as well as his two other young *Grandsons* --- Nichols and Nathaniel; were also there. Charlie, an old friend of Clarence's, was there too and sang *Ave Maria* as Peg and Lucy walked down the isle.

The ceremony itself was short and sweet; the dinner, extravagantly out of this world. Helen and Clarence embraced as they accepted each other with open arms. Harley gave his *Blessings*, provided the entertainment and picked up the tab for both *Honeymoons*.

All in all, it was a memorable event. Especially when Sexy Sarah blushed as Harley sang a song, which he dedicated to her --- *Crabs In My Mustache*. Everybody was on the floor rolling and holding their aching guts; even *Sorry Sarah*. The party ended as the band played another song that Harley also sang --- *The Last Dance of the Night*, which solicited attention as the floor was packed.

The following morning, the four newlyweds departed on their honeymoon. Lucy was very nervous; fear of flying. Actually, she was never in an airplane before; by choice.

Unfortunately, her father died in a routine flight, which crashed while he was in the Air Force. She was eleven at the time and vowed to avoid the vehicle; which robbed her of her daddy. Thanks to Peg, it was the *Trouble Bush*; that gave her courage to face her fears. She carried that burden long enough.

When the plane landed at Honolulu International Airport; Lucy giggled in delight as she actually enjoyed the ride. She was sorry that she declined previous chances and realized that she literally missed out on certain opportunities as destiny is a winding road. But, she learned in the course of her lifetime not to cry over spilt milk. *What's done is done*, she thought; *'Live and Learn'*; *'Love and Enjoy Life'*. Hence, she vowed to face her fears and never to be pessimistic again.

"Aloha!" "Aloha," echoed the traditional greeting of salutations --- Hawaiian for *Love*; from the *Natives* as they placed lei's of garland --- Hibiscus Blossoms of showy flowers and leaves around all of the vacationer's necks. They also crowned all the women with a wreath on their heads. Half of the *Amigos* and their spouses felt at peace amidst the floral-scented sea breezes and tropical warmth. It was an unforgettable moment of breath taking beauty.

It was in a little boutique on Oahu, nicknamed the *Gathering Place*, where Peg found simple treasure. Its pleasure was truly

Spiritual; a Naked Truth. Not many realize it as they take it for granted, but oh do they bitch when so often times --- *Shit Happens*. Lucy recognized its value as they bought one hundred tee-shirts; sporting words of wisdom --- *Grace Happens*; as they wanted to *Spread the Word*.

The two weeks flew by before they knew it; as they stayed active. Sight-seeing during the day --- *Waikiki Beach, Diamond Head, Pearl Harbor and Sunset Beach* just to name a few. The islands were simply gorgeous, palm trees swaying in the wind. They snorkeled in *Hanaumu Bay* on the southeast coast, parasailed in the southern *Koolau Range* near the *Nuuana Pali Lookout*; where the view of the windward coast is enchanting. They even took a *Circle Island* tour and visited a pineapple plantation.

At night it was dinner, drinking and dancing --- luau style; Kalua pig, the sacred bowl of poi, sweet potatoes, Luau or laulau (salted butterfish known as escolar combined with either pork, beef, or chicken which is wrapped in taro leaves), Lomi salmon, tropical fruits - pineapple, mango and papaya as well as haupia, a traditional coconut milk-based Hawaiian dessert. All the traditional Hawaiian dishes were absolutely succulent. The newlyweds loved the beat of the Polynesian drums and the allure of the seductive Tahitian dancers. Ironically, *Jack* was neglected as Mai Tai drinks were in style. The rums and creme de almond tasted great in the pineapple juice, but they snuck up on you.

Maybe it was the alcohol, but they thought that they died and went to *Heaven*. They shared spectacular sun-rises and sun-sets everyday, found seashells by the seashore, built sandcastles as they day-dreamed and found --- themselves by the time they left Paradise. They even came back a few times to watch the tide come in and wash the sandcastles away.

Incidentally, Peg and Clarence managed to sneak away, late one night and successfully complete their promise again; as they made *Love* and skinny-dipped in *Peace*. Ironically, the last night turned out to be the funniest as both Clarence and Henry decided to play a prank on each other. Unfortunately, on the first day, Henry got sunburn on his bald head and had to buy a hat. Thus, on the last day, Clarence couldn't resist the temptation as he spotted a hat with a long ponytail attached to it. He had the shop keeper inscribe Hank on it.

Henry was a good sport as a sense of humor builds character. He put it on and wore it, but by the end of the day; he returned the favor. The front of Henry's new shirt read --- *With It, Again!* The back read --- *Truth is akin to Cool as both are Repulsive to the Un!*

Clarence laughed as he thought that Henry was reminiscing in nostalgia, trying to be *Hip* once more. Suddenly, the old hippie handed Clarence his present; also a tee shirt. The front simply read, --- *It*, the back read --- *Almost Cool by Association!*

They were a sight to be seen, especially with their newly pierced-ears. They were the *Odd Couple*, *Groovy* and *It*. They danced together and Clarence won the *Limbo Contest*. Without doubt, they were the life of the party and Peg and Lucy had the pictures to bare witness.

Both Peg's and Lucy's houses sold while they were away in Hawaii. Fortunately, they each got their asking price. In fact, Lucy's sale included the entire contents.

Peg gave her furnishings to Helen. What she didn't want; went to charity. Unfortunately, Thomas O'leary was diagnosed with liver cancer while they were gone. He was already on *Chemo* and radiation by the time they returned home.

Sarah gave the new wives a belated wedding present --- a set of *BenWa Balls* each. She professed that she never left home without them. Then she confessed that she was in *Love* with Jacques.

"I adore him and worship the ground that he walks on; as he knows where my *G-Spot* is hidden."

Peg and Lucy busted out roaring until Betty butted in; as she was ease dropping with Eva and Edna. The three sex-triplets had puzzled looks on their faces?

"What is a *G-Spot*?" Betty asked earnestly.

Sarah got the honors as she educated the less fortunate. The two newlyweds politely excused themselves nonchalantly embarrassed. As they were exiting the room, the other four were giggling like a bunch of teens.

Peg just shook her head silently as she couldn't believe how naive or sexually deprived they lived. It was hard to believe that they were all married once and that two of them actually gave birth? She wondered *if any of them ever had an organism.*

Sarah was their inspiration as she created a new outlook on life. They were turning into *Sex-pots*, all dolled-up. She was their role model as all three of them wore mini-skirts, wigs and make-up galore. Her word was God when it came to sex as they worshiped her experience. They couldn't wait to explore her advice as she suggested that they buy a curved *G-Spot-vibrator* from *Erotic Delights*.

The *Amigos* were shooting pool at one of the two pool tables when the call came in. Clarence was elated. He finally had his *Girl*. Brandie just gave birth to Baby Mayan Angela. Sarge sounded the *Call for Celebration* and the entire *Commune* partied. Even Chi stopped by for a few.

The first year passed in spite of the ups and downs as *Social Security* proved to be a caring congregation; a *Mecca of Love*. For they came a long way, shared both the good and the bad --- *Together* as a *Family*. But what surprised them all was the fact that they sustained for themselves as the businesses were booming.

Peg's great sense of humor was an asset in balancing her multi-faceted-responsibilities. She overcame each and every challenge of her endless tasks, on a daily basis. She was the backbone of the *Commune* and she knew how to throw a big party.

At the *Anniversary Celebration*, Peg and Lucy presented the *Four Amigos* with a token of appreciation from the *Tribe* for playing a major active roll in daily operations. The *Comrades* were proud as they sported their new ponchos. Each had his name stitched on his. To top it off, they were also given their own sombreros. They looked *Bad --- Armed Ambries*.

Old Carlos was in his glory when somebody popped in a CD

of Spanish Music. He was ready to go in his wheel chair, shaking his maracas, sporting his own poncho and sombrero. He was the oldest resident at ninety-three, yet as healthy as a horse except; for a broken foot.

The women took turns wheeling him around as he drank tequila. A few even sat in his lap. Sarah flashed him her tits as she made his day and he felt like the *Fifth Amigo*.

It was a day they would never forget. Carlos was quick with the draw as he showed Sarah his *Gun*. Sarah was in *Love* again, at least for a minute; as he had a whopper --- hung like a horse. Consequently, Sexy Sarah nick-named him - *Numero Uno Macho*, and he was proud as she screamed:

"Ooh-Lala! You want to cha-cha-cha with me?"

Everybody roared with laughter. But, Eva, Betty and Edna; all gave *Sexy Sarah* the *Evil-Eye*. His tool intimidated their curiosity with desire. Ironically, he was over-looked but now; he was considered as fair game, new meat and eligible.

It was a Sunday after the traditional brunch; when the *Amigos* decided to go to the park and feed the pigeons. Suddenly they spotted him --- *King-Wine-O*; laying in the grass, brown bag in his hand, talking to himself, having a *Good-ol-Time*.

"Poor bastard," Max pointed. "Self-neglected abuse; he's pathetic, I wonder how long it's been since he had three hots, a bath and a cot?"

"I don't know. Let's go over and ask him." Clarence suggested as they approached him with unduly caution.

Startled, Joe sat up. "Want a drop!" he offered generously.

"No thanks." they echoed simultaneously.

"Are you hungry?" Henry asked sympathetically.

"I'm OK." Joe answered as he extended his hand and introduced himself politely. He told the guys that *'His name was Old Joe McCoy, who had no family and that he was a Free-Spirit, blowing in the Wind from town to town --- pursuing Destiny.'*

SOCIAL SECURITY

He considered himself: '*A legend in his own mind, a self-taught blues singer*'.

"Have a listen!" he offered without hesitation as he whipped out his harmonica and sang -- *Brown Bagged Wine*.

BROWN BAGGED WINE

(*King Wine-O*)

Sitting on a park bench
Laying a little low
Watching all the people, hustle as they go
Off to work, it's a steady job
A routine rut and guess whose stuck?
It ain't me --- I'm free
I'm the King and I do my thing
Brown bagged wine, --- feeling fine
The more I drink, it lets me think
I have plenty of time
All the time
For me and mine --- brown bagged wine

Laying in the tall grass
Watching it grow
Figure out why --- hell nooo
Mother Nature, it's a steady job
A routine rut and guess whose stuck?
It ain't me --- I'm free
I'm the King and I do my thing
Brown bagged wine, --- feeling fine
The more I drink, it lets me think
I have plenty of time
All the time
For me and mine --- brown bagged wine

Laying on my death bed
Feeling a little low
Afraid of dying --- hell nooo
Human Nature, it's a steady job
A routine rut and guess whose stuck?
It ain't me --- I'm free
I'm the King and I do my thing
Brown bagged wine, --- feeling fine
The more I drink, it lets me think
I have plenty of time
All the time
For me and mine --- brown bagged wine.
Day and night, it feels right
Me and mine, brown bagged wine
Have-in a good ol time,
All the time.

    The *Amigos* were moved by Old Joe's sincerity, in spite of his situation. They were impressed with his simple philosophy of life. They clapped when he finished his song. Henry took a twenty dollar bill from out of his pocket and Joe was so happy that he did a jig.

    Suddenly, Sarge had an idea as his *Heart* was inspired. He called his friends over to the side for a huddle. They conversed in conference and all agreed. Joe was ecstatic; as they adopted him then and there and he became a member of the *Commune*.

    King Wine-O was welcomed with open arms and smiling faces when they arrived back at *Social Security*. Sexy Sarah offered Joe her hospitality after asking him if he had the *'Irish Curse'*.

    "Hell No!" he replied.

    "Prove It!" she responded back. "Take me for a ride in the O-Zone."

    Once he found out what the *O-Zone* was, he politely refused, but he was a good sport as the *Three Sex-pots* were more curious than ever. Everybody roared in delight as Sexy Sarah answered Betty's question: "What's *The Irish Curse*?"

"All potatoes and no meat." she answered as Old Joe blushed, pleaded the fifth with his silence; until he burst out laughing along with his new *Family*. He had nothing to prove as a few imaginations went wild.

Needless to say, he fit right in. In fact, he was so pleased to have a home and a family that he actually quit drinking; cold-turkey. He adapted and became a tea-totter and assumed position as head gardener, an acquired perfection which he learned in his travels.

Old Joe and Thomas O'leary became friends. Joe felt sorry for him as he was having a hard time dealing with his treatments. Sometimes his pain was unbearable. He consulted with the *Amigos*; about growing some marijuana to ease Thomas' pain.

"Why certainly," was their reply, "anything to help Thomas, but no selling it."

One fine day, while spraying his *Special Plants*; he spotted a familiar face --- a new resident. *"Anna,"* he whispered?

He couldn't believe his eyes? Talk about fate, destiny --- coincidence. It was a *Miracle*, a second chance encounter; a *Dream Come True*. Ironically, it was a bit spooky; synchronicity, no mere chance coincidence as he got the chills --- down his spine.

Actually, he thought that *she was deceased*. But as it turned out; she was a victim of robbery --- knocked on the head and left for dead. Nobody knew who she was for years as she suffered in amnesia. Eventually, her memory came back --- a decade later.

She searched for Joe. But he vanished by choice as he went searching for her until he gave up --- *Hope* and turned to the bottle. It became his only friend or family for the last thirty-five / forty years until a few months ago.

It was a tender moment. A time for hugs and kisses, tears and laughter as brother and little sister reunited. Anna professed her faith; *that she knew that they would find each other before death.*

She dedicated her life --- searching for Joe. She utilized the internet, talk-shows, public records, etc. She even prayed everyday. In fact, she was praying when he spotted her. They were destined to meet again.

She was grateful to God for answering her prayer and to the *Commune* for being so generous in accepting her as she had very little income. Joe shared her sediments --- exactly as he confessed that he *Loved* it here. He apologized for being so weak and giving up *Hope*.

"Blame is irrelevant in *Life*." she replied as they embraced --- looking into each others eyes, tears of joy spilling down both faces. "We mustn't feel sorry for ourselves." she continued. "It's a useless waste of time. It's like hurry and worry, fret and regret which are misconceptions of time and lead to depression and anxiety. Time is what you make of it."

"Let's make the best of the time that we have left. We are so lucky! From now on, let's enjoy life fully – Always."

Joe agreed as they kissed and then, they just sat there holding hands, reminiscing as they bonded in admiration; appreciating their second chance miracle. Suddenly, they were interrupted by Marge who was confronting her troubles; thanks to a renewed spark of hope and a lot of courage as Max was curiously eye-balling Anna from behind another *Trouble Bush*.

Joe spotted him and laughed to himself as Anna inquired about Marge. He enlightened her, but not before he gave Max the *Evil-Eye*. Max abruptly disappeared.

When Marge left, Joe exclaimed; "Rumor has it that they castrated the sinister bastard that raped her while he was in jail. But first they raped him and eventually killed him. I hope he was alive when they cut off his balls."

"What goes around comes around," Anna replied. "It's called *Karma* and, it ain't prejudice. I like to call them *Karma-Krispies* and SHAZAM --- destiny replies accordingly as *Karmic Retribution* is a *Fact of Life*. If not, in this life-time; then perhaps the next; but --- Eventually."

"In the meantime we all have to live with our conscience. For as Edgar Cayce warned --- 'the laws of the universe continue to operate even when ignored.' 'Every act, good or Bad, is recorded in a Journal of Life, the Akashi Record; the Annals of Humanity'"

◄ SOCIAL SECURITY

"You believe in reincarnation?" Joe asked his little sister with a startled look on his face.

"I most certainly do!" she insisted without any doubt. "It's the only thing that makes any sense to me. Why, don't you?"

"To be perfectly honest with you, I never really thought about it Sis." he admitted ardently with an opened mind.

"Believe it or not, many great minds believed in reincarnation, including *Einstein, Ben Franklin, Plato* and *Edgar Cayce* himself ---- the renowned *'Sleeping Prophet'*. If you're interested," she continued, "I have many intriguing books on the subject. In fact *Einstein* proved in his theory that matter never dies as it just takes on a new form --- *Conversion*."

"It sounds fascinating!" Joe replied with excitement.

"In fact," Anna continued, "I am a proud member of Cayce's *A.R.E organization (Association for Research and Enlightenment)*, in Virginia Beach, Virginia. I also believe in *Holistic Healing* and *Spiritual Growth*. You should check it out. Doctors from all over the world go there to research his readings."

"Maybe someday, we could go there together? I'd love to be enlightened. Please pick out one of his books for a novice layman."

That night she obliged her brother with a book about Edgar Cayce's life --- *There is a River*. He was overwhelmed as he spent half the night reading it. The next morning, he admitted that he was hooked on Cayce; as he wanted to read more about his life endeavors.

As luck would have it, she had a whole library of books concerning his remarkable predictions. After all, she was an adamant follower of his readings. After a few weeks, Joe had a new outlook on both life and death.

Anna became Joe's companion in the *Garden* as they shared the responsibilities. He laid out the *Genesis* and the *History* of *Social Security* for her. He even warned her to stay away from Max. But little sisters never listen to older brothers as they have to find out for themselves.

Max put the move on Anna and she accepted as they began dating. Eventually, they were inseparable. Old Joe McCoy was a bit jealous as if he lost his best friend since she was spending so much time with Max.

He respected her judgment; however he was a bit overprotective of his sibling. Especially, since he heard rumors that Max was married and divorced three times because he couldn't keep his pecker in his pants. He decided to take action.

Thus, he warned Max with no disrespect intended; that he better treat her like a lady or else, he'd stick *El Caramba* up his *arse*. Joe made it perfectly clear that he wasn't about to put up with his malarkey or shenanigans. His point was well taken as Max didn't push his luck by disobeying Joe's wishes.

He respected both Joe and Anna and would never jeopardize their friendships. Besides, he didn't want to get in a heap of trouble. Hence, he never even joked about sex in front of Anna; let alone make any naughty moves.

Frankly, he knew that *Old Joe* was from the *old school; old fashion,* when it came to romance. He lost his sister once but now he was here to protect her; reputation and all. He insisted on courting and marriage before *hanky-panky*.

Ironically, it was Anna whom seduced Max. She insisted that he take her to a motel like some teenagers; sneaking off. Although Max was scared of *Old Joe*, his hormones couldn't resist provoking temptation. Especially since she assured him that she'd handle her brother.

Joe was pissed at first but after all; she insisted: "This is a *New Millennium;* the *Age of Aquarius* is about to begin and besides, I'm a big girl now. I'm just trying to enjoy the rest of my life like we agreed."

Joe apologized to both Max and Anna and gave them his *Blessings*. They accepted and announced that they were engaged and the *Commune* had a double celebration. Coincidently, Sarah and Jacques also decided to tie the knot as settling down seemed to be the thing to do.

SOCIAL SECURITY

Sarge was a bit uneasy. Perhaps he was somewhat jealous; perhaps he was sick and tired of the advances from the *Three Sex-Pots*, whom were hot to trot. For he and Joe were declared fair game as Betty, Eva and Edna were like cats that were itching to be scratched and on a mission --- *Gotta Get a Man!*

Actually, it was at the *Christmas in July Party*; when they proved to be extreme. They were dressed-up like *Santa's Little Helper's* --- short mini-skirts, crotch-less panty-hoes' and come-get-me pumps on. They also sported long red-tee-shirts; with the words *'Boy Toys'* on them, a present from Sexy Sarah.

Joe was playing Santa Claus and the *Three Sex Pots* kept jumping in and out of his lap; asking for *'Naughty Christmas Presents'*. Actually, they were dying to know. The *Irish Curse* was driving them mad?

Old Joe was somewhat offended but tolerated their lucid behavior since they spiked his cups of tea. Sexy Sarah taught them many tricks in regards to getting a man. She even taught them how to give a proper *Blow-job* on a willing resident who had no complaints.

Hence, they were flirting with their tongues in several ways and, it didn't involve words. Eventually, Joe ended up in Eva's bed and woke up with a hang over and lipstick all over his body. Rumor has it that she offered to give him a *Gum-Job*. Rumor also spread fast that Old Joe did not have the *Irish Curse*.

Betty and Edna were jealous when Eva and Joe hooked up; so they set their sights on Sarge after they left the party together. Sarge saw the hunger in their eyes, a lust for *Love*. Betty told him that if he found her *G-Spot*, she'd *Toss his Salad*. He declined the offer, only to be propositioned by Edna who stuck her tongue in his mouth and then down his throat.

He pushed her away and gave her the cold shoulder, but she grabbed his neck with both arms and slid her tongue into his ear. She then offered to take him *Around the World*. He jerked away and politely refused. As he proceeded to leave the building, Betty gave him the flickering tongue again from across the room.

Frustrated but determined, they didn't abandon their mission as they approached Carlos. After all, he was *Numero Uno Macho*. He had plenty to go for. Surely, he could satisfy both of them whom admired experience. The ninety-three year old gladly accepted their invitation to the *O-Zone;* for a three-some. They gave him some *Viagra*.

Three weeks before their scheduled trip, Sarge got a call from Aspen. *Paradise Lost* experienced a big fire and their trip was postponed. All were disappointed until Chi showed up with *Good News*. Both *Prudent Paradise* as well as the state, settled the class-action lawsuits --- out of court.

After investigating, they uncovered several other rapes over the years and a lot more abuse. Its secret wrap-sheets / records were ignored and or covered up or bought off. Hence, *Social Security* was loaded as each resident would receive one million dollars from each claim for their trauma, fear and neglect. All that was pending; was the three individual suits pertaining to --- Marge, Thomas and Max. And they were another fashion.

The *Commune* was excited, as the amount was a most welcomed surprise. Perhaps it was the title --- *Millionaire*, which impressed their *Ego's*. Perhaps it was a matter of principle --- *Compensation;* which they deserved without a doubt. But eventually, the commotion wore off as they were already happy. All but Marge, it would take more than money to salvage her *Peace*.

In the mean time, Sarge Yelled --- "The bar is open, drinks are on me."

Thomas was the life of the party as he passed out his joints. Even Marge smoked the marijuana as the whole *Commune* got stoned or drunk and pigged out on pizza and wings. Marge even laughed as she cackled like a silly old hen. Everything seemed so funny to her. Ironically, she forgot about her troubles, at least for a little while; thanks to the *Wacky Tobaccy*.

CHAPTER **Seven**

Confrontations

Chapter 7   Confrontations

Summer turned into autumn and Sarah and Jacques, Anna and Max were married in a double ceremony on the grounds and spent their honeymoons in Hawaii. They too, were impressed with the *Islands* as they also found themselves --- *Spiritually* and expressed their *Love* physically.

On the last day, Sarah made a promise to Jacques "You can have breakfast in bed every morning, all you can eat --- Me! But," she added, "its self-service."

She even got a tattoo on her inner thigh inscribed with --- *Eat Me, Anytime*. She showed it off proudly to everybody and anybody that wanted to see it when they returned home.

Winter was just around the corner when some of the cats had kittens and dogs --- puppies, again. The new life brought excitement throughout the *Commune* until they realized that they had a surprise problem. The fleas were dealt with swiftly, but that wasn't what he was concerned about.

"Who's going to feed and tend to all these animals when we're in Mexico?" Sarge asked as they were eating lunch in the mess hall.

"Mexico?" echoed throughout the room with confused looks on all their faces.

"I just got a call from a friend," Sarge enlightened, "mud-baths

SOCIAL SECURITY

and hot-springs! We got to take a vote. There is an opening in three weeks at *El Rio Caliente Manida,* but they need a deposit."

"Yes," echoed unanimously without any doubt!

Carlos was so excited that he threw his sombrero in the air; stood up and did a *Mexican Hat Dance.* Then, he flashed his manhood. Everybody started to laugh until Clarence suggested.

"We better hire some professional animal sitters."

"Let's get rid of the whole bunch." Max interrupted sarcastically.

"Bite your tongue." Anna argued their case defensively. "They're part of the family."

"Relax darling." Max replied. "I'm only kidding."

"I'll make some calls in the morning," Peg promised as she and Clarence left to go shopping. Sarge excused himself to make his phone call to confirm their reservations.

Clarence and Peg bought ponchos and sombreros for all to be worn on their Mexico trip. Later that night, Lucy was in her room, secretly stitching names on each poncho and talking to Clarence when Peg came in with the news.

Unfortunately she told them that: "Marge is susceptible to pneumonia again and she's still sensitive to her intimidating memories. They are profound and conflicting and she is confused and expiring. She has bronchitis and she looks pathetic --- dying in misery, guilt and shame; weeping bitterly."

Clarence was utterly stunned as he resorted to drastic measures. Outraged, he went up to Marge's room, knocked on the door and entered after he got no reply. He looked straight into her eyes as she lay there in bed; shallow, sad and distraught with tears rolling down her face.

"Shit Happens!" he shouted as he confronted Marge as an act of *Love.* "So get over it. Quit dwelling on the past. Quit feeling sorry for your self. Forgive! Forgive God and yourself and that monster that tormented you. --- Now, ASAP."

Marge was flabbergasted, completely startled as she cried out loud with mix signals in an emotional tailspin; as she reached for his hand. "Oh, I. I. I, oh please help me, please."

She knew that Clarence was kind, considerate and humble. Why then, she wondered; *why is he yelling at me?* It was hard to grasp let alone understand; especially under her circumstances and her physical condition.

But suddenly, as she held his hand with a death-grip, she realized that *he was right*. He was only trying to talk some sense into her. She had carried this baggage of animosity; anger, guilt and shame; long enough. It was time to face herself and confront her troubles --- *Now*; before she met her *Maker*.

It was a defining moment; irresistibly natural. Peace at Last? Hopefully! But it was a *Divine Option* --- As --- *Forgiveness* is a *Choice*.

"*Have Faith*," she whispered to herself as she focused in on *Death's Door* --- lingering semiconscious between *Two Worlds*.

One minute, Clarence looked like a shadow of a figure, the next; she'd seen shadows and heard voices --- *Beyond*. Ironically, she was scared of *Death*, but she felt at *Peace* as she hovered in and out of her own body. One minute, she was lying in the bed, the next; she was floating above her hollow shell, staring at herself and Clarence. It was a phenomenal experience. Suddenly, her favorite poem --- *Footprints*, flashed in her brain like some God-send.

FOOTPRINTS

(Author Unknown)

One night a man had a dream,
He dreamed he was walking along the beach with the Lord.
Across the sky flashed scenes from his life.
For each scene, he noticed two sets of footprints in the sand.
One belonged to him, the other to the Lord.

SOCIAL SECURITY

When the last scene of his life flashed before him,
He looked back at the footprints in the sand.
He noticed that many times along the path of his life there was only one set of footprints.
He also noticed that it happened at the very lowest and saddest times in his life.
This really bothered him and he questioned the Lord about it.
"Lord, you said that once I decided to follow you,
You'd walk with me all the way.
But I have noticed that during the most troublesome times in my life,
There is only one set of footprints.
I don't understand why when I needed you most you would leave me? "

The Lord replied, "My precious, precious child.
I love you and would never leave you.
During your times of trial and suffering,
When you see only one set of footprints,
It was then that I carried you. "

Marge felt somewhat relieved as Clarence sensed that death was imminent. She tried to smile as Clarence pulled a chair by her bed. Her face was consumed with worry and fear and an oxygen mask.

"You look so sad my *Dear Friend*; so terrified. Are you afraid to die?"

She nodded --- Yes.

"You haven't spoken for over two years, except to the *Trouble Bushes*. Don't blame yourself. It wasn't your fault. But, you must forgive the *Bastard*."

Marge smiled as if to acknowledge that his rational was correct.

"Death should be a *Peaceful Transition*." Clarence continued. "Don't take your mental anguish with you. Leave it here. Think

CONFRONTATIONS

Flowers! We both know the *Joy* that they give you."

Suddenly, he flashes a bunch of *Roses that were hiding* behind his back; which he robbed from a vase in the hallway on his way up. Tears were rolling down her face as he handed them to her and kissed her forehead. He then proceeded to make up a story about *Flowers --- Samantha's Paradise*. Her face lit up instantly like a child at Christmas time.

Samantha's Paradise

"Once upon a time, not so long ago --- right here on *Earth;* little Samantha had come a long way in her *Spiritual* journey through her young life. Ultimately, she proceeded to *Love Flowers*. Everyday throughout spring and summer, she would visit Gram-Ma's Garden.

Anticipation was routine as Samantha knew that Gram-Ma would let her pick 1 or 2. Sometimes, 3, 4, 5, and once, 6, 7, 8, 9, 10, 11 and 12 --- a whole dozen! They were so beautiful and her *Mother* was always surprised --- time and time again; when she brought some home for her!

Gram-Ma was such a kind old soul with a green-thumb. She could always grow more --- said she:

'Go ahead --- indulge, pick 1, 2, 3, 4, 5, or 6. *Smell their Smell, Savor their Beauty; Enjoy!*' And believe it or not, Samantha surely did --- always. For the *Flowers* made her *Day* and *Night*. She even dreamt about Gram-Ma's precious passion.

Perhaps that's why Gram-Ma called her Garden --- *Samantha's Paradise*. After all; little Samantha, would literally get lost in this *Field of Dreams,* this *Paradise of Beauty, Awe and Wonder.*"

Marge rolled over on her side and wiped the tears from her eyes. Clarence sensed that she was compelled by his little tale. He smiled at her and she smiled back again as he continued.

"I guess it would be safe to say that Samantha actually inherited Gram-Ma's fancy for *Flowers* as she became one with them and, they were her *Friends*. She put them in vases, wore one as a corsage

SOCIAL SECURITY

and even kept one in her hat and both of her socks."

"Sometimes her cat *Tig Tig* would come and hang out with her in the Garden. Animals know a good thing when they see it as they appreciate *Mother Nature*. But, Samantha knew *Tig Tig's* little secret? He just liked to hide way-way-way in the back and take a nap in the shade! There were so many *Flowers* in Gram-Ma's Garden that --- *Tig Tig* blended right in *Samantha's Paradise* as you could not find him unless you knew where he actually was. And that's the way *Tig Tig* liked it --- *At One with the Beauty, Awe and Wonder of Being.*"

"Samantha *Loved Tig Tig* as much as she Loved Gram-Ma and her Flowers. She would never give up *Tig Tig's* hiding-spot. For nobody but her and Gram-Ma knew about it. No body except the *Flowers*, the *Birds*, *Bees*, several *Squirrels*, 3 *Trees*, the *Sun*, *Moon*, and the *Stars*. Yes, sometimes *Tig Tig* would sleep there on hot *Summer-nights*. Wouldn't you iffin you knew where it was? After all, isn't every body searching for a little *Paradise* --- here on *Earth*? "

Marge laughed and shook her head yes. Clarence knew that he was making headway --- progress in route to *Peace*. He paused for a brief moment and put his hands on top of her hands. She reached for his two hands and gave gentle squeezes of appreciation as he obliged them both and continued as they locked fingers.

"Samantha was a very lucky little girl and she knew it. She was happy and grateful that she was blessed to have Gram-Ma, *Tig Tig* and her *Paradise of Flowers*. She couldn't imagine her life without them. But ironically as life is so irony, so unpredictable; Samantha got the surprise or shall we say, shock of her life --- *Reality* as all the Flowers were going bye-bye? Poor *Tig Tig* started to hide-n-sleep in a *Tree*--- with the *Squirrels*."

"Slowly but surely, Samantha knew deep down in the *Heart of her Heart* that something wasn't quite right. Little by little; first 1 or 2, then 3, 4, 5, 6 --- began to wilt and whither --- away. Samantha was so upset; she did not know what to do?"

"Unfortunately, she kept her trouble to herself. She never expressed her concerns to anybody. Not even Gram-Ma or *Tig Tig*;

whom continued to hide in *Trees* --- daily. Maybe he was troubled too since he became a *Watch-Cat?* He wouldn't sleep anymore. Instead, he spied suspiciously."

"Alarmed by *Tig Tig's* verifying indication, Samantha did the only thing she could think of. She sorta tried to *Pretend* and *Wish* and *Hope* it --- *Trouble; Away.* She even prayed to God for Help. Unfortunately, sometimes His answer is *No?*"

Marge let go of Clarence's hands to wipe the tears from her face. Evidently, his point touched home. He kissed her on the cheek and proceeded on.

"But finally, one sad day, Gram-Ma found Samantha in her *Garden of Paradise* --- sad as sad can be? 'What's a matter Sweetie?' Gram-Ma asked."

"'They're gone,' replied Samantha sadly, 'every last one?' Gram-Ma just laughed as she took the wilted bunch of *Flowers* from her hand."

"'Relax,' Gram-Ma continued with mercy. 'Take a deep breath or two or three. Let me *Enlighten* you girl. After all, life is an education. Nature is our greatest teacher. As I see it, death is a perfect example. Every *Living-Thing* must die. *Death* is but a *Test of Character*, in the *Fullness of Time.*'"

"'Oh No', Samantha yelled; 'No, no, no, no; not you Gram-Ma!'"

"'Hush-hush Sweet Samantha, even me. It's a *Fact of Life*, it's a natural situation. Don't make such a fuss or an ordeal over it. When you lose a *Loved-one* to death, you must carry on your *Spiritual Journey;* as each and every one of us is here to learn. Both life and death are mysteries? But *Life* is *Pure Energy,* and it is a scientific fact that energy never dies; as it merely transcends and changes form.'"

"'Inevitably, there is a *Time to Live* and a *Time to Die. In-Between Time;* we get to enjoy the *Flowers, Birds, Tig Tig* and *Each Other* --- *Quality-Time.* Blessed is he whom rejoices in the *Beauty, Awe* and *Wonder of Being!* Blessed is whoever learns to live and die *Gracefully* as you become one with *Eternal Peace and Harmony!*'"

SOCIAL SECURITY

"Samantha started to cry as she jumped into Gram-Ma's arms. 'I Love you Gram!'"

"'I Love you too!' Gram-Ma replied. 'Cheer up my little darling, there is a *Time to Laugh and a Time to Cry*. Next year, there will be new *Flowers* to treasure; a *Gift from God* to us. Until then, we get to *Indulge in the Memories!*'"

"THE END"

When they made eye contact, Marge had a big smile on her face. She pulled the mask away from her face and whispered: "Thank You," as Clarence hugged her. Then with tears of joy in her eyes, she continued to speak soft and slowly.

"I can let go now in *Peace*, a *Happy Ending*; as *Grace Happens!* I'm moving on to *Paradise* to be at one with *God* and the *Flowers, Sam and Samantha. I Love You* and everybod;" were the last words that she murmured as she died with her *Eyes Wide Open* as well as her *Heart, Mind and Soul*.

Clarence bent over and kissed her on her silent lips. He closed her eye-lids, and said a small silent prayer as he felt relieved that Marge made *Peace* with *her-Self*. Her anger, fear and hatred; mental anguish vaporized instantly, as she let them go before she died; via *Forgiveness*.

She had the power to pardon the misguided soul that beat, raped and abused her; all the time. But unfortunately like most of us humans; she was too stubborn to let it be. Hence, Alexander Pope realized: 'to err is human, to forgive divine'.

Clarence put the *Flowers* in her hands that were folded in her lap before he exited to announce her passing to all the others.

"She looked fine in the *Garden* this afternoon." Anna broke the silence as all were shocked.

"The Doctor said that she had walking-pneumonia." Clarence clarified. "God only knows how long she was suffering. The poor woman never complained about anything. She was so congested and her lungs were full of water. It must have been oh so painful; just to breath."

"God Bless her Soul." Henry shouted. "Her last two years were a reoccurring nightmare."

"She's at *Peace* now." Clarence assured. "She spoke and forgave God, herself and the bastard before she passed on. She left her troubles behind and sent her *'Love and Thanks to All'*." he fibbed a little.

"Amen." yelled Max.

"I'll put the flag at half-staff and meet you all at the bar." Sarge insisted. "This calls for a celebration as Marge would surely approve."

Everyone charged to the bar in the memory of Marge. Unfortunately, the party was a bummer as they tried to pacify grief, but it can't be fooled. You got to let it take its course.

One by one they retired unannounced, until Sarge found himself; alone. He went out on the porch and looked up at the stars in the sky and wondered why? *Why we live, why we die?* Suddenly, he remembered a poem which his mother sent him when he was in *Korea or was it Nam?*

It was before the accident. She wrote it for him; a little outlook on the way life works --- sometimes? He came to cherish it as a goal, his life's dream to be fulfilled as he played his part in destiny. It gave him inspiration to fight for what is right for his country as he kept re-enlisting in spite of the fact that war is hell. Thus, *'Life'* got him through some hard times.

LIFE

You live, you die
But who, who knows why?
First, you're born into this life
Before long, you've a husband or a wife
Both face the good and bad
Both have times happy and sad
Together you make love tender and warm
Before long, a child is born

SOCIAL SECURITY

He lives, he'll die
But who, who knows why?
You brought him into this life
And soon, he too will have a wife
You're getting older
Tired of looking over your shoulder
You've made many, many mistakes
But by now, you know what it takes

Now, now you know why
Why people live, why people die!
Life, life is the reason
And it can happen in any season

Soon, soon you'll die
And he, he'll wonder why
But some, someday he'll know
And I hope he has a long way to go
Because life; Life is Beautiful.

Unfortunately, the memory of his dream depressed Sarge as it was unfulfilled. He felt as if life didn't play him a fair hand. He blamed it on the Wars. He went back inside and found his old guitar lying behind the bar. Earlier that day he got an urge to play it, but he broke a string in the process. After he fixed it, he was interrupted by the phone call about the Mexico trip and hurried to the mess hall to break the news. He forgot all about it; until now.

He picked up his old guitar and started to strum it; feeling sorry for himself. Horrific war scenes danced in his head as he felt so sorry for all of his fellow veteran-brothers; whom are plagued by demons of the past. God only knows what they have to go through; especially when they come back home; limbless and or with tragic memories that they have to deal with, not to mention live with for the rest of their days and sleepless nights.

Far too many Americans don't realize the price of war? But,

Freedom, Isn't Free! Besides casualties from IEDs, mortars and claymore mines, including death; there is divorce, bankruptcies, broken bones and broken families. Then there are veterans who are disabled with lung disorders, caused by *Agent Orange, depleted uranium,* titanium or other toxic composite particles. There are also, those poor souls who suffer from tinnitus, *post-traumatic stress* disorder and *Friendly-fire.* And, let us not forget about all of the people at ground-zeros; who are affected, including far, far too many innocent lives. Unfortunately, the numbers are growing daily and too many *VA Hospitals are over-burdened and under-staffed.*

Suddenly Sarge started to play a song that his old *Pal*, Pat wrote; to relieve his guilt and shame. As he sang *'I Have Met The Enemy, And He Is Me Is'*; he felt as some burden was lifted. *War is HELL.*

I Have Met The Enemy, And He Is Me

By: Patrick Arthur Gordon

>Every night they come again
>The dogs of war, that never end
>Drag me back into those places in my mind
>I've come to realize, I'll never leave behind
>
>When every day is just survive
>How can you say: You're a live
>Acting strong so others, think that I am brave
>When deep inside I'm scared, I'll meet an early grave
>
>(Chorus)
>And I won't live that lie again
>This God Damn war has got to end
>Battles rage in dreams, too horrible to keep
>As I'm facing my demons each time I try to sleep

◂ SOCIAL SECURITY

Is this the future I deserve
Every night a war to test my nerve
It seems I've won some ghoulish, consolation prize
A ticket back to hell, each time I close my eyes

(Chorus)
And I won't live that lie again
This God Damn war has got to end
Battles rage in dream, too horrible to keep
As I'm facing my demons each time I try to sleep

(Repeat Chorus, and end)

After the song, he downed a Jack and went to bed

The next morning, Clarence notified his Grandson --- Chi about Marge's demise; since he handled all of her legal affairs. Chi came over; latter in the afternoon to read her last will and testament. Evidently, unbeknownst to most of the *Commune*, she met with Chi three days prior; upstairs in her room.

Peg arranged the meeting per Marge's request. She gave him *Power of Attorney* and accepted an offer in her law suit. That's when she made out her final will and testament.

She was loaded, including stocks and bonds. She had no blood family alive. Chi elaborated that she lost both her husband and a daughter, Sam and Samantha in the same year --- 1950 to *TB (Tuberculosis)* the dreadful consumption. She never remarried and therefore, she left every penny to *Social Security*; in annual installments via a trust fund.

"Like I told Clarence three days ago," Chi continued, "her husband and daughter were both cremated. Hence she too wished to be cremated and her ashes spread throughout the *Garden*; including the area by *Old Joe's Special Plants*."

Everybody was extremely touched by Marge's last testimonial. "She acknowledged that she *Loved* the *Commune* and thanked everyone for their care and concerns," Chi continued.

CONFRONTATIONS

Anna suggested that they dedicate the *Garden in Memory of Marge*. Clarence recommended that they name it *Marge's Paradise*. Everybody agreed with the two ideas.

Sarge stated that he too: "Wanted to be cremated and have his ashes spread out in the *Garden* as well; since he had no family."

Henry professed that the: "*Commune* was his *Family*." He got no argument.

Max exclaimed --- "What's good enough for Marge is good enough for me!" Eventually, all agreed to a *Family Tradition* --- *Marge's Paradise* as their final resting place.

"Incidentally," Chi informed, "Marge settled for $67,000,000.00 cash up front."

"What about mine?" Max asked curiously.

"Yeah, and mine," Thomas dittoed?

"They made an offer this morning for both of you. Do either of you want to discuss it in private?" Chi asked professionally.

"Spit it out!" Max demanded.

"Yeah, I can't take the suspense." Thomas confessed nervously.

"$5,000,000.00 cash for you Max and Thomas, you get $50,000,000.00 cash!"

"Hot Damn," Max yelled. "Settle!"

"Woo Hoo; Hallelujah, where do I sign?" Thomas asked with a joint in his hand.

Needless to say, Thomas paid for a round of drinks in spite of the fact that money didn't really matter to any of them anymore. Chi had one with the *Commune* in honor of Marge and then he left to make arrangements for her cremation; but not until they decided to lay her out for a day in the living room down the hall. It would take a few days before they got her ashes.

Clarence suggested that everyone wear their *Grace Happens* tee-shirts; since it was amongst Marge's final words on her deathbed. Everybody promised to oblige; even Chi who had tears in his eyes. Needless to say, the atmosphere was gloomy --- under the spell of grief as it was the night before.

Perhaps Max and Thomas were somewhat overwhelmed by

their settlements as the former got --- drunk and the later -- stoned. Except for the two of them, nobody else felt like partying as Marge was on their minds. Thus, they opted to go about their business and deal with grief in their own way.

Later that evening, Clarence was at the piano, tickling the ivory, deep in thought. *It's funny how the loss of a Loved-One makes you think. Life is a challenge indeed and I surely had my share of its ups and downs; blood, sweat and tears.*

He thought about *God, man and nature; mind, body and soul; mental, physical and emotional; Father, Son and Holy Spirit?*

He never realized that there were so many names for the *Trinity*. He wondered how many more he could think of and, how they actually affect society as we know it? *Steam, ice and water; wisdom, intellect and intuition; spirit, blood and water; is, as and at?*

"Hmm," he whispered out loud; "Very interesting!" He continued tickling and did some more thinking; *faith, reason and mercy by grace; super conscious, conscious and sub conscious; as well as super ego, ego and id?*

Perhaps, he concluded; *perhaps it's no small wonder that there are so many different religions in this world or that we have resorted to separation of church and state as well as science and religion; as we settle for physical, mental and spiritual anguish.*

"What is the common goal?" he asked himself; "Survival? Enlightenment? Is all fair in *Love* and war and survival? What is *Truth*? What is man's *Duty*? Why do men have different values, different senses of direction? And, why do some have the audacity; to think that they are the *Chosen People*?"

Peg watched silently as he was talking with himself, deep in thought. He started to play *Chop-Sticks*; to calm his thoughts and emotions. He knew that *'Thought is Energy'*. ** *'That 'consciousness is intelligence in action and all consciousness has feeling'*. (** Harold Sherman *'You Live After Death'*)

He remembered reading that man is *** *'one of many appearances of the thing called Life and that we are not its perfect image. For it has no image except Life and Life is multitudinous and* *emergent in the stream of time'.* (*** Loren Eiseley 'The Immense Journey')

He also read somewhere that *Mother Earth Her-self; is a Living Organism ---- GAIA.*

Peg joined him in *Double-Chop-Sticks*. He smiled as he welcomed her company and elaborated on his thinking, regarding the **Trinity**. Then he asked her.

"Do humans really believe that we are created in God's image? That God looks human? Or; that the *Human Race* is *Superior* in our estimated --- 13.5 billion-year-old universe? Talk about conceited. Go figure?"

Peg laughed and then, suddenly, Clarence had a *Divine Permeation*. "Someday," he prophesied, "mankind will believe; they will *B4 H.E.A.R.T.!* They will believe in God, self and each-other. Ultimately, man is but the *WORD of GOD*. Man is a *Living Bible*. Man is but, *AS;* he is --- *Functionality*."

Peg welcomed his revelation but she was somewhat skeptical. "It sounds like wishful-thinking." she surmised. "Man is so damn peculiar. What you see is what we achieved --- Together."

"Exactly," Clarence agreed but he insisted, "I have faith in mankind. Be patient. God is patient as he lets us do our own thing. Unfortunately man has been labeled and classified as a noun."

"But in actuality, we are more than just a person --- *AS;* action speaks louder than mere words --- both good and evil speaks for it self. Man is but; *AS;* he is. Someday mankind will realize that we are one --- with God. Each of us is a little god who must live with each other and face our self; eventually."

"Little devils, sounds more like it," Peg joked sadly. "An *Un-divine Comedy*. Ironically," she continued, "mankind pathologically worries about individual rights and neglects their personal responsibilities and obligations. However, selfishness and greed are poor excuses."

"'Opinions and excuses are like ass-holes'," Clarence responded. "We always have one as philosophy is the epitome of man. But, it's what makes us so unique; it's synonymous as a finger-print. Actually, there aren't two that are exactly the same. Hence, Cicero exclaimed: 'O philosophy, you leader of life'."

"I often wonder where we are headed." Peg interrupted with concern. "Apparently, philosophy is in fact so ambiguous, but so are politics, science and religion. I guess it is *Human Nature*."

"After all, there is surely a gap between policy and practice, between sin and crime, between morals and morale as ethics, are suspect in the name of economics. Especially since man has a hard time practicing what he preaches. For how many mean what they say and say what they mean?"

"Man is at a crossroads," Clarence replied, "obedience or moral choice? *Maya* or *Truth!*"

"Maya?" Peg asked.

"Illusion." Clarence clarified. "We create our own *Reality*; as we see what we want to see and hear what we want to hear."

"Wanton arrogance," Peg exclaimed.

"Perhaps," he replied, "but perhaps the *Classical Greeks* adopted the appropriate terminology --- 'Divine Madness'. For mankind has progressed to make such a 'To-do' out of *Nut-ting* or -- *Chaos out of Peace*. Unfortunately, men worry about composure and reputation and yet, they can't compose themselves properly as they are torn between *Maya* and *Truth*; as logic takes precedent over *Humanity*."

"Hence, ST. Augustine surmised: 'Two cities have been formed by two loves; the earthly by the love of self; even to the contempt of God; the heavenly by love of God; even to the contempt of self?'"

Peg paid attention to detail as Clarence bared his *Heart and Soul*.

"Ultimately, we are all *Blessed* with *Reason* and *Free Will*," he continued. "But unfortunately, most choose to ignore their other *Blessings* --- *Intuition* and *Conscience*? Alas confusion and repercussions manifest as reckless thoughts collide."

"It's a battle of left brain verses right brain, *Intellect* verses *Intuition*. Instead of working together in *Cooperation*; they compete. Man must *Trust* his *Conscience*, which is also more than a dormant noun; and learn to recognize thy own invading enemy within as the source of our own problems. Personal conflict is the result of *Ego*; a parasite, which everybody hosts as *Ego* manipulates *Soul*."

"It seems as if we don't acknowledge either of their existence?" Peg concluded without doubt. "Humans choose to ignore both their *Conscience* and *Intuition*. I wonder why?"

"Ironically," Clarence clarified, "man is baptized by Logic; --- Divine Bait as Curiosity is the Original Sin. Without a doubt, God planted a seed; - Temptation, when he warned: 'Don't eat of the Tree of Good and Evil.'"

"'And the Lord God said: behold, the man is become as one of us, to know good and evil.... But lest he put forth his hands and take also of the tree of life. Thus ... the Lord God sent him forth from the Garden of Eden. ' ---Genesis 322-23'"

"The Logical Fall of Man!" Peg shouted: "AS each is so obsessed with finding his own *Tao*; or *Way* through *Life*. Thus, we are in the midst of a logical revolution since logic is the unclear, ever-present, prominent and pre-dominate function of all mankind --- AS --- to each his own involved method to his own possessed madness."

"Precisely," Clarence professed with a twinkle in his eyes. "We are possessed by our own thoughts --- *Formulated Ignorance*; *The Forbidden Fruit*. Thereby, we are guilty by *Reason* and *Reasonable Doubts* as *Logic* and *Free Will* unite into *Choice*; a license to freedom, ambition, agility, emancipation, independence and individualism."

"Alas, society as we know it is man-made by choice, a quagmire of collective *Egos* competing in the name of zealous pride, the trade-mark of human-beings. Consequently, it is but a human travesty with a mess of troubles per each individual *Ego*, the invisible intimidator; *The Keeper of Our Own Crypt*. Shame on us as we proudly sport our own *Fig-Leaf*; confounded and dumbfounded in *Spiritual delinquency*."

Peg nodded in silence as he elaborated.

"Peculiarly obsessed, we cogitate, reflect and theorize immaturely as each of us gets so wrapped up and absorbed in our own little secular worlds. Ironically we long for attention, wanting to belong and yet, be different at the same time and stand-out; --- *Look* --- *it's me*. Sometimes we compromise with our own dignity, at the expense of *Humanity*? Far too many try to impress others by pretending to be something that they aren't."

"Unfortunately, we are confronted daily with temptation; enchanting risks, greed, erotic appeal and vices. Thus, it's no small wonder that so many get lured, lost and trapped in unfathomable uncertainty. Infatuated with both physical and sense gratifications; some even end up living in a nightmare of sensual indulgence as they attach without commitment, without thinking about consequences."

"To add insult to injury," Clarence continued, "certain somebody's --- the so called experts and institutions; try to instill standards, convert and conform us to *The System* as technology flexes its muscles and computers do the thinking for us. Ironically, many unworthy hypocrites make a living --- preaching some so called *Holy Gospel* of platitudes or ridiculous rhetoric to us, we the *Lost-Souls*."

"Alas, we are engrossed in established policies, lost --- stuck somewhere in-between reason and faith, between science and religion; a compromising condition, as the privileged few; the secular powers that be, backed by *International Capital*, play god."

"Woe is he," Peg shouted, "whom --- settles in the *'Waste Land'*; of *'Conformed Confusion'*. Oh is we, appeasing pawns --- blind fools in our chosen illusion just as *Robert Fisher's 'Knight in Rusty Armor'*. For *we hurry and worry about making a living as each assumes his leery position in; 'The Assigned Establishment'*."

"It's *No Wonder* the *World* is so *Fucked-Up*." Clarence surmised. "We have grown accustomed to tenacious beliefs, judgments and habits as we con-form into a niche in the *Name of Approval* and or Acceptance as we long to be *Loved*. How ironic is that as *Life* is, but an encounter and endurance through God's wonders and our woes."

"However, mankind wasn't born to be manipulated or controlled like a herd of cattle. Unfortunately, man doesn't utilize the readily availability of his preconscious - a *State of Grace*, a reservoir that is always *Ready, Willing and Able to Assists* the *Eternal Moment*.

Addicted to *'Denial'*, we are burdened by doubt as we avoid the *Truth* like some plague. But, vulnerability is merely a product of ignorance. Peace is within everybody."

"Ultimately, there are two major undistinguishing factors; a dichotomy governing all of the reins of existence --- *Fear* and *Faith*. They pertain to all relationships; business, government, marriage, friendship, etc. It is all based on trust and creditability as well as distrust and doubt. When intimidation gets involved; chaos is inevitable. All outcome; both causes and effects derive as a direct result of either or and; are measured by two prevailing indicators or two classifications --- *Good and Evil*."

"Essentially," he added, "*Either / Or*; is the *Significance of Choice*, as we all contribute --- *Willingly*. Be it pilgrims, pirates or the parasites, the good, the bad or the ugly. For *Life* is a *Rainbow of Efforts*. Possibilities are endless, as ingenuity and peculiarity are unique. Unfortunately, one man's *Bliss* provokes another to tease as *Envy* is akin to *Jealousy*."

"Ironically," Clarence continued with tears in his eyes and a lump in his throat, "mankind will continue to fear each other until they have faith in each other. Destiny awaits our command. Chaos is but an option."

"Salaciously, man is unpredictable by nature, but savage by choice as poverty is so unnatural; an absolute abomination. Thus, we best Beware of the *Fury, of a Republic Scorned*. Hence, cunning old *'Fury'* warned in *'Through the Looking-Glass, and What Alice Found There'*, --- *'I'll be judge, I'll be jury, I'll try the whole cause and, condemn you to death.'*"

Peg shook her head as Clarence got his point across clearly. She realized that historically, man used the *Word of God* as both a source of pleasure and peace and as a tenant of fear and damnation. Ironically, the establishment's man-made-laws are still subjected to, technicalities and double standards; as public perception is blinded by trust.

Unfortunately, governments are manmade, but the *System* itself; is predicated on cooperation. It is in fact backed by man's rule of law through intimidation and force if necessary. But then again; so were many governments before these. Governments always fear the *Power of the People.* Eventually the People Wake Up.

Perhaps, she thought to her-self silently as she remembered the Bible. *Perhaps life as we know it is inevitable; because Love is the Law --- 'Love worketh no ill to his neighbor; therefore love is the fulfilling of the law,'* (Romans 13:10). Suddenly, she realized that God does Love us and, that He lets us learn how to Love at our own pace.

Thus, she pondered to herself; *each must reexamine his own life as both good and evil actions, speak volumes. Ironically though, some don't believe in God at all, while some are Soul-Searching and still, others have surrendered to conformed ignorance. It's so simple and yet profound?*

"Peace is a mutual effort!" she exclaimed. "Negligence is malignant. Arrogance is insulting, detrimental, and counters to purpose and principles of *Humanity.* Ultimately, we all long to be *Loved* as we are afraid of being alone, but we're also afraid of getting hurt. And yet, we continue to hurt each other?"

"Unfortunately," Clarence tried to clarify; "Fear is life's greatest mystery while faith is its greatest secret. However," he asked whole heartedly, "what is the difference between a *Mystery* and a *Secret?*"

Peg stood up and walked over to a bookshelf and grabbed a dictionary. "According to *Mr. Webster's* definition," she explained, "'*A mystery is something not secret or beyond understanding.*'"

Clarence scratched his head as Peg fingered through the book, then informed that: "He defines a secret as '*a specific key to a desired end.*'"

"Brilliant," Clarence shouted as Mr. Webster answered his question --- *'What's the big mystery and what's the big secret?'* "Ironically, there is no big secret or big mystery when it comes to *Fear* and *Faith* as fear is inferior to *Faith.* Fear is nothing more than a lack of *Faith!* Hence * '*He whom cannot accept faith, is doomed to a life of doubt.*' (*Miracle on 34th St)."

"What can be simpler?" he asked. "It all depends on your

CONFRONTATIONS

desired end. Thus, the *Truth* shall overcome and we shall overcome! But, only --- when we want to? Because fear, like all innovation and inventions; is a by-product of imagination. Actually, it is only a matter of perspective. Hence, Ernest Hemingway surmised: '*Cowardice, as distinguished from panic, is almost always simply a lack of ability to suspend the functions of the imagination.*'"

"In the future," Clarence continued, "Man will realize that God is everything. Man is but part of the puzzle, a little god. God is Love. Life is but an *Evolution of Love*. Humanity; is the bottom line --- *Divine Prosperity*. We must learn to embrace the *Power of Love*."

"Ultimately, life is a matter of truth or consequences; as *Denial* is the *Anti Christ*. It leads to typical none-sense if not evil or pretence. Gratitude, generosity and compassion are *Graces from God*; which co-exists with envy, greed and jealousy --- sins of man. These are the forces behind *Good and evil*. They define our personalities, refine or corrupt individuality and determine the destiny of mankind."

"Thus, we either have faith, trust and hope in *God's Graces*; which bring *Peace* and *Harmony* through *Love*, or fall prey to the sins of man through ignorance as fear, hate and doubt. Hence, '*I yam what I yam*', and you are what you are. And, if and when we are all in fact what we are all supposed to be --- '*One for All and All for One*' --- *Divine Zest*; then and only then will we have *Peace on Earth and Good Will for All*."

"Phenomenally, to sum it all up, man's true essence is of *Sacred Decree* --- LOVE. God IS Love! Love IS where He's 'At' and, Man will find Peace 'AS' he 'IS' 'AT'; One with God --- a *Celestial Connection*."

Peg was most definitely amazed as Clarence's *Sermon* was movingly insightful. Suddenly, she recalled *Arthur Miller's Play* ---- '*Death of a Salesman*'. Perhaps the '*wife*', summed it up best when she realized that:

'A man can't come into this world with nothing and then go out with nothing! A man has to add up to something!'

"What is the sum of mankind?" she asked Clarence.

"When ignorance is ignored," he replied, "stupidity is justified. Ironically, '*Popeye the Sailorman*', came closest to being *At One with God* as he would always profess: '*I yam what I yam*, and that's all that I yam'. He believed in himself for what he was with his moral righteousness as he fought in the *Name of Justice*."

"He took on the '*Goons*', whom were indistinguishable from each other; including *'Alice the Goon'*. Spinach was his symbolic *Special Manna,* a panacea for his invigorating power when he; 'can't stands no more'. Thus, man cannot live by bread alone as *God told Moses that His Name was Yahweh* --- translation, '*I Am Who Am'* --- *Divine Guidance.*'"

"Unfortunately, man's third-eye is blinded by a semblance of freedom." Clarence continued. "The value of *Humanity* is underestimated. However, eventually common sense will be obsolete as man utilizes his *Cosmic Sense* and finds his place in *Nature* as the *Laws of Nature and Human Nature in Harmony.*"

"Perhaps *Joseph Campbell* summed it up best:

'*Follow your bliss*... As life is not a problem to be solved but a mystery to be lived. '*Cause*'; you are that mystery which you are seeking to know.'"

"In essence," Clarence elaborated, "man must learn to *Love* and *Respect* himself before he can commit to his *Divine Obligation*. Ironically, in our quest for *Truth*, we are both the *Fool* and the *Hero* as the system requires our cooperation. Thus, we only fool ourselves when we look for other heroes or saviors."

"Blessed is he whom '*Knows Thyself*' and, Blessed is the '*Outcast*'; he whom was not afraid to '*Stand to Center for Shame in the sight of his fellow gulls*'. Hence, *Jonathan Livingston Seagull* proclaimed:

'*the only law is that which leads to freedom* '. Perhaps he was ahead of his time as he realized that the: '*price of being misunderstood --- is being called God or devil.*'"

Peg just shook her head again; mesmerized as Clarence was getting deep. She couldn't help herself as she quoted *Immanuel Kant* out loud:

"'*Two things fill me with awe; the starry heavens above, and the moral law within.* '"

Clarence smiled as Peg continued by citing *Kahlil Gibran:*

" '... we cling to the earth, while the gate or the Heart of the Lord stands wide open, we trample upon the bread of Life, while hunger gnaws at our hearts. How good is Life to Man, yet how far removed is Man from Life?'"

"Unfortunately," he interrupted, "contemporary man believes in logic, questions his faith and at times his own sanity as he can't fathom or perceive miracles. Insidiously astute and empirical, he appropriately demands instant confirmation or verification which he also confutes as 'mystical ecstasy is rendered to hysteria'. Unfortunately, man is a pathological believer whom interprets to satisfy ideal convenience as we believe at will."

"Ironically," he continued, "the *Trinity* applies not only to religion, but science also. Perhaps *Father Teilhard de Chardin* was right when he stated that:

'Science and Religion would remain enemies as long as they remained strangers. For in actuality, they could supplement each other, even complement each other, as the specifics of Science clarified the speculations of Religion.'"

Suddenly, Clarence began to laugh.

"What's so funny?" Peg asked.

"Attitude, attention and awareness," he replied. "It's a matter of perspective as interpretation and perception are enigmas? Perhaps there is no greater mystery than man himself. It's no wonder why we turn to science, religion and myth for answers. Rumor has it that Cain killed his brother Able."

"Has *Intellect* killed *Intuition*? Are we doomed in the *Age of Reason*? Where is this '*Ambrosia*'; food of the god's which gives immortality? What is the '*Special Manna*'? Have we forgotten that there were *Two Trees* in the *Garden of Eden*? "

"I never thought about it!" Peg admitted with excitement. "But, you are perfectly correct --- 'So he drove out the man; and he placed at the east of the garden of Eden cherubim's, and a flaming sword which turned every way to keep the way of the tree of life.' --- Genesis 3:24"

Clarence smiled as Peg dug deep and quoted from Blake's

poetic revelation ---'The Marriage of Heaven and Hell.'

"'The cherub with his flaming sword is hereby commanded to leave his guard at the tree of life, and when he does, the whole creation will be consumed, and appear infinite, and holy, where as it now appears finite and corrupt. This will come to pass by an improvement of sensual enjoyment. But first the notion that man has a body distinct from his soul is to be expunged. If the doors of perception were cleansed, every thing would appear to man as it is, infinite. For man has closed himself up, till he sees all things thro' the narrow chinks of his cavern.'"

"Historically, man is so oblivious, reckless; so malicious and ruthless with reality." Clarence interjected. "Good intentions don't always produce best results. Especially when greed gets involved as man is dishonest with him-self. Poverty is excruciating proof."

"Unfortunately, we humans can be oh so lazy as many get lost in convenience? Perhaps it's the *Nature of the Beast* --- dualism; Good and Evil. Prudence is the bottom line. Trust your conscience to be your guide."

"Is Conscience a noun or a verb?" Peg asked perplexed.

"As a verb," Clarence replied, "thinking is involved per intellect. But as a noun --- *Intuition;* man already knows wrong from right, as intellect is inferior to *Intuition.* For what is imagination without destination? What is fear, when you have *Faith?* What is faith without God? What is greed when there is no need? Perhaps it's no small wonder that the *Heart* is the international symbol for *Love.*"

"Perhaps," Peg surmised, "we are all like *King Arthur* as passion is our magical sword ---'*Excalibur';* in our '*Quest for the Holy Grail'* --- *Spiritual Perfection, Love, Truth and Peace?*"

"There have been many tales written throughout history about man searching for *Truth.*" Clarence responded. "Take the sailing of the *Seven Seas* for instance. How many different references are there?"

"*Joseph Campbell* believed that *Myths* are *Sacred*. Ironically, science professes evolution while religion preaches *Adam, Eve,* the infamous *Apple* and the *Devilish Serpent*. Both are believed to be true depending on one's belief. But, in Greek Mythology, *Prometheus the Giant* was crucified for stealing *Fire --- Reason* as *Truth* from *Zeus* and giving it to mere mortal mankind as *Hope* floated to the *Top of Pandora's Box* and escaped as a *Last Resort*."

"And," he continued, "Jesus was a rebel messenger, who had *Divine Audacity*, as he stood up to established authority with his *Beliefs --- Blasphemy*; and humbly walked with the --- *Cross*, our burden, the *Woodwork* --- to *His Death* ; professing *His Message* that the --- *Truth is Within Each and Everyone of Us as All Humans have Eternal Life*."

Peg was overwhelmed by the different legends. "Were *Jesus* and *Prometheus* referring to the same *Truth*?" she asked sincerely.

"Not quite," Clarence responded profoundly. "It's like comparing apples and oranges, but remember as rumor has it --- where '*The Apple*' got us. Actually, *Prometheus* gave man the *Divine Bait*; *Reason* which also led to the *Fall of Mankind; thanks to Pandora*. But *Truth* is beyond *Reason*."

"Jesus was telling man to look deeper as the *Truth lies Within All of Us*. There is *Hope for Mankind*. But, like an orange; you have to dig inside, peel away past the skin. Hence, '*know ye not that your body is a temple of the Holy Spirit which is in you*'. I Cor.6:19"

"Jesus died in the Name of '*Gestalt*'- '*Good Grief*'." Clarence assured. "For time is neither here nor there as *Energy* is but perpetual motion --- *Vibrating --- Accordingly*. Thus, precognition and retro-cognition are but sensuous states of *Awareness --- In Tune with the Infinite* as all is a part of this *Great Divine*. Hence, Jesus promised:

'*he that believeth on me, the works that I do shall he shall do also; and greater works than these shall he do.*' (John 14:12)."

"According to the *Hindu Religion*," Clarence tried to elaborate further, "*Being* is but *Energy* and *Energy* varies in its degree through our '*Seven Charkas*', which emanates the *Human Aura* as to how enlightened a person is. Thus, when a man balances his *Seven Wheels of Energy* or *Seven Charkas*, he will realize *Peace*."

"And," Clarence asked, "what about *John's Vision of The Book of Revelations* as the great *Tribulation of the Seven Seals*?"

"I don't know." Peg admitted. "What about it?"

"According to *Edgar Cayce*," Clarence continued, "whose advice both *Thomas Edison* and *Nikola Telsa* sought and cherished; the *Seven Seals* are the *Seven Charkas of Yoga* in man as the *Great Tribulation is Within Man Himself*."

"It proves your point that *Man is at War* with self." Peg deducted as she though of 'Pogo'. 'We have met the enemy, and he is us.'

"*Carl Jung* believed that *man's charkas were gateways of the conscious.*" Clarence added specifically. "Unfortunately, so many of us are lost or stuck at one of our *Seven Seas* as we are the captain of our own ship; who is overwhelmed by irresistible, captivating sensation; movements, thoughts, memories and dreams as *Intuition* is neglected and or ignored. Marge was a perfect example until she utilized her *Heart Charka*."

"Very interesting," Peg was fascinated as she appreciated how enlightened *Emerson* truly was and shared it with Clarence.

"'Standing on the bare ground....All mean egotism vanishes. I become a transparent eyeball; I am nothing, I see all; the currents of the Universal Being circulate through me; I am part or particle of God.'"

"The *Heart Charka* is the whole key." Clarence testified. "It's emotional in nature and akin to *Intuition* as *Love is Divine*. Someday it will unite man's three lower charkas which are physical in nature with his three upper charkas, which are mental in nature via the Central Nervous System --- *Gray-Matter*."

"Thus, the left brain which is *Intellectual --- Yang*, our Western side and the right brain --- which is *Intuitional --- Yin*, our Eastern side will work in *Harmony* as man will be at *Peace. Intuition* is the *Holy Grail.* It is our *Congenial Birth-rite*; a *Consecrated Blessing in Disguise.*"

"*Sir Charles Sherrington* called it 'The Enchanted Loom', The Brain and Mind Connection, Our Virtual Vista, the Central Nervous System --- our two separate Brains and our Seven Charkas which will Unite our Conscious and Unconscious Minds, the Individual with the Universal."

"It sounds promising." Peg hoped. "A *Divine Synchronicity*, a literal meeting of Intellect and Intuition as Intuition is the Tree of Eternal Life. But, it seems so complicated?"

"We are almost in the *Age of Aquarius*; The Age of Miracles." Clarence assured. "Man makes life so complicated as we try to avoid the rules. But, like *Edgar Cayce* proclaimed: *'the laws of the universe continue to operate even when ignored.'* Thus, *Eternity is Watching!* Man's rules are inferior to God's as Jesus proclaimed:

'there are three that bear witness on Earth, the Spirit, and the water, and the blood: and these agree in one.' (I John 5:8)."

"*Love* is the answer to all of man's problems. *Love* shall over come --- evil, fear and doubt as *Love* ensures *Faith*. Eventually, mankind will learn to believe in *Thee* --- in *God*, self and each other as mankind is the *Living --- Collective Bible --- Unfolding in the Fullness of Time*. Marge found the *Faith* to let go and *Forgive* and she *Realized* that *'Grace Happens'* as she found *Peace* through *Love*."

"Someday, mankind will balance his *Mind, Soul and Body*; or *Spirit, Water and Blood* and thereby --- develop and utilize his *Third-Eye*. Blessed is he whom can see his own *Aura*. For your *Aura* is but a reflection; a distinct emanation of your *True Self*. Evil is but wrong living as it is *Live*, spelled backwards."

Peg was proud of Clarence as his rational made *Perfect Cosmic Sense*; tolerance, respect and mutual understanding. It was so simple yet profound and intriguing. Subconsciously, Mankind has the *Cosmic Blues*; but he also has access to *The Burning Bush* --- Existential Certitude, a *Central Core of Being*. She found new meaning in:

'Seek and Ye shall Find, Ask and Ye shall Receive, Knock and the Door will Open'.

She kissed him and excused herself since she had to go to the bathroom. Suddenly, she thought of her favorite motion picture, *The Wizard of Oz*. *'There's no place like home.'* *'There's no place like home'*; kept popping in her mind.

But she wondered, *where is home? Heaven?* The *Garden of*

SOCIAL SECURITY

Eden? Is *Heaven on Earth* possible with so many --- *'Lions and Tigers and Bears --- Oh My'*? She laughed as she surmised to herself; *perhaps life is a jungle, however who made it that way?*

"After all these years," she asked Clarence before she left. "Why do we continue to act like a bunch of little *Munchkins*; so immature as we actually believe in a physical yellow or should I specify --- *Golden Brick Road?* Pacified by lollypops; broken promises, drugs and booze; we accept as we bestow honor, prestige and trust on our *Mayor* --- the political pukes as well as *Wall Street*, and the *Federal Reserve;* since we need them to lead, reassure and control us like a herd of animals."

"Alas" she continued furiously, "domesticated, We --- the People have forgotten that we are all *Blessed* with a *Heart* and a *Brain* --- *Complements* of our *Divine Wizard*. Hence, it's no wonder that the parasites continue to underestimate us; as they insult our intelligence and assault our intuition, while we fear --- lost and frightened like imbeciles or *Imp-A-Souls*, searching for a Wizard of Oz, a *Guru* or a *Cult Leader*."

"Fear Not!" Clarence assured. "Someday, mankind will muster the *Courage* to unite his *Heart* and his *Brain* and *Act Naturally*. For the alarming inequality of existence is a motivating cause for concern. It's our sacred duty, our mission to accept the challenge in the name of *Humanity* as the road to freedom --- *Home* is paved with *Truth*."

"But first, each must decide which *Witch* he is; a *'Good Witch'*, or a *'Bad Witch'*? For *Home* is where the *Heart* is! Eventually, our *World* must choose to *Unite*."

Peg smiled. She felt relieved, but Clarence knew better since she was all bent over, holding her stomach.

"You best hurry before you piss your pants." he warned. "I'll be up later."

She exited as quickly as she could under the circumstances. Clarence sat there in utter silence for a few minutes. He thought about how happy Marge was before her dreadful ordeal. He was glad that she passed in *Peace*. He said a few prayers for her.

Suddenly, *T. S. Eliot* consumed his mind. ---- *'Music heard so deeply that it is not heard at all. But you are the music while the music lasts.'*

He smiled as he vowed to adhere to *Joseph Campbell* as mankind must ---*'follow his Bliss'*. It is our duty as each and every one has work, to do.

I intend to make a difference! He promised himself. But first, I must compose in honor of Marge.

BELIEVE IN THEE

The Awakening (Believe in Yourself / God)

There is a book, with a guarantee
Glory be, Salvation is no mystery
So take a look, take heed, spend some time and read

You gotta take control
Trust with your heart and soul
There is no free ride
Trust your conscience to be your guide
And believe in Thee
You gotta believe in Thee
And if you believe in Thee
Then destiny, you'll achieve your destiny
So follow your dreams and pay your dues
Consider in love, the steps you choose
Cause some you'll win but when you loose
Ride the waves through your blues
Ascension, Ascension, fear, regret and greed; will fools
Ascension, Ascension, intuition is the key
Fly free --- on the Wings of Truth
So believe in Thee, Just believe in Thee
Then destiny, you'll achieve your destiny

SOCIAL SECURITY

There is a book with a guarantee
Glory be, Salvation is no --- mystery
So take a look, take heed, spend some time and read

You gotta take control
Trust with your heart and soul
There is no free ride
Trust your conscience to be your guide
And believe in Thee
You gotta believe in Thee
And if you believe in Thee
Then destiny, you'll achieve your destiny

TAG ---Ascension, Ascension, intuition is the key
Ascension, Ascension, fly free --- on the wings of truth
So believe in Thee, just believe in Thee
Then destiny, you'll achieve your destiny

CHAPTER

Peace and Closure in Paradise

Chapter 8   Peace and Closure in Paradise

The following morning, Marge was laid out in her own bed at *Social Security*; in the living room. She was wearing a blossom print dress as well as her 'Grace Happens' tee-shirt. The residents paid their respects throughout the day as *Flowers*, graced the whole building.

Chi showed up at 4 PM with Brandie, Jim-Jim and Baby Mayan. All four sported the tee-shirts as did the *Minister* and the rest of the *Tribe*. The *Minister* led a few prayers via a *Sermon* and *Blessed* everyone. Chi and Clarence delivered the *Eulogy* and Peg sang *Believe in Thee* followed by *Amazing Grace*. There wasn't a dry eye in the *Commune* as even Baby Mayan cried as did Jim-Jim; who was a brat and got his feelings hurt.

The hearse came at 6:30 PM to escort Marge to the crematorium. Chi and Brandie paid their final respects before they left with the two kids. Clarence and Peg drove along with Marge. Max, Anna, Henry, and Lucy followed in one car, Sarge, Old Joe, Eva, Sexy Sarah and Jacques in another. The rest of the gang piled into the bus. Once she entered the insinuator; they said a few prayers and left, destination --- Mr. Denny's.

Chi was presented with Marge's ashes a few days later, in a solid-gold-urn. Jacques cooked up an extra special brunch on Sunday.

◄ SOCIAL SECURITY

After they ate, the *Tribe* went to the *Garden*. There, there was a huge arched sign attached to a trellis with the words inscribed: 'Welcome to Marge's Paradise'; 'Our Garden of Remembrance!'

Clarence got the honors as he spread her ashes throughout the entire *Garden*, including the area where *Old Joe's Special Plants* grew. Old Joe wheeled out a Japanese Cherry Blossom Tree to commemorate Marge. Several residents helped him plant it. Afterwards, they all drank Bloody-Maries and Mimosas' as Thomas and Old Joe toked together.

Suddenly, there was a big commotion as well as a putrid odor. Thomas was yelling and screaming as two nurses wheeled him away --- against his will. Clarence scratched his head with perplexed concern; a habitual act of intuition. He had been denying it but his conscience was getting to him; not to mention his nose as his memory served him with --- review, examination and scrutiny.

Ultimately, Thomas was out of control as he lost complete control of his bodily functions --- shitting and pissing himself repeatedly. Unfortunately, this was the forth or fifth uproar this week or so. Ironically, not only did he lose his dignity, but also his regard for others as he had no sense of shame.

Clarence was dumbstruck. *Is Thomas addicted*, he wondered? *Perhaps he is a chain-toker, but is it justified by his pain? Or, does he just like getting high?* He was warned about being discrete with his special medication and yet, he flaunts it proudly?

"When is enough, enough?" he asked himself. Can Thomas cope without it? Does it jeopardize our Commune? Would prohibition be betrayal? Damn drugs were responsible for my son's death. Clarence was beside himself.

He decided to *consult with the doctors and staff, which were a special tight nit group*.

Peg analyzed Clarence's worry.

"His body is shutting down." she explained. "It's part of the process. I'm surprised that he still breathes on his own. He won't be smoking his stash much longer. Soon, he'll be bed-ridden as advancing cancer entails chronic pain which is a sad situation."

◄ 144

"Bedridden," Clarence shouted in shock? "Why over the last couple of weeks; he has been the life of the party? He didn't even get to cash his settlement check yet? Talk about raining on your parade."

"God works in strange ways," Peg reminded him. "Many times, people seem to get a second wind before they degenerate. It will only get worst; his condition will surely deteriorate. We must watch him closely as he shall become confused and isolated from the world around him. Soon, depression, anxiety, fear and frustration; will take their toll."

Clarence was speechless as he was getting his consultation now.

"Soon," Peg continued, "he will need an injection every four hours, probably --- Morphine. Unfortunately it is addicting as a compulsive, overpowering crave for not only relief from pain, but for its psychological effects as well."

"Ultimately, Thomas knows that it's only a matter of time as he is dying. But, like Marge; will he accept it or try to deny it and fight till the end? Hopefully, he knows that you can't ignore *Death* as it is but a *Fact of Life*."

Clarence trusted her judgment and left it at that. He kissed her on the forehead and said, "Thank You." Then he asked, "Do you want to go to the beach, I have to clear my head; unwind."

"But of course," she replied and, off they went.

It took another week or so, but Peg proved to be right. Slowly but surely, day by day; Thomas got worst until finally, he was bed-ridden. He was on oxygen. The pain got worst by the minute; especially since he was diagnosed with emphysema.

"No more smoking." The doctors warned. Consequently; be that as it may, he was delighted with the morphine.

The *Commune* was concerned. They felt sorry that Thomas wouldn't be going to Mexico. However, he insisted that they go and have a good time. He promised that he'd be here waiting --- when they returned.

SOCIAL SECURITY

He wanted them to bring a video camera. They agreed. He was incoherent when they left several days later. All were excited in spite of Thomas' situation as they accepted the fact that he was dying. Besides, he insisted.

Carlos was like a little kid, waiting for a present. He left Mexico over seventy years ago and had never been back since. Back then, he couldn't read or write; he barely spoke English.

Thus, he never kept in contact as time seemed to slip away. Unfortunately, there was never enough money to return *Home* for a visit. He barely made enough money to survive here in the USA.

Ironically, he was born in a small village near Guadalajara, where they were landing. The *Amigos* promised to take him on a special trip to look up his hometown. He prayed that he'd find a long lost relative or some new offspring.

The residents of *Social Security* looked like gang members at the airport before they entered their private plane. They got a lot of laughs and stares. Lucy managed to sweet talk her way into the cockpit as she was no longer afraid of flying but most curious as it made her feel closer to her father; as if he were there beside her.

The flight took off on time as scheduled. Clarence was glad that it was a non-stop flight.

The stewardesses' went out of their way to make everyone comfortable and happy. Their lunch was fantastic; as if it were home made. Even Jacques gave it his thumbs-up.

Clarence felt guilty as well as selfish. He expressed his feelings to Peg. "How many mean what they say and say what they mean?" he asked her.

"What do you mean?" she asked back.

"Society takes words for granted." he tried to explain. "But words are complicated by the *Living Word* --- *Man*, himself. Death is a scary thought."

"It's a personal transition, but nobody should be alone when they die. I should have stayed with Thomas. I should be there to hold his hand as he --- *Passes On*."

Peg smiled as she reached for Clarence's hand. They were

PEACE AND CLOSURE IN PARADISE

kindred souls. Suddenly Clarence insisted: "I must go back! His words were but an excuse; permission, but he's probably scared to death about dying."

"*Permission* is as *Sacred* as *Sacrifice*," Peg assured. "It is a sacrifice in its own rite. Respect his wishes. Thomas didn't want to ruin the trip for anybody."

"Sometimes, it's good to be alone. Thomas's permission was a *Gift* to all of us; from his *Heart*. It made him feel better in spite of the fact that he is surely dying and probably scared. "

Clarence just listened with discern as Peg continued. "Thomas is in God's hands now. Unfortunately, he could suffer for months, even more. I'll make a phone call when we land and have *Hospice* stay with him till we return."

Clarence smiled with doubt but Peg kept right on encouraging him. "We have our hands full; we have over five dozen or so *Family Members* to keep our eyes on. They all look up to you for guidance. We must all stick together. This is a chance in a lifetime; let's make it memorable."

Clarence reached over and stole a kiss as a voice sounded out --- loud and clear over the intercom. "This is your *Co-Captain* Lucy speaking. Get your asses in you seats and your belts on. Prepare for landing."

The total flight took about five and one half hours. When they landed, they fit right in except for the custom stitching; as a bunch of locals were also sporting ponchos and sombreros. Carlos actually jumped for joy; after he bent down and literally kissed the ground. He then proceeded to hug and kiss everyone in sight as he became the center of attention at Guadalajara International Airport.

He conversed with everybody and anyone --- in Spanish, dropping family names and word about; where he'd be staying. A taxi-bus was waiting in the parking lot. Peg called *Social Security* and arranged for *Hospice* to assist Thomas while the *Tribe* was loading into the taxi-bus.

Their resort --- *El Rio Caliente Manida,* was 25 miles away. Carlos's hometown --- Tlaquepaque, was only fifteen minutes away.

He was anxious but they had a schedule to keep. Clarence promised to bring him back tomorrow.

Carlos understood but insisted that he had to visit *Tequila Volcano* before they left Mexico. He said that it would bring back memories since he played there often as a kid on his uncle's farm near the Town of Tequila.

"*Tequila Volcano*," Sarge asked? "It's no wonder that shit knocks me on my ass. What's it made out of --- Volcanic Ash?"

Clarence and Carlos laughed as the bus driver explained that "Genuine Tequila is only manufactured in one of two municipalities; either that of Tequila or that of Arandas, northeast of here. Many a brawl has broken out because of arguments; about which is best. You better believe that we take pride in our *National Beverage*."

"I am a defender of Senor Jose Antonio de Cuervo." Carlos Sanchez bragged. "My twin hermana, Teresa and I tended to the Agave Tequilana when we were jovenes."

"Well then," the driver answered, "you are in luck as the town of Tequila is near El Río Caliente *Manida* and the Cuervo family is still very active in the town."

Carlos was in his glory, he only hoped that someone was alive --- old enough to remember him. Pedro, the bus driver apologized for not politely introducing himself properly. Then he explained that: "The town of Tequila itself; dates from soon after the Spanish conquistadors arrived in the area, led by the barbarous Nuno de Guzman. Legend has it that its name supposedly derives from '*Place of Tricks*' or '*Place of Those Who Pay Tribute*'."

"It lies in the shadow of an imposing 9000 foot volcano." he continued. "It is a 10 mile drive from the center of town on a cobble stone road to the top of *Tequila Volcano*. It provides breath-taking views, overlooking the country side. Rapid changes of flora occur with increasing altitude. You can see over five dozen species of birds on a good day --- including the exotic Mot-Mot, Orioles, the Squirrel-Tailed Cuckoo and hummingbirds. The tropical plants are so tranquil --- the Bougainvillea, Jacaranda, Montezuma Pine and Tropical Palm; just to name a few."

PEACE AND CLOSURE IN PARADISE

"Mucho Gracias! Mucho Gracias!" Carlos thanked Pedro for the memories.

As the bus rolled out of the airport, Pedro welcomed everybody over the microphone as they were practicing their Spanish on each other. "Bienvenidos a México!"

"Mucho Gracias! Mucho Gracias!" they echoed.

He then introduced himself and stated that he'd be their guide. Needless to say; everybody was excited.

"You'll Love our climate here in Mexico!" he assured. "National Geographic rates it among the top two on *Earth*. This area is known as *Eternal Spring* and the weather is always on your side here. Your next destination, *El Rio Caliente Manida,* is a magnificent 60-acre getaway."

"It is nestled in the foothills of the Sierra la Primavera; an ancient volcanic valley surrounded by ex-volcanic mountains and the vast green Primavera National Forest. This forest is an ecologically protected nature reserve; covering over 76,000 acres of which consists mainly of pine and oak trees atop rolling hills occasionally separated by narrow, deep canyons with grassy meadows. El Rio Caliente itself is *'The Hot River';* perhaps one of our country's best-kept secrets."

"It maintains a mineral-rich stream which offers hikers a soothing, natural hot-bath. But, enter with caution as there are several different temperature zones in the many areas. Ironically, it is only a few yards wide and conveniently shallow for wading."

"Seek and you will find a spot where a blasting hot spray will give you a natural soothing hydro massage from bubbling mineral water. You will think that you died and went to *Heaven*. *El Rio Caliente* literally boils its way out from deep underground in the Primavera Forest, running through cool, pine-covered hills and eventually, it cools to become the Ameca River which then curves westward for 130 miles until it spills into the Pacific Ocean at Puerto Vallarta."

"Soon," he continued, "we will be passing through the village of Primavera (Springtime) and the Primavera Forest itself. Our ETA will be about an hour. At 5,000 feet above sea level, our air is clean and clear. Enjoy the tranquil view of the varied ecology"

The companions were at *Peace*. The landscape was pristine; an oasis of beauty, so soothing to the eyes, so nurturing and natural. They felt safe and comfy as if they were on another planet. It was no wonder why so many were taking pictures and videos. Especially since it was easy because the bus had no windows and everyone was trying to stick their head out.

They couldn't wait to get deeper into this exploratory expedition, but soon they were deeper and deeper into a rural and poor countryside. They were driving on a small and very bumpy dirt road; stopping frequently to make way for livestock and caballeros on horses, Pedro seemed to know everyone and waved frequently.

Suddenly, they a saw picturesque compound up ahead! A large gate swung open and the bus drove in as Pedro announced: "Welcome to *El Rio Caliente Manida*; a rustic nature getaway! You are about to be pampered beyond belief."

It was if they were entering a magical paradise; secluded, laid back and an unassuming environment.

The grounds were beautifully maintained and seemed enormous. It was incredible. Everything looked lush and green, with beautiful, colorful flowers dotting the grounds as well as water fountains and bird-baths. The road leading to the office was cobbled and lined with a large garden of vegetables on each side, and the hot river, (El Rio Caliente) running under a small bridge.

When they got off their bus, they were greeted by a friendly warm staff and overwhelmed by hospitality. The sanctuary had a lot to offer as it was a hot springs, health spa and nature resort. All the cottages were charming, but simple and so clean and fresh-smelling. They displayed hand-crafted furniture, pretty woven fabrics, their own fireplace and a private geo-thermal tub/shower.

There were three heated mineral lap pools, three private (his and her) mineral plunge pools, the *Volcanic Aztec* steam room, two whirlpools and hot-tubs as well as a massage, beauty and health complex. And, there was modern pluming. Lucy, Sexy Sarah and Peg had to pee. They entered one of the bathrooms that had six toilets in it. Suddenly, there was a loud scream, followed a second or two later by another scream and then, a bunch of laughter. Peg got scared, since she could imagine what was going on?

"What's wrong?" she yelled to her two friends. "Are you two OK?"

"Oh it's nothing." They echoed back.

Peg was confused until she flushed and --- Surprise --- it was an unforgettable, memorable moment from a toilet, which flushed and cleaned you with steaming hot water.

Of course, nobody told the others as they got their surprise latter. The *Amigos* joked amongst them selves; about getting their balls boiled. Even Sexy Sarah acknowledged that it was a new experience for her and her privates.

Old Joe was impressed with the organic vegetable garden. Eva, Betty and Edna wanted to go horse back riding, but decided to wait until after dinner. Peg and Lucy made an appointment for a detoxifying mud-wrap, facial, pedicure and manicure.

Sexy Sarah couldn't keep her eyes off the young senores. She was flirting with a handsome masseur. Jacques was a bit jealous but his eyes wandered just as much as the senoritas' were gorgeous. Suddenly, there was a big commotion around the pool area. The guys were going wild as Gabriella was practicing her belly dancing.

The more they hooted, hollered and whistled; the more she giggled, jiggled and wiggled. It was electrifying. She had so much energy; she could have danced all night, but cena was being served and, all were famished. Gabriella promised to entertain later and give lessons to the ladies.

After dinner which was fresh, filling, and delicious; Eva, Betty and Edna organized a horseback excursion. About a dozen others participated. Gabriella kept her promise and the guys kept their eyes on Gabriella. All but Sarge; he was nowhere to be found.

Sexy Sarah was jealous. She felt deprived until she learned the art. She mastered the technique naturally. Peg and Lucy tried as did a few others, but they all gave up. Eventually, the excitement got boring.

The Sunset was unforgettable. Except for Sarge and the trail-

SOCIAL SECURITY

riders, all others watched it from the pools; sipping freshly squeezed juices.

Henry proposed a toast to the *Sun*.

Carlos added, "Salud; Health / Cheers!"

And, Max didn't hear a word as he was lost --- practicing the *Art of Doing Nothing*.

Clarence felt much better; the complex was so unpretentious, so unspoiled --- pure and intoxicating. They didn't need any alcohol. He took one look at Peg and he knew that he'd get lucky; later tonight. She had that look --- sparkles in her eyes and the atmosphere was so romantic and inviting.

He was glad they came. He could get addicted to its simplicity. It was contagious. He only wished that Marge and Thomas were here. He felt sorry for Thomas and, he missed Marge. Ironically though, he laughed as he thought --- *'She gone. But, she ain't gone.'*

"Did you see that spectacular Sunset?" Eva queried with excitement as they returned from their remarkable adventure. "It was breath-taking; soothing for the *Soul*."

"It surrre wawasss," Lucy stuttered before she jumped right back into the heated pool.

"It's a cool fifty-degree winter night," hollered one of the lifeguards.

"That's why we have fireplaces and don't forget the *Volcanic Aztec* steam room," another shouted!

Everybody started to laugh as nobody dared to come out.

"Psychophysics," shouted Gabriella. "It's all in your head. 'Mind over matter'; --- Psycho kinesis. You have control over your body. That's one of many *Secrets in the Pilgrimage of Life*. Never underestimate the *Wisdom of the Ages*."

Clarence got out of the pool --- immediately. He was freezing, but he kept his *Cool* or should we say *Cold* --- hidden as he wanted to set an example. Soon, one by one, the others followed as Gabriella and the life guards clapped, laughed and cheered.

After they made *Love* by the fire; Peg thought about what

Gabriella had said --- *'mind over matter'*.

"Man must make an effort," she realized out loud, "to make your theory work. We must take control of our own lives. Self awareness is a marvel."

"*Thales* hit the nail on the head," she said, "when he proclaimed: *'Know Thyself.'* We must observe, examine and choose --- It's either *Self-Deception* en-route to *Self-Destruction,* or *Self-knowledge;* en-route to *Self-Liberation --- Enlightenment.*"

Clarence smiled; he was both pleased and proud that Peg wasn't a self-centered fool. Without a doubt, she *'Believed in Thee';* as she respected *'Cosmic Consciousness'*.

"Self-discovery is astonishing," he assured. "Man is but an extension of good and evil. Patience as well as persistence; are both *Sacred,*" he rolled over and hugged and kissed her before they fell fast asleep --- embraced together, naked by the fire.

They woke up early in the morning and took a walk by the Rio Caliente; *Hot River*. They were surprised as half of the *Commune* was already there --- admiring the awesome steam; lingering as it collided with the fresh air. Eventually it rose slowly --- up, up and away past the mountains, to make room for an encore.

After breakfast; Clarence, Carlos, Max and Henry rented a car. They had business to attend --- in the *Name of Closure* for Carlos. They couldn't believe all of the eye-candy that was lingering around as they passed the pool. Sarge was still nowhere to be found. But, he left word at the mess hall; that he was looking up some old friends.

"Maybe he has some --- Hot Senorita?" Max surmised.

"Perhaps," Clarence interjected; "he must have been here before. How else would he know about this Paradise?"

"Lucy saw him last night," Henry added. "He was talking to some younger guy --- up on the hill. He waved to her from a distance."

The map seemed simple enough. Clarence drove as Max and Henry were the co-pilots and Carlos delighted in his glory. The countryside was stupefying, even more beautiful; than it was observed from their bus ride. Perhaps it took the eyes time to adjust as their brains had to identify through indulgence as they acclimated --- Naturally and culture shock wore off.

They stopped in the village of Primavera before they proceeded to Carlo's hometown. He wanted his presence to be known. He left word at local businesses that: "Carlos Sanchez, edad noventa y tres, whom hailed from Tlaquepaque; was looking for family and old friends."

He was told that there were several Sanchez families on the outskirts of the village. In fact, Jose el barbero was a Sanchez. Needless to say, they all scurried off to the barber shop in a flash.

Carlos introduced himself and they exchanged family history.

"Believe it or not," Jose proclaimed, "my great second cousin on my father's side --- Teresa Ortez, edad noventa alguna cosa; lives ten, twelve miles away on a big farm with her hija --- Maria. She is the niece of my Great-Great Grandfather Mateo Sanchez."

"Si! Si, mi Tio Mateo! Tio Mateo!" Carlos shouted as he hugged and kissed his great second or third cousin.

"Take me to see my hermana gemela Teresa! Gustar! Gustar," Carlos demanded --- elated beyond belief as he passed a bottle of tequila; which he bough from somebody at the airport.

"Bebida! Bebida," he insisted as Clarence took a swig so that he didn't offend him. Henry and Max obliged as well; even though they promised the girls that they wouldn't drink on the trip. Jose made it unanimous.

Tension mounted on the short drive to *Closure*. Carlos was thrilled and anxious but nervous as he braced himself. He confessed that he never believed in his wildest dreams that he'd be reunited with Teresa.

"Would she be mad at me for not coming home sooner," he asked all jittery?

"Better later than never," Clarence assured; calming the worry on his face.

"Cousin Teresa is a saint." Jose informed. "She'll --- *Welcome you with open arms!* She doesn't get mad at nobody, no how. *Everybody is Always Welcomed to her house."*

PEACE AND CLOSURE IN PARADISE

The adobe farm house was huge but worn. A dozen people lived in it, including --- Maria's Grand-son Pablo and his wife Paula, their seven children and one nephew --- Carlos. The furnishing, were plain and simple. There was no running water or indoor bathroom. A rooster, chickens, goats, pigs, cows, dogs and cats littered the area as well as several junk cars. They were poor to say the least.

Teresa was so excited that she fainted when she embraced her brother. He thought that she died of a heart attack, but Jose brought her around to a glorious reunion as he splashed some water from the well on her face.

"No worry, Ma-Ma as healthy as a caballo." Maria exclaimed, "too, too much excitement, a shocking, unexpected visit. She'll be alright," she continued as she gave her mother a cup of agua.

"Carlos, Carlos; mi hermano perdido largo," Teresa cried. "Adonde os esconder? Nosotros pensamiento os finado."

"No! No, I'm alive!" Carlos answered, "mi aca! Hallar mi familia!" he continued as he picked up one of his little great, great, great nephews.

The *Amigos* had tears in their eyes as it was oh so touching. Carlos passed his bottle around and even Teresa had a swallow. Paula fetched some lemonade and home-made deserts as she was a good hostess. She explained to the guys that Teresa didn't speak any English.

The reacquainted siblings; Carlos and Teresa chattered a mile a minute as if nobody else were there. She told him that she raised twelve children and; that they were all still alive. He had sixty-two nieces and nephews thanks to Teresa; not to mention all the cousins, on his Uncle Mateo's side.

Not bad considering the fact that their mother died giving birth to them. Their father died shortly thereafter in a farm accident. Unfortunately, Teresa's Husband Miguel died ten years ago, but they had had a productive life together.

Carlos told her that he would be in town for another six days, but she insisted that he not leave her sight. "Usted viene a casa Carlos! Usted no va otra vez! Amo a muy gran Carlos."

SOCIAL SECURITY

She was glad that Carlos was happy and alive and well as they sat there holding hands. *The Amigos* were anxious to get back as they felt out of place. Pablo offered to take Carlos back whenever he decided. They all agreed, but Carlos called Clarence to the side.

He wanted him to call Chi and have him draw up papers for a will for his realized long lost and or forgotten family. Clarence explained that it was more complicated than that as he would need all their names. He suggested that maybe he might want to transfer cash. After all, even if he only sends half of his $1,000,000.00; that would surly go a long way down here in Mexico. Carlos agreed to wait and talk personally with Chi.

As *The Amigos* headed back; Peg, Lucy and Old Joe took turns manning the video camera. They captured the beautiful scenery as well as the activities. But, you had to be there to realize the significance.

After all, how can you emphasize the appreciation of the *Art of Doing Nothing,* a state of dreamy relaxation? Ironically, simplicity is foreign back home ---- where hurry and worry dictate as a matter of conformed obedience. Poor Thomas didn't know what he was missing.

Joe got close with another resident --- Patrick; who was also Irish. Joe elaborated on how glad he was to be here, not to mention a *Member* of the *Commune*.

"So many grow old, cold, miserable and calloused," he explained, "but *Social Security* taught me how to *Love* again. I never wanted for much except the chance to see Anna again. I never realized what I was missing in regards to *Family* and a sense of belonging. And then, *Miraculously;* Anna appeared! I was flabbergasted."

Patrick knew that Joe was homeless for years. He stated that they were *both lucky* and that he *shared his sediments exactly*: "Friends and family are the most precious things in life; besides one's health. *Social Security* is a *Treasure*. We are millionaires thanks to Chi."

"But that doesn't matter," he continued; "I've been there before --- way, way back when a million dollars was worth something. I was on top of the world, so to speak; --- cars, houses, wife, mistress, family and friends. I was king of the hill in my neighborhood. But then, suddenly --- overnight, puff, I was broke as life is one big gamble."

Joe sat there --- listening as Patrick summarized his life. "I lost everything as my business went under. I wallowed in disbelief and denial. But the hardest part about being down and out; were all the excuses. I blamed everybody but myself. Ironically, I even made up excuses for my friends and family whom snickered and avoided me as if I had the plague."

Old Joe enjoyed his little chat as he could relate to Patrick's poetry with the same sediments. People use to avoid him like a leaper as money talks and appearance speaks loud and clear. He use to want to disappear as people actually pretended that he wasn't even there anyway.

Thus, he Thanked God for *being here --- Now as well as for his reunion with Anna.* Perhaps, he thought to himself, *maybe someday Patrick will be lucky too and perhaps; find someone from his past. Second chances are sacred. Doubt kills dreams.*

The *Amigos* arrived back at the retreat in time for lunch. They were exhausted and ready for a siesta, but decided to eat first. The *Commune* was pleased when they heard that Carlos was staying with his sister and a bunch of relatives.

"It's funny how life's path twists and turns and yet; can come full circle." Old Joe stated with delight. "Peace entails a bit of closure."

Everybody agreed between bites as they devoured their meal. They spent the rest of the day relaxing as they took advantage of *Mother Nature* as well as the accommodating facilities. *Eternal Spring* was the place to be and they were, enjoying every minute of it.

Several days past too swiftly; between hiking, biking, bathing, shopping; sight seeing and doing nothing. Sexy Sarah and the three *Sex-pots*; all got their belly buttons pierced like Gabriella. They sported their new solid gold earring and bikinis as they sunbathed by the pool. Some of the guys were drooling as they took a gander at all the young eye-candy with fantasying thoughts like dogs in heat. Ironically the four *Sex-pots* thought that they were the *Bathing Beauties.*

Sarge was scarcely seen and there was no word from Carlos. The following morning, the gang ventured to *Tequila Volcano.* Sarge made the trip, but he got hammered; drunken shit-faced, three sheets to the wind.

When they returned to Rio Caliente, Jose Sanchez was there waiting --- with sad news as Carlos died earlier that afternoon in his sister Teresa's arms. Apparently, his heart gave out. The *Commune* was stunned as Betty and Edna cried for their *Lover.* Sarge felt sick as he went to sleep it off --- somewhere.

Jose expressed his family's gratitude as they had a wonderful three days with Carlos. "God works in mysterious ways." he said, "but, it was as if Carlos was on a mission as he just had to come *Home to Rest in Peace."*

Clarence asked about the arrangements and assured him that they'd be there to pay their last respects. He also informed him that they would be leaving Mexico in two days. Jose thanked him and said that there would be a celebration tomorrow after the burial near the farmhouse.

That night, Clarence called Chi with the news. He gave him the heads-up on Carlos's wishes. Chi assured him that there were ways to transfer the money and avoid inheritance taxes. He would set up a charity fund from one nonprofit organization to another.

The following morning; both *Families* paid their respects. The funeral was simple and dignified. A Padre gave a *Special Sermon.* Clarence said a few words on behalf of the entire *Commune.* He also stated that they would plant a *Tree* in *The Garden of Remembrance,* in *Honor of Carlos.*

Betty and Edna cried like babies. His *Mexican Family* was confused as they couldn't comprehend which one was his *Lover.* Some; giggled, others were shocked and stunned as rumor spread fast.

There was plenty of food, singing, dancing, tequila and *Mexican Beer*. During the celebration, Peg who spoke fluent Spanish, accompanied by Clarence; had a private meeting with Teresa and Maria. They were overjoyed as they decided to divide the money equally among their entire Family.

"Mucho Gracias Jesus," echoed out of their mouths!

They were told that Chi would fly down to Mexico next week with the paper work. It would be another month or so before they got their money. They couldn't wait to tell the *Families the News*. Needless to say, it was a *Dream Come True* --- Pasmoso as the celebration turned into a *Celebration*, Thanks to Carlos Sanchez.

The following morning, the *Four Amigos* were all up early --- watching the steam condense --- Naturally. They decided to take a quick drive in the rent a car. Sarge grabbed a bottle of Tequila from the stash in his room. They opened it at the small cemetery; poured a little on his grave and *Toasted* --- "Hasta la vista Carlos! Paz estar con usted!"

When they returned back to the retreat; everybody was practicing their *Meditation* and or *Yoga*.

Clarence laughed to himself as he realized that *Carlos wasn't the only one that found Peace*. He wondered, *what are the others thinking about*; as they were lost in deep thought?

Perhaps they were just trying to accept the fact that it was almost time to leave Paradise? Some sat with their legs-crossed-Indian-style on hand-mage rugs while others were gazing haphazardly into space; lying in their hammocks. Or, perhaps, they were just content with being alive --- Now? When they finished their newly discovered routine; there was a special brunch before the return trip --- Home Tomorrow.

As they were eating their lunch, Peg and the gals showed the guys a hand-made super large hammock that they bought for Thomas. The all laughed and thought that he would *Love* it. Then Max told the girls that the guys bought him some Tequila which he wanted. Everybody agreed that he probably needed it, but they also hoped that Thomas would get a chance to enjoy both gifts.

That night, they had a barbeque for supper. It went on and on into a festivity of dancing and celebration with fruit juices and Mexican foods. Gabriella and Sexy Sarah were the life of the social interaction and entertainment until Max jumped into the heated pool naked.

"Go Baby, Go!" Eva, Edna and Betty escalated it into a hullabaloo when they egged him on and on; just a hooting and a hollering as Anna them the *Evil-Eye*.

Everybody laughed and laughed as Anna joined in; when Henry pushed her into the water. One by one, everybody jumped in, with their clothes on. Max was oh so embarrassed when he got out. Henry had all the towels in his hands and refused to give him one. Poor Max streaked back to his cabin in his shrunken birthday suit.

The following morning, everybody packed after they ate their breakfast. Unfortunately, they sadly said their goodbyes to their new friends and thanked the staff. As the plane took off; all had tears in their eyes as Carlos was on their minds. It was a memorable trip indeed as they --- *Mastered the Art of Doing No-thing and, Enjoyed It!* It was a *Journey* of a *Lifetime*.

CHAPTER **Nine**

Compassion, Mercy and the Confession – Plus

Chapter 9   Compassion, Mercy and the Confession – Plus

"This is your *Co-Captain Lucy*, Get your asses back in your seats and prepare for a safe landing."

Everybody busted out laughing as they did land safely at the Buffalo Niagara International Airport. The day driver was there waiting in the corporate bus; to meet the anxious gang. It was a fantastic vacation but it was also great to get back home. After all, *'there is no place like home'*.

When they got to *Social Security*, most were tired from jet-lag and went straight to bed. Others just relaxed and did nothing. Clarence and Peg headed upstairs to check on Thomas.

Unfortunately, he was sleeping, but at least he was still alive! Peg thanked the lady from Hospice and assured her that they would *take care of him now*. She replied to Peg: "He's a fighter, but he has good days and bad. Some are better than others. Some are unbearable for him as he cries like a baby."

Thomas *Loved* his new hammock. Two of the maintenance men rigged it up for him in his room. In fact, he laid in it the very next day and even drank some of his new *Tequila* and watched the videos that were taken of the trip.

Unfortunately, he had to be lifted in and out of it, but that wasn't a big chore since he weighed less that 100 lbs. Sexy Sarah gave him a signed autographed picture of Gabriella which put a smile on his thin face. Then, she did a *Private Belly Dance* for him which made his day.

A few weeks past and Thomas insisted on lying in his hammock during the day as he watched the Mexico Trip videos over and over again. He became a belly dancer expert as he sipped on his Tequila. Sexy Sarah was a good belly dancer but according to Thomas; *'she could use a few more lessons from Gabriella.'*

The *Four Amigos* were playing pinochle, shooting the shit; when Henry announced:

"Rumor has it that Thomas can't take it any longer. He hallucinates often --- *Talks to Marge?* He says that 'he doesn't want to die --- *All Doped Up!* But, he just can't take the pain or make it stop without the morphine.'"

"Frankly, he wants to die with a clear head. He even told one of the nurses to spill out his *Tequila*. He keeps begging the doctors for *Euthanasia*. However, they decline --- citing Dr. Jack Kevorkian's predicament."

"What about *Hypnosis*," asked Clarence? "It's worth a shot; mind over matter."

They all agreed. They consulted with the doctors whom thought that it might be a good idea. Dr. Gloria Talbert, a Clinical Psychologist and close friend of Peg's, agreed to put Thomas under.

Initially, it worked. Unfortunately, Thomas was getting bored and tired of waiting for death. He was lonely as he longed to participate, but was too weak. Eventually, he asked for *Euthanasia* again --- constantly as he accepted his fate --- Death.

"Existing is Not Living," Thomas insisted seriously to Clarence. "The *Thrill* is gone. I'm agonizing in *Shame* --- piss and shit in my pants as I speak --- reeking. It's pretty bad; when you can't stand your own smell. Release me Please, Please; I'm begging you for a rite of passage. Just bring me *El'Caramba.*"

Clarence had a lump in his throat and an ache in his chest / Heart as he felt for Thomas's predicament. *Shit,* he thought to himself. *Someday I might be in the same boat. I'd probably want death too.*

"I'll talk it over with the *Amigos*." he promised before he left as Thomas smiled --- Sincerely.

"I chatted with Thomas this afternoon and I sympathize with his plight." Clarence stated as he dealt the cards. "A right to die is as sacred as a right to live. He's not crazy, senile or drugged. He's desperate and as ironic as it sounds; he should have the right to choose --- his own death."

"Death is but a fact of Life," he continued. "Unfortunately, so many are afraid to deal with it, let alone face their own death. But not Thomas O'leary; he's begging for it. He needs a little help from his friends."

"What do you have in mind?" Henry asked reluctantly.

"He wants a gun." Clarence replied. "But we can't afford a suicide as we don't need any negative publicity."

"As I see it," Sarge interjected. "Death is inevitable, *Life* is but an option. Truth is simple. Death is the bottom line as man is born to die. Why suffer in prolonged agony. We must grant his wish in the Name of --- *Mercy as Free Will, a Right to Die*."

After discussing Thomas's grief; they decided to get involved in conspiracy. Sarge grabbed four plastic stir-sticks and cut them into different sizes.

"Who wants to go first," he asked as he held *Destiny in his Hands?*

Henry lost; he was the unlucky participant with the displeasure to execute misery.

Nervously he stuttered --- "Ga Ga God, wha wha whata I gotta do?"

"Nothing," Sarge responded. "Fuck God. We give him credit when things are going good, but where was He or Marge's Guardian Angles for that matter --- all those times when she was being raped? And where was God when Thomas was pulverized by that sick bastard."

"I'll take care of it. I still have one ball left. I got plenty of practice in Korea and in Viet Nam. Sometimes man has to do God's dirty work."

SOCIAL SECURITY

"Thanks." Henry was relieved as he wiped the sweat from his brow.

"Forget about it." Sarge replied. "I'll see you guys latter. I have to take care of something."

After Sarge left the complex; Henry felt much better, but, "How is he going to take care of it?" he wondered out loud.

"He knows what to do." Clarence assured most definitely.

"Where does he go everyday without exception," Max asked redundantly concerned with curiously again?

"I haven't the vaguest?" Henry answered. "It's as if he is living a double life. He is always gone at least a few hours a day."

"And what about; on the Mexican vacation?" Max added. "He only hung out with us the last two and a half days."

"Awe, he's just a private sort of guy." Clarence defended. "Mind your own business. He probably looked up an old fling in Mexico. He traveled half the world you know. What, are you two jealous? Perhaps someday we'll get to meet his *Lover*, perhaps --- *Lovers*. If not, then --- so be it, but I bet he has a lot of wild escapades to talk about."

"I'm hungry." Max changed the subject.

"Me too," Clarence agreed. "Let's get some *shitty-canoes.*"

"Yeah," Henry agreed unanimously, "I can go for a few of them scum dogs."

When they got back home, the guys were too nervous to do anything; let alone go to bed. They decided to wait up for Sarge as they watched TV. Henry got instant heart-burn in anticipation but blamed it on the Texas hotdogs.

Sarge rolled in about 1 AM, waved to his *Amigos* and headed up stairs.

"Why is he so damn secretive?" Max asked, "When is he going to do it; tonight?"

The other two shook their heads in ignorance as Sarge was up in Thomas's bedroom. Sometimes a man has to do what a man has to do for his buddy; honor his passionate plea for death. Sarge learned this during the war on the battle field. He was no virgin.

Alexander Pope overshadowed his mind with inspiration; *'this long disease, my life'*, as Thomas looked up at him and smiled in deadly anticipation; waiting for relief - Freedom. Sarge bent down with tears in his eyes and a deadly pillow in his hands. He removed Thomas' oxygen-mask and sent him to his maker.

"Adios Amigo," he whispered as Thomas gasped for his last breath. Sarge bit his tongue, tasted his own blood and left the room.

He returned to the family room to his anxious, confused, nervous and concerned *Amigos*. He knew from experience that it was easy to kill somebody, but hard to live with it.

"Get the Jack." he snapped. "It's a done deal; a sad ending to make a *Dear Friend Happy*."

"Amen!" echoed out of the other three mouths. They all toasted to Thomas --- confidently. They promised not to tell anybody about their involvement as some secrets are meant to be secret.

"Speaking of secrets," Max asked nonchalantly, "what did you mean about having one ball left?"

"My right nut got blown off in Viet Nam." he confided sadly.

They all started to laugh at Sarge's misfortune as they just couldn't help themselves. Ironically, neither could he as he laughed so hard that tears were rolling down his face. After all, it had been over four and a half decades ago.

"It was a *Napalm bomb*," he explained, "ironically, *Friendly Fire* from a *SkyRaider* in the village of Trang Bang, 25 miles North West of Saigon. Most of the right side of my lower body was burned, blistered and scarred."

"I laid there dying, agonizing in and out of consciousness until I was captured by the VC. They actually saved my life. Unfortunately, I developed an infection but at least I didn't die. That's why I never wear shorts."

"You mean our own military plane fucked you up?" Henry asked shaken by surprise.

"Shit happens." Sarge answered.

"Can you get it up?" Max was curious.

"I'm gay. Sarge admitted. I like it in the ass."

A thunder of silence --- swept the room --- until --- suddenly, Henry inquired: "You're a fucken-fairy?"

"Watch your mouth." Clarence interjected instantly as he fumed. "He's our Pal."

"I'm sorry." Henry apologized, "I never imagined. You hid it so well."

"I was embarrassed." Sarge fesses up and came clean. "I was a P.O.W. in Nam for three years, but I was considered M.I.A. until I escaped. The Viet Cong use to beat me. A few raped me. Most of them laughed at and made fun of me because I was deformed and functional; on part time basics."

"The war changed my sex life, my dreams and my views. There were many times when I thought about suicide. Psychologically, I still struggle to keep my sanity. Jack helps."

The other three *Amigos* were stunned. They didn't say a word as Sarge continued with his confession.

"I've been seeing Melvin now for over eight years. I never met anyone so gentle or more sympathetic than him. He's fifteen years younger than I am, but he *Love's* me and I *Love* him! He's my only *Family* besides *Social Security*. We had a secret rendezvous in Mexico for the first five days. He is the one who found the place."

Sarge's declaration brought tears to their eyes. He was a survivor whom was dealt a tough hand and deals with it. He is *Family* and they *Love Him for who he is.*

"Lucy seen you talking with some younger guy." Henry remembered.

"That was my Melvin." Sarge admitted, "My *Soul-mate*. We get along well together and whenever people get along; it is a *Beautiful Thing*."

"It's a *Divine Blessing*." Clarence insisted. "*Peaceful co-existence is a Miracle amongst God's Miracles --- Human Beings.*"

"Amen!" they all agreed.

"Where does Melvin live," Clarence asked?

"He lives with his Mother who is an invalid. He takes care of her

24 / 7 as he works from home on the internet. He has his hands full but he doesn't have the *Heart* to put her away."

"Does his Mother know about the two of you?" Max inquired.

"She was disappointed at first; being Catholic and having dreams of *Grand-children*. And then, there's the fact that I'm a *Negro* and he's *Caucasian*; that was a bit of a culture shock to her. But, I think the biggest let down was her passion for piano. She has a portable keyboard that she plays, propped up in her bed."

She had visions of playing --- one day for Melvin as he walked down the isle with his bride. She still practices even though she accepted us as a unit in the *Eyes of God*. She *Loves* Melvin. I only hope that she doesn't resent me."

Silence prevailed as the conversation ended until Clarence stood up and broke it as he padded Sarge on the back and said: "Good-night; it has been one heck of a day."

On his way up the stairs, he yelled back --- "Call Melvin in the morning and tell him that we'll be right over to help him pack. He and his Mother are moving in --- Immediately."

Instantly, Sarge cried --- Tears of Joy. Deep down, he knew that the *Amigos* would understand and accept him for what he is. But first, he had to accept it himself. He was glad that he finally did. He downed another shot as did the other two.

"Does Melvin know about the *Book-making Operation?*" Max asked with concern.

"He's cool." Sarge replied. "He was at Woodstock. He still tokes occasionally."

"I thought that you were against drugs?" Henry interjected with surprise.

"How the hell do you think I survived two wars? A little herb ain't so bad. Shit, Marijuana was legalized in Hawaii for doctors to prescribe it to the terminally ill, but I believe that that got over turned."

"So I heard," recalled Max. "Perhaps Cannabis should be legalized. Our farmers could make a fortune growing Hemp for clothing. When I was in the Bahamas years back; I bought some clothing made from *Hemp*. It was so soft and durable and it didn't shrink."

"Someday pot will be legalized." Henry predicted. "Over a dozen states already legalized its use for medicinal purposes. And many states are easing the penalty for criminal possession of pot as prisons throughout the US are over-crowded. In fact, many prisoners who were arrested for pot; are being released early because the federal mandated drug sentences were modified."

"And," he continued, "President Obama is considering a shift on the U S war on drugs. His drug czar, Gill Kerlikowske called for an *'end to the war on drugs'* and said the drug problem in this country *'should be a public heath issue and not a criminal justice issue'*. Unfortunately, the wrong people have been arrested throughout the years on this so called *'Drug War'*?"

"Meanwhile," he continued, "California is now considering the decriminalizing of marijuana and taxing it to offset its massive budget deficit. Perhaps Governor Arnold Schwarzenegger realizes that *Prohibition* doesn't work. It only ensures organized crime. It is the root to evil. We should educate and regulate, not eradicate drugs, booze, illicit sex or gambling. Hence, Gov. Schwarzenegger acknowledged: 'That it's time to debate whether to legalize and tax marijuana.'"

"Vices give the people a way to --- Cope and the secular powers that be; know it." Max was adamant. "Ironically, so do virtues as the churches preach God and promote salvation, bingo, etc. while the states are obsessed with more and more lottery revenue not to mention taxes. And then, we have the organized underworld which thrives on gambling, sex, and the smuggling of drugs as well as illegal aliens; with a little help from their friends --- corrupt politicians as well as immoral judges and law enforcement officials."

"Money is man's god." Sarge interjected. "As long as the secular powers that be; are making a profit, nothing will change. Corruption will continue unless we unite and make a difference."

"Have you ever wondered how drugs get into this country?" he asked. "A commodity of choice; can you spell lucrative? Can you smell *Mena*? Drugs are a national disaster which is responsible for crime and prostitution as junkies must support their habit. Drugs ruin lives; just ask Clarence."

"I can vouch for that," Henry confessed. "When my wife died, I got hooked on *Heroin*. I almost lost everything; including my kids. If it wasn't for my sister Linda; they'd of been raised in an orphanage or by the state foster program. I sold everything I owned and was in hock up to my ears. I over-dosed and was found unconscious by Linda who called the ambulance and had me committed for a drug addiction. I've been clean now pret' near thirty years except for weed."

"Wow?" The other two *Amigos* were shocked since they never knew Henry's past plight.

"Ironically," Sarge continued the conversation, "I'm surprised that Clarence lets *Old Joe* grow his *Special Plants*; considering that his son *OD* on drugs and died. Unfortunately, drugs are easy to get and the total market in opium, heroin, cocaine and marijuana combined in the USA; generates a gross volume of business in excess of well over $100 billion US a year. The importing, sale and distribution of drugs is an enterprise that generates more revenue than any of the largest multinational corporations in the world. It makes the gross volume of illegal drugs in the US greater than the gross national product of all but a dozen nations in the world. The '*Powers That Be'*, are making a fortune. "

"'*Power corrupts*'." Max shouted.

"'*Absolute power corrupts absolutely*.'" Henry added. "It leads to greed and paranoia."

"The whole legal system needs an overhaul." Max demanded. "Far too many are in on the take; complicity, collusion? Our government is at the mercy of a secret government, which hides behind *National Security*. Ironically, *Corporate Security* is the name of the game. If the public knew the truth, there would be riots, chaos; mayhem --- civil-war in the *Name of Several National Disgraces that have infected the World*."

"It's hard to trust a government which adheres to an on *A Need*

SOCIAL SECURITY

to Know Basis." Henry was adamant. "It's even harder to respect a system which has double standards and special privileges. Ironically, some are innocent until proven guilty; as others are guilty until proven innocent."

"Unfortunately," Sarge reminded; "there are those whom are beyond prosecution --- no matter what? It's a damn shame. Take the case of Ollie North for instance; he was convicted of a felony, but miraculously, it was overturned on a technicality."

"And, back in 1992, George Bush Senior; pardoned his bosses, former Defense Secretary Casper Weinberger and five others who had either been indicted or convicted of charges in the Iran-Contra affair. Unfortunately, rank does have its privileges; especially when they get caught."

"By the way," Sarge continued, "Ollie North lived in a million dollar house, with a state of the art security system. He listed $5,000,000.00 in assets when he had the Balls to run for the Senate as he vowed after his nomination: 'they will never see Ollie North crawling up the steps of Capital Hill to kiss their big, fat rings!' How did an officer in the USMC acquire so much net worth?"

The Amigos were fuming as Sarge poured another shot of Jack and reminisced further out loud. "Former Vice President Spiro Agnew was indicted by the FBI for taking cash from contractors (kickbacks). But he made a deal; he resigned and got pardoned by Nixon. Is it any wonder why Tricky Dick pardoned him? We had Watergate, but Nixon was not a Crook? After all, he, Nixon proclaimed: 'When the president does it; it's not illegal!'"

"History is paved with dirty secrets and cover-ups." Henry assured. "It is hard enough to go to the process and actually impeach somebody, but it is a National Disgrace when that person gets pardoned. I don't believe that Vincent Foster committed suicide. And, I do believe that the Monica Lewinsky sex trial was a big ploy --- blown out of proportion, to divert attention away from the White Water Scandal which ended up swept under the rug. Talk about a Miscarriage of Justice; Obstruction of Justice is more like it? It's much bigger than we'll ever know."

COMPASSION, MERCY AND THE CONFESSION – PLUS

"To add insult to our system of justice," he continued, "Clinton was not a perjurer? Thanks to his definition of sex; our young kids think that it is OK to engage in oral-satisfaction as STDs are out of control --- Oral Herpes, Pharyngeal, and Oral Wart Virus. After all, he set a precedent and he was the *Prez*, so it must not be sex as he testified."

"I wonder how he defines the word pervert." Max inquired sarcastically. "Maybe he could teach Sexy Sarah a thing or two about cigars."

They all laughed together as Sarge asked. "I wonder if he had an *O-zone* in the *White House?*"

They all laughed again until Max fumed. "Perjury is serious. It undermines the backbone of Humanity / Truth. Ironically, in the not so long ago past, man would testify by holding his testicles. Hence, the origin of the word *'testify'* is rooted in *Honor* of the *Sacred Family Jewels* --- man's testicles. Would you risk your balls, at the expense of perjury; as off with your testicles is in the back of your mind?"

"Absolutely not," The *Amigos* testified as they held their *Family Jewels!*

"Unfortunately," Sarge stated sadly, "when it come to those who are above the law; far too many times, it never goes to trial. Look what that Scum Rosty did. He was one of the most powerful members of Congress, but in 1994 he was indicted by a Federal Grand Jury on 17 felony charges alleging he plundered nearly $700,000.00 from our government over a 20 year period and had ghost employees kick back paychecks to his office. He was facing 110 years in jail and $365,000.00 in fines."

"U.S. Attorney Eric H. Holder Jr. described Congressman Daniel Rostenkowski's (Chairman of the Ways and Means Committee) conduct as a 'betrayal of the public trust for personal gain.' And then he had the balls to offer him --- the *Chairman of our Ways and Means Committee*; a plea-deal to one felony and six months in jail? If you think that was a dumb offer, you're not alone. Cause, so did Rosty as he refused and fired his lawyer?"

"Why did Holder offer him a plea deal?" Max asked as the

others shook their heads with suspicions.

"They don't want us, we the people to know what's going on." Sarge answered. "They were afraid to go to court. They were afraid that he would talk. Go figure? Especially after he claimed; *'that he had behaved no differently from most other members of Congress'*. Hush! Hush! It's a classic example as 'Power corrupts and Absolute Power corrupts absolutely'. Talk about Leverage; *A Vault Full of Dirty Secrets?*"

"How much time did he finally serve? " Henry asked offended.

"In 1996, he pleaded guilty to two felony counts of missing public funds in a plea bargain. He spent a whole 451 Days in a Federal Minimum Security Prison --- Halfway House." Sarge answered with disgust. "And, oh yes, by the way --- he was still entitled to his annual Federal Pension of $104,000.00."

"It's just the tip of the ice-berg." Max assured. "Why was J. Edgar Hoover --- a *Drag Queen*, allowed to persist with all his personal secret documents and insists that there was no *Mafia*; which he hung out and associated with during his 50 year regime? When he died, U.S. Government Auditors audited his estate and found $900.000.00 which he stole from the public. Ironically, his name is on top of some FBI offices as if he was some *Hero*? Every time I see it, I want to puke; it's a disgrace. His name should be on a *Wall of Shame*."

"Yap, I read about that in 'Official and Confidential: The Secret Life of J. Edgar Hoover'." Henry remembered. "Rumors of Hoover's homosexuality were rampant but suppressed during his lifetime. That book also claimed that Hoover did not pursue organized crime because the Mafia had blackmail material on him. The author, Anthony Summers also named a source who claimed to see 'Hoover at a party in drag; a fluffy black dress, very fluffy, with flounces and lace stockings and high heels, and a black curly wig.'"

"She, the source; also stated that: 'He had makeup on and false eyelashes.' she said that: 'Hoover was introduced to her as Mary' and that he, Hoover responded; 'Good Evening'. She acknowledged that she saw Hoover go into a bedroom and take off his skirt. There,

COMPASSION, MERCY AND THE CONFESSION – PLUS

'young blond boys' worked on him in bed."

"And, that wasn't the last time that she seen him as a cross-dresser. A year latter, she saw Hoover again at the same Plaza Hotel. This time, the director was wearing a red dress. Around his neck was a black feather boa. Alas, it wasn't until after his death that Americans learned J. Edgar Hoover was a secret transvestite. I guess that it was too embarrassing for the FBI."

"I also read a book about the CIA that made me cringe." Henry continued with shocking revelations. "It was entitled: 'The Man Who Kept the Secrets, Richard Helms and the CIA by Thomas Powers, N.Y. Knopf, 1979. I learned that Ex CIA Director Richard Helms was caught lying about a CIA operation that killed Chilean President Allende. When Helms was indicted and threatened with conviction for perjury to the Senate, he made it quite clear that in order to save himself; he would make public every dirty secret he knew. Alas, they took him serious as he was permitted to plea-bargain; a suspended sentence plus a fine that CIA Exes' Association paid for him'? Hush? Hush, Again and Again?"

"Democracy as we know it is a charade. Sarge professed. "The CIA is akin to the *Calloused Infrastructure of America*. Ultimately, it is the backbone of a top-secret government within our government. Unfortunately, when knowledge is distributed on a need to know basics, it is a double—edged sword with jaded edges; a 'Doctrine of Plausible Deniability'."

"But," he continued, "'*Ignorance is NOT Bliss.*' By ignoring them; we lead them into *Temptation* as they can deliver *EVIL* upon *Us*. Mena is the prime example."

"How" he asked as he tried to connect the dots, "how can we fight a '*War on Drugs*'; when '*The Powers That Be*', are involve --- smack in the middle? Barry Seal was a 'notorious gunrunner, international drug trafficker and covert C.I.A. operative extraordinaire', who was at the center of the 'Iran-Contra Affair'; drugs for arms scandal; which operated out of Mena, Arkansas while Bill Clinton was the governor of that state. This *covert operation went to* Nicaragua in CK123 Cargo planes amongst others with weapons and CIA employees and returned from Central America, loaded with cocaine; which was then dropped over Arkansas and Louisiana for distribution to larger U.S. cities. Who profited from the sales of those drugs is the big mystery?"

"Unfortunately," Sarge sadly informed. "Two teenage boys, Kevin Ives and Don Henry paid with their lives as they were murdered because they found some of the drugs being dropped from the sky from one of these planes. Their murders were covered-up for the longest time by the *'Powers That Be'*. The cover-up investigation extended to every level of government involving local, state, and federal law enforcement agencies."

"As a result of intense investigations and documentations," Sarge was fuming, "According to a Penthouse article entitled: 'The Crimes of Mena' by Sally Denton and Roger Morris; 'Seal's legacy includes more than 2,000 newly discovered documents that now verify and quantify much of what previously had been only suspicion, conjecture, and legend. The documents confirm that from 1981 to his brutal death in 1986, Barry Seal carried on one of the most lucrative, extensive, and brazen operations in the history of the international drug trade, and that he did it with the evident complicity, if not collusion, of elements of the United States government, apparently with the acquiescence of Ronald Reagan's administration, impunity from any subsequent exposure by George Bush's administration, and under the usually acute political nose of then Arkansas governor Bill Clinton.'"

"In fact," Sarge continued, "people began coming forward and alleging under sworn statements that Clinton profited from the operation at Mena by laundering money through the newly created Arkansas Development Finance Authority. Hmm; I wonder if Vincent Foster's alleged suicide and the Whitewater Development Corporation scandal had anything to do with *Mena?* Anyway, amongst others that were involved in this operation were 'George Bush Senior, Oliver North, Dewey Clarridge (CIA Agent), John Pointdexter and Caspar Weinberger'."

"Ironically," Sarge continued to connect the dots as all the major

COMPASSION, MERCY AND THE CONFESSION – PLUS

players (*the Elite Powers That Be*) are interconnected in cahoots; "Barry Seal was assassinated on February 19, 1986 in Baton Rouge, Louisiana. Unfortunately, this put an end to the most important investigation in history of the USA involving the DEA. Seek and you will find who he was willing and wanted to testify against. And it is no surprise whose names popped up in the investigation of his assassination and their possible involvement. Guess whose private phone number was found in Barry's wallet when he got shot? If you do a Google Search on Drugs & Mena, you will get sick to your stomach; an *Immaculate Deception*."

"JFK's assassination made me sick to my stomach!" Henry was livid. "Did you see the documentary that the CIA doesn't want you to watch?"

The Amigos shook their heads --- No as Henry continued. "It is entitled: 'The Garrison Tapes' by John Barbour. You can see them exclusively on Mark Allin's website http://www.AboveTopSecret.com. Ironically, no other source of media will show this but you have a right and ought to see it! Check it out at http://media.abovetopsecret.com/media/1956/The_Garrison_Tapes_Part_1/."

"Incidentally," Henry added, "both JFK and Abe Lincoln believed in our *Country's Constitutional Power* to create and issue its own currency / money; without going through any *Privately Owned Bank* and both got assassinated? President Lincoln wanted to issue the '*Greenback Dollar*'. And, President Kennedy issued an *Executive Order # 11110*; that would strip the *Federal Reserve Bank* of its power to loan money to the US Federal Government, which would put it out of business."

"That's it!" Max yelled. "America should declare bankruptcy, tell the *Federal Reserve Bank* and its cronies to go *Fuck Them Selves* and then print its own money backed by the *Will of Its People*; ingenuity. In all honesty, what is money or credit for that matter if it is not based on *Trust*? I sure as hell don't trust the *Federal Reserve Bank*. Our forefathers printed '*In God We Trust*', on our money."

Both Henry and Sarge were amused, yet infuriated at the same

◀ SOCIAL SECURITY

time since destiny is corrupted by such evil pukes. Especially when 9 trillion dollars cannot be accounted for by the Federal Reserve Bank? Thus Sarge exclaimed: "Ron Paul proposed a bill to audit the Federal Reserve (HR 1207) and it now has 179 co-sponsors, and the numbers keep growing! You should see the video at http://vodpod.com/watch/1612055-federal-reserve-steals-9-trillion-dollars and his website at http://www.ronpaul.com/on-the-issues/audit-the-federal-reserve-hr-1207."

Henry and Max promised that they would check it out. Suddenly, Max realized what old Abe Lincoln foreseen and shared it with his two buddies. "Lincoln issued *Greenbacks* because he was in a bind with the *Civil War* and he eventually realized who was really pulling the financial purse strings of America as well as the rest of the world; the *International Bankers*. He foresaw what was at stake and knew what was in store for us, we --- *The American People*; if he didn't act. Thus, he proclaimed:

'The government should create, issue and circulate all the currency and credit needed to satisfy the spending power of the government and the buying power of consumers..... The privilege of creating and issuing money is not only the supreme prerogative of Government, but it is the Government's greatest creative opportunity. By the adoption of these principles, the long-felt want for a uniform medium will be satisfied. The *taxpayers will be saved immense sums of interest, discounts and exchanges*. The financing of all public enterprises, the maintenance of stable government and ordered progress, and the conduct of the Treasury will become matters of practical administration. The people can and will be furnished with a currency as safe as their own government. Money will cease to be the master and become the servant of humanity. *Democracy will rise superior to the money power.*'"

Without a doubt, Henry interrupted as his adrenalin was a flowing, and his brain was thinking. "We are in a bind today. And by the way," he excitingly proclaimed incidentally: "ironically, JFK's executive order was never directly reversed, but in 1987, Ronald Reagan signed Executive Order 12608; which revoked a key section of Executive Order 11110, essentially nullifying it. – (http://www.ronpaulforums.com/showthread.php?t=135003)."

"BUT any president can reissue another Executive Order and reinstate it or modify it; to get this country out of the fucken mess that we are in. That is if he has the balls to implement or enforce it. It gives the *Treasury Department, the Constitutional Power* to create and issue currency - money - without going through the *privately owned Federal Reserve Bank*."

"Unfortunately," he continued, "it must be too risky for any president to chance it as the *Elite Powers That Be* can get away with murder? The *Immaculate Deception* is a *Powerful Intimidator* as President John Kennedy's murder was the biggest *Cover-Up* in US history. The *'lone assassin' / 'Magic Bullet'* theory; is plain bullshit."

"Conspiracy seems to get the job done." Sarge surmised. "But, I don't believe in coincidences. Especially considering whose names and connections; keep popping up. Did you know that John Kennedy Jr. was going to run against Hillary Clinton for Senate in New York before his death in July, 1999?"

The guys shook their heads no. "Unfortunately, Sarge continued, "he died in a mysterious plane crash? Ironically, it was ruled an accident, but further investigation will prove contrary. You would be shocked if you knew the actual facts and what he was up to. Check it out on the web some time. http://whatreallyhappened.com/RANCHO/CRASH/JFK_JR/jj.html. You'll also learn some startling facts about the Watergate break-in and its relation to the death of his father JFK. Nixon resigned to protect just WHY the crime had been committed."

"What was Kennedy Jr. up to besides deciding to run for Senator?" asked Henry.

"Well, for one," Sarge replied, "John Jr. was the only Kennedy to publically acknowledge that he believed a conspiracy in his father's death. In fact, he published an article by Oliver Stone, in his magazine, *George*, about assassination, conspiracies, and lying history books. And John Kennedy Jr. vowed in his last editorial in

"George"---'the fight against the forces of evil this summer.'"

"It sounds as if he was fed up with all the bullshit." Henry surmised. "Just like we are now; *God Bless his Soul*. The mere threat of entering politics and exposing evil-doers via a national magazine is a bold statement. He must have ruffled some feathers. I'm sure he wanted the Truth to be known or at least confronted and then; he's dead? Go figure? He must have been on to something? Perhaps he was a threat to the *Powers That Be*, the same *Bastards* that killed his father!"

"Damn Straight." Max fumed as this pattern of historical injustice was absurd; sad prime examples of powerful positions that seem to be above the law as they coordinate to cover their asses. "If you really want to get sick, you should read: 'Circle of Death: Clinton's Climb to the Presidency by Richmond Odom'. And by the way, there were more deaths after his book was published." he cried as he worried about the future of *Humanity*. *What evil lurks in our own government* he wondered as he quoted *Herbert Hoover's warning?*

"'We may commit suicide from within by complaisance with evil, or by public tolerance of acceptance with evil, or by cynical acceptance of dishonor. These evils have defeated nations many times in the past'."

"Abuse of power is ghastly evil, contrary to *Humanity as Trust is Sacred*." Henry assured lividly. "Ironically religions con us out of our money in exchange for *Hope* as they prey upon our guilt and shame while the politicians rob us blind. And, let us not underestimate science and technology."

"I was reading through some old magazines at the public library just last week and I came across several articles that are eerie by today's perspective. 'In 1931, *Nikolai Bukharin*, president of the *Soviet Academy of Sciences*; addressed the *International Congress* on the *History of Science* in London with this question: 'shall science enslave the masses or serve them?'"

"Go Figure? Food for thought as class does have its privileges. Today, health insurance determines treatment as disease is a multi-billion dollar industry. Unfortunately, prescription drug manufacturing is a highly lucrative business with almost no competition; thanks to the merger of Bristol-Myers with Squibb?"

"Instead of trying to wipe disease out; they are pushing pills to maintain and control diseases; with side-effects that are worst than the disorders themselves. How many of us in this *Commune*, have family members and or friends; that are fucked-up for the rest of their lives or almost died not to mention those that did die because they trusted their doctor? God bless their souls."

Both Sarge and Max agreed as they reminisced in anger. In fact, most of the *Commune* did know of somebody that was affected in some way or another if not them selves. It is very sad when you can't trust your doctor.

"It's a damn shame that our so called FDA does such a shitty job." Sarge was adamant. "It's awful scary. Perhaps its (FDA's) people that are in charged should be held responsible. Ironically, they approve some shit and disapprove possible *Miracle drugs* that are being used in other countries; with no side affects what so ever. But then again, money talks in this elite world of the *Powers That Be*."

"The bastards approved Aspartame," *he continued*, it's an artificial sweetener which is substituted for sugar in our diet sodas / pop, gum, foods, etc. Scientific study proves that it is poisoning people world-wide. It is accused of being the major cause for all kinds of disorders and diseases."

"According to researchers and physicians studying the adverse effects of aspartame, the following chronic illnesses can be triggered or worsened by ingesting aspartame: Brain tumors, multiple sclerosis, epilepsy, chronic fatigue syndrome, Parkinson's disease, Alzheimer's, mental retardation, lymphoma, birth defects, fibromyalgia, and diabetes. The book 'Prescription for Nutritional Healing,' by James and Phyllis Balch, lists aspartame under the category of 'chemical poison'.

Aspartame is also responsible for very serious adverse reactions including seizures and death. Other documented side effects that have been reported to the FDA --- over the years include: headaches

SOCIAL SECURITY

/ migraines, dizziness, seizures, nausea, numbness, muscle spasms, weight gain, rashes, depression, fatigue, irritability, tachycardia, insomnia, vision problems, hearing loss, heart palpitations, breathing difficulties, anxiety attacks, slurred speech, loss of taste, tinnitus, vertigo, memory loss, and joint pain."

"In fact," Sarge presented his case convincingly, "doctors are testifying against it internationally; in courts and in front of governmental authorities, but to no prevail --- so far in the USA. But that is about to change; according to http://www.mpwhi.com/main.htm. It is banned in a few countries."

"Don't forget about the so called preventive vaccines." Max fumed. "My nice is all messed up with *Autism*. She was perfectly fine before she got a couple of vaccinations?"

"My great nephew was medicated. Henry admitted sadly. They said that he was *Hyperactive* and labeled him as / or accused of having an *Attention Deficit Disorder (ADDA)*. I got him out of that school after I seen a powerful documentary entitled: 'GENERATION RX' by Kevin P. Miller."

"It opened my eyes. It investigates the collusion between drug companies and their regulatory watchdogs at the FDA and focuses on the powerful stories of real families who followed the advice of their doctors - and faced devastating consequences for doing so. You should check it out at http://www.generationrxfilm.com/synopsis.htm."

"Kids Need Plenty of exercise, *Love*, attention and understanding;" Sarge interjected, "*Fresh-air, Nature;* a good old fashion game of tag or hide & seek, kite-flying, sports, etc. They don't need those medications; they have to burn off an extra excess of energy. Like Clarence always says; '*they need plenty of Love and Understanding.*'"

"With all of the anger, violence and uncertainly parading in this world today; children are getting stressed with anxiety, depressed and confused as adults are fucking up their world to be." Henry surmised. "Coping is but a struggle on a daily basis; especially with the threat of massacres in their schools."

COMPASSION, MERCY AND THE CONFESSION – PLUS

"Unfortunately," Max analyzed, "Both adults and children are being treated for depression in order to cope? Depression can be very serious but these drugs can be addicting and some can cause suicidal urges; especially in teenagers. When I feel depressed, I too, get a *Longing for Nature*; fishing, bird-watching, a walk in the woods or perhaps a round of golf. A Breath of fresh air works wonders for the soul. Outdoor activity is a *Blessing* in disguise as these simple solutions clear my head. So, why is everybody pushing so many drugs to get by?"

"When I got mad as a kid;" Max continued, "I took it out on the baseball. If I acted out of line; I got my ass kicked. If kids act up today; they get sent to a shrink?"

"Doctors get a percentage from the drugs that they prescribe, a residual income." Sarge enlightened. "Years back, when my *Mother* was still alive; it got to the point --- when I had to rush her to the hospital. She was so doped up; taking thirty different pills from five different doctors? She almost died. The hospital contacted all the doctors involved and it was a mess. There were no *computer RX* records back then. Even today, drug stores lack a data-base to communicate; in order verify if a prescription was filled for a specific person or not. Alas God only knows how many die each year because of dangerous drug reactions and counter actions to multi-drug combinations?"

"People are dying for no reason." Max's temper boiled out loud. "We trust our doctors and the pills that they give us; are killing us? People, especially our children, are being subjected to and injected with deadly mercury and other toxins? Wake up; the "Mad Hatter" went crazy--- from mercury poisoning! This is like some population control?"

"We buy over the counter drugs; such as the 'PM' drugs and our livers get fucked up?" Max was beside himself. "Far too many people are taking high profile advertised diet pills; which are constantly being recalled, because they too are fucking up people's livers; because they are dietary supplement and its manufacturers, are not required to seek FDA approval."

"And then," he continued: "we have far too many people dying because they have no health insurance and therefore can't afford

SOCIAL SECURITY

to seek health care. It is a senseless disgrace in this 21st Century! Unfortunately, people don't realize that there are many natural remedies for disease; instead of pills; alternative medicines."

"Health care is bankrupting this country!" Henry fumed aghast. "We need an affordable *National Health Care System*. Medicaid is fraught with fraud. If doctors lost their license for illegal billing practices; that would surely make them think twice. No ifs, ands or buts. Just don't do it!"

"The country is already bankrupt!" Sarge assured sadly. "We can't afford the interest on our *National Debt,* let alone support the two wars on terrorism."

"We were bankrupted by design." Max insisted. "In the name of a *New World Order*, the elite *Powers that Be,* wish to establish a *One World Bank;* ultimate command and control of the masses. We have been served a calculated agenda of false hope via deception and or fear; with greed as the ultimate bait as corruption, conned the world."

"*When Will Americans Wake Up?*" Henry wondered out loud. "It's hard to grasp, perhaps even harder to interpret yet understand, but someday *Wonderland,* will take on a new meaning as mankind stops wondering and --- '*I'll be judge, I'll be jury'. Said cunning old Fury; 'For I'll try the whole cause and, condemn you to death.'*"

"*Glory Be When the Voice of Dissension Speaks Loud & Clear!*" Sarge Yelled.

"Societies come and go." Max replied. "Governments fold and unfold accordingly as greed, apathy and deprivation --- *Ignorance*, takes its toll. For people are the backbone of both society and government. Thus, government better take care of its people or else."

"The government is turning its back on us." Sarge interrupted. "They cut welfare and *Medicare* and promote gambling and *Corporate Welfare*. I often wonder where all that state lottery money really goes. Here in New York, it is supposed to go for education, but I don't think so."

"We pay taxes upon taxes. Where does all that generated income actually end up? Why did we ever allow the US Government to use money from the US *Social Security* funds; for the general funds?

COMPASSION, MERCY AND THE CONFESSION – PLUS

Why do we allow *US Corporations* to set up their *Headquarters* overseas as they avoid paying *US Taxes*?"

"Soon our *US Social Security System* will run out of money and nobody wants to address this problem? But, it is a *crisis* and it better get acted upon --- Soon or else? Can you imagine? Talk about an uprising? Perhaps our government should run a *National Federal Lottery* to *help support* our *Social Security System.*"

"Unfortunately," Sarge continued, "our whole income tax system needs an overhaul. It has so many advantages that benefit the rich and the almighty corporations. Ironically, the tax code has so many different questionable possibilities that even the IRS and tax experts can't agree on certain issues? Do you know what I mean?"

"Yep; I, I, I, hear ya!" Henry agreed as he was fuming inside and Max nodded with a disgusted look on his face. "Perhaps we should redefine the term --- *Enemy of the State*? For who's State is it any way? Whose Government is it? Economically, the USA is fucked as there is indeed a fine line between *National Security* and *Corporate Security* and, that line is *Greed*; the *Commonwealth of the Elite Few*. Why they can't even account for the *$700 Billion TARP Bailout Bill*? They aren't even sure where a lot of that money went?"

"It is insulting, blatant stupidity --- when the people entrust their *Faith and Fate to the Powers that Be*; for all the wrong reasons." Max assured. "*Abuse of Power* is evil and irresponsible. No government can survive if it continues to avoid issues or turn its back inhospitably on its citizens. A sure tell tale sign is when a Government addresses --- social, economical and political matters as *Law and Order* problems; self-serving excuses of *Special Interests*, to maintain control in the name of *Secrecy and Shame.*"

"Beware of a *Government* that doesn't meet expectations or maintain confidence." Sarge warned. "Eventually, the majority always wakes up from *Wonderland*. Someday mankind will stop wondering why *Social Injustice*, exists on this *Planet of Plenty*. Why inequality exists. Beware of the *Fury of Poverty*. There is no greater motivation than *Hunger --- Momentum of Survival.*"

"It's the fucken lobbyists, corrupt politicians and bankers as

◂ SOCIAL SECURITY

well as *Wall Street;* an elite den of thieves, that caused this mess." Max elaborated. "And now, poor President Obama has his hands full dealing with the fallout of our economic bomb from fraud, bad investments, bad judgments as well incompetence; reeking --- havoc; as foreclosures, failed banks, frozen credit, failing corporations, loss of jobs and the jeopardy of the 'Big 3 Auto Makers'. If Obama can't get our political pukes to act soon, we will have a *One World Bank.*"

"Greed has become contagious as it is a *Dog Eat Dog World.*" Henry joined in. "I hope this $800 Billion Stimulus Package ensures long term economic growth. *Abe Lincoln* envisioned America:

'...this nation under God...; with its democratic principles as --- The Last Best Hope of Earth!'"

"He also had a horrific fear," Sarge warned,

"'The money power preys upon the nation in times of peace and conspires against it in times of adversity. It is more despotic than monarchy, more insolent than autocracy, more selfish than bureaucracy. I see in the near future a crisis approaching that unnerves me and causes me to tremble for the safety of my country. Corporations have been enthroned, an era of corruption in high places will follow and the money power of the country will endeavor to prolong its reign by working upon the prejudices of the people. Until the wealth is aggravated in a few hands and the republic is destroyed.'"

"How ironic is it that Abe fought so hard to free the slaves and now we have the first black president of the US; facing his horrific prediction?" Henry surmised.

"I think we shall see riots, chaos, depression and a revolution before we see a *One World Bank.*" Max was adamant. "Communism fell and now, it seems as if capitalism is hanging by a thread. What's next, socialism?"

"Is it any small wonder why capitalism defeated communism?" Henry asked more livid. "Ultimately, in 1959, Soviet leader *Nikita Khrushchev vowed* that: '*Deception and drugs are our first two strategic echelons in the war with capitalism.*' Mysteriously, somehow, some way --- the elite powers that be, '*the imperialists*'; have managed to turn his theory into a reality?"

"Perhaps they joined forces so to speak --- the chosen few and chosen few; in the name of profit as capitalism thrives on drugs and deception; deceives and betrays the public of the entire world. Welcome to our nightmare --- *Inhumanity*; impunity of the evil elite as greed has escalated from reason to madness."

"Perhaps," Sarge advised, "perhaps it's no small wonder that the world has mixed feelings about America? Thanks to our political, economical and diplomatic actions per corporate motives. Can you spell sanctions? Are we not responsible for our government? Isn't out government supposed to answer to us --- *We the People?* "

"Unfortunately," he continued, "war generates money. Ironically, obsolete / inferior weapons are a gazillion dollar enterprise. Some like to play god as they play one country against another for *Special Interests*. But," he warned sadly, "nuclear weapons are a different animal which jeopardizes life itself."

"Thus, *Hanson Baldwin's* CFR address best be heeded. *'We have opened for all time the lid of Pandora's Box of evils. We cannot push the genie back into the box. We may not like it, but we must face it. Atomic bombs, biological agents and other weapons of mass destruction are now a permanent part of man's society; and no perfect physical system of control is possible for all these weapons.'*

Both Henry and Max nodded in agreement. Suddenly Max began laughing. Sarge and Henry were both offended as the topic was no laughing matter. Perhaps that's why they say not to discuss politics or religion when you are drinking.

"What's so funny?" Henry asked bitterly.

"A poem that I wrote a few years ago; do you want to hear it?"

"Poetry," Henry sighed shaking his head?

"Go ahead, spit it out." Sarge gave permission.

CAPITAL HILL

(The show must go on)

Our government is the circus.
Our politicians are the clowns.

> The press has a field-day with the coverage.
> We, the people are the audience.
> The performance is sad, entertaining and quite amusing.
> But, how long can it go on?
> Who's going to pay for production?
> And, what will the ultimate price literally be?

"Precisely," Henry exclaimed! "President Obama better heed *Abe Lincoln's* prophetic warning about *'enthroned corporations'*. Are we not in; *'an era of corruption in high places'* as he predicted? Is the *'money power of our country endeavoring to prolong its reign by working upon the prejudices of not only our people'*, but people all over the world?"

"*'Will the wealth be aggravated in a few hands'*? And, will our *'republic be destroyed'*? Who stands to profit from this emerging so called *New World Order; International-Imperialistic-Corporations*? Will Average Joe or Mom and Pop stores be able to survive in spite of major corporate control?"

"Enough is enough --- already." Max interrupted. "If he doesn't straighten this mess out soon; we, the *Amigos* best enlist Chi and take action and lead a march on Washington with both the young and the old in the *Name of Humanity*. Or else, someday soon, the shit is going to hit the fan literally. We can no longer deny *Truth*."

"Unfortunately, denial is inexcusable ignorance." Henry added all the evidence. "War, oppression, injustice, inequality, corporate welfare, hatred, racism and exploitation are *Divine No No's*. Political and economic-tyranny are *Divine No No's*. Poverty is absurd in this age of abundance. It's unbelievable?"

"Freedom entails responsibility, "Sarge warned." Man is responsible for each other. Arrogance is insulting, detrimental and, counter-to purpose and principles of *Humanity*. What we have is but a *Semblance of Freedom*. They want to control us like a herd of cattle."

"Ironically," he continued, "far too many walk around shaking their heads in disbelief like a bunch of confused idiots. Is it any wonder why so many feel desperate and depressed? Unfortunately,

COMPASSION, MERCY AND THE CONFESSION – PLUS

they know that they are getting fucked over and lied too. But they either choose to ignore or deny; by convincing themselves that: *I can't do anything about it?* People seem to be shell-shocked by insecurity and uncertainty."

"It's as if we are becoming programmed robots." Max agreed as he remembered some years back; a story on national TV about a corporation that just implanted a microchip, the size of a sliver with medical data on it in the arm of the inventor. He shared the details with his pals.

"His history can be read on this microchip with a scanner and it works. Soon thereafter, they wanted to market it further as they proposed it for kids as a safety precaution to keep track of them as well as old folks whom are senile or dementia. There was also talk about it being used for airport security workers as well as nuclear power plant personal."

"It sounded good at first, but what else would it lead to? Thank God that a group of people got together and did some investigating. They found out that some rats got cancer from this invention and the company's stock is now worth pennies on the dollar."

"Oh yeah, I remember hearing about that." Henry recalled. "Their stock was very hot at first and going through the roof. I almost bough some of it, but I had my own ethical doubts. I remember there was also talk of a *National ID Card* and that scared me to death."

"I then wondered how long it would be before it was mandatory; before we were all required to have a chip embedded in each of us as well as a *National ID Card*, for our own safety or shall I clarify --- keep track of us like a herd of cattle? Would our financial data be required, race, sexual preference? What about our religion, our medical records, etc. etc.? Would they also be required information?"

"Would we be able to buy or sell without the 'Mark of the Beast'; as the Bible predicts? 666? I'm glad that I turned my stocker broker's advice down."

Suddenly Sarge interrupted, "PU! It stinks; it's as if every day is like *Thanksgiving.*"

"Thanksgiving," echoed out of the two *Amigos* mouths --- simultaneously?

SOCIAL SECURITY

"You guys never heard the *Thanksgiving story?*" Sarge asked as they looked so dumbfounded, shaking their heads no.

"Well then, let me enlighten you."

PU ---- Shameless

It's Thanksgiving Day, and Papa Tony is carving the turkey. His whole family is sitting at the dining-room table watching him. Suddenly, Papa Tony lets out a loud, smelly-old-fart. Some laughter breaks out.

"You a Pig You," Papa Tony says, shaking his finger at Grand-ma!
"You gotta No Shame?"

Grand-ma puts her head down with instant tears in her eyes; hiding her face. Uncle Joe laughs and shouts:

"Let's all have a Toast to Grand-Ma!"

They all drink their wine and dinner goes on as if nothing had happened.

"Poor Grand-ma," Max sympathizes.

"Poor us; is more like it." Sarge corrected. "How can we pretend that our government; is *A-OK* when in fact; it is corrupted by lobbyists, soft money, international capital, loopholes and technicalities. We laugh at *Plausible Deniability* but someday mankind will be crying; as *Anarchy* is a *Real Possibility.*"

"Class has it privileges." Henry admitted. "But, necessity speaks for itself. You have to fight for your rights or else you're fucked. *The Haves* best help the *Have-nots;* or else this country will be divided. Have we forgotten that; our country, the USA, was founded on dissension and conspiracy?"

Then, Henry recited the beginning of the **Declaration of Independence:**

'When in the Course of human events it becomes necessary for one people to dissolve the political bands which have connected them with another and to assume among the powers of the earth, the separate and equal station to which the Laws of Nature and of Nature's God entitle them, a decent respect to the opinions of

COMPASSION, MERCY AND THE CONFESSION – PLUS

mankind requires that they should declare the causes which impel them to the separation.

We hold these truths to be self-evident, that all men are created equal, that they are endowed by their Creator with certain unalienable Rights, that among these are Life, Liberty and the pursuit of Happiness. — That to secure these rights, Governments are instituted among Men, deriving their just powers from the consent of the governed, — That whenever any Form of Government becomes destructive of these ends, it is the Right of the People to alter or to abolish it, and to institute new Government, laying its foundation on such principles and organizing its powers in such form, as to them shall seem most likely to effect their Safety and Happiness....'

(Check it Out http://www.ushistory.org/Declaration/)

"They best come together soon." Max agreed. "Somebody better address and challenge / modify the greedy evil corruptions before it's too late. Laws must evolve just as man evolves. Some precedents are obsolete and many new ones have to be established."

"But," he continued with troubling concern, "lawyers and judges are just too damn closed minded, busy, corrupt, and or obsessed with the past? Even constitutions must evolve; conform to their time. And, why are *Federal Judges Appointed for Life*? If Obama doesn't address these issues, our current *Troubles*; then we must question authority."

"Damn straight." Sarge agreed as Henry nodded.

"Unfortunately," Henry shared a bit of advice that he read in a book entitled: *'When Heaven and Earth Changed Places'*, by Le Ly Hayslip, "Man can no longer afford to: *'Put material things above people, vengeance before love and greed before God'*."

"Denial," he continued, "is the *anti-Christ*, which ensures hypocrisy not democracy. The world is so fucked up cause man made it that way through manipulation, exploitation and deprivation as *Greed* interferes with *Need*. Mankind best heed her warning."

"You guys are all talk and no action." Clarence interrupted the conversation.

"How long have you been there?" Max asked with surprise.

"I forgot my glasses and got mesmerized by your discussion. You

SOCIAL SECURITY

guys were so engrossed that you didn't even notice that I was here. So I copped a squat and eavesdropped. It is very interesting, so profound and yet scary. So what are we going to do about it?"

"What do you mean?" Sarge responded abruptly.

"Hey, we conquered *Hell*. Didn't we," he replied? "United, we addressed the issues and got involved. We took the time and energy to make change. But these issues are of a greater magnitude. It is becoming a matter of *Survival*. Let's devise a game plan. *Glory Be When We, The People Unite, Get Involved And Act!*"

"Don't get wrong, *America is the Greatest Country in the World!* But, we sold our souls to the devil. We as a *Nation* are so far in debt; I feel sorry for our Kids and Grand-kids. The damn lobbyists, corrupt politicians and corporations are ruining the *American Dream*. Their disregard and or disrespect for the US *Constitution; the principles of which this Country was founded upon; is a National Disgrace*. They are taking away our *Freedoms* little by little and enslaving us economically."

"Unfortunately," he philosophized, "mankind in general has to do what he has to do; to survive. We are living in uncertain times. When people get desperate, they will resort to desperate measures; cunning, wit and not so legal talents."

"They will; that they will." Henry agreed.

"Ironically," Clarence elaborated, "audacity and arrogance can be devastating. The *'haves'* are vain and blinded by their very own vanity, living the life of *Riley*; lost in their own world of prosperity and contentment. While the *'have-nots'*; are also lost in their own little world of miserable desperate circumstances. Pre-occupied, they are frustrated; woe and sorrows as they are confronted daily with uncertainty that can seem overwhelming. Far too many times; too many of them have to decide whether to --- buy *food* or pay for their health insurance, the gas or electric bill as priorities vary accordingly?"

"Alas, they too are too busy as they hurry and worry about their own personal problems, daily reality; eking out an existence. They don't have the time or take the time or summon the energy to stop and think about how they can get involved. They've become careless about politics and ignore the audacity and arrogance of

COMPASSION, MERCY AND THE CONFESSION – PLUS

the so called system, not to mention the problems of the world; since they can't do much about it anyway."

"Furthermore, they desperately watch; wait and see and hope for better days. They are infected with doubt. They pacify their conscience by giving to charities and voting for our *two-party-farce*. Perhaps they pray and go to church. But, what else can they do? They believe that their fate is in the hands of *Destiny*. Someday, mankind will realize that we as a whole create our own Destiny."

"We too can watch with the best of them; wait and see and do nothing about it. But, as we learned from experience; silence becomes consent. Evil must be confronted --- always. We must demand accountability, in spite of plausible deniability and pretentious intentions. Governments are man-made by *We the people*. We must revive their Hope. We best inspire them to Unite. Together, we can make a difference before it is too late."

"It's our responsibility as the secular powers that be --- *Fear* the power of a crowd, the power of the people; the power of conscientious objection and discontent. United, we must take charge of our *Destiny*, again. We all have to take the time to get involved. Someday, *the Voice of Dissension Shall Speak Loud & Clear!*"

"United, *We the People* can demand change or make change by addressing issues; corruption, corporate greed and shady deals, poverty, *Humanity*, etc. etc. The world as we know it; is changing because of technology. Every year we are losing more and more jobs to foreign countries. We as a nation must adjust. We must start producing goods in this country again. *Energy* should be our *Top Priority*! We mustn't let technology do the thinking for us. We all have our own *Brain*."

"Perhaps technology is moving to fast for man to adjust to or comprehend. Granted, our world is getting smaller and smaller --- everyday as we are all connected; inter-net via computers, satellite TV, cell-phones, etc. etc. But, *Love* is the bond that shall sustain this connection. Love of Humanity; as we all have a *Heart*."

"*Love is the Law of Eternity*. Someday, man will practice Jesus' Golden Rule ---'Love God with all his heart, mind and soul and his neighbors as himself' --- *Literally*. Until then; the world will continue to be *Fucked Up*."

SOCIAL SECURITY

"Fuck that God shit." Sarge objected angrily again as he has his doubts about God. "Men created this mess and man must correct it. Unfortunately, far too many *citizens are uninformed and or illiterate about the particulars of our government.* But, a dog licks his balls because he can."

"Poverty, corruption, neglect and abuse all exist because we continue to allow them to exist. Ultimately, resistance of temptation is but a matter of preference. It is an option of choice; 'to do' or 'not to do'. Haphazardly, mankind has grown accustomed to and has taken a *Shine to Greed* in spite of the fact that Humanity is a matter of co-dependency. Compassion is vital to Humanity."

"Exactly my point," Clarence answered as he cited an *Old Jewish Proverb:* "'this evil that belongs to me, is my responsibility.' Too few take the time to scrutinize or study themselves as a source of danger which --- lingers inside of man --- *Himself*. Collectively, mankind as a whole creates *Destiny;* both good and evil as reason is responsible for cause and effect --- both consciously and unconsciously. Denial is evil as it ignores criminal intent."

"Man invented corruption and mankind as a whole *Fucked Up this World*. But fear not, as there is always *Hope. Humanity* is the Answer To and For *Humanity*."

"It is our *Duty* to do; what *ought* to be *done* or *else;* poverty and corruption will escalate until it is too late as both are our liabilities and obligations --- Always. WE must question authority and stand up for *Humanity*. *Humanity* is a *Cause;* which should *cause talk* and arouse awareness – world-wide."

"Unfortunately," Clarence continued, "Abe Lincoln, JFK, Dr. King, RFK and Malcolm X all got assassinated for getting involved as they fought for *Civil Rights*. God Bless their Souls. Human rights refer to the basic rights and freedoms to which all humans are entitled, including *civil and political*. We must muster the *Courage* amongst All of Us to make *Change*. We must be Willing to Help the Unfortunate Victims of Circumstances Beyond Their Control."

The other three guys just sat there in silence with tears in there eyes as Clarence preached *FDR's Message:* "*Glory Be:*

COMPASSION, MERCY AND THE CONFESSION – PLUS

' When the World is Free Everywhere, Free to speak and express himself, Free to Worship God in his own way, Free from Want and Free from Fear --- Everywhere, All the Time!'"

"Amen!" echoed' throughout the room as Clarence emphasized his thoughts about *Freedom and Truth*.

"There is a fine line between religion and politics. Perhaps *Gandhi* put it best when he came face to face with the *Spirit of Truth*. Thus, he proclaimed:

'To see the universal and all-pervading Spirit of Truth face to face one must be able to love the meanest of creation as oneself. And a man who aspires after that cannot afford to keep out of any field of life. That is why my devotion to truth has drawn me into the field of politics; and I can say without the slightest hesitation, and yet in all humility, that those who say that religion has nothing to do with politics do not know what religion means.'"

"Ironically," Clarence acknowledged, "I stopped at a local coffee shop last week and overheard a conversation that a few collage students were having and boy did they make me think twice."

"Why, what were they discussing," Max asked with wonder?

"They showed me two websites on their laptop and they blew my mind. I learned that in March, 2005; a secret meeting was held at Baylor University in Waco, Tex., between President Bush, Mexico's President Fox and Canada's Prime Minister Martin. *On their agenda was a plan to replace the dollar with the 'Amero' via 'The Security and Prosperity Partnership of North America' (SPP)*; a natural extension of the North American Free Trade Agreement (NAFTA)."

"This '*Amero*', is a new consolidated currency that is supposed to replace the U.S. dollar, the Canadian dollar, and the Mexican peso. In fact, the *Amero* was proposed by Robert Pastor; vice chairman of the CFR - *Council on Foreign Relations*."

"Wa wa what," Sarge was livid? "Just like the European Union and the Euro?"

"Maybe we should trade our dollars into pesos now?" Henry was concerned.

"They already bankrupted the USA." Max cried. "The people just

SOCIAL SECURITY

don't know it yet. Soon our dollars will be worthless. Then we can use them for toilet paper."

"Do you think it's too late Max?" Henry inquired sadly?

"Relax," Clarence tried to assure them somewhat. "Mexico is in worst shape than we are here in the US and its economy will probably collapse before ours. Why the hell do you think all of the illegal aliens are sneaking into this country?"

"Unfortunately," he added, "these illegal aliens are bankrupting California; especially because of medical health issues at hospitals. To add insult to injury, soon we are going to have to deal with all the drug wars and the gangs that are getting in and getting out of control. Someday, soon, we are going to need our *National Guard* to guard certain boarders of ours."

"But anyway, supposedly, immediately after the adoption of this 'Amero'; the living standards and wealth of the citizens in all three countries will be completely unchanged. However, as the devil is always in the details; ironically this North American Union, a so called *'trilateral partnership'*, is envisioned to create a super-regional political authority that could override the sovereignty of the United States on immigration policy and trade issues."

"In fact," Clarence continued, "The US Government even set up a website- http://www.spp.gov/; explaining this new security plan and details, pertaining to the movement of people, capital, and trade across the borders between the three NAFTA partners. And, there is also an 'Amero' website; http://www.amerocurrency.com/."

"And, the *Council on Foreign Relations (CFR)* is pushing for this trilateral approach. Rumor has it that the reason President Bush did not secure our border with Mexico; is that his administration was pushing for the establishment of this *North American Union*. Helter Skelter; the CFR has proposed the creation of a North American Customs and Immigration Service which would have authority over U.S. Immigration and Customs Enforcement (ICE) within the Department of Homeland Security."

"God damn those bastards," Henry cried out loud. "What the hell are they up to now? They do have a plan? Lincoln was right."

Clarence got up with his glasses in his hands and headed back

COMPASSION, MERCY AND THE CONFESSION – PLUS

upstairs. Half way up, he stopped and said: "I think we should all count our *Blessings* tonight; say a few prayers and think about making a difference while we sleep. It's our duty to get involved, but President Obama deserves a chance. Something is up and only time will tell."

"Perhaps," he continued; "perhaps we should concentrate on poverty? Let's declare a war on both drugs and poverty; which are hurting our children and ruining lives. Let's enlist the children in our *Cause* for *Humanity*. They are our *Future* and if we don't *Act Now; God Help Us.* "

Then he said, "Goodnight, my Amigos."

Sarge grabbed another bottle of *Jack* from behind the bar. He started to pour, but both Max and Henry declined as they had had enough. They were overwhelmed to say the least; Thomas' death, the threat of the sovereignty of the United States and almighty dollar; were too much to digest for one night.

They followed Clarence's lead and went up to bed. Sarge sat there all alone, sipping his double shot of bourbon on the rocks; in private gratification. He felt at *Peace* in spite of the fact that he just killed his friend and the frightening fate of America.

He was elated that he confessed his secrets as a heavy load was lifted from his chest. Ironically, he had no guilt about playing god and sending Thomas *Home* to 'the Keeper of the Stars'. Suddenly, he wondered if there was a God or two or three; as the *Universe* was so precise. He knew one thing for sure. He didn't believe in hell. For hell; was man-made; --- Korea, Viet Nam, *Prudent Paradise*. At least he had the privilege as he was instrumental in eliminating one.

He realized that evil was just *wrong living* as it is *Live* --- spelled backwards and devil was *Lived;* ---spelled backwards. He poured one more drink and went out to the porch to look up at the *Stars* and the *Moon*. They were so enchanting, so serene and picturesque. He *Loved* life in spite of its adversity, its mysteries, staggering contradictions and surprises.

"*Good Luck Old Buddy,*" he whispered as he held up his last shot in a toasting gesture and drank it down before he headed

SOCIAL SECURITY

upstairs to call Melvin and tell him about the *Good News* as well as the bad; Thomas' demise.

Upstairs, Clarence couldn't sleep as *death, corruption and the New World Order;* were on his restless mind. *The world seems to grow madder and madder by the day as all of his friends were dying. But, at least they lived a full life.*

Tears rolled down his face as he thought of his teenage son *William who died of a drug overdose when he was 18 years old.* Clarence never got over it. Peg caught him crying a few times as he blamed himself for not seeing the signs.

He told Peg that he felt that he should do something to help other parents prevent drug abuse. Perhaps now was the time? Clarence went to his desk and grabbed a small note-book and a pen.

Suddenly, he realized that *he had to get rid of Old Joe's Special Plants.* He was more determined now than ever before; to finish the short story that he started ten years ago entitled *Surprise.* He read what he wrote and liked it a lot. But, it needed some work.

He vowed to give it top priority; a pet project and finish it before he died. Then he said a few silent prayers and tried to fall a sleep. Unfortunately, he had too much on his mind as he remembered when *America got an unwelcome surprise as the 'Twin Towers' were destroyed in New York on 9/11.*

Terrorism hit home on that dark day as Americans got a rude awakening --- beyond belief. But in her unsettling time of crisis, we *RE-United --- Together in the Name of Patriotism;* in spite of our different beliefs. Life went on in uncertainty as the press prolonged fear --- world-wide as panic and disbelief focused on anthrax, a new house-hold word.

As always, poverty persisted as did corruption; however we Americans realized a different out look on life. The Evil-Doers caused chaos and confusion but they underestimated the American People.

Priorities changed as *Family and Friends,* hugs, hand-shakes and kisses became important again. In essence, reality set in as life is so fragile yet precious. Our *Flag,* our *Symbol of Freedom* was appreciated again. We were *Proud of Our Country* in spite of all of its faults.

COMPASSION, MERCY AND THE CONFESSION – PLUS

Clarence continued to toss and turn and returned as his mind wandered farther. He just couldn't shake the worldly troubles that were haunting his mind; *terrorism, war, corruption, greed*. Anxiety was beginning to take its toll as he pondered the future of mankind.

Who is going to pay for these sins? Who's going to pay for this war on terrorism; he wondered; our children? Our children are our future, but this world is so fucked up. They are overwhelmed by violence.

These wars in Iraq and Afghanistan will continue to cost the USA a fortune not to mention our 11 trillion dollar National Debt that continues to increase an average of $3.75 billion per day. Will the US survive? Will Mankind survive? Iraq's oil production was supposed to cover the cost of that war, but that is now dismissed as bogus?

Clarence's mind had a hard time trying to comprehend all these troubling issues facing our world today. He felt sorry for our troops. So many are being deployed for the third and some for their forth tour of duty --- overseas to fight for what?

He believed that it is just a matter of time, a short time before President Obama reinstates the draft. Especially when you consider the situation concerning Iran and Israel as well as the 'West Bank' and North Korea's statement that it is ready to declare war. Add the invasion of Pakistan by the Taliban; as they want their hands on their *Nukes*; to the mix and it is definitely a recipe for disaster if not World War III.

He cringed at his thoughts not to mention *all the temptations that corrupt our entrusted officials; the opportunistic hypocrites operating under false pretenses with hidden agendas*. Suddenly, *Ezekiel* entered his mind --- *'Without vision, the people will perish'*. Sarcastically, he had an eerie thought as he despised former vice-president Dick Cheney. Especially since he was reading (The New Pearl Harbor by Michael Ruppert) --- *Alas, what if the US did let them planes hit the Twin Towers, etc. on 9/11? Was that part of their grand plan?* Many believe that President Franklin D. Roosevelt and other high ranking members of our government let the Japanese bomb our ships at Pearl Harbor in 1941 on purpose; so that we would get into the war.

Ironically, guess who was on the board of directors of a company providing electronic security for the World Trade Center, Dulles

◄ SOCIAL SECURITY

International Airport and United Airlines on 9/11/2001, according to public records? Marvin P. Bush, former President George Bush's younger brother! Surprised? Coincidence?

The security company was called Securacom, but now it is named Stratesec and it was backed by an investment firm, the Kuwait-American Corp., also linked for years to the Bush family. According to its present CEO, Barry McDaniel; the company had an ongoing contract to handle security at the World Trade Center "up to the day the buildings fell down." The company lists as government clients 'the U.S. Army, U.S. Navy, U.S Air force, and the Department of Justice', in projects that 'often require state-of-the-art security solutions for classified or high-risk government sites'.

Clarence was outraged as he cringed again in anger in regards to all of this information that is available to anybody that is interested in investigating it further. *How*, he wondered and *why does the Bush family name keep popping up in such awful events*? But, what really bothered Clarence the most was when he remembered a shocking website about the *Bush Family*: http://www.oldamericancentury.org/bushco/bush_crime_family.htm, which painted an ominous picture.

Earlier that day, Clarence saw a video which featured Richard Gage's interview with KMPH Fox 26 in Fresno, CA, on YouTube; which added insult to injury. Architect Richard Gage is a member of the American Institute of Architects, and founder of Architects and Engineers for 9-11 Truth. He believes that the destruction of the three World Trade Center high rises on 9-11, were an inside job. He and 700 other architects and engineers have found evidence for explosive controlled demolition, and are calling for a new investigation. After visiting his site at http://www.ae911truth.org and watching the video at http://www.youtube.com/watch?v=oO2yT0uBQbM Clarence was convinced that 9/11 was a well organized plot to manipulate America into action.

He believed that the *Elite Powers that Be* loved to instill fear as a means to maintain control. But he also knew that they fear panic which is unpredictable. He continued to toss and turn as he tried to fall asleep and forget about uncertainty.

His thoughts were rambunctious as he fell into subconscious

dreamland —lost, astray, deep in a dark, enchanting forest. Confounded by doubt and fear, he chose to flee from our world, since it was so cruel and corrupt. Drifting away, running scared, angry, confused, bewildered, and yet entranced by this mystical woodland, he shouted out loud —

"Why, God? Why?" Suddenly, he saw an incandescent light, particles of hope, dancing, peeking through the thick trees ahead of him. Curiously, he anxiously hurried toward that radiant area. The closer he came to this brilliant glow, the brighter it got.

Finally, he was out of the woods as he reached his focal point in a most beautiful Garden of Ether / Eden, which he could have never imagined. Astonished, as he assimilated his attitude, attention, and awareness; he knew that he was on sacred Holy Ground, some harmonious realm — ineffable paradise.

Spellbound, he fell to his knees — mesmerized, amazed, overjoyed, and in a state of awe, beyond pure contemplation — exultation. Embraced by an exuberant feeling of Pure Perpetual LOVE —divine chemistry — he melted in rapture as he felt the presence of Sacred Holiness. His heart beat in tune with overwhelming yet soothing, soft music — bliss, which hailed from the Ultimate Divine.

Nonchalantly, he looked up into the sky, and there she was, totally refreshing and as clear as the full moon entertaining the darkest night --- The Virgin Mary, Mother of Jesus, hovering amongst a cloud, floating closer and closer toward him. She was so beautiful, so immaculate — a bare testimonial of the absolute as a luminous white aura surrounded her completely. In fact, she looked as if she were made of light.

Ambushed by relentless peace, happy tears rolled down his face. Her elegance was so bright that he felt unworthy to look at her. He turned his head away. He wanted to stare, but he couldn't until she assured him,

"Fear not; relax. Your heart is pure and you may look as your eyes won't hurt."

Ironically, she didn't talk. Their minds — in fact, their thoughts — were engaged in communication as if by some visible sound waves, vibrating, emanating, and attracting and exchanging together as if magnetized. Mental telepathy!

She smiled and told him,

"Your thoughts are true to your heart, and what you're thinking, is right and just."

Ironically, she warned, "time is running out, but the world isn't ready yet. Be patient. You will know when the time is right," she assured.

Then she quoted Apostle Paul: "'**Proclaim the Word; be persistent whether it is convenient or inconvenient...for the time will come when people will not tolerate sound doctrine'.**"

She finished by encouraging him to do his duty in the name of World Peace and Humanity.

"Soon," she promised, "the world will be ready, willing, and able as it is desperate for Love; so follow your Heart and Live your Dream!"

Overwhelmed and excited in a state of ecstasy --- an emotional overload of pure-high; he awoke with water in his ears and salt in his mouth. He wiped the tears from his face and gently shook Peg to wake her up and tell her all about his *Blessed Experience*. Half asleep, she replied:

"That's nice," and rolled over --- back to sleep.

Clarence was more determined than ever to; make a difference. He realized that he couldn't run away from the troubles of the world any longer. *Denial* is evil. Denial is the *anti-Christ*. He must rise to the occasion. He visualized a *World of Peace* in his *Mind's Eye* and *Now* was the time to go for it.

He vowed to do his homework and make a game plan. He would create a website to enlist the *Children* and their *Parents*, *Grandparents*, etc.; to *Get Involved*. Suddenly, he thought of *William Ellery Channing*; 'There are seasons, in human affairs, of inward and outward revolution, when new depths seem to be broken up in the soul, when new wants are unfolded in multitude; and a new and undefined good is thirsted for. These are periods when --- to dare is the highest wisdom.'

He smiled to himself as he knew that with a whole lot of *Faith* and a *Little Help* from his *Friends*, Chi and *B4HEART.com*, Thy Will, Will Be Done.

COMPASSION, MERCY AND THE CONFESSION – PLUS

In the morning, Clarence discussed his *Dream* with Peg. She had forgotten all about it as she didn't even remember; being woken up. Clarence refreshed her memory as he re-elaborated and she was fascinated.

Peg was proud as Clarence was so sincere and excited about the *Dream*. He showed her his notes and the manuscript that he started years ago. His book wasn't finished yet; but it was clear what he was trying to do.

She agreed with his website idea; www.B4HEART.com and promised to help him get it up and running. She also *Believed* that *United Together* with the *Help* of the other *Amigos* and the *Commune*; they could make a **Difference;** just as they did for *Social Security*. They decided not to tell the others until they got the website up and Clarence finished his story.

At breakfast, word spread fast that Thomas perished in his sleep. Nobody suspected the contrary. Clarence tried to call Chi to make sure about a will or if he had had any family, but he was in Mexico meeting with Carlos's family.

As far as anybody knew, Thomas had no relatives to speak of. He worked on cruse ships; his entire life. He would brag that he circled the globe several times and that he had kids all over the world. But, he never stayed in one place long enough to establish any relationships.

Originally, he was from Jamaica. His Father was an Irish Sea Captain whose ship was lost in a storm right after he married his Jamaican Mother. He died before Thomas was born. Hence, both Thomas and his Mother had a tough life and she too; died when he was young. Thomas worked many odd jobs until he got scared off by some *voodoo* when he was a teen and never went back. Something about some walking zombies?

Peg reminded everybody that he wanted to be cremated and have his ashes spread throughout *Marge's Paradise* in the *Garden of Remembrance*. She ordered two *Special Trees* to be planted, one in *Honor of Thomas* and the other in *Honor of Carlos*. Chi could make the necessary arrangements --- Tomorrow when he got back.

After breakfast, The Four *Amigos* took two vans over to Melvin's house and helped him pack. He and his Mother moved in that day --- to *Welcomed Arms and Smiling Faces*. Melvin's Mother, Viola was tickled pink. She had heard so much good about the place.

Both fit right in. Melvin moved into Sarge's room and Viola into Marge's old room. She liked her new motorized-wheel-chair and the fact that there were elevators to cruse the entire complex. The *Garden* brought tears to her eyes.

Rumor spread fast about Mel and Sarge; sleeping together. It was a hoot as there was some snickering and bickering. But, after all, Sexy Sarah was *Bi-Sexual* as was Jacques (AC /DC); who gave Melvin a double take. Sarge spotted it and gave him the *Evil Eye*.

Thomas was cremated two days later after a simple ceremony at *Social Security*. As it turned out, he had no known family and left all his money to the *Commune*, via a will which was entrusted to Chi. Old Joe planted the two new *Special Trees* near *Marge's Tree*. A week or so later, Thomas's ashes were scattered throughout *Marge's Paradise*.

One month later, there was a *Special-Surprise-Wedding* for Melvin and Sarge --- *Theirs*. Viola, arrange it all. She trick them into getting all dressed up; under the assumption that they were taking her to some fancy restaurant; in her new motorized wheel chair.

They became suspicious, when they seen Mel's Minister and others assembling together, chatting in the huge dinning room that was all decorated. Viola confessed when Melvin accosted her for an explanation. She gave each of them, their own matching silver *Wedding-Ring* and, *Her Blessings*.

Both Sarge and Melvin were overjoyed as she played the *Baby Grand Piano; Here Comes the Bride-s,* as her son and his *Lover* --- walked down the *Isle, Together as a Unit* in the *Eyes of God* in spite of the fact that it wasn't legal in the eyes of our laws.

Clarence held a toast to the newlyweds. He announced that the *Commune* would pay for their *Honeymoon in Hawaii*. Both Sarge and Melvin cried again as did Viola, Peg, Lucy, etc; etc.

An old friend of Melvin's; Adam was invited to the ceremony and sang a song entitled 'In My Mother's Eyes'. When he finished singing, there wasn't a dry eye in the place. It was a touching tear-jerker under the circumstances.

CHAPTER **Ten**

The Awakenings

Chapter 10   Thee Awakenings

While the newlyweds were away; Clarence worked tirelessly on his short story. There was a plane crash in a nearby town, where everybody on board died. It was such a tragic ordeal.

Mel and Sarge boarded their plane back home as their honeymoon trip ended. Mel was nervous about landing home in Buffalo's weather after last week's plane crash. Sarge tried to calm his nerves but his topic only made him more nervous.

He told Mel as he reminisced about his last trip to Hawaii: "I was stranded here a few extra days on 9/11 as the FAA shut down all airports in the US. It was so eerie; nobody knew what to expect next or how long we would be here? Confusion and silence persisted as everybody was trying to observe and understand what was happening. Tormented by uncertainty which fueled suspicion, everyone was nervous as fear was evident on everybody's face."

"When I got home, the flags that hung on all the houses gave me a sense of wonder as threats became reality. I wondered if this was the beginning of World War III. I even prayed --- God Bless America!"

"I seen it all on TV," Melvin remembered.

"I was in Paris at the time. I'd probably be there still; if my mother didn't get sick. But such is life as I found you because I came back home."

"I'm glad that we found each." Sarge replied as he reached for Mel's hand.

"I know that you don't believe in God, but you got to *Believe in Something*." Mel responded. "The 9/11 attack was awful shocking. Its terror was enough to drive us back to God and to each other as its evil united Americans --- Again! Unfortunately, America smelled blood; --- Its Own!"

"But these wars on terror could go on forever in the name of God or Allah; as Jesus' *Words of Wisdom* are ignored. Israeli and the Palestinians are obsessed with the biblical West Bank and the Gaza Strip; as tensions in the Mid-East escalate off and on year after year. The terrorists antagonize the situation as they call for a *Holy War* as other countries encourage and train them. They want the US right smack in the middle of a *Jihad* as the *Oslo Accords* are forsaken."

"War is hell. Man is blinded by religion." Sarge interjected. "But religion is man made. Dogma, ritual obedience in the name of fear, guilt, shame or even eternal damnation; it messes with people's heads. It's ludicrous when men declare war in the name of God. *Karl Marx* called religion: *'the opiate of the masses'; a medicine which contains --- Opium.*"

"Osama bin Laden and his al-Qaida terrorist network are a bunch of devils." Melvin agreed. "They are twisting a sacred religion to promote themselves. They degrade their women and brainwash their young with anger and hatred."

"Their children," Sarge warned, "will haunt us as they are conditioned to be *Anti-American*. Can you imagine a society where kids are forbidden to sing, fly kites or make snowmen? The Taliban regime is as corrupt as it gets as it ensures misery and poverty and abuses its youth and women."

"Their disregard for life is a tragedy; promoting suicide is insane." Melvin assured. "Life is a preparation for death, but all must respect life as *Life is Precious*. Life is God's gift to us so that we can learn to Love!"

"I do, I do *Believe in Something*," Sarge confessed again. "I just don't believe in religion. It's all very simple. I believe in *Love*. The bottom line is that *God is Love* and *Love is Truth*, which *Relates to All*."

"To ignore God as Love is a selfish abdication of responsibility to each other. God is not a double-edged sword, nor a pawn to be used in the name of man. The skeptics deny *Truth* as the sinister reinforce fear and despair."

"I Love You Roman!" Melvin replied.

"Me too," Sarge admitted as the stewardess brought them their breakfast.

The three *Amigos* were waiting for Mel and Sarge when they landed at the airport. They were sporting their ponchos and sombrous since it was 62 degrees; an absolute abnormality for Buffalo, New York in February. They had a surprise for Melvin and Sarge. It was Lucy's idea as she and Peg went shopping and bought an outfit for Mel. Lucy did the personalized stitching.

The guys insisted that both Sarge and Mel put their ponchos and sombrous on; which they packed into the trunk of Henry's old ragtop. Melvin was proud as Clarence handed him, his and welcomed him as the *Fifth Amigo*. Both of them had tears in their eyes as they obliged, then headed off to get their luggage.

On the ride back to *Social Security*; after they packed all of their suitcases in the trunk of the car, Sarge and Mel enlightened the guys with the details about their wonderful vacation. Melvin showed them the pictures and Max joked about Mel's pink Speedo's. As it turned out, Sarge bought them for him. Everybody laughed. Mel informed that they bought trinkets for the whole *Commune*.

They exchanged a bunch of small talk as well as the disastrous plane crash, abnormal weather for the past few days and the fact that Mel was nervous about landing until the pilot announced the forecast for arrival home. Henry got anxious and stated that he too was a bit nervous. He elaborated that he and Max were doing some serious thinking and research while they were gone as Clarence was too busy working on his book.

"We spent a lot of time on the internet and checked out the two websites that Clarence told us about. They are but; rude *Awakenings*."

"They are both troubling to say the least." Max stated alarmingly as he agreed with Henry.

"What are you talking about?" Mel asked with concern. "What websites?"

"He's talking about the Amerocurrency.com and the SPP.gov websites." Sarge reminded him. "Remember Melvin, I told you all about them."

"Oh, oh yeah, I forgot? It is scary, I checked them out too. I guess I was lost in the excitement of our wedding and getting ready for our trip."

"Well, anyways," Henry rein-formed. "It is frightening indeed; a real hush, hush operation. The media doesn't even mention either site. They are either ignorant or dumb as dirt as they ignore them."

"Censorship by ownership," Clarence assured. "They want to sneak it in; in spite of the fact that the websites are already up and when it happens; it's not their fault if --- *Nobody Challenged It*. Nonchalantly, they don't want to confirm it or deny it."

"They want a done deal." Henry insisted, "A smooth transition."

"Why doesn't the president address this?" Mel queried. "Perhaps he knows more than we ought to know? Maybe the *System* is on the verge of collapse? Maybe they fear the ultimate panic and then a run on banks; that goes out of control --- World-wide? Perhaps they are just stalling for time?"

"Whatever," Max insisted. "But, America as we've know her is about to change. Like always, '*The devil is in the details*'; somewhere in their evil scheme. The more I think about this, the more it smells fishy."

"Fear of the unknown is only natural," Clarence explained. "But, change is necessary as we are headed up *Shit's Creek*; knee deep. I don't know what they are up to and I surely wonder myself what the outcome will be? I never trust any government; however chaos and anarchy are scary thoughts."

"What is scary is the focus on their main detail itself. *The replacing of our USA's National Central Banks as well as Mexico's and Canada's National Central Banks with the North American Central Bank.*" Henry warned.

"Ah-ha," Sarge yelled, "That is a problem! We already gave up the *'Power to Coin Money and Regulate the Value Thereof'*, and that contributed to both conspiracies; which led to Lincolns' and JFK's death. Now, they want to take our Country's right to print *Federal Reserve Bank* money freely at will? How dare they?"

"The big question is: who will govern, control and oversee this so called new *North American Central Bank.*" Clarence tried to solve their concerns.

"And, what's going to become of our $11 Trillion Dollar National debt? And whose is going to pay for it and how? Better yet, who the hell owns it?"

Clarence paused for a minute as he scratched his head and then continued as the other *Amigos* sat scared into silence.

"Remember what Thomas Jefferson warned:

'Banking institutions are more dangerous to our liberties than standing armies. If the American people ever allow private banks to control the issue of their currency, first by inflation, then by deflation, the banks and corporations that will grow up around the banks will deprive the people of all property until their children wake-up homeless on the continent their fathers conquered.'"

"Slavery," Sarge asked shouting somewhat offended with grave concern in an alarming manner?

"Or indentured servants; to say the least?" he fearfully added."
No, No, No, Not if I can help it!"

"Only the white people," Henry joked as Sarge chuckled out loud with disgust. "Ha, ha, ha".

"It's no laughing matter!" Max reminded them. "One of the stipulations attached to this proposed merger of the banks is that all three countries must not incur persistent budget deficits."

"Or else what," Mel asked sarcastically yet, serious? "How the hell is the USA going to live within it means when *she* can't even afford the interest on *our National Debt* now?"

"And, what happens when the *US Social Security System* runs out of money because the *Powers that Be* squandered it?" Clarence inquired.

"These issues are *Cause for Concern* and shall surly lead to revolt and riots as chaos if not addressed sooner or later." Henry surmised. "It might even lead to another civil war; if states like Vermont opt to secede from the union?"

"They are prepared for riots." Max enlightened. "I was in several chat-rooms the other day and rumor has it that there are F.E.M.A. prison camps setup, stocked and ready to go throughout the entire USA on Federal bases; just in case. It's all part of the plan. It's an ugly scary thought."

"I also found some information about a man named Michael Maholy who after 20 years of serving the New World Order agenda for America from within the CIA and Office of Naval Intelligence; is spilling the beans. He has been hiding and remains underground now for 13 years. He decided it was *Time to Tell America the Truth. He* wrote a series of articles back in 1995-1996 entitled 'THE PIPELINE,' exposing names, locations and activities in the CIA drugs out of South America. Michael had been a major role player in the infamous CIA drug smuggling black ops in South America, (Columbia S.A.).You can read about him in 'Defrauding America' by former federal FAA inspector and whistleblower, Mr. Rodney Stitch. Check out http://www.defraudingamerica.com."

"In fact," Max continued, "Michael Maholy worked directly under pseudo-'Patriot' Ollie North and Bush Sr., then head of the CIA. When asked about the so called F.E.M.A. (Federal Emergency Management Agency) Prison Camps by Pamela Schffert, an investigative journalist with a Christian perspective; he replied: 'Oh, all of us in the CIA knows all about the concentration camps in America and their purpose! We all know that their purpose is to terminate 'resisters of the *NEW WORLD ORDER*' under *Martial Law!*'"

THE AWAKENINGS

"Pamela was blown away by Michael's blunt revelations concerning the *NWO* and their *Martial Law* agenda." Max was furious, "He not only elaborated on the *FEMA Camps* and their grim purposes. He confirmed many other reports that she was investigating; boxcars with shackles, guillotines and more."

But what scared Max the most was a new law that was signed by George Bush in October, 2006 in a private Oval Office ceremony. Public Law 109-364, or the 'John Warner Defense Authorization Act of 2007' (H.R.5122). It allows the President to declare a 'public emergency' and station troops anywhere in America and take control of state-based National Guard units without the consent of the governor or local authorities, in order to 'suppress public disorder.' Alas, the *President* can utilize the use of the *Armed Forces in Major Public Emergencies* and declare *Martial Law*.

The Amigos were shaken by his undertaking.

"Do you remember *Blackwater*; the corporate *Goon-squad / Mercenary firm* that our government likes to hire to do its dirty work?" Sarge asked. "They will surely be ready, willing and able to stand guard over *We the People* in these prison camps. Ironically, they sent our National Guard oversees and pay these guys, outrageous salaries as they mussel about with car blanch authority."

"They abused our citizens in New Orleans during and after Hurricane Katrina. Talk about outrageous. They will do anything for money."

"Yeah," Henry interjected, "they slaughtered and abused innocent Iraqi citizens for no reason if not paranoia. Our government finally agreed to turn a bunch of them over to the Iraqi Government; to stand trial according to Iraqi Law. Last week, they changed its name from *Blackwater to Xe*, but, that won't erase its history. Who the hell do they think they are?"

"Fortunately," Clarence interjected with *Hope*; "cooperation is the name of the game. *The Amero will never get off the ground without the cooperation of the peoples and the powers that be know this.* That is why Canada has established a special police unit, to enforce this project and Mexico has pledged both its military and their Federallies? All three countries promised to work together to realize this union."

"God help us," Melvin shouted as Henry turned into the gates of *Social Security*.

"I'm sure the Mexican citizens will cooperate, but," Clarence continued, "will the citizens of the USA or our servicemen for that matter; cooperate? Do you think that they will put their own family members in these prisons? No, I don't think so, but I do know that our government has been drafting people from all over the world; into our armies and making them citizens on the quick."

"It sounds like they are either getting desperate or have plans for these new citizens." Henry surmised.

"It sure should make us think twice." Sarge warned. "I remember an old Nazi tactic; how they enlisted local police and transferred them to other parts of their country in the name of Nazism / Patriotism / National Security and then, tricked and or black mailed them to do what ever they tell them to do; by either using their family members as hostages or by promising to take good care of them. What choice do they have? They surly know to run a police state by making people do ghastly things to enforce their ill will."

"Talk about a *Police State*; I went to the casino last week with my nephew Tim, who stopped in to visit me." Max butted in lividly. "He graduated last year and had a hard time finding a decent job so he joined the Marines. He stopped by to see me before he went off to boot-camp."

"'Semper Fi'," Sarge yelled, "God Bless his *Soul*. We're going to need him on our side."

"Amen," Echoed throughout Henry's vehicle as Max got back to his story:

"Well anyway, we went over to Canada to the Fort Erie Race Track & Casino. I won $300.00 bucks and took him to the *French Ballot* and then we tried to come home across the US Boarder. We had a hell of a time; getting back over into our own country."

"Why, what happened?" Melvin asked with concern.

"The US Custom Agent was a prick. We both had picture IDs,

our driver's licenses and my nephew had his birth certificate. He wanted to know why I left the USA without my birth certificate. I told him that I lost it over thirty years ago. I then showed him my VA Medical Picture ID and he laughed."

"He said that; *'it didn't mean anything.'* Who the hell does that young piss-pot think he is? That was a US Government issued identification card and my driver's license is a NY State issued identification card. What was he thinking? I had to show proof as to whom I am in order to get those two IDs in the first place."

The *Amigos* just sat there silently listening to Max vent.

"Don't get me wrong as I do understand that he was doing his job. But, I felt like I was being harassed. He checked me out on his computer and found nothing."

"I don't have any criminal record. No warrants out for my arrest and; he still gives me this shit. He was rude and nasty mean."

"He told me to *'either get a passport or an enhanced New York State Driver's License.'*"

"He then warned me, *'not to leave the country again without one or else!'*"

"He even went on to say that I was: *'now warned and this time; he would let me slide back in to my homeland as he was giving me a break.'*"

"I was afraid to ask or else what? I didn't want him harassing us any more. I heard that the custom agents have the authority to tear you car apart --- looking for drugs and that they don't even have to pay to fix it or put it back together for that matter. What's this country coming to; paranoia, Russia?"

The Amigos were all upset to say the least.

"They are trying to set a precedent," Clarence assured. "Actually, New York is one of the states that was chosen and agreed to be a guinea pig; especially since it is a boarder state. I heard that they just optioned this so called enhanced license a few months ago. It was supposed to be put into effect almost a year ago but was delayed for some reason."

"Let's go inside and check out this so called enhanced license

SOCIAL SECURITY

on the internet." Henry suggested.

They all agreed as they stormed the *Commune* and headed straight upstairs into one of the offices with a computer. The *Five Amigos* gathered together anxiously around the monitor, longing for answers. Mel typed in the words: *Enhanced NY Drivers License;* in the Google Search box; ounce he got the internet up and running. Then he clicked on the *NY State DMV* website option.

Sarge took over and when he clicked on the information about this new mandated *'Liberty'*, license, he got sick to his stomach.

"Hmm, it appears as if New York State is in fact one of their first attempts at a US Police State. The bastards have succeeded in issuing a recognized; National ID." he fumed as all of the *Amigos* were in shock.

Hence, low and behold, according to the NYS DMV:

'A NYS Enhanced Driver License (EDL) or Enhanced non-driver photo ID card are options available staring **September 16, 2008** *to NYS residents who are U.S. citizens. An Enhanced Driver License (EDL) serves as a secure driver license, identity document,* **proof of U.S. citizenship** *and* **NYS residence, and a Western Hemisphere travel document all in one.**

The information went on to state that:

An enhanced document can be used for **land and sea border crossings only**, *instead of a passport, as an accepted method of entry to and from the U.S., Canada, Mexico, Bermuda and the Caribbean. An EDL* **cannot** *be used for* **air travel** *to other countries.*

After doing a little more research on the net; they found out that this new enhanced license is optional for now, but it also has a *REID Chip* embedded into it. All information on this chip can be read instantly via a scanner. Reality set in as *National Security* was hard to grasp. Who or what are the potential threats and to whom or what are these dangers aimed at?

"What information is on this chip?" Mel asked. "How accurate is that information? What information will be on it in the future? And what legal rights do we have to see and challenge this information if any?"

The *New World Order;* was looking like a real possibility in the *Eyes of the Amigos.*

"The Elite *Powers that Be;* are close to realizing their dream." Henry warned. "They're not only laying the ground work; they are already starting to enforce policy? God Help us! I bet that our social security number is on all of these new licenses."

"Damn, I need a drink," Max insisted as everybody else agreed again.

When they got down to the bar; Sarge set up the usage, a round of four JD's and a red wine for Melvin.

"How far will this policy go?" Clarence wondered out loud. "They already have a strong hold on education and the so called free press. And, the damn lobbyists have their dirty hooks in both the democratic and the republican parties as they hedge their bets. It doesn't matter who wins anymore as money talks."

"The media makes a fortune from both campaigns." he continued. "Our system of checks and balances is a joke when our politicians get the checks and the lobbyists hold the balance. It's a willful betrayal of our trust."

"It's pretty sad when you have to learn to read between the lies." Mel objected with concern. "Our free-press / media is subjected to sanction by ownership while our educational system is curtailed through stipulations from foundations with grants and scholarships as our laws are bought and paid for. Society is meticulously cultivated as we are brainwashed by design."

"They seem to regulate everything but policy." Henry surmised. "Go Figure? It's sacrilegious when corporations get to regulate themselves and when the media needs press passes to be present at major press conferences; especially considering the possibility of planted press questions."

"How long," he continued, "will it be before the government reads our E-mails or sets limits on what we can say? How long before they tax and regulate the inter-net? Cyber Censorship? Will they be able to deny internet access to certain people that are deemed undesirable to their policies?"

SOCIAL SECURITY

"If we're not careful, the new anti-terrorists laws will eventually ensure a *Police State*." Max warned. "What rights are we willing to relinquish next; client-attorney-privilege, free speech? Are we willing to give up our *Civil-Rights* for *National Security*?"

"How long will it be before we have to give up our right to bare arms and turn all of our guns in?" Sarge was infuriated.

"Huh? Oh No, No, No, No," Max was adamant. "I sleep with El'Caramba."

All *Five Amigos* busted out laughing out loud until Mel riled them up again.

"I wouldn't be surprised if they try to regulate and limit ammunition; bullets, shotgun shells etc. With computers, they can keep track of how much ammo a person has in stock and set a limit on the amount that is allowed to be owned in a specific time period. With a few modifications, they put an expiration date on all legal projectiles and then require that they be turned in; if not used by that date. Thereby, if you ever get caught with outdated ammo or ammo that does not have a date on it; they could fine you and charge you with possession of illegal ammunition."

Suddenly, Sarge stands up and asks; "When are *We the People*; going to question policy, stand up to authority, the *Powers that Be*?"

"United we stand!" Clarence insisted.

"Divided, we fall." Max assured. "It should become mandatory that every US citizen carries a gun, if he so chooses; except for convicted felons. That would surely make people think twice before they act. We have the *Right to Bare Arms* so that we can protect ourselves from intrusion or invasion from any entity; be it a person or a country; including our own government, if it trespasses on our *Human Rights.*"

"Amen!" echoed from the mouths of the other *Four Amigos*.

"It's getting critical." Henry enlightened. "We must become the *Watch-dogs* of our *Liberties*. We must not tolerate corruption or injustice."

"Will they cry *Terrorism* every time somebody speaks out against

THE AWAKENINGS

government *Policy* or its special interests?" Mel asked sincerely. "In the name of the *National Security Act*; what is defined as treason? Whistle blowers? Will they be arrested or labeled as trouble-makers or instigators? Don't dictators regulate social behavior through fear and intimidation? Is slavery inevitable again?"

"Slavery is the epitome of evil. People are now enslaved by economics," Sarge was disgusted. "*Evil* is when any government or establishment --- in the name of god or any secular power that be; imposes its will or ulterior motives on others as it influences thinking so that it can control resources, especially money."

"Especially *Human Rights*," Clarence warned. "Basic necessities such as food, water, and shelter --- are vital to existence; *Survival*. Poverty ain't prejudice and it is at the *Mercy of Humanity*. Can you imagine if corporations got control of the world's drinking water?"

"I can't believe that people actually pay for bottled water today." Max chuckled. "If you told me fifty years ago that someday people would pay one or two dollars for a bottle of water; I would have laughed you off as crazy."

"With advertising, people are conditioned at will; especially the younger generation." Clarence clarified. "Ironically, in the beginning of civilization; it was a matter of survival to learn how to store water in containers. Today, it's a fashionable appeal and convenient. Corporations and cities are making a fortune selling ordinary tap water."

"People can be so naive." Henry agreed.

"Brainwashed by design," Sarge elaborated. "But remember what Benjamin Franklin warned: 'When the well's dry, we know the worth of water.'"

"Who's brainwashed," Peg asked as she and Lucy entered the room carrying a large welcome home cake for Mel and Sarge? They were followed by the rest of the *Commune*; anxious to see the newlyweds.

"Far too many of us," Clarence replied with a disgusting look on his face. He dropped the subject and did not elaborate because of all of the commotion; hugs and kisses, hand-shakes and small-talk, etc. etc. It was if they were gone forever.

Suddenly, Melvin ran out to Henry's convertible to retrieve one of the suitcases. He was excited about passing out all the small gifts for the *Commune;* an assortment of jewelry, hats and tee-shirts. But he was especially proud to present his new *Family* with a special plaque that he bought for them all.

Clarence hung it over the fire place; right next to the *Peace Pilgrim's Plaque.* Everybody loved it. It simply read: 'Live Well, Love Much, Laugh Often'.

They ate pizza and wings as part of their celebration routine and then, devoured the cake. Somebody put some music on, but Clarence turned it off and made an announcement. He told them that he had *had a Dream* and then he shared his *Blessed experience with them.* Everybody thought that it was a beautiful ordeal, but nobody understood its relevance or importance?

Clarence then told them that he wrote a short story entitled: *Surprise,* about a *Worm* named *Oouey Gooey;* that wanted to declare war on drugs and poverty and promote *Love and Peace World-Wide.* Everybody wanted him to read it out loud so; he went upstairs to his room to get it.

Subsequently, when he got back, he gave the loose-leaf book to Peg, whom volunteered to read it. She told her audience to get comfortable since it would take at least an hour and a half to oblige. One by one people scurried about like little children getting ready for a bedtime story. Most ran to the bathroom first and then, off to get pillows, blankets and snacks.

Twenty minutes latter, after elbowing for space, everyone was comfy and cozy; ready and willing to listen. Some were on the couches waiting anxiously, others stretched across the floor cuddling together like typical kids anticipating a feature presentation. Peg proceeded to recite from Clarence's manuscript.

Synopsis

Two cousins, Chi and Jimmy, spend their summer vacation on their Grandpa's farm in Western New York and get the surprise of their life. It is a defining moment as they get enlightened, thanks to Oouey via B4HEART — *Humanity Envisioned And Realized Together*. For *Oouey Gooey* is a simple worm with a simple plan — *Love!*

He believes in miracles as he pursues his dream. He is but a blessing in a state of grace that is opposed to drugs and devoted to peace. As an ambassador of hope and goodwill, he knows that *Children*, are our *Future* and that '*Hardcore Rap Music*' as well as aggressive video games and the glorification of acts of aggression portrayed via our main stream media; TV, movies, etc; have robbed us of a *Generation of Progress*, via violence, anger and hatred.

His mission is to start a revolution, a spiritual revolution to save mankind from greed, poverty, hunger, drugs, and corruption in the *Name of Humanity*. Intuitively, Oouey believes in a spiritual evolution — that someday mankind will in fact, be enlightened as we evolve to a higher state of *Moral Consciousness*.

He is not a democrat or a republican but an Earthling with a wife named Olga and twenty-three offspring. They live in the *Rose Garden* in Delaware Park in Buffalo, New York.

Oouey has a motto which he adopted from *Peace Pilgrim*; 'To Overcome evil with Good, falsehood with Truth and hatred with Love'. He wants to spread these words-of-wisdom, world-wide; via dialog and interaction. But, Oouey needs your help. So, spread the word to all of your friends about his mission and his website!

Chi and Jimmy make a pact and take a vow with Oouey as they promise to B4HEART and Declare War on the Drug Epidemic, which is infecting our cities and schools and ruining Families. — www.B4HEART.com

This is the first in a series of *Spiritual Enlightenment* for the whole family, with work progressing quickly on the follow-up. It carries a *Message of Hope* as it presents an opportunity with interactive substance, to make a difference; if you are willing to accept the challenge. It is both captivating and compelling as it demonstrates family and social values, little lessons in life.

Surprise, will move and inspire both child and parent as it entertains the simple joys of life --- *Fun; Nature* --- fishing, horsing around and worms; which leads to the ultimate surprise as *Oouey* prepares to make the world a better place for all to live in. Never underestimate the element of *Surprise*.

When Peg finished reading the *Synopsis*; everybody was quite impressed. They were proud that the *Commune* displayed *Peace Pilgrim's Words of Wisdom;* over their fireplace. Peg informed them that www.B4HEART was up and running *Live!*
They all wanted to get involved and were excited about their *NEW Mission*. Especially since Lucy passed out *B4HEART* tee-shirts for everyone. Clarence suggested that everybody stand up and stretch for a few minutes and put on their new shirt; if they wished. He was sporting his.
A few minutes passed as all sported his or her tee-shirt and Peg proceeded with *The Legend;* behind *Oouey's Mission*.

The Legend

It all started way, way back in the so-called *'Garden of Eden,'* with Adam and Eve, who *Oouey's Greatest Granddaddy*, Ebenezer Worm (whose name implies Divine Help or Deliverance) tried but failed to warn and enlighten. For he attempted to prevent and later conquer evil as he stuck his neck out of *'The Apple'* and shouted: "Excuse me, Madame," just before the *'Original Sin'* or first bite.

But, Eve was so intoxicatingly engrossed, so enthused and relished in the process that she didn't notice or see him, and she almost bit Ebenezer's head off. In fact, *Grampa Gooey* was too slow, and he lost his tail in the inevitable act. Thus, *'Curiosity'* is the *'Original Sin'* that led to the *'Logical Fall of Mankind'* per *'Choice'* or *'Free Will'*.

THE AWAKENINGS

Some say it was a miracle that he didn't lose his life in this historic event. But, perhaps God did have mercy on poor ol' Gramps since he was on a sacred mission; actually trying to warn both Adam and Eve with a slice of advice. For he knew of God's little secret. He knew that if man indulged in the *'Apple of Good and Evil;'* then man must also partake of the *'Tree of Eternal Life'*.

Unfortunately, since he didn't succeed in averting the misdeed, evil manifested, and *Grampa* grew aghast. To make amends, he spent the rest of his life trying to get both Adam's and Eve's attention. But, they were too proud and salacious to listen as evil persisted and escalated.

Thus, on his deathbed, in front of his entire family, he made them all promise and take a solemn vow to erase evil and pass the word on to their offspring. Hence, *Oouey* believes that he was deemed by fate as a duty to fulfill his Greatest *Grampa's* death wish — to avenge the *'Logical Fall of Man'*.

When Peg finished reading *The Legend*, the *Commune* was even more excited. They wanted to enlist their families too. They wanted all of their Grand-children, nieces, nephews, etc to get involved.

Peg had to calm all of the commotion that lingered about so that she could continue with Clarence's story. Clarence watched all the faces filled with wonder as Peg read on and on. He could tell by all of the different expressions; that their minds were consumed in anticipation as *Oouey* enlightened not only Chi and Jimmy but *Them!*

Peg read on and on as Clarence gathered up 3 different drawings that he had had an artist; paint for the new website. He had copies for everybody. He also brought www.B4HEART.com up on several of the *Commune's* laptops; ready for the gang to check it out as Peg finished the last paragraph of *Surprise*.

Ultimately, Oouey knows that 'Life' is but a 'Process of Spiritual

◀ SOCIAL SECURITY

Evolution' en route to 'Enlightenment' as mankind evolves to a higher state of 'Moral Consciousness'! Intuition is but the 'Divine Nature of Being'. With a little help from his Friends and YOU, he believes that his Greatest Granddaddy, Grampa Ebenezer's Dream, his dying wish; will finally come true --- 'A Little Heaven on Earth!'

Please, do your part in the name of 'Love'.

B4HEART—
Humanity Envisioned And Realized Together.

The End

When the story was over, Clarence got a grateful round of applause from his *Family*. Peg ran over to Clarence, gave him a great big hug and kiss and said: "The characters are brilliant and will surely spark the interest of children. I know a publisher."

Max busted out laughing as Lucy passed out the copies of artwork as well as B4HEART Badges. He proclaimed that: "*Oouey*; looked like Clarence and *Olga*; like Peg."

◄ SOCIAL SECURITY

The Rose Garden in Buffalo, New York.

THE AWAKENINGS

Everybody agreed and thought that both *Oouey* and *Olga* were cute. They also agreed with Peg; that *Surprise* should be published. Especially since *Children* are our *Future*. Clarence felt a bit shy but decided to publish under an assumed pen name using a pseudonym. He chose Robert James Karpie.

While the *Commune* gathered into several different groups around the laptops to Check Out *B4HEART.com;* Clarence made another announcement:

◄ SOCIAL SECURITY

"I will donate 10% from of all of the profits from *www.B4HEART.com* as well as the profits from *Surprise;* to St. Jude Children's Research Hospital.

I made a promise to *St. Jude* and I intend to keep it every year; on the same date on an annual basics."

"Amen!" echoed throughout the room as all agreed that it was a *Great Cause for Concern.* Sexy Sarah wanted to be a *B4HEART Babe* and Henry a *B4HEART Dude.* So did everyone else; according to their sex. Sarge suggested that the *Amigos* go and see Chi in the morning and enlist his help and support. Again, everybody agreed with him and with Lucy's idea about breakfast at Mr. Denny's tomorrow morning.

When the bus rolled into Mr. Denny's at 8AM for their planned breakfast; it was a sight to be seen as both the *B4HEART Dude's* as well as the *B4HEART Babe's;* were wearing their shirts and badges proudly. All the customers and waitresses wanted to know who Oouey and Olga were and some wanted a B4HEART tee-shirt. They were told that they could order one on B4HEART.com and that they would find out all about Oouey and Olga on the site as well.

When the bus got back home to *Social Security;* everybody scurried about again like little children. Many of the residents called their *Loved ones* to tell them all about their *New Mission.* The *Amigos* piled into Clarence's old Buick; destination --- Chi!

On the way there; Max got a call from his doctor's office. His doctor wanted to see him later that afternoon; have a *Heart to Heart Talk.* Max was shaken with fear as a sinking feeling fell in the pit of his growling stomach. The other *Amigos* could see by the look on his face that he was scared.

"Relax Max." Clarence tried to calm him down as they pulled into the parking lot of Chi's office building. "He probably just wants to read you the riot act about drinking. Maybe he wants you to go on or change your diet."

"Yep, I agree, I do agree," Henry tried to reassure. "Don't worry about it."

Max took a couple of deep breaths; trying to ease his racing heart. "I guess I could afford to loose a few pounds." he replied as they exited the car.

The *Five* inspiring *Reformers* marched into Chi's office --- unannounced. They opted for a meeting of the minds as they were all wearing B4HEART badges. They had a radical proposition and their colors on. They sported the B4HEART tee-shirts with the words 'Humanity Envisioned And Realized Together'.

Chi seen that look in their eyes; he knew that he had had his hands full as he seen it before. They were on a *Mission* --- hardcore serious and loaded for corruption. *The Amigos were ready to Rock n Roll.* They had pressing issues that needed addressing.

"What's up?" he asked as he prepared himself for war again.

"There is a fine line between *National Security* and *Corporate Security!*" Clarence fumed.

Chi scratched his head and listened attentively as Clarence continued. "In the *Name of Greed*, *Corruption* exists at the expense of *We the People*. When *Top Secret,* benefits the *Elite Powers That Be*, monetarily; *Chaos* is enviable. It is time for a change. If not now, when?"

"Now is the Time!" Henry answered. "To paraphrase Eldridge Cleaver: *'If your not part of the solution, you are part of the problem'*. Therefore, it's time to B4HEART."

"B4HEART?" Chi asked as he read their shirts again without thinking about it - again.

"Humanity Envisioned And Realized Together!" Melvin verified verbally.

"Wow, now you guys want to *Save the World.*" he surmised without doubt as he sensed the *Passion* in their *Eyes* and *Faith* in their *Hearts*.

"The world is all Fucked-up." Max added angrily to the conversation. "Our government is all Fucked-up. The *System* is out of control. It's time for *Reform*."

"It's time for a *Wake-up Call*." Clarence clarified. "Frankly, the system itself is consuming us; we the consumers. We are becoming slaves economically as our *Individual Rights & Freedoms* are cannibalized from within our own government."

"God help us if we laugh now and cry later." he warned. "Ultimately, *Life* is a matter of Good verses evil! Unfortunately, *Truth* is akin to *Cool*, as both are Repulsive to the *Un*."

"Millions of people have lost their *Nest Egg* and or *Job*; because of fraud, corruption and a system that is incompetent." Sarge was adamant. "Bernie Madoff is a mad man who made off with billions of dollars of people's money by operating a Ponzi scheme. Ironically, our whole financial system itself, the Federal Reserve; is one big Ponzi scheme. America is actually bankrupt. Our national debt is somebody's wealth, but, nothing from nothing equals NOTHING. Actually, it is worthless. We can declare bankruptcy and rise to the occasion by issuing American money backed by American ingenuity. But first, we have to get rid of the corrupt bastards that allowed this to happen."

"We're willing to give President Barack Obama a chance," Max backed off a bit. "But if he doesn't straighten out this mess; we got plans. We'll organize a *Million Earthlings for Humanity March on Washington, DC for both the Young as well as the Old!*"

"We will support Oouey for President and Olga for Vice-president in 2012 under the *Symbolic B4HEART Purple Party*. Our two-party-system is a farce. It is but a mere distraction, a pathetic circus as a *New World Order* is being ushered in; right under our noses, in front of our eyes.

"Ironically," Henry elaborated, "politicians worry too much about being politically correct and utilize double talk in the name of their party. It's a *Immature rivalry*. Unfortunately, too many of them are so blinded by greed that they don't even realize what is going on --- in the *Name of a New World Order* with a *Globalist Agenda which* is creating a network of international laws to regulate, control, and dominate nations. This ultimate *World Government* would include the merging of the EU, the almost up and coming North American Union and the proposed Asia Union; under the auspice umbrella of a *United Nation* takeover via *Martial Law*."

"Many people laugh at this idea," he continued. "But presidential candidate Ron Paul responded --- back in November, 2007 at a CNN GOP debate and set the record straight when asked about the rumor in regards to creating a North American Union in the mold of the European Union. Dr Paul replied by explaining that: 'it is ludicrous to call the very real NAU movement a conspiracy theory'."

"Alas, 'The CFR exists, the Trilateral Commission exists,' Mr. Paul explained. 'And it is a 'conspiracy of ideas,' this is an ideological battle. Some people believe in globalism, others believe in national sovereignty. And there is a move on toward a North American Union, just like early on there was a move for a European Union that eventually ended up. So we have NAFTA and a move toward a NAFTA highway, these are real things.'"

"The mainstream media backs off, down plays and even --- cover-ups these issues in an attempt to keep them off the public's radar screen." Sarge warned. "But, Americans are organizing and getting enlightened as they are fed up with rhetoric, lying, double talk, and blind fools. You mark our words. Americans *Love* their *Freedom*. But little by little we are becoming less free. Far too many are in fact becoming economic slaves. Tempers are beginning to flare. America is like a big volcano, waiting to explode."

"Ron Paul is one of the few that tells it like it is." Clarence interrupted. "Maybe we should tar and feather corrupt politicians. The *United States Electoral College* should become obsolete. It's too easy to steal an election. I'm not a damn democrat or republican. I'm an *Earthling. Oouey and Olga are both Earthlings.*"

"Who the heck are Oouey and Olga?" Chi wondered out loud while contemplating their voice of dissension.

"Clarence had a *Dream!*" Henry informed. "And he wrote a book entitled *Surprise*."

"And we got our own website www.B4HEART.com!" Clarence was proud.

"Hold on guys; what dream and what book? And again; who the heck are Oouey and Olga? I'm a bit confused. Please enlighten me, but one at a time."

SOCIAL SECURITY

"Check out our website --- B4HEART.com," Clarence suggested. "You will find out all about *Oouey* and *Olga* and our *Mission*. Human-beings, world wide, are *Thirsting*, and *Hunger* for *Love*! We plan on *enlisting* the *Children to Save this World. Love is the Answer.* If we don't *Unite via Love*; eventually we will blow up this entire planet."

Chi brought up the site since his grandfather insisted with solemn words of warning. He observed and got an instant educated guess in regards to their *Goal / Grand Plan*. Their enthusiasm was very contagious and their website persuaded him.

He laughed with delight as he *Loved* their new *Mission*. It seemed exciting and stimulating. He also thought that *Oouey and Olga were cute and agreed that they looked somewhat like Clarence and Peg*. He also believed that *Children would relate to them Willingly*.

"Count me in your inspired endeavor!" he exclaimed proudly. "You guys really do have something special here. Especially since the *Heart Emblem* is recognized world-wide as the sign / symbol for LOVE."

"We do have an obligation to our *Children*." he continued. "They are our future and we must encourage them to B4HEART. They must step up to the plate. I shall do my part to *Help Promote World Peace, Prosperity and Human Rights*. B4HEARTers are but *Peace-Makers* irrespective of their religion!"

"Unfortunately, religion is the source of most conflicts and conflict will continue until all religions as well as science respect each other. Ironically, wars are fought in the name of their certain God? But, Love is universal; it is the one golden common denominator that is recommended by all religions; in one way or another." Chi was on the same wave length as his *Amigos*.

"Without *Love*; the people will perish." Clarence warned. "Love makes the world go round. I believe if we *Avow by Love World-Wide*; the *Universe* will make itself know to us via *Contact*. UFO's; hover over this planet constantly, shaking their heads in vain; fruitlessly waiting patiently for *Earthlings to Wake-up and Love* before we blow up our planet --- *Earth* to *Smithereens*. In fact, they are trying to give us messages via *Crop Circles!* You can learn all about it at http://www.cropcirclesecrets.org ."

"Someday soon", he continued; "The US Government is going to come clean with *UFO* disclosure. Too many other governments are speaking out and releasing countless sources of footage. It's just a matter of time, but what will it mean in regards to *Religion* and to *Science*; for that matter? If there are such things as *UFO's*, crafts from other *Planets*; their existence will surely add new meaning to our *Belief Systems*."

"Last year," Melvin shed some light on the topic, "the Vatican newspaper did a story about UFO's and Aliens entitled: *'The extraterrestrial is my brother'*. In an interview, the Rev. Jose Gabriel Funes, the Jesuit director of the Vatican Observatory and its chief astronomer was quoted as stating that: *'How can we rule out that life may have developed elsewhere? Just as we consider earthly creatures as 'a brother,' and 'sister,' why should we not talk about an 'extraterrestrial brother'? It would still be part of creation.'"*

"The Rev. Funes stated that: 'Ruling out the existence of aliens would be like *"putting limits"* on God's creative freedom and that believing that the universe may contain alien life *doesn't contradict our faith.'"*

"And," Mel stated his case even more convincingly, "let us not forget what Dr. Edgar Mitchell proclaimed. He was the Lunar Module Pilot for Apollo 14 and he also walked on the *Moon. He* confessed 'I happen to have been privileged enough to be in on the fact that we've been visited on this planet and the UFO phenomena is real…. It's been well covered up by all our governments for the last 60 years or so, but slowly it's leaked out and some of us have been privileged to have been briefed on some of it.'"

"These statements," Mel surmised, "should surely make people think twice about other forms of life outside Earth; even intelligent ones. What do they know? And, why all of a sudden are they trying to change their tune in regards to the theological implications of the existence of alien life?"

"Unfortunately, people believe in what they are led to believe."

Sarge interrupted. "But if seeing is responsible for believing; --- someday mankind will realize that we are not alone. It will surely cause them to reconsider existence as we know it."

"Amen," echoed throughout the room as they all pondered what they have seen on TV and personal experiences. Suddenly, Chi confessed. "I too believe in *UFO's*, but I also believe that there are other planets that are far more advanced then we are; who have evil / sinister ulterior motives. I just *Hope* that the *Loving Planets* can keep *Them under Control* and *Earth out of Harms Way.*"

"Unfortunately, there is a lot of *evil* in this *world.*" Chi continued; "And I'm sure that there is a lot of *evil* on other planets in the *Universe* too. We may have a monopoly on evil but not an exclusive. For I also think that there are planets that are more primitive than ours; that will create their own evil if they allow greed to interfere in route to so called progress."

"Ironically, consciousness has a way of being polluted as reason and free will dictate. Ultimately, I believe that consciousness is what occupies the entire universe / universes. Perhaps death is but a transition into one of these universes. Regardless, I believe that consciousness never dies and that *Love* is the cosmic connection that translates eternal consciousness. Now what's this dream you had Pa and what about your book?"

Clarence shared his *Dream* with Chi and his *Amigos* and Suezy whom entered the room unexpectedly. Both Chi and Suezy were intrigued with his *Blessed Event*. Then Clarence gave Chi a copy of his manuscript.

Suezy made a copy for her self. Both promised to read *Surprise* with curious anticipation. The *Amigos* were thrilled to have both Chi and Suezy on board.

"We have one more concern for you to check into for us." Max didn't forget with worry on his face. "Actually, we have two websites for you to check out and investigate the situation."

Henry went over to the computer and brought up both http://www.spp.gov and http://www.amerocurrency.com.

Chi was somewhat familiar with both the rumor of the *Amero* and the so called *North American, Canada, Mexico Treaty?* But he confessed that he never really paid any attention to either of them. But after seeing the websites; it was his *Duty to Investigate Further*. He remembered when they formed the *European Union and the Euro*.

All of the *Amigos* thanked Chi for his support. He promised to get back to them shortly and urged them to *Keep the Faith* and *Spread the Word – B4HEART*. He also vowed to check into why the mainstream media never addressed the issues in regards to this *Amero* which was proposed by Robert Pastor; vice chairman of the CFR and the *North American Union* that is also supported by the CFR.

Chi was more than curious. He was really suspicious since nearly every person elected as president of the United States since 1952; when the CFR was formed; and nearly every opponent, has belonged to this secretive, globalism-oriented organization known as the Council on Foreign Relations – (CFR). By the way, the CFR also supports the idea of a *New World Order of One Government*.

Chi wondered why President *Obama was surrounding himself and appointing diplomatic positions to members and former members of the* CFR and the Bilderbergers Group. Ironically, the Bilderbergers Group helped create the Euro. Do you Believe in Coincidences? Did you know that President Barack Obama was on the Senate Foreign Relations Committee?

On the way home, the *Amigos* stopped for lunch. They wolfed down their scum dogs. Suddenly, Henry had an idea. Scum-dog tee shirts for people who commit sins against *Humanity*. They decided to build a website --- B4HEARTsWallOfShame.com.

Max drove off to his doctor's appointment after they arrived back at *Social Security*. He refused the company of each and everyone of his *Amigos*. He was scared but wanted to be alone.

It was supper time when Max returned home from his consultation with tears in his eyes. The Guys braced for the worst; bad news? They knew he was sick. They saw him cough up blood on several occasions. He always blamed it on his ulcers. He drove around the city in a daze for an hour or two after he got the news.

"What's the prognosis?" Clarence asked with sincere concern.

"Dick-Do," Max answered.

"What the Fuck is Dick-Do?" Sarge asked all confused.

"My stomach sticks out more than my dick do." he laughed until he cried, coughing up blood into a red stained hankie. The other *Amigos* pretended to laugh. They realized that he really was sick.

"Shit," echoed throughout the room as they realized that Max was on his way out. His worst fear had come true; Max had to face it --- Death was on the horizon. He had been coughing up blood; off and on since Mexico. He though that *it was the tequila*. He finally summoned up the courage to see his physician, blood-work, more tests, etc.

Terminal Lung Cancer was the diagnosis. **"Six months, maybe a year;"** was the answer to his ultimate question. He felt like drowning his sorrows with Jack Daniel's but changed his mind. Ironically he laughed as he realized that *he had taken life for granted*. Unfortunately, daily living itself was becoming a chore.

He overlooked his simple freedoms. The natural expressions such as a cough, a fart, a laugh, a sneeze, a shit or piss as well as a breath and a cry; which had become painful and bloody issues --- energy, that must be expressed and released. Soon, some would become unwanted interruptions; embarrassments as he too would loose control.

"I gotta make the best of it." he insisted. "Shock and Depression are for the weak. I had a full *Life, Family/Amigos ---- The Commune*. I had a hand in creating something *Beautiful*. Shit, we even destroyed *Hell*. Maybe I can stretch it to two, maybe even three years."

The Guys were all speechless and sick to their stomachs. Max excused himself to go up to his room. He didn't know how to break the news to Anna.

Up the stairs Max went and down the hall until suddenly ---- an evil altercation sent him into flashback mode. The community's comfort was disrupted. Max is seeing *Red*.

"Leave her alone, you degenerate bastard." he shouted as a new orderly had Anna pinned up against the wall by her throat because she bumped into him by accident.

"Piss off Pops, you old bastard." The low-life warned. "Mind your own fucken business or I'll give you something to worry about."

"I'll give you pops." Max retaliated with the memory of his broken leg on his mind. As Max advanced to confront the assailant; he turned around and punched Max right on the jaw.

Max went flying into a medical cart and landed on the floor, cart on top of him; medicine, band-aids, gauze, etc. etc; all over the place.

"Semper Fi," he yelled with scissors in his hand as he jumped up swinging the weapon into the heart of the scum --- killing him instantly without thinking.

Max went into shock. In fact, he fell to the floor and rolled into a ball; like the fetal position. Anna was scared silent. She panicked but was desperately relieved that Max wasn't injured. She held him and rocked him like a baby as they both cried next to the dead body.

As luck would have it; it was still supper time and the entire staff was eating in the mess hall. Sarge came up the stairs.

"What the hell happened?" he asked dumbfounded. "I thought I heard some yelling or commotion of some sort."

"Max went berserk because that thing was roughing me up after I bumped into him by accident. Then he hit Max and Max retaliated as he killed him dead. What are we going to do?" she cried as reality set in.

"Get some of the plastic that we use on the beds and a bucket and a mop and blanket ASAP."

"OK! OK!" she replied as she hurried and scurried about.

"Max, Max! Pull yourself together." Sarge slapped his face till he responded. "Have a sip of this." he ordered as he handed him a flask of JD.

"Thanks, I needed that. What did I do?" he asked.

"You executed a useless piece of shit."

Anna returned with Sarge's requests. Sarge told Max to help him wrap the body in the plastic and then the blanket. His plan was to hide the body on the third floor office so that they could think. Max and Anna cleaned up the blood while Sarge wheeled the crap in a wheel-chair into the elevator and upstairs.

Sarge helped them finish up when he returned before anybody else came up. Then he calmed them both down as he told them that Chi would take care of it. He said that he hid the body so that nobody would panic and besides, *Social Security*; didn't need any scandal.

Next, he called Chi on his cell phone. He told him that there was a situation that needed his attention. Then the three of them finished the Jack Daniel's before they went down to find the other *Amigos*.

Chi was there in a flash. He met the desperate *Amigos* at the bar --- where Sarge was filling Clarence, Mel and Henry in with the details. Max was in a daze, distraught and incoherent. Chi was confused as he heard them talking about getting rid of some body as the solution --- the easy way out?

"What's Up; my *Amigos*," he asked all concerned?

"Sorry, false alarm." Sarge lied since they didn't want to involve him.

Chi scratched his head with perplexing doubt. He knew that they were lying. Perhaps ever hiding something, but he trusted their judgment. After all, they trusted him with everything else.

"Alright then, but what's this about a body?"

"Oh, the cat," Clarence also lied. "Max ran Willy over by accident with the car. He's afraid to tell Lucy that he's dead because she is so damned sensitive. We're going to bury it and tell her that it ran away."

Chi didn't believe a word but decided to play along with them for a while anyway.

"Honesty is the best policy." he advised. "Tell her the Truth."

Suddenly, Max came to his senses.

"I got six months to live?" he cried. "I killed an orderly whom was abusing Anna. I lost my head. I have lung cancer. Call the police; I want to confess. God, I need a shot."

"Relax Max." Chi suggested as he went to pour him another shot. The other *Amigos* were startled as they forgot all about the cancer. They didn't care about the piece of shit upstairs. Chi was speechless as he too drank.

"What's the cat's name?" he asked.

"He was new. His name tag said Leonard Wilson." Sarge answered. "He had Anna by the throat because she bumped into him. Max saw him and went crazy. He punched Max in the jaw; knocking him onto the floor as a medical cart fell on top of him. Max went berserk and responded with a pair of scissors; instant death. It was purely self defense if not temporary insanity."

"Where is the body?"

"I hid it on the third floor and we cleaned up the mess."

"It sounds as if you all had temporary insanity." Chi surmised. "We have to call the police, confess the panic and the attempted cover up. It's the right thing to do. We'll straighten it all out. Everything will work out."

"What about *Social Security*?" Clarence asked. "Will they shut us down?"

"No way, its reputation is spotless. There will be an investigation, but we'll keep it as quiet as possible. You better get rid of Thomas's *Special Plants*; especially since he passed on. And, why don't you can the book making operation for a while. You most certainly do not need the money."

"I had Old Joe dig them up them this afternoon." Clarence replied as they all agreed to give up *Sarge's* old hobby; the *Booking Making Operation*. They also decided to discontinue *1900-Sex-Chat*; which was becoming a *boring obligation*. After all, they had something more important to concentrate on now; *B4HEART*.

The police came, including the homicide division. They took statements and pictures. Max was arrested for manslaughter and the other four *Amigos* for *Stupidity in the First-Degree* --- obstruction of justice.

They were released on bail the next day. They told Chi all about B4HEARTsWallOfShame.com. Their pictures were in the paper again as the press had a field day. *Social Security* was in jeopardy. Its future was in Chi's hands. Everybody prayed that he was in God's Grace.

A few months went by as Max hung in there; thanks to the support of his *Family*. The Press backed off. Chi had his hands full. He Prayed for *Fortitude; the strength to persist, the courage to endure.* He also Prayed for his *Amigos* as well as the *Commune* and for America, one nation under God.

Unfortunately, Chi was losing faith in President Obama as he is keeping up with executive tradition --- *Immaculate Deception*. He has been in office just over four and a half months and he is already resorting to *Abuse of Power?* He decided to fire AmeriCorps inspector general Gerald Walpin for *Doing His Job*. A violation of the *2008 Inspectors General Reform Act*, which Mr. Barack Obama himself --- co-sponsored into legislation back when he was a senator. This *Inspectors General Reform Act*; requires the president to give Congress 30 days' notice, plus an explanation of cause, before firing an inspector general. Will Cover-Ups ever cease to exist?

Apparently, President Obama doesn't like where an investigating was leading --- to in regards to Kevin Johnson, the former NBA star who is now mayor of Sacramento and his personal friend who he enjoys playing basketball with. Thus, Mr. Walpin was issued an ultimatum and given one hour to resign or be terminated as per President Obama's orders. He steadfast refused to resign, because in the course of his investigation, he found Johnson and his program *St. HOPE*, which was implemented at City University of New York; had failed to use the federal money they received for the purposes specified in a grant and had also used federally-funded AmeriCorps staff for, among other things, "driving ([Johnson) to personal appointments, washing his car, and running personal errands."

Gerald Walpin came to the conclusion that Johnson and *St. HOPE* should be subject to suspension and possible permanent debarment. Consequently, according to the *Sacramento Bee*, if Mr. Kevin Johnson, mayor of Sacramento; was found to have misused federal money in the past: "Sacramento would likely be barred from getting federal money -- including tens of millions the city is expecting from the new stimulus package -- because Mayor Kevin Johnson is on a list of individuals forbidden from receiving federal funds."

Iowa Republican Sen. Charles E. Grassley, Ranking Member of the Committee on Finance; described Walpin's work as "legitimate" and "meritorious" and professed to Alan Solomont, head of the Corporation for National and Community Service, which oversees AmeriCorps: "Inspectors General have a statutory duty to report to Congress. Intimidation or retaliation against those who freely communicate their concerns to Members of the House and Senate cannot be tolerated. This is especially true when such concerns are as legitimate and meritorious as Mr. Walpin's appear to be." Sen. Grassley expressed his concern via a letter that Walpin was fired in part for complaining to Congress about interference in the St. HOPE probe by the top management of the Corporation.

Chi was infuriated about President Obama's decision as well as his shady association with ACORN and the way that that investigation is being handled. By the way ACORN, the Association of Community Organizations for Reform Now, is changing its name to COI -- Community Organizations International? Does this sound familiar?

As Chi searched the net for more information, he became even more upset when he learned that Barack wants to give the *Federal Reserve* more *Power*? Why would you give more Power to the culprit that didn't do its job in the first place at the expense of us, We the People? The mere words --- *Power, Regulate* and *Over-sight,* scared the shit out of him; considering the fact that they can't account for $9 trillion plus dollars now?

Chi wondered whose side Obama was on? He gave him the benefit of the doubt when it came to hanging out with Rev. Jeremiah Wright for over 20 years and not realizing his racial, radical as well as hateful convictions. Perhaps he thought, maybe people are right in regards to his birth certificate. Even Lou Dobbs questioned the legitimacy of President Barack Obama's birth certificate on CNN. Everybody's talking about in the media from Larry King to Rush

SOCIAL SECURITY

Limbaugh? After all, you have to be born in the USA to become president of USA.

Chi continued to search and found more and more startling facts. He learned a long time ago that you have to learn to read between the lies and he realized that American history is indeed paved with *Immaculate Deception*.

Suddenly, Mark Twain entered his mind: "If you tell the truth you don't have to remember anything." Then he found a quote on the internet by Donald Rumsfeld: "There are a lot of people who lie and get away with it, and that's just a fact." Alas, a Criminal *Travesty*; here is something to think about:

1. The FDA Approval of Aspartame?
2. North Korea Ominous Warning that it: 'Will use its nuclear weapons - both to defend itself and as an offense against those who seek to attack the country'?
3. Swine flu vaccine scam / poisoning: in 1976?
4. Swine flu scares in April 2009?

Here are some alarming facts:

Donald Rumsfeld was the Secretary of Defense under President Gerald Ford from 1975 to 1977 and again, Secretary of Defense under President George W. Bush from 2001 to 2006.

In Regards to # 1. The FDA magically changes it mind and Approves Aspartame?

The FDA refused to approve aspartame for sixteen years because it triggers brain tumors—violates the *Delaney Amendment;* that makes it illegal to allow any residues of cancer-causing chemicals in foods. From 1977 to 1985, Rumsfeld served as Chief Executive Officer, President, and then Chairman of G. D. Searle & Company, a worldwide pharmaceutical company based in Skokie, Illinois. In January 1981 Rumsfeld told a sales meeting, according to one attendee, that **he would call in his chips and get aspartame approved by the end of the year.**

Shortly thereafter, in 1981 the FDA commissioner's authority was suspended by. the new President of the USA, Ronald Reagan; on his first day in office. One month later, he appointed a new FDA commissioner. Four months later, the new FDA commissioner, Dr. Arthur Hull Hayes (Rumsfeld's old friend); **defying FDA advisors**, approved aspartame for dry foods.

It was his first major decision? In November 1983 the FDA approved aspartame for soft drinks. It was Dr. Hayes last decision? Supposedly, he was under fire for accepting corporate gifts; thus he left the agency and went to work for GUESS WHO? He became Searle's senior medical advisor for their public-relations firm. Aspartame name was changed to *NutraSweet*. **Rumsfeld received a $12 million bonus.**

'Prior to the approval of aspartame, the FDA sent two specialized teams to G.D. Searle and found a ghastly 95% level of misdirected testing; concealed tests, collusion between corporate and their company-funded research; withholding of material facts; alterations of records: lying to investigators, lost records, no records; falsification of reports, bribery, poor test methodology or design...' --- by Arthur M. Evangelista, a former FDA Investigator in his Open Statement Concerning The Artificial Sweetener, Aspartame.

In Regards to # 2. *Some people will do anything for money? ABB and North Korea?*

Donald Rumsfeld was on the board of a technology giant --- ABB when it won a deal to supply North Korea with two nuclear power plants. Rumsfeld sat on the board of directors of ABB, from 1990 to 2001, when he became Secretary of State again. ABB is a European engineering giant—based in Zürich, Switzerland. In 2000 this company sold two light-water nuclear reactors to North Korea.

The sale of this nuclear technology was a high-profile, $200 million dollar contract with Pyongyang, Korea. Weapons experts warned that waste material from these two reactors could be used for so-called 'dirty bombs'. According to Wolfram Eberhardt, a spokesman for ABB; Rumsfeld "was at nearly all the board meetings," during his decade-long involvement with the company.

Rumsfeld does not recall the $200 million dollar deal being brought before the board at any time. *(Denial or selective memory or a blatant lie?)* But ABB spokesman Björn Edlund told Fortune (magazine) that "board members were informed about this project." In 2002 Defense Secretary Donald Rumsfeld declared North Korea a terrorist state and a target for regime change. ABB no longer has any involvement with the North Korean power plants.

In Regards to # 3, and 4 - *Tamiflu and Swine Flu terror* - Propaganda from friends in Washington and other high places to instill a scenario of panic by fear-mongering.

Donald Rumsfeld has long standing intimate ties with the big pharmaceutical companies that have and will reap millions more in profits from these new *Swine Flu Scares*. 'Tamiflu', is an antiviral prescription medication, in pill form. So far it is supposedly, the most effective treatment for combating the new swine flu as well as protecting health care workers who may be exposed to it. This drug is made and marketed by Hoffmann–La Roche Holding AG of Switzerland, but was developed by Gilead Sciences Inc. of California in 1996.

Ironically, but not surprisingly, Donald Rumsfeld - as a major stock holder and former CEO of Gilead Sciences Inc., the sole patent owner of Tamiflu, antiviral drug now being stockpiled by the Defense Department and other agencies - stands to make millions again from this new Swine Flu Panic. The US federal government is one of the world's biggest customers for Tamiflu at the tax-payers expense. Former Sec. of State George Schultz — CFR, Trilateral, and Bilderberg member, was also on the board of Gilead Sciences. According to *Fortune*, Shultz turned a neat $7 million profit in 2005 in insider selling of some of his Gilead stock. Incidentally, there is also another treatment called *Ralenza?*

At Rumsfeld's urging, in 1976, President Ford called for a national inoculation against swine flu. The $135 million program proclaimed that 'every man, woman and child'; should be vaccinated. Huge amounts of vaccine were produced and distributed quickly and the government assumed all liability from side-effects.

Several older people died within hours, after taken the shot; from heart attacks. There were also reports of the vaccine touching off neurological problems, especially rare 'Guillain-Barre' syndrome.

Eventually, the government suspended the program, after inoculating 40 million people for a flu that never came.

In 2005, President George W. Bush pushed for and won $7.1 billion in emergency funding to prepare for an influenza pandemic that was not even yet on the horizon. Remember, Donald Rumsfeld was Defense Secretary at that time? The United States placed an order for 20 million doses of *Tamiflu* at a price of $100 per dose. It cost the taxpayers around $2 billion. *Conflict of Interest?*

Also, in March 2005, Britain's Tony Blair, ordered the UK Government to buy enough Tamiflu drugs to supply 14 million of its British citizens.

In 2006, George Bush signed into law the Public Readiness and Emergency Preparedness (PREP) Act as part of the 2006 Defense Appropriations Act (HR 2863). This law; lets the HHS Secretary declare any disease an epidemic or national emergency requiring mandatory vaccinations. But, nothing in this Act lists any criteria that warrant a threat. Nor does it list any potential penalties for those who balk and or refuse to get it. Maybe quarantine and? Check out 'Readying Americans for Dangerous, Mandatory Vaccinations' **by Stephen Lendman at**:

http://www.globalresearch.ca/index.php?context=va&aid=13925

Do You See a Pattern Here?

And now, the *World Health Organization* is hyping up the hysteria by declaring a *Swine flu Pandemic;* warning that governments worldwide should launch emergency response plans for late 2009 or early 2010 as a pandemic is "imminent."? Eventually, we shall see how many billions our US Government will spend on Swine flu this time?

Dr. Ron Paul Says 'Flu Hype' Designed To Scare Americans http://whatreallyhappened.com/content/ron-paul-md-swine-flu-scare

Swine flu is Hogwash! Read the story http://us-constitutionalist.

SOCIAL SECURITY

blogspot.com/2009/05/swine-flu-hogwash.html.

Hype, Caution, Bullshit or Genocide?

US Government health officials are planning to spend up to $2 billion to buy about 160 million doses of vaccine for the 'Fall' of 2009 – ' Winter' of 2010, to prevent Swine Flu.

A presidential panel warned on 8/24/09 that Swine flu could kill up to 90,000 Americans - most of those kids and young adults, this fall and winter.

The 21-member President's Council of Advisers on Science and Technology's 68 page report, a so called – " plausible scenario" - estimates that: as many as 1.8 million in the U.S. will be hospitalized, and up to 300,000 victims will land in intensive care units.

Incidentally, by donating land in New York City, Rockefeller was instrumental in the decision to locate the United Nations headquarters in the United States. David Rockefeller is the chairman of CFR. Both the CFR and the UN are calling for a drastic depopulation program. Are these Swine Flu shots made to save people or kill people? Will the UN enforce Martial Law if we refuse to take their Swine Flu shots? What if we resist their New World Order of One World Government? Hmm!

After doing a little investigating, Chi became a believer in the *Immaculate Deception theory*. He couldn't believe all the cronyism, collusion, favoritism and lies. For instance, on September 14, 2003 on NBC's Meet the Press, Dick Cheney said, "And since I left *Halliburton* to become George Bush's vice president, I've severed all my ties with the company (Halliburton), gotten rid of all my financial interest. I have no financial interest in Halliburton of any kind and haven't had, now, for over three years." Ironically, the ex-vice president conveniently forgot to mention (*lies of omission*) that he continued to receive a deferred salary of over $150,000 per year while maintaining 433,333 shares of unexercised stock options from *Halliburton*.

Halliburton Corporation, who's former CEO is Ex-Vice President

Dick Cheney; has so far gotten billions of dollars worth of US construction contracts in Iraq and else where. In January 2004, it got a no-bid cronyism and favoritism contract from the US Army. Soon there after, it over-billed the US Government by about $27.4 million dollars for meals for our troops. It has evaded paying US Taxes, admitted and or was accused of bribes as well as doing business with foreign counties which were forbidden at the time by our US Government to do business with. Halliburton also over-billed the US Government while Dick Cheney was CEO.

The US bombed the hell out of Iraq and the US taxpayers are paying Halliburton to rebuild it? Is it just a coincidence that Cheney's closest political friend is Donald Rumsfeld? Sad but true, both men got rich off the US taxpayers. Check out the Cheney/Halliburton Chronology at: http://www.halliburtonwatch.org/about_hal/chronology.html

Chi also found countless websites in regards to the so called *Amero* and the *North American Union*. It is definitely a possibility; especially considering the United State's economic situation and its past history of *Immaculate Deception*. In fact many citizens are taking this very seriously. Chi heard several news stories on both TV and the radio about Americans stocking up on ammunition. Many stores and gun dealers across the USA are reporting that they are running out of *Ammo* as soon as it comes in. Some people are waiting in line for hours.

Unfortunately, Americans have lost their faith in our government as well as our system of justice and the rule of law? Many people are waking up and talking about it --- chaos, martial law, anarchy; if the U.S. dollar collapses; then what? Ironically, we are becoming slaves economically as our *Individual Rights & Freedoms* are cannibalized from within by own government; an unforgiving act of *Immaculate Deception*.

Many Americans realized that it is time to support and defend the U.S. Constitution again! United, it is time we implement the system of *'Checks and Balances'*; which were designed by our founding fathers as they established a *'Separation of Powers'*, on purpose.

◀ SOCIAL SECURITY

Ultimately, the *'Power'*, was designed to be shared between our three branches of government and each branch has the right and the duty to challenge the actions of the others; a safe guard to prevent excessive power grabs by either the judicial, legislative or executive branch of our government. Ironically, our forefather's greatest fears are coming true? Why? Because --- *'We the People'*; have fallen asleep. We have forgotten about the *'Power of the People'*; our Duty to Question Authority and Demand Answers. We should not fear our government; they should fear us, We the People!

Frankly, Americans are pissed off and want to --- *Restore America!* On April 15th, 2009; hundreds of thousands of citizens gathered in more than 800 cities and voiced their opposition to out of control spending at all levels of government. It was organized in all 50 states by Americans from all walks of life. These *'Tea Parties'* were a true grassroots protest of irresponsible fiscal policies and *intrusive* government. TaxDayTeaParty.com was the home of these protests, and will continue to be an online gathering place for a new generation of grassroots activists who are committed to effecting positive change in their communities.

Evidently, believe it or not, peaceful demonstrations and protests do seem to work and the proof will soon be fought in the courts as our states are finally fighting back in regards to mandatory federal laws and taxes. Also in April, 2009; Montana passed a law --- A message of dissent that --- guns and ammo made in, and which stay in Montana shall not be taxed or regulated in any way by the Federal Gov. No more licenses, permits or background checks. This law will go into effect in Oct, 2009. Utah and Texas are going to do the same thing and another dozen states are watching and thinking about it as The United States begins --- *To Unite Again!*

It is time to take action. Besides republican Ron Paul's *Campaign for Liberty*, some of our other elective representatives are trying to do their duty. Take Congressman Dennis Kucinich for instance, he is a democrat from Ohio who wants to restore the rule of law and hold former President George Bush and his administration, including former VP Dick Cheney; accountable for their alleged abuses of power and violation of national and international law. He introduced several Impeachment Articles of Resolution, including one against Cheney and a so called: *'35 Articles of Impeachment against President George W. Bush'* as well as a single article to impeach President Bush, accusing him of deceiving Congress to convince lawmakers to authorize his invasion of Iraq.

In 2006, President Bush is said to have purchased a 98,842-acre farm in northern Paraguay, between Brazil and Bolivia. Paraguay is one of the few countries in the world which has promised not to prosecute American troops or government officials on War Crimes charges! Is he ready to escape prosecution by the World Court?

Unfortunately, although Dennis Kucinich rallied support; it seems to have fallen on deaf ears. I guess that the good old boys stick together --- till death do they part? But, he vows not to give up just because they left office. He still has a website up and running, if you want, you can sign his petition at: http://impeachment.kucinich.us/petition. He will personally deliver it to your Congressperson!

In Congress, Mr. Kucinich has authored and co-sponsored legislation to create a national health care system, preserve Social Security, lower the costs of prescription drugs, provide economic development through infrastructure improvements, abolish the death penalty, provide universal prekindergarten to all 3, 4, and 5 year olds, create a Department of Peace, regulate genetically engineered foods, repeal the USA PATRIOT Act, and provide tax relief to working class families. It surely sounds as if he wants to address and conquer the chaos that is plaguing America today.

Chi felt somewhat relieved. He knows that there is always *Hope*. We the people can make a difference by uniting together. He logged off of the internet and then went to the fridge to get a beer. He turned the radio on to his favorite country station and got a good laugh when Billy Currington was singing his song entitled *'People Are Crazy'*. Hence, Chi had a new favorite song; "God is Great, beer is good and, People are Crazy."

Ironically, Chi thought of *Thou Shalt? Must we slay him or tame him?* And then he laughed again as he knew that someday soon, he'd be on some terrorist watch list as *Big Brother* is getting nervous because *Uncle Sam* is out of control. But, he vows not to give up.

Intuitively, Chi knows that it is our *Duty* to get *involved* and make a *difference* before it is *Too Late*. All of us must unite, organize and fight for our God given fundamental rights, liberties and freedoms by taking a stand together. We must reposition, restore, preserve and ensure America's solvency or *Answer* to our *Children*. Frankly, our government is full of crap. It stinks and it's time to change the dirty diaper. It's time WE get rid of all the *Shit!*

We owe it to God, to ourselves and to each other. Until then, *Life* as we know it --- *Is what it Is;* as we settle for the *consolation* of HOPE. But, 'Peace Is Within' all of Us! Mankind controls his own destiny - Collectively.

Hopefully, *Life* will go on in *The Name of Humanity.* Regardless, *Life* is but a *Collective Constellation of Continuous Consciousness* --- *Lingering Eternal Energy* --- *Longing for Peace.* For man's true essence is of *Divine Decree* – *Unconditional Love.* Glory be when, humans finally realize that God is Love!

The End

The New Mission via B4HEART --- A Spiritual Revolution

The New Mission via B4HEART — A Spiritual Revolution
Think Purple; It's Time To Get Involved & Act!

"…Over the last 50 years, U.S. government has grown too big, too corrupt and too aggressive toward the world, toward its own citizens and toward local democratic institutions. It has abandoned the democratic vision of its founders and eroded Americans' fundamental freedoms." --- By *Ian Baldwin and Frank Bryan in* the Vermont Commons

www.B4HEART.com is up and running. Check it out and do your part --- B4HEART –
Humanity Envisioned And Realized Together!

"I refuse to accept the view that mankind is so tragically bound to the starless midnight of racism and war that the bright daybreak of peace and brotherhood can never become a reality... I believe that unarmed truth and unconditional love will have the final word."
Martin Luther King Jr.

If you are serious about making a difference in this world; then please check out all the websites that were listed in this book and spread the word. Together, they add up to something, something

SOCIAL SECURITY

awful ugly. These sites were created to help stop the insanity; which is destroying America!

These are not democratic (blue) or republican (red) issues. Ironically, both the democratic and republican parties fight and squabble with each other in name of their so call *Party*? It is a ridiculous spectacle, so childish. Think *Purple (Humanity)*; as we must *Unite Our Country* again. Wake UP!

If you want to read how entwined our government is with evil; read 'The Family: The Secret Fundamentalism at the Heart of American Power' by Jeff Sharlet. He names; names of both Democratic and Republican Congressmen and Senators who have some explaining to do. The list also includes names of other high ranking officials as well as high profile deceased people including a Supreme Court Judge and the countries that they are involved with --- in conspiracy.

It is a shocking disgrace. We have to stop these bastards. This so called secretive cult – 'The Family', 'teaches Washington lawmakers that people chosen for leadership are above morality'. They have their own evil specific religious beliefs as well as their own agenda and a systematic process. We must vote these scum of the Earth out of office. Check out Mr. Sharlet's website at www.JeffSharlet.com.

Last week President Barack Obama met with his so called North American Free Trade Act (NAFTA) partners --- Mexican President Felipe Calderon, and Canadian Prime Minister Stephen Harper in Guadalajara, Mexico. Amongst other things; they discussed Free Trade, the swine flue and the world's economic crisis. I wonder if they discussed the 'Amero'?

Ron Paul is now talking about mandatory swine flue vaccinations? There have been many sightings of NATO troops doing exercise throughout America? Word is that they are being housed at old / obsolete US Military Bases? Why is Obama trying to push this new Health Care Bill in so fast? They best take their time and get all the details. The devil is always hidden somewhere in the details. Remember what happened to most of the 'Stimulus Package Money'? They can't even account for where most of it went?

These are Great Causes for Concern! The shit is about to hit the fan. We must be instrumental in stopping it --- Chaos. I feel sorry for those that laugh and sneer and think that everything is A-OK. They either live in denial with their head in the sand or they are too naïve to understand. WAKE UP!

It is time to address matters of conspiracy and corruption at the highest level. *Silence is Denial.* We best get to it and stand up to these criminals. America is supposed to *Stand Up for Freedom!*

Remember *our Declaration of Independence!*

'When, in the course of human events, it becomes necessary for one people to dissolve the political bonds which have connected them with another, and to assume among the powers of the earth, the separate and equal station to which the laws of nature and of nature's God entitle them, a decent respect to the opinions of mankind requires that they should declare the causes which impel them to the separation.

We hold these truths to be self-evident, that all men are created equal, that they are endowed by their Creator with certain unalienable rights, that among these are life, liberty and the pursuit of happiness. That to secure these rights, governments are instituted among men, deriving their just powers from the consent of the governed. That whenever any form of government becomes destructive to these ends, it is the right of the people to alter or to abolish it, and to institute new government, laying its foundation on such principles and organizing its powers in such form, as to them shall seem most likely to effect their safety and happiness.'

Preamble to US Constitution:

'We the People of the United States, in Order to form a more perfect Union, establish Justice, insure domestic Tranquility, provide for the common defence, promote the general Welfare, and secure the Blessings of Liberty to ourselves and our Posterity, do ordain and

◄ SOCIAL SECURITY

establish this Constitution for the United States of America.'

(Note, there are misspellings in our US Constitution - http://www.usconstitution.net/choose.html)

It Is Time To ACT!

Congressman John Conyers has proposed extending statutes of limitations on the Bush-Cheney crimes *(before they magically escape down the rabbit hole)*. You Can Help make this happen at http://www.peaceteam.net/action/pnum933.php. In his 487 page report, titled 'Reining in the Imperial Presidency: Lessons and Recommendations Relating to the presidency of George W. Bush'. Congressman Conyers, who is the House Judiciary Committee Chairman; warned: "To fully preserve and protect the rule of law, the statute of limitations must be extended now." He called for a fair opportunity for them to be actually investigated by a real prosecutor. His report also contains 47 separate recommendations designed to restore the traditional checks and balances of our constitutional system.

9/11 was a *National Disaster,* but is it an *International Disgrace?* Sign the petition and demand Congress --- to re-open up a new and truly independent investigation of the *9/11 Immaculate Deception.* Go to http://www.ae911truth.org/ and get involved.

Act now, make a difference. *Glory Be When the Voice of Dissension Speaks Loud & Clear!* You can order a colored *Wake Up* greeting-card and print any message that you want inside of it. You can address it to your Congressperson or Attorney General Eric Holder and ask them to appoint a Special Prosecutor to investigate and prosecute Bush-Cheney.

You can also *Spread-the-Word;* by sending a message to all of your friends or any body-else that you might think of whom could help fight in the Name of Truth. All you have to do is type your message --- on your computer, inside of the card. They are shipped the same day that you order one; at midnight and only cost $1.99

THE NEW MISSION VIA B4HEART — A SPIRITUAL REVOLUTION

cents plus the price of a U.S. stamp and can be mailed anywhere in the world for 50 cents. Order your cards today at *http://www.A-National-Disgrace.com* . They are copyrighted by © **B4HEART Publishing.**

I personally; as a *Former Marine*, am calling on all of my *Fellow Americans* and, especially my *Veteran-Brothers*, to step up, fall in, unite and get *involved* and help *stop* this *Madness*. It is time to address these issues, hold the political pukes responsible for their actions and bring them to trial if necessary. There are far too many liars, conspiring thieves and murderers. We must also make sure that they don't hide behind a so called 'National Security'. And, if and when they do get convicted; make sure that there is not a pardon or a miraculous overturning of their convection on a technicality.

A Message of Hope! You can also visit B4HEART.com and order colored tee-shirts, badges, etc., from Oouey and Olga's Store!

Truth is akin to Cool as both are Repulsive to the Un!
http://www.A-National-Disgrace.com

In closing, I can't emphasis enough how vital it is to address 2

SOCIAL SECURITY

major issues and make a few suggestions. I don't have the answers. But, at least I am mindful of the situation and realize that these problems must be confronted and addressed Now!

1. Our *'Social Security System'*, is running out of money. What can we do? How about a *National Federal Lottery System* to help tackle this problem. Or, maybe we should legalize a *National Sports Betting System* like they run in Las Vegas and *Tax the Winnings* like OTB does, plus a service fee like the 5% vig.

Believe it or not, vices generate big money. Sex, drugs and gambling are multi-billion dollar enterprises. The state of Nevada proves my point. There is no personal income tax in the state on Nevada. It has the lowest tax rate of any state in the nation. There are NO state income, inheritance, gift, or estate taxes, while franchise and inventory or corporate taxes are levied. Nevada leaves your money where it belongs, in your pocket.

But, why is Nevada allowed to operate this way? They proudly promote all of its vices; while other states abide by a set of different rules? Why do the other states farm out their gambling joints to the Indian Nations and or so called off shore gambling boats? New Jersey has some freedom?

Wake up your state legislators; tell them that your missing out on live sources of incomes that are going on anyway, some how at some time in your own back yards. I for one; would go for taxing the internet. I would start with all the porn sites and gambling sites. I would also set up a system to monitor them via a new x.com-system for adult fun and tax it.

Maybe we should also legalize marijuana like Arnold wants to do in California. The farmers could make a fortune; here in our own country and our government could tax them. We could become the *Hemp Clothing Manufactures* of the world. I personally owned some Hemp clothes and they were some of the softest, most durable clothing that I ever owned and they did not shrink.

Hemp Facts
(Serious Consideration is Recommended for its Golden Potential.)

The U.S. Constitution and Flag, two of our most cherished symbols were made of hemp before it was prohibited. Hemp was second to tobacco as the crop to grow in early America. The demand for tobacco in England, kept the farmers busy with this cash crop. Many of our forefathers were *Hemp Farmers,* including George Washington and Thomas Jefferson. Both men were high on hemp as an important crop to replace and rotate with tobacco.

Before we lost such an important right, namely the control of agricultural production; Hemp was a vital resource to America's *Economy* and *Everyday Necessities.* Unfortunately, Prohibition has a way of profiteering for the *Powers That Be.* Our early American soldiers wore uniforms made of Hemp as were the tents; which they slept in. Our ships' sails were also made from Hemp as were the ropes that hoisted them up and the maps that the Captains followed and the log-books that they recorded their voyages in.

As you can see, Hemp was utilized for many projects; from bibles, books, and canvas for paintings, to postcards, gloves and clothing. It was not just any string that connected Ben Franklin to the clouds above for his famous experiment with a key, it was hemp string. Hemp was responsible for 'Demonstrating the Identity of Lightning and Electricity'; from which Franklin invented the lightning rod.

'Hemp is also a pain-reliever and an effective treatment for anorexia, arthritis, asthma, epilepsy, AIDS, glaucoma, menstrual cramps, migraines, nausea and other ailments. Hemp is a safer substitute for many over-the-counter and prescription medicines. The human brain appears to have receptors for hemp's active ingredient, THC. And hemp medicine is now legal in California and six other states that have passed medical marijuana bills in some form.'

For more info, visit **http://www.hempmuseum.org.**

Hence, we could use all the revenue from the (4) sources that I mentioned; to bail out our *Social Security System* until it gets back

◂ SOCIAL SECURITY

on its feet. Then, we could apply our newly found fortune to maintain our infrastructure, roads, bridges, etc. which if not addressed soon; will be the destruction of America as a World Power. But, we must be carful to keep Greed and Corruption from infecting these programs.

Never the less, our infrastructures are truly a National Disgrace. According to the American Society of Civil Engineers (ASCE); the nation's roads, bridges, levees, schools, water supply and other infrastructure are in such bad shape that it would take $2.2 trillion over five years to bring them up to speed. Alas they released a 'Report Card for America's Infrastructure' which averaged "D" for 2009.

We best heed the warning from ASCE: *'A healthy infrastructure is the backbone of a healthy economy. In these challenging times, infrastructure is essential to reviving the nation's fortunes, and in maintaining our high quality of life.'* Alas, its president D. Wayne Klotz proclaimed:

"We've been operating on a patch-and-pray system…" Da? Wake Up America!

2. We have to stop our addiction to foreign oil. Over two thirds of our trade deficit is a result of our dependency on other countries for this fossil fuel. We have to Start Producing Products, right here at Home in America. Especially when it comes to energy; so that we can become a self sustaining nation!

It has been over Forty Years since the United States has had an Energy Plan? Meanwhile, China is buying up all of the Future Reserves in Oil? If you don't believe me, do a little research. It is awful frightening to say the least.

Our dependency on this foreign oil puts us at great risk and it is our own damn fault. We have to demand that our elected officials take action and get this country back on the right track. Our desperate need for foreign oil is a double edge sword. It destroys the Environment on one hand; while it is also destroying our Economy and jeopardizing our National Security; that requires oil to protect ourselves.

THE NEW MISSION VIA B4HEART — A SPIRITUAL REVOLUTION

We have many great minds in this country with ideas that need backing. Unfortunately, the *Powers That Be;* have a way with keeping them silent? A perfect example is Paul Pantone who invented the GEET Fuel Processor which you can run a car on 80% water or more. When Pantone refused to sell out on his patents and technology, he was framed for securities fraud and railroaded to a mental ward at the Utah State Hospital in March of 2006 until May 2009. Now, Paul wants to spread the word about his Geet Fuel Processor again. To get a free copy of one of his plans, go to http://www.geet.nl/free-geet-plans.php. Read all about his abuse.

Sad but true, the *Powers That Be* are cruel cold-hearted lost souls. They resort to anything to protect their interests. Ironically, all we have to do is look at many of the inventions on the past for answers. Believe it or not micro-wave-ovens and Velcro were invented in the early 1940's and were finely utilized decades later? A lot of inventions were suppressed on purpose by critics and disinformation.

Incidentally, Nikola Tesla wanted to give the World Free Power. He discovered the alternating current of electricity AC and he designed the first hydroelectric power plant in Niagara Falls in 1895, which was the final victory of alternating current. With the backing of J. Pierpont Morgan, Tesla built the Wardenclyffe laboratory, including its famous transmitting tower in Shoreham, Long Island between 1901 and 1905.

This huge landmark was 187 feet high, capped by a 68-foot copper dome which housed a magnifying transmitter. It was planned to be the first broadcast system, transmitting both signals and power without wires to any point on the globe; discharging high frequency electricity that would turn the earth into a gigantic dynamo which would project its electricity in unlimited amounts anywhere in the world. Morgan withdrew his funding when he realized: "If anyone can draw on the power, where do we put the meter?" Alas, when Tesla died on January 7th, 1943 in the Hotel New Yorker; the FBI raided his two-room suites and confiscated all of his papers and discoveries.

◄ SOCIAL SECURITY

Maybe you have and Idea or an invention or know somebody that does? We have to start somewhere and get the word out and what better to start with than producing our own energy and saving energy. America was *Built on Ingenuity*!

There are Many Alternatives to Oil --- Natural gas, Wind (Windmills), Solar Powered Energy, Nuclear (Nucular), Electric cars (electric batteries), Hydrogen / Water and Coal which can be turned to a cleaner form of energy and which we have plenty of. *'Necessity is the Mother of Invention.'* Now is the Time. It is time to tap into our own resources and use our own *Natural Reserves*. By the way; we are the *Saudi Arabia of Natural Gas,* which can easily replace oil with a few modifications on all of our vehicles.

Maybe we can get back on track by reinventing our railways. For the most part, the system is already laid out. We should reinvest in drop-off-points / stations; where our truckers can pick up goods delivered by our trains. And, what about our old ship-yards; they are just sitting there rotting away as eye-sores?

Anyway, here are two ideas that would make a difference. T. Boone Pickens is leading the way. He proclaims that: *"America is blessed with the world's greatest wind power corridor and abundant reserves of clean natural gas."* Natural gas is half the price of oil; is 50% cleaner and could power all of our vehicles.

Check out his Plan at: http://www.pickensplan.com/act Sign up and join his Army to Save America! To learn more about him, go to: http://tboonepickens.com/

Don't believe the myths about Alcohol Fuel. Get the Facts! Check out the benefits concerning Alcohol Fuel; including a Greener Planet and Watch the Video!

http://www.truth-about-alcohol-fuel.info

Henry Ford designed his cars so that they could run on Alcohol Fuel. Prohibition was instigated, backed and funded by gasoline magnate John D. Rockefeller to drive the alcohol fuel companies out of business. He helped the so called movement of holy rollers to get organized and backed them financially as they decreed that 'demon rum' was to blame for the ills of society.

Ironically, many affluent people with influential connections and resources made a fortune selling *Booze* on the *Black Market*; bootlegging beer, importing illegal rum, gin, whisky, etc. and or moonshine during the so called dry-years of prohibition. It was a *Bloody Industry* – literally. But, the *Fear of Alcohol Fuel* was the real reason for *Prohibition* which made it *illegal to produce or transport alcohol*.

Get the Facts!

http://www.truth-about-alcohol-fuel.info

And on a final note, my heart goes out to the brave people of Iran, who are risking their *Lives* by protesting and demonstrating in a gallant effort, through-out their country; concerning among other issues, suspicions of voter fraud as a rigged election. Perhaps, the election is an excuse, but they have to start somewhere as they have tasted *Freedom* and they don't like what is happening in their country. Alas they are being brutalized as they are beaten with batons, clubs and chains, tear-gassed, shot at and even killed for standing up for their rights. Last night, protesters were being rounded up in the middle of the night.

Today, there are several reports of people being chopped up with axes and slaughtered like meat as others are thrown off bridges in Tehran. All because of their *Courageous Effort* to win some *Freedom*! God Bless all of you brave *Souls* and especially your *Soccer* team who risked their *Lives* and or perhaps *Freedom* by wearing their *Green Campaign Color / Symbolic arm-bands*.

We are in historic times now. Internet communication is changing the world. It is fascinating to say the least, when a suppressed country can get their message out and, the world can watch it unfold and cheer for them; as they display incredible acts of courage in spite of the lethal violence that they face for their civil unrest. But watching and cheering is only a start. The Iranian People need our support --- Now.

How can the world just sit back, watch and do nothing after watching --- Neda Agha-Soltan, a 26-year-old woman; who was shot dead during anti-government protests in Iran by a sniper. It was captured on video and transmitted via the Internet. It spurred an outpouring of grief from angry mourners in Iran which has fallen on deaf ears? Her family was told by the Iranian government to remove mourning banners outside their home and not to eulogize her at her grave.

Unfortunately, the *United Nations* chooses to sit back and do nothing in regards to the appalling *Deadly Force;* massacres that are being used to crush this peaceful democratic up-rising. More proof that the U.N. is in fact a worthless farce. However, I do believe that someday; we will have to confront the U.N.; here at home in the USA.

To read why; the United Nations is a useless failure: http://www.philforhumanity.com/Why_the_United_Nations_is_a_Useless_Failure.html.

Ironically, we did not hesitate to use stealth methods as we helped to over-throw Iran's democratic government in 1953 to suit U.S.'s own economic and strategic interests. The CIA, backed by the British, masterminded the coup d'état; after Iran's Prime Minister Mohammad Mosaddeq nationalized the Iranian oil industry, which was run at that time by the British-owned Anglo-Iranian Oil Company. Mr. Mosaddeq was passionate for his country's freedom and opposed to foreign intervention in Iran. History, sometimes, does speak for its self as *Freedom* does have a price. Mohammad Mosaddeq paid the consequence; he was imprisoned for three years and subsequently put under house arrest until his death.

Shortly after Obama's inauguration in January, 2009, Iranian President Mahmoud Ahmadinejad demanded apologies for 'crimes'; he said the United States had committed against Iran, starting with the 1953 coup. As a result, President Barack Obama is breaking barriers. He was the first president ever to admit in public

--- US involvement in that Iranian coup in 1953. President Obama responded by confessing at a speech to the Muslim world in Cairo in June, 2009. It was a major composition, an act of atonement as a gesture of peaceful redemption to the Iranian people when he declared: "In the middle of the Cold War, the United States played a role in the overthrow of a democratically elected Iranian government."

As an American citizen, I am asking all Iranians to forgive us, we the American citizens; for the atrocities that were inflicted upon your country by our CIA and certain --- Powers That Be --- in the name of Special Interests / Greed; which not only control our own country, but the entire world. They have over thrown many governments in the past; and got rich in so doing without conscience. Ironically, the same bastards have unfortunately been robbing the American taxpayers; whom finance their operations and in so doing, are literally destroying and bankrupting this country for a long, long, long time as well. And they will continue to do so; as long as we continue to let them. Their ultimate goal is to control everybody via a New World Order of scared ignorant slaves.

Wake Up America! Wake Up World! We must fight for our Rights and Freedoms --- Always. God Bless America. We are the Last Great Hope for Humanity. But we are running out of time. *Peaceful Co-Existence* is based on *Trust. United We Stand!* Together we can destroy the *Elite Powers That Be* and their diabolical plan – *A New World Order;* as they need our cooperation – *Fear and Ignorance.*

Breinigsville, PA USA
24 September 2009
224642BV00005B/1/P